WHEN MAMA'S GONE

by Richard O. Jones

D1706704

Published by Milligan Books, an imprint of Professional Business Publishing

WHEN MAMA'S GONE

Published and Distributed by:
Milligans Books (an imprint of Professional Business Publishing)
1425 W. Manchester, Suite B,
Los Angeles, California 90047
(213) 750-3592

First Printing, March, 1998
10 9 8 7 6 5 4 3 2 1

ISBN 1-881524-16-7

Cover layout and design by Jah'Key Lucien
Back cover photo by Rose Mary Mallett

Dedication

To the absent Black Father: I dedicate this book to you in the hope that through these pages you come to realize the golden beauty of parenting. No, fatherhood is not for sissies. However, to the real men separated from their little ones, let it be known, your children need you. You may not be as prosperous as the man next door, or as educated as you had once planned to be, but in the eyes of your children-you are their father. If you can give them nothing else, give them your love and they will be proud of you. No matter how long your absence or the reason, it is never too late to let your children know that you love them. Don't allow the rift between you and your children's mother rob them of their paternal heritage and you of your dignity. Children that have not seen their father in decades still long to know he loves them. Ending this cycle of waywardness in the Black family is mandatory for you as a man. Each situation is unique. Nevertheless, let us do away with the myth that Black men are irresponsible fathers. The truths of the matter is-Black men love their children too.

To the absent Black Mother: First there is God, then there is motherhood. In some children's lives, unfortunately, there is no God. However, there is always motherhood. In the eyes of the child, you were their first link to life itself. When the dire circumstances of the world separate you from your children, give them God. Pray for them and constantly let your children know that you love them. Do not be ashamed of yourself if their father or another person has custody. God is not finish with you yet. Be the best absent mother that you can be. I dedicate this book to you because I am keenly aware that the burden on Black women is heavy and many fall in harms way. Be of good cheer and return to them in a due season, a stronger and more loving mother, with all things decent and in order.

To the single Black Mother: You are singehandedly responsible for more successful career minded, intelligent, spiritual, and honest adults than any other woman on earth. For no other woman had to endure and overcome such formidable odds. Walk tall Black single mother. I dedicate this book to you because you are my mother, my sister, my friend, and my first teacher. Thank you.

To the single Black Father: I dedicate this book to you with pride. You are the heartbeat of a new phenomenon. You are the leader and provider God created. It is the steadfastness and sound mind of responsible men like you that'll make a positive different in the next generation. Your sons will learn from your example to be accountable. Your daughters will learn to accept no man that is less than the high male standards in which they have become accustomed. Society has given you a dirty rap for too long. It is time to dispel the myth. Thank you.

WHEN MAMA'S GONE

Acknowledgments

As I reflect on the many near death experiences in my life, including but not limited to spiritual death, from causes self induced to causes accidental, I thank the loving grace of Jesus Christ for sheltering me. When I deserved an obituary, He gave me a book. Thank you Lord.

All homage and due respect to my courageous mother, who endured the formidability of single motherhood   after prematurely forfeiting the carefreeness of her youth and the opportunities of higher education. Though jobs were scarce and wages low, mother epitomized the ethics of hard work, and embedded in me a good measure of   survival instinct. Through her demonstrations of 'Tough Love', I was always clear on the fact that society did not owe me a 'Rose Garden'. Mom I thank you for not molding me into a 'whining wimp.'

To all my children: Thank you. You are the preeminence of inspiration in my life. In all that I do, I see your faces. Before I act on an idea or impulse, I ask myself, "How would I want my children to behave under similar circumstances?" That's my secret formula for practicing good judgement. Yolanda R. Jones; Rochelle E. Jones; Jennifer C. Jones; Roxanne C. Jones; Darren O. Jones; and Brandi O. Jones, I love you. And it is my sincere prayer that I've shown myself worthy of your love.

During my single parenthood I was privileged to receive memorable and thought provoking words of wisdom from several sources. Four such sources were more impacting than others:

(1) Thank you Sister Patrica Hill, the First Lady of Cochran Avenue Baptist Church in Los Angeles, a spiritual counselor, wife and mother of two, who said, "Try not to get 'too' upset with your girls, Brother Jones. There are some things that daughters go through, God doesn't intend fathers to understand. Just trust Him."

(2) Thank you Dr. Rosie Milligan; author, publisher, businesswoman and mother of three, who said, "I measure all men by the high moral standards of my father, Simon Hunter. If a man doesn't carry himself in a manner that resembles the character of which I am accustom, I do not waste time on him".

(3) Thank you Jah'key Lucien; psychiatric social worker, poet, talk radio commentator, computer graphic designer, and mother of two, who said, "Richard, don't be such a dictator! Share in the housework. In doing so, your girls won't grow up thinking it's their duty to cater to men. If you train them to be subservient to you, they will be subservient to men in general. Which means, they will be attracted to 'insecure' men that expect maid service."

(4) Thank you Manuel C. Jackson, a longtime friend, electrician, husband and father of two, who said, "Don't you go poking your chest out farther than you oughta. Black women have been toting the load for absent fathers since slavery...Ain't nobody threw 'them' a ticker tape parade."

Special thanks for literary contributions: Paul V. Wilson, proofreading; Michelle Kennedy of M and R Enterprises in Long Beach, California and Carry-on Productions of Orange County, California for compiling the manuscript; Evelyn C. Tennell, retired school teacher, travel consultant of Travel Treasures in Los Angeles and Marcie Eanes, author and poet of Hawthorne, California for editing.

Thank you Rev. Barbara Nixon, of The Sacred Holy Ghost Temple, for your prayers. Thank you Rev. Bill Landrum, of Lynwood, CA. for sending me a Bible during my incarceration.

Special thanks to the clubs and organizations that provided me with a regular poetry platform: Soulvisions Productions; The Frontline Poets; Our Authors Study Club; The Writer's Corner; Speaker's Etcetera; John-Nays Christian Coffeehouse; Cebu 'African American/Philippino' Restaurant; Colonel Allen Allensworth State Park in Tulare County, and James and Pam Jacobs for my 'Gospel Brunch' performances.

Very special thanks to the Joyce Bryant of Safety First Company in Cleveland, Ohio for arranging my first out-of-state book signing for my book 'Tips Against Crime Written From Prison.' My self-confidence was fortified tremendously.

Very special thanks to Judy Banks, associate producer of the *Oprah Winfrey Show*, for making my guest appearance possible. And thank you Gil Cofrancesco, field producer at NBC, for making my national TV appearances possible on CNBC, *The Today Show*, and *The Leeza Gibbons Show*.

Kudos and accolades to Superior Court Judge Candice Cooper, the magistrate that sentenced me to prison, and District Attorney Chief Investigator Mel Wesson, the lead officer in my fateful arrest, for appearing as guest on my public access cable TV show entitled, 'Tips Against Crime.'

5-10-98

To Scot & Kim,

Your father is an inspiration to my Christian Fellowship. I hope his beauty is shown in your

Richard D. Jones

Preface

We have labeled Black men throughout the span of time as deadbeat dads. Our Black race in particular and the world overall has been exposed to negative images of our forefathers and brothers for so long that our lack of responsibility is expected. However, contrary to the racist propaganda, ignorance, and media hype, Black fathers are rising to the occasion of responsible single fatherhood in record numbers.

Many issues may cause a unit to separate. Sometimes it's in the best interest of the children that a dishonorable father is removed from their daily environment and upbringing. This autobiographical account was written to give you, the reader, a rare look at the other side of the Black man's image as a father.

This story is a candid view of a man's struggle with worldly and godly principles, while rasing his four daughters as a single parent. Richard Jones, who is an atheist with a criminal lifestyle, marries Annie Mae Champs, a devoted Christian. This paradoxical marriage drifts apart on moral issues. In his quest to give his daughters a positive female role model, following the death of their mother, Richard Jones staggers along a spectrum of unethical live-in housekeepers to an unfaithful live-in lover. However, Annie had implanted godly seeds in his mind and returns through visions to cultivate them.

Jones who was raised by a loving and hardworking single mother, with a volatile streak of tyranny, was now struggling to be a nurturing dual parent. He discovers that parenthood is a heavy burden without God but is reluctant to abandon his beliefs and criminal activities, which was his only source of income.

The Jones girls experience the instability of separation during the prison incarceration of their father, which landed them in foster homes and extended periods with distant relatives. The mistakes and poor judgements of their father brought many indignities upon them, leaving deep-seated resentment.

Upon his prison release, Jones fights to reunite with his daughters and dispel his negative image. Outwardly, Jones portrays a man with unshakable confidence, but in reality he is more apprehensive than he dare reveal. The mental visions and words of his departed wife, Annie, continues to revisit and guides him through rough times.

This book takes you into the mind and life of a dedicated criminal plunged into single parenthood due to unfortunate circumstances. His yearning to become the father he never had, and make sense of his situation, channels him to thoroughly examine his past and spiritual beliefs. In in search of a better life Jones transforms from criminal to crime fighter, and from a con man to a poet. Tough realities are explored and harsh truths are exposed.

Chapter 1

*T*his was the first funeral my daughter had attended. Yolanda fought to be strong. Even in this traumatic situation, the funeral of her mother, she was trying to be the *son* I always wanted. I felt guilty for the death of my wife. When I realized my daughter was ashamed to cry in my presence, my guilty feelings doubled.

We arrived the morning before the funeral and stayed the night in the home of Hanna Mae, my dead wife's oldest sister. Though she and her family were gracious, I felt they knew I lured their beloved Annie into a life of crime, which ultimately caused her early death.

They held the funeral in their family church. One of Annie's uncles was the pastor, and two of her brothers were deacons. The sounds of hearts breaking and tears flowing throughout the small country church were beginning to penetrate my calloused ears. I desperately tried to block it all out. My mind was on my daughter, Yolanda. "For heaven's sake! ," I thought, "get it over. Stop prolonging the inevitable."

"The Lord giveth, and the Lord takes it away," Pastor Leon Champs told the congregation from the pulpit. "This is not our home. As sand in an hour glass, we all are just passing through. No one knows the day or moment, but we're all going home. Someday! Get right with God now. I tell you. Tomorrow may be too late!" "The choir had sung, only minutes earlier, an emotional song that had the whole church sobbing," I thought. "Now this!" I hated the idea of crying publicly, and wanted Pastor Champs to speed the service along.

"If you need to say I love you to somebody," the good pastor continued, "you better say it now. If you need to say I'm sorry to somebody, you better say it now. This may be your last day, I don't know."

I held Yolanda tighter as we sat on the front pew with a few members of the immediate family. The last time Yolanda saw her mother, about two weeks ago, she was alive and well. I frantically wondered how she would react, seeing her mother this way. "Oh God," I silently lamented, "Let's get this thing over with."

Yolanda began to tremble beneath my embrace. "Oh God, stop the trembling. Don't let her cry. I don't think I could stand it if she cries. Oh Lord, it's too late. Her eyes are watery. My eyes are watery. My Lord, tell me what to do."

Thoughts ran rapidly through my head as two ushers approached and opened the casket. The service had been more than two hours long and now finally the grand finale. Was I ready? Was anybody truly ready? There lay the tall, slim, 32-year-old creamy chocolate, brown-skinned woman, with a speckle of acne, whom I had married ten years earlier. She lies before us as a beautiful precious stone, sculptured into the image of a bronze classic goddess. They were viewing Annie Mae Champs- Jones for the last time on this side of life. They dressed her for the occasion. Annie's family put her to rest in a gorgeous white gown. It was more beautiful than her wedding gown. I started to cover my daughter's eyes with my hands but found myself frozen in shock. My eyes became fixed upon the long fatal gash across her forehead which was too severe for the mortician to hide.

"Oh my God! Not my sister Annie Mae! Don't take Annie Mae, a female voice directly behind me loudly proclaimed. Please, Sweet Jesus! Don't take my big sister." Then I knew it was Annie's younger sister, Ella. The two of them were very close.

Suddenly, Yolanda broke from my grip and ran toward her mother. Hanna Mae intercepted her with open arms and hugged her dearly. However, an endearing hug was not enough to restrain her 4'5", 70 pound niece. Tears were flowing down Yolanda's young tender face with the passion and torment only an agonizing child would know. She screamed as if her soul were on fire.

"Mama, Mama, Mama, get up! Show them you're not dead!" She darted toward the casket with such momentum that I nearly fell when I rushed forward and encircled her waist with both arms. Yolanda began kicking and screaming, trying to free herself. "Mama, please get up. Mama, Mama, please!"

An older woman sitting across the aisle from me fainted, and one usher rushed toward her. A choir member began praying loudly as tears poured down his face, while the other choir members sat silently.

Approximately 30 vehicles caravanned to the family graveyard. They laid Annie to rest next to her mother. This was my first time riding in a burial procession, but I witnessed many passing along the city streets of Los Angeles. Usually, a half dozen motorcycle escorts would stop traffic and expedite an uninterrupted motor chain. When there's an extra long motorcade, waiting motorists would become impatient. Annoyed drivers do not respect the procession and break the chain. However, in Natchez, Mississippi, they amazed me to the point of fresh tears. The Black and White people of Annie's home surely won my heart. No one waiting for the procession to pass, interrupted the chain. Other motorist honked their horn and waved as a goodbye. Men and women on the sidewalk stood still until the procession passed. Many men removed their hats and covered their hearts. At first, I thought it was a coincidence, but block after block, and mile after mile, the reverence continued. It was as if the body of royalty was passing by. Perhaps I lived with a queen and was too inebriated to notice, I thought.

Two hours later, all was calm. Peace reclaimed its rightful place. The emotional storm that wreaked havoc on The Champs Family had passed, leaving behind one casualty. The survivors gathered at Hanna Mae's home and feasted on a banquet of pot luck meals that would cause a gourmet chef to salivate. Twice as many relatives and friends attended the 'After-Service' ceremony. Annie's loved ones shared childhood stories of happier times with

3

Yolanda. This made her laugh, and I was truly grateful to them.

Liquor was plentiful, but I dared not touch a drop among new acquaintances. In the South, how well he holds, his liquor determines the measure of a man. Everyone I knew in Los Angeles was aware that I didn't know how to behave once I began to drink. I saw no need to expand my dubious alcoholic reputation to Annie's hometown. Therefore, I decided to remove myself before the temptation became too great. I quietly slipped away from a huddle of brothers and cousins arguing over whose hunting dog was best or which university had the better football team.

In the kitchen area, I joined a couple matriarchs preparing more meals and asked about the distance to the nearest market. They were Annie's two aunts, Louise and Ida. "No need to go wandering off down these dark roads," Louise, the oldest of the pair snapped. "Everything ya wanna eat is right here."

"Now Louise, don't ya go and start meddling and minding his business," Ida said. "Rick has a lot to sort out, ya know. Ain't gone be no picnic raising 'em chillun 'lone with no wife and all." Then she pointed through the open window while holding a large butcher knife and said, "Just walk yonder no more than a mile or so and turn left at Paxton Road. No more than another mile, maybe two and you'll run into Kirby's Place on the right-hand side."

Louise immediately butted in, "Kirby's closed! Ida, you oughta know that. Yo' boy owns the sto' and he's sitting right there in yonder telling some lie or another." "Woman hush!" Ida replied. "Don't you know nothing? His wife done been put away. Let the young man get sometime alone. If Rick wanted something to eat or drink, would be no need of him leaving."
"I reckon so," Louise humbly replied. "Don't mind me none, Rick. You just run along and take your time 'bout getting back, if you have a mind to. That gal of your'n will be all right." Ida stood silently at the opened door.

The afternoon spring air was warmer than I expected Mississippi to be in February. Mid-70's was just my kind of weather. The freshness of the breeze gave me a sense of vitality. I walked briskly with my head held high.

4

However, I felt remorseful. Many pathetic past choices I have made were whirling inside my head and chanting insulting remarks. Repeatedly, I tried to silence the voices and focus on the highlights of our marriage. Annie and I surely kicked up our heels a time or two, and that's what I wanted to remember. Yet we also fought. Our love faded years ago. However, Annie's childhood commitment to a lifelong marriage and my ambiguous sense of fatherhood kept us hoping for a miracle.

Faster and faster I walked until finally I broke into a trot. The passing motorist gave me curious looks. I suppose that running down the road without being chased by The Klu Klux Klan was unusual for a black man. On the other hand, in this small close-knit community, my entanglement was no secret and the looks were compassionate ones. The trees along the road yielded to the freshness of spring. Huge houses were spread out approximately 500 yards apart. Most were beautiful homes eclipsed by an occasional rear shack.

As I continued to jog, visions of Annie playing with her siblings upon the rolling hills put a fragrance of solace in the breeze. The knowledge that Annie had grown up within the framework of a Norman Rockwell painting lead me to conclude that her short life was not in vain. She had played on the hills where the Lord finds sanctuary.

The physical and mental exercise did my spirit well. I arrived at Kirby's Place within thirty minutes. However, it was farther than Ida had suggested. The closed store was no more than a bait and tackle shop. I sat on an empty bench outside to catch my breath before the long walk back to the house. After a few moments of rest, I rose and resumed my excursion in a slower gait. I figured I would wander another 30 minutes farther than my starting point and then do an 'about face'. Though I tried to focus on plans, my concentration left no space for anything or anyone but Annie. Our first meeting became vivid in my mind. I allowed thoughts to drift on yesteryear's currents.

During an evening walk in mid-city Los Angeles, I noticed an attractive young woman approaching me from the opposite direction. She was only ten yards away and I wasn't prepared with a line. If I had seen her a half block away,

I would've been ready. My favorite pick up approach, when streetwalking, was to move up from behind. This gave me the opportunity to study the female prior to making contact. If there was enough space between us, I would duck into a store until she passed, then follow for 20 or 25 yards before swooping down.

I had been living nearby on Kingsley Avenue for several months, but this was my first time noticing this fine ornament. This tall, slim, sexy creature had a natural glide and swayed with the gracefulness of a young gazelle. Her big brown eyes reminded me of the cherished prize marbles I carried in my pocket as an eight-year-old kid. I showed them off and made the other boys envious. Nevertheless, I would never trade or enter them in a shooting match. She wore a modest full length black vinyl coat which she buttoned up to the collar and knee high brown vinyl boots. She "definitely" was no slave to fashion. My intuition declared that this godly sculpture, with the innocence of acne sprinkled generously upon her face, was the pure hearted woman that I longed for in my life. There was no more time to think. This was the decisive moment.

We made eye contact. I smiled and made my move when she smiled back. "Hi," I began. "May I speak to you?" She stopped and puzzlingly asked, "About what?" "I only want to talk to someone," I said while trying to sound homesick. "I just moved here, and you're the first person that I felt an impulse to meet. May I walk with you?"

"If you want to," she responded with a smile, "but I'm only going to Kingsley." "Hey, that's a coincidence," I pointed-out, "I live on Kingsley!" "Oh really!" she cheerfully replied, "I do too." I reversed my direction and began walking her home. "How long have you lived in L.A.?" she asked. I lied and said, "About four months," adding, "Everyone's so stuck-up here." "They sho' is!" she exclaimed. "I told my Aunt Lana that and she said I wasn't friendly." "Where are you from?" "Mississippi! Natchez, Mississippi!" she boasted. "We don't act all funny with folks." She continued, "I've been here most of a whole year and still don't

6

hardly know nobody. Nobody nice, that is. The girls don't talk to ya' and the boys, they'll talk to ya' but they mostly smoke weed and don't work. What 'bout you?" she blurred, "Do you smoke weed and don't work?"

I lied again, on two counts, "No I don't smoke weed, and yes, I work."

"Where you work at?" she asked.

"I'm employed at the Crocker Citizen National Bank Data Processing Center as a computer operator. I've been there for over a year." Although they had recently terminated me from the bank, I still referred to the job as my place of employment when meeting new women.

"I thought you said you ain't been here but four months," she quizzed.

"Yeah, I most recently returned to Los Angeles four months ago, but I lived here before. The bank gave me my old job back."

"Well they sho' must like you," she said merrily.

"Yeah they like me all right," I said, "Like me just fine."

By the end of our five block walk, I discovered her name was Annie Mae Champs. She graduated high school two years earlier, and received a one year scholarship to attend a beauty college in Iowa. After graduation, her family wanted her to return to Mississippi, but Annie wouldn't hear of it. The sound of the big city was calling. Whether it was in Chicago, New York, or Los Angeles, Annie determined that she became a successful hairdresser.

She chose Los Angeles because there were more movie and television studios, and each hired many hairdressers. Besides, her father's sister lived here. When I asked for her telephone number, Annie told me that Aunt Lana didn't allow her to receive phone calls from more than one man. In her Aunt's eyes, Annie committed a carnal sin by having two men calling, within her first three months in town. Aunt Lana called her father in Mississippi and told him that Annie had turned her home into a whorehouse. Because of this, she refused to give out the telephone number anymore. "Instead," she said, "I'll call you." I rushed home and waited for her call. While I waited, three other calls came in. The fourth one was hers. We talked for two hours. Before we said goodnight, I persuaded her to allow me to meet her the next evening at the bus stop where she exited each work day. I was to be there between 6:15 and 6:30 p.m. I began meeting her daily and walking her home. She would always call me later and we talked for hours. On the fifth day of our acquaintance, as I was walking her home for the fifth time, Annie said, "My Aunt Lana wants to meet you."

"Do I have to?" I joked. "If you wanna take me out, you do," Annie giggled. We laughed at our foolishness. A date with Aunt Lana was set for 8:00 p.m. Annie and her aunt were impressed with my punctuality. The meeting went quite well. Aunt Lana was a piece of cake. She thought I was a college graduate with a bright future at the bank, a man from a stable home and Christian upbringing. I left an hour later, under the pretense of getting ready for work. They were under the false impression that I worked the graveyard shift.

Over the next few weeks, Annie and I became inseparable. We went to movies, the beach, long rides, and restaurants. I even prepared dinner for her in my apartment twice. The day after I met Aunt Lana, Annie gave me their telephone number. She said that Aunt Lana didn't want her to give the number to any other man, until I was no longer calling. It was thrilling to know that I was the only man dialing her number.

This young woman was the most exciting female I had ever met. It was refreshing just to know a woman who wasn't connected to all the social vices Los Angeles offered. This young woman didn't cheat, cuss, or lie. We did very little necking during the infancy of our friendship. It really didn't bother me, for a while. I had an ace in the hole. When a cold shower wouldn't do the trick, I had Norma. Norma was the woman from my last intimate relationship. We had recently broke-up, although I was still privileged to conjugal rights.

Through patience, I learned to understand and respect Annie's reasoning. I remembered my days in St. Louis when I was sixteen and Stella Barrs was fifteen. We went darn near all the way, often. Stella Barrs wasn't a tease nor was Annie. Their Christian upbringing strongly influenced both. Additionally, they knew their fathers cared for them. At 19-years-old and 2500 miles away from home, Annie's teachings were still with her. She was terrified of becoming pregnant and earning the shady distinction of being the

8

first unmarried mother in her family. Though Annie's body was as appetizing as a large bowl of succulent fresh fruit, she seemed oblivious of her splendid physical attributes.

Our premiere night of erotic consummation occurred at my apartment after a six-month courtship. When Annie returned home about two o'clock the following afternoon, her aunt had reported her suspicions to their folks back home.

"Don't say a word to me!" Aunt Lana snapped at Annie. "Just call yo' daddy." Annie's father demanded that she respect his sister's house or move out. Since she was unmarried and didn't know how to behave herself, he advised that she would be better off in Mississippi. Annie called me later that evening. "Aunt Lana has taken her door key," she cried, "and she wants me to move out."

The winter of 1970 in Los Angeles was reminiscence of any sweltering summer day in the Midwest. The weather forecast was reaching the high 80's to high 90's during the entire Christmas season. Annie and I walked along the beach shore several nights a week. While she worked during the day, I searched for an apartment befitting a fledgling bachelorette. Since Aunt Lana repossessed her door key, Annie was under new house rules. If she wasn't home by 10:00 p.m., her aunt would not open the door. That was quite all right with us, because the deceit of my night employment still enjoyed its secrecy, therefore, we were never together after 10 o'clock.

My intimacy with Norma became a lame duck affair and had drifted into cool platonic waters. Now that Annie was seeking her own apartment I had no doubt that she and I would become closer. However, I questioned my ability or desire to remain monogamous. My inadequate preparation for mature and responsible adulthood preconditioned me to assume the measure of a real man was in how hard he hit with his fist and the number of women with whom he slept. For all I knew, any man with one woman was considered henpecked. Well, I had fallen in love and was willing and ready to be labeled henpecked, or whatever.

9

A week passed and Annie still hadn't selected an apartment. I convinced her that most apartment managers wouldn't rent to a single young woman unless she was rich, white, or had super credit references. The only option was for us to pretend to be married. After that, when we met the various landlords, I introduced Annie as my wife.

Boy, oh boy, was she picky. I tell you, she found more reasons to reject an apartment than I ever imagined. I soon became suspicious of her sincere desire to continue living in California. The Champs family was constantly telling her to come back home, and her aunt was increasingly giving her a hard time. "Okay Rick," she would say, "I won't be so picky tomorrow." The next day, her same sense of logic would prevail.

Finally, Annie chose a small single apartment with a wall bed in the living room. When we rented the apartment, I instructed the landlord to put the rental agreement and rent receipt in my wife's former name for tax purposes. Consequently, all paperwork was in the name of Annie M. Champs. Annie promptly gave me a key. The selling point wasn't the cheap rent, the convenient location, or proximity to stores and buses. Nor was it the new paint job, nice furniture, or paid utilities. The Crocker Citizen National Bank Data Processing Center was only two blocks away, and she suggested, "You can come by during your hour lunch break at 3:00 a.m. and I'll fix you something to eat."

That's when it hit me. My lie was about having a job was about to be revealed. I didn't intend on getting out of my bed every morning at 2:30 a.m., then rush to Annie's place for an hour lunch break before pretending to return to work. The obvious solution would be the one I chose: By week's end they would fire me for something beyond my control.

When Annie was only two years old, her mother died because of a car accident. Though her father remarried during her adolescent years, Annie nor her siblings liked the idea of their father having another woman in the house. Therefore, the relationship between Annie and the step mother never blossomed.

Our first Christmas together was a memorable one. My mother gave Annie step-by-step instructions on cooking an intimate Christmas dinner. Annie prepared a festive turkey dinner with all the trimmings. We invited about ten guests, my mother, her date, my two sisters and their mates, and a few friends.

Hanna Mae, Annie's oldest sister, became the Champs' family matriarch after the death of their mother. She treated Annie like a dependent child, which hindered her preparation and emotional maturity for womanhood. Not only did Annie display naiveness, she also lacked etiquette and culinary skills. Incidents that would embarrass the average person struck Annie as amusing. One example involved Christmas dinner, Annie seated guests at the table while I carved the turkey. I noticed the plastic bag which contained the gizzards, kidneys, and neck, was still tucked snugly in the cavity of the fowl. I purposely dropped the fork which held the turkey in place onto the floor, then asked Annie to wash it for me. While she was doing so, I joined her at the sink and discreetly whispered, "You left the guts in the plastic bag . . . "

"What!" she interrupted, getting everyone's attention. She chuckled and retorted, "Rick said I left the guts in the plastic bag!"
"What?" all the guests said at once. Harry, my sister Tammie's husband, took his fork and fished out the dripping bag. My mother ended up recooking the turkey. Annie didn't feel a thing.

Once, my buddy Curtis and his date Wyleen, were visiting us. Muhammad Ali was fighting in the ring for the first time since refusing to be inducted in the military. They transfixed us to the television screen, when Annie and I saw a mouse run across the kitchen floor. Curtis and Wyleen didn't see it. "Ahhh!" she blurted excitedly, pointing her finger, "There he is Rick!"

Wyleen and Curtis, who were lying on the floor, scanned the room following Annie's finger until they spotted the fleeing rodent. Our guests quickly moved from the floor onto the sofa, with their feet propped upon the coffee table. They thought it was so funny. I covered my shame by laughing with them. There were several seemingly insignificant episodes of frivolous and asinine behavior. However, Annie and I spent so much time alone, most people never

11

knew Annie marched to the beat another drummer.

It wasn't long before I had more clothes at Annie's apartment than my own. She thought I was putting clothes in her closet for a quick change, but I was slowly moving in. It had been three months since I told her my concocted employment dilemma: My position at the bank became uncertain due to an influx of overseas investors. However, the bank offered a free training program for their computer operators that would qualify them as computer programmers in eight months. The catch was, the trainees must move to San Francisco, California, which is nearly 500 miles away. I agreed to move. They scheduled the next training class to begin in sixteen months. Meanwhile, I collected unemployment insurance. (So much for the lie.)

I never shared with her that I was really working with a gang of crooks who specialized in bank fraud. My role was to supply the bank account numbers and customers' signature to a con man called Pretty Willie. His female accomplices' ripped-off the bank accounts through forgery. Before being dismissed from the bank, I obtained valuable information. However, as I began to fall deeper in love with Annie, I became more inclined to get a regular job and be the honest and decent man all Black women deserved. Therefore, after another four months of concealing my true character, I confided in Annie and assured her I would change my lifestyle.

Annie was elated that I decided to get a job. She came from a long line of hard working people. In her eyes, a real man worked and provided for his household. It didn't matter what kind of work he did if it were honest. She was truly proud of me. I could see it in her face.

During dinner one evening, Annie gave me some exciting news. She was pregnant. Never in my twenty-three years had I impregnated any girl or woman to my true knowledge. I always wanted to be a father. Most of my friends were fathers, even as teenagers. In fact, I had begun to suspect my fertility. Since my lovers were casual affairs, except Norma, who was consistently on oral contraceptives, I rationalized that Annie was the first woman who I dated that didn't take birth control pills.

"Annie," I gasped with a swallow, "if you'll marry me, I prom-promise to to be be aaaa good father and husssssban-ban . . . But did ya ya seee a doc-doctor?"

"Yeah," she mumbled and sighed, "I didn't want us to get married because of this, but 'cause ya *really* want to."

"I do want to. Please believe me, I do," I pleaded. "We can go to Las Vegas within the next couple of days," I suggested, "and get married or whenever you want. Then I moved closer to her, and asked in all seriousness, "Annie, will you please marry me?"

"Yes Rick, I will marry you," she said, and then cried. I began calling her Ann after she agreed to marry me. Neither of us liked her birth name of Annie.

My mother, and sisters, Elaine and Tammie, liked Ann more than any of my previous girlfriends. They talked Ann into postponing the marriage a few months until they could plan a big wedding reception. Actually, it was my mother who did all the planning with my sisters' support. Ann and my mother set the date for October 9, 1971, which was four months away. Meanwhile, Ann and I moved to a cozy, one bedroom, furnished bungalow. She quit her job as a wig stylist, because the smell of hair spray nauseated her. The liquor store, in which I had become employed as a delivery man, was only a ten minute walk or a one minute drive from our home.

My new father-to-be status was the most exciting time of my life. Watching Ann's stomach and breast swell was miraculous, but dealing with the mood and appetite swings took some getting use to. My work shift was from 6:00 p.m. to 2:00 a.m., and I dropped by our residence three or four times a night. My purpose was twofold. Not only did I get an extra few moments with the future mother of my children, but I also got to stash the mounting storehouse of liquor which I stole from my black employer.

I wasn't proud of myself for stealing from a black business, but my values were twisted. No pride in black enterprise, oh, I talked a good game, but when it came down to it, a dollar was a dollar. I knew I could easily sell my loot whenever I wanted. Unfortunately, my deep-seated desire to be a crook was deeper than I realized.

13

One evening while working in the store, Curtis came in as he frequently did, but this time he had some valuable information. He told me, his sister, Charolette, who was a Public Assistance social worker, said Ann and our unborn baby was entitled to public aid benefits through the welfare program. This was hot news. That meant semimonthly checks, food stamps, and free medical insurance. "That's Grrreat!" I exclaimed and gave him five.

The very next day I drove Ann down to the welfare office. I schooled her on what to say. Within a week, she had a full month county check in her hand. Knowing the money would be coming every two weeks gave me little reason to continue working at the liquor store. Nevertheless, I stayed because of the liquor I stole.

One of my favorite liquor store delivery customers was a middled-age couple, whose names were Jamal and Trudy. I delivered liquor to them at least once a week. Jamal and I would talk jazz. He had a great jazz collection. After knowing them a few months, during one of my deliveries, Jamal asked me to sit a while longer and have a soda.

"No, I better head back."

"Just a minute Richard," Jamal insisted. "I want to help you make some easy money." Of course that made me relax. "What's up?"

"Do you have insurance on your car?" he asked.

"No, Why?"

"A friend of mine," he began, "is retiring after 30 years driving truck for the Compton School Board. He wants to fake an accident before he leaves, that way, they'll have to pay him retirement and worker compensation, and benefits."

"How do I fit in?" I asked.

Gamble said, "I will arrange for him to hit your empty car tomorrow night. He'll take your name and driver's license number back to his job and report to them that you had five other people in the car when he rear-ended you." He continued to explain things. "The next day you and your buddies go to the attorney I send you to, and to the doctor he sends you to. In a short time everybody will have some money."

14

By this time, his <u>Mongo Santa Maria</u> recording was thumping. Mongo had his bongos on fire. "Sounds fat to me," I said in full agreement, "but will my car still run?"

"Yeah," said Jamal, "he's only gonna damage the trunk a little." We planned to meet the next night at 11:15, behind a line of closed warehouses near Jefferson and Exposition Boulevard.

All that next day, I tried to convince Ann to be a passenger in the fake accident. She would have no part of it. I grossly exaggerated the expected amount of money five times, but futilely. Frankly, I was disappointed in myself for not having any influence on my future wife's decisions. That was a disgrace in the circle I traveled. I wasn't too sure that I wanted to plan my life with *"Honest"* Ann. Since I quit screwing around with other women, I no longer had the personal acquaintances to fill my the car with people. That was disgusting. If only I had five women. What a wonderful case it would be. I could get at least half the money in the car. I decided right then, I wasn't gonna get caught with just one woman again.

Timing was important, so, I contacted Harry and gave him the low down. He gave me enough names to fill the car. Tammie had long moved into her own apartment with their elementary school age daughter, Karen. I thought about getting Norma involved but my better judgement screamed, "No Way! She's too vindictive!" Months passed since I had seen or heard from her. That was the way I liked it. All went as Jamal planned. Two days later six fraudulent accident victims sat in a Beverly Hills lawyer's office reciting scripts.

Ann had a full-term pregnancy. Our first daughter was born early in '72. Our nuptials took place in a small wedding chapel which was in the upstairs rear of a mid-city flower shop. We invited a handful of our friends and family members to the wedding. The reception, which my mother hosted in her rented, spacious, two story, four bedroom home, was packed wall-to-wall with guests. All brought wedding or baby shower gifts. There were plenty of food, booze and people . . . all at my mother's expense. She even gave me one of her rings to give to Ann. It was a beautiful day. Ann was the life of the party. Everyone loved her.

Some men there with dates flirted with other women, and some women with dates flirted with other men. Three or four drug dealers, several gamblers, con men, and even a prison escapee was there. As I looked around, I was startled at the revelation and realization of the den of misfits I just bestowed upon Ann's future. Tammie got drunk, as usual, and was dancing like a wild nymphomaniac. Those who knew her best, tried to ignore her. The others enjoyed the shameful spectacle. Whenever Tammie got a drink or two in her, she transformed right before your eyes, into a 5'2" mouth of vulgarity, especially in the presence of Mommy. She wasn't satisfied at any social function until she cursed out our mother or embarrassed her beyond full recovery. She, like me, couldn't remember a thing the next day and was completely oblivious to the morning reports. For Tammie and me, both alcoholics in denial, one glass was too many, yet one bottle wasn't enough.

My baby sister, Elaine, was a great dancer. Everybody loved to watch her. She would have lots of fun until someone pointed a camera in her direction, then she would run like the house was on fire. If she happened to observe two secluded people whispering and laughing, Jesus Christ himself couldn't convince her that they were not talking about her. Only a miracle could make her stay. On this day she stayed, thanks to the insistence of her new gambler, abusive, and controlling boyfriend, Kenny. He called himself, "Sweet Ken, From the Sugar Bin." Kenny was an alcoholic and habitual losing gambler. Elaine loved him dearly.

After several months of marriage, and a newborn child, I felt above menial labor. Ann wanted her own furniture and appliances. Our furnished one bedroom home no longer suited our taste. Though we had a few thousand dollars in the bank, I felt desperate for cash. A husband and father had to provide, and a liquor store just couldn't do it. I counted the days before my accident settlement would rescue us. Meanwhile, I stole five blank money orders from the job, then bought a check writing machine from a local pawn shop. The stolen money orders would finance new furniture.

While waiting for the settlement, I began a mail order home-study course on accident investigations. I became familiar with all the legal and medical terms involving accidents. Part of the course covered claim adjustment. A claims adjuster worked for an insurance company. That wasn't for me, but I wanted the knowledge. The course included twenty-four volumes of law books. I loved studying law and it made me extremely popular with my family and friends.

Every time there was some type of civil or unresolved legal matter in their lives, I became the advisor or mediator. I wrote business letters, resumes, letters of complaint, employee grievances, filed court papers, and advised motorists and pedestrians regarding liability for their accident cases. When the word got out I was the man to talk to about cases before you saw a lawyer, my phone stayed busy. My service was free, but just for friends and family or their friends and family. I was determined to learn all this course had to offer regarding accidents because I knew there was a future for me in fraudulent accidents if Jamal's caper panned out. To have a good hustle would be a dream come true.

One evening, during a quick stop home between deliveries, Ann told me that Harry wanted me to call him at his cousin Garrison's house. Garrison was a good hustler, though he specialized in conning women. He owned a TV repair shop, a record shop, an income tax preparation service, and a night club, within the past five years. Garrison was now in the record recording business and he had a studio on Sunset and Vine in Hollywood. I had passed the word that I wanted to go into some kind of business when I received my settlement. Garrison was going to set me up with some guy who arranged phony credit. I dialed the number. "Hey man," Harry said. "The dude is here now. Can you get here within fifteen minutes?" "How much is it gonna cost?" I heard Harry cover the receiver and ask "How much?" Then he spoke to me, "Bring $250 and you'll have A-1 credit in two days."

Chapter 2

*G*arrison lived only a five-minute drive away . . . I was there in three. A trio of men was in the den playing cards when Garrison's wife Liz announced my presence. "You can go back now Mister Richard," his Filipino wife said in her broken English accent. Liz was about 25, an extremely beautiful and shapely young woman. Harry told me that Garrison married her overseas when he was a 30-year-old soldier, and she was 14. I never quite understood why he cheated on her. She was loyal, docile, and the mother of his four children. Liz addressed all the men as Mister and the women as Miss. She even called her husband Mister Garrison.

"What's happening fellas'?" I said as I grabbed a seat at the table. Everyone halfheartedly spoke. Then Garrison asked, "You remember Hamilton, don't you?" "Yeah, sure," I replied nodding to the middle-aged bald, plump and well-dressed gentleman across the table. Hamilton was Garrison's business associate. "So Hamilton, you're The Man!" I acknowledged.
"I'm the Man," he smiled. "What ya' need?"
"I just need some good credit," I explained, "I don't have *any*."
Hamilton played his card and won the game of Tonk. "That's ten dollars a piece y'all owe me," he boasted to Garrison and Harry with a sarcastic grin. "Ya' know Richard," he said, "no credit is worst than bad credit." I figured anytime some hustler tells you how difficult getting something done, you're gonna get screwed.

"It's just like a house," he began. "It's much easier to sweep out a house than build a new one."
"So you'll build me a new house for $250," I stated for assurance sake.

19

"That's right!" Hamilton assured.

Our discussion continued in the presence of Harry and Garrison but that was all right because we all knew each other and no strangers or blabbermouths were around. Hamilton told me that for $250, they would allow me three calls. That meant three different merchants would get a favorable telephone credit rating, anything beyond three would be more money. I paid him the money and he instructed me to wait two days before coming by his used furniture store on Western Avenue to get my credit information. I left moments later because I still had a liquor delivery in the car.

When I visited Hamilton's Used Furniture Store two days later, everything was ready. My new credit history was very impressive. According to the documents, I had paid off a bank loan, car loan, and furniture store within the last two years. On another account, I had only three remaining payments due to a finance company for a $5,000 personal cash loan. Also, I was a six-year employee for a well-known moving and storage company as a truck driver and earned four times my true salary at the liquor store. The name was an alias I created for myself.

For the next two weeks, I studied the information; bank account numbers, furniture store account numbers, dates, addresses, names of businesses, salary and starting date. Ann to quizzed me. I learned the entire sheet within a matter of hours, but such a scam amazed me so that I kept studying the information in disbelief. I triple checked the figures to see if the financial calculations were correct; Thirty-six months times $189.56 plus 4% interest with a $381.98 balloon payment, after making a $400 down payment . . . Wow! The figures checked out!

I was really killing time while anxiously awaiting my accident settlement. I called the law office every week until the secretary finally asked me to gather all my passengers and come in to discuss the settlement offer.

The six of us went in the very next day and walked away with a check for $800 each. After my five passengers paid me $200 each, I had a total of $1,800. Harry charged each of the four women 50 per cent of their $600 which brought his total up to $2,000. Of course, this pissed me off with Ann again. I could have had more money if she had been involved with the case. However, when she realized how easy it was, she agreed to be in the next one.

Meanwhile, we went furniture and apartment hunting. We found a new apartment building which still had several unoccupied units. We rented a beautiful three bedroom unit on the second floor with a fantastic view overlooking West Los Angeles. I printed up the stolen money orders which I had saved for $300 each and used them as down payment for furniture, coupled with my fraudulent credit. Between two stores, we elegantly furnished our entire home with major appliances, a child's bedroom set, our bedroom set, living room, dining set, and office furniture.

I had everything delivered to a cheap east side apartment rented for that purpose. I rented a U-haul truck and moved everything out the next day. The cost of our furniture was more than $12,000. To think I stole it all was exhilarating. My expenses were few, and came out of my accident settlement. Therefore, everything truly was free. That same week, I selected a brand new 1972 car and paid $500 down, on approved credit, and drove it home an hour later.

When I reported for work later that evening, I was still driving my '65 Rambler with the trunk smashed in. Driving a new car to a low paying job only arouses suspicion and jealousy. However, I really didn't care about that since I planned to quit at the end of the work week anyway. I told the owner that I found another job and would be leaving. He thanked me for the notice. I liked him a great deal and regretted stealing from him. I rationalized my doing it because of the high risk factor of working in a liquor store, especially where lots of drug users hung around. However, the truth was, I came to steal.

In the spring of '73, I finished my home study course and begun to send resumes to more than 50 law offices in Los Angeles to offer my services as an accident investigator. Approximately 15 - 20 lawyers replied to my letters. I had some business cards printed in an alias, introducing myself as: Richard O. Brooks, Accident Investigator. All of the attorneys that met with me were accident specialists, also known as ambulance chasers. Their offers were very similar. Each needed a sign-up man. In other words, when the law office had a client that couldn't come into the office, they would call my office and put me on the case. For each person that I signed and referred through their office, they would pay me $25 - $75 if the case turned-out to be a good one. Additionally, if I signed up new cases that I sought myself, each person covered by the accident would be worth from $250 - $350. Each lawyer suggested that rear-enders were the best. None of them actually told me to go out and set up phoney accident cases.

After my marriage, I became more active in meeting women. Although sex was far from being the motivator, it served as a fringe benefit. Many hustles I set up were designed to appeal to low income working women. I sold high quality, brand name fashions, including cosmetics, jewelry and lingerie. I even had an inventory of children's clothes and toys. All this was a front to meet women.

Two or three times each week, I would leave my house at 5:30 a.m. just to cruise the main streets and look for working women standing at bus stops. I would offer rides to many of them and most accepted. My new car was an influencing factor. By 9:00 a.m., I would return home. I would also cruise for woman walking early in the morning in stormy weather, because they were prime suspects to be in need of financial help.

Occasionally, my route took me by various welfare offices to pick up the young black women. These particular ladies had a deeper need than poor working mothers. They soon became my preferred choice. I also set up an avenue to widen my circle of male associates, especially ambulance and tow truck drivers. I would approach them anytime and anywhere for the sole purpose of making them my accident pipeline. For every case they referred to Richard O. Brooks, Accident Investigator, I would pay them $50 - $100 depending on the injuries and the insurance coverage.

Eventually, I installed a second phone number at home because the calls were too many for Ann to handle herself. The new telephone was considered my phone and was connected to a phone answering machine in my office. The answering machine held 40 calls. Each day I would have to rewind the tape because it reached its limit. People were calling for everything from liquor to accident referrals. Lawyers were calling, sending me to the neighborhoods their white investigators didn't venture into. For example, if a black person called the attorney and stated they were an accident victim but didn't have transportation to come into the office, the likelihood that they would send me was great. If they happened to dwell in a crime infested community, my chance of being referred was an absolute. I played the accident game for more than 15 years and not once was I referred to white families.

I dreaded the attorneys' phone calls after awhile because most of their referrals were dry runs. Whenever that happened, they did not pay me for my time. Over time, I realized that most black people entertained exaggerated and wrong expectations following an accident. They accused me or the lawyer of selling them out to the insurance company. When five independent witnesses told me that my client ran the red light, I had no choice but to report my findings to the lawyer (my employer). Naturally, he would decline the case, which meant I received no money from him, and a good cussing out by the client.

It got to a point that I was only accepting attorney referrals with an ulterior motive. I would enter the home browsing around to see what the family needed, in hopes of selling them a new air conditioner, television, stove, etc. or even use them in a future set up car accident. This method turned every referral from the lawyer into a customer or future accident victim for my interest. This new approach made many friends and casual affairs.

Then I got smart. In rare instances, when they sent me on a call that might be a good case, instead of writing an accurate report and earning $25 - $50 per client, I would falsify the report. When the lawyer determined the case was no good, he would decline it. Then I would go back to the client and tell them that I knew a better attorney, a black man, that would take their case. The attorney I took them to was Dewey P. Summer. He would pay me $300 a client. He, in turn, referred them to the Metropolitan Medical Group which had a black administrator named Gilbert Williams. Dewey referred a great deal of his clients to Ike's Body Shop, another black man, for their auto body repairs. (Dewey P. Summer, Gilbert Williams, Ike's Body Shop, and Ike are not true identities.) I received $300 from Gil for each patient, and $200 from Ike for each customer.

When I was sure that there were ten women in my social circle that I trusted and met my requirements, I purchased ten used cars in one month. The cars ranged in price from $300 - $500 and all in good running condition. Then I arranged with each woman. I paid for the insurance, but they had to be willing to fake a car accident. Ann and Norma were among the ten women.

My wife was tired of driving my old '65 Rambler anyway. I took my time and found her a sharp '66 Thunderbird for only $500, which she loved. I then transferred the title of the Rambler to a female crime partner. After all the insurance policies were in effect, once a week I staged rear-end, six passenger, car accidents. I had an endless supply of people anxious to file a false insurance claim. Many cases were taken to white attorneys in the high rent district. After they wrecked all ten cars, repaired, and settlements collected, I cleared more than $40,000 within a few months. Every three or four months I would have another ten cars to give away to ten different, grateful, owners.

One morning after a meeting with Gil, I left his office and discovered an empty parking space where I parked my car. Though I hadn't made one car payment in the eight or nine months, I assumed someone had stolen it. I called the police, and within a few minutes they told me my car had been repossessed. Since I used an incorrect address on the credit application when I purchased the car, I couldn't figure out how they nabbed me. This baffled me. If they knew my home address, they could've followed me. I couldn't figure this one out.

The next day, I went to Hamilton with the cash for more credit under a different name. A week later I was driving away from a Buick dealership with a brand new '73 Regal. This was the first year of production for the Regal;

it was all black, in and out; plush leather interior; a two-door sedan with whitewall tires. On my trip home, men and women were smiling, waving, and giving me the thumps up sign as a way of validating my choice.

My mind was focused on how I could keep this car beyond the six-month disability car payment insurance I purchased through the dealer. It would be a cinch to fake an accident and gain six months payment relief. Well, I had a lot of time to figure that one out. For now, I had more pressing matters.

Harry phoned me the night before with the news that Juanita, one of his marginally sane girlfriends, was furious with him for kicking her butt. He had a well-known reputation of keeping his feet warm by cramping them up a stupid woman's buttocks. Juanita never complained until now. This time she was threatening to call the insurance fraud unit and blow the horn on our racket. Harry had put this fool in several cases and now she was seeking revenge. Harry called himself a player and couldn't even slap his own woman around without jeopardizing others. How revolting!

Ann loved me too much to stoop that low. I might have to sleep on the sofa for a week or so if I slapped her or pushed her around for some small infraction. She may even call the police, which she had done once, but never to report matters that would lead to prison. Frankly, I hated arguing or fighting but my life experience taught me no other method of problem solving . . . especially under the influence of alcohol. Coincidently, Ann called the police on me a week before Harry's problem with Juanita.

After they repossessed my car, I took it for granted that I would drive Ann's car until.I bought another. What a shock I was in for. She said no. I was so disgusted that I left the house twice and conducted my business by bus. Then one night about midnight I wanted a bottle of wine. I told her that I wanted the car for a few minutes. Ann flatly refused. I pushed her aside and snatched the keys from her purse and stomped out of the house. I was so angry that I forgot my wallet and had to leave the wine on the counter and return home for money. When I got back, Ann was in the bedroom and so was my wallet. I hated to go in, but did without exchanging words. As I was about to leave, the doorbell rang. I wondered who in the world would be visiting us at nearly 1:00 a.m.

"Who is it?" I called through the door.
"It's the police!" I opened the door.
"What's the problem officer?" I asked. "We're here to see Mrs. Annie Jones." One of them said, "Is she here?" "Yes, I'm Mr. Jones, what's the problem?" "We have a stolen vehicle report," the second officer said, "Can we speak to Mrs. Jones?" I yelled to Ann to come out of the bedroom.
"Did you call the police madam?"
"Yeah, he took MY car!" She said, pointing her finger at me. The officers looked at each other. "Is he your husband?" one asked.
"Yeah!" she pouted, "But that's MY car. I never drive HIS!" "Are the two of you presently living together?" the other one asked.
"Yeah!" she fretted, "But I told him. Don't take my car! And he went to the store." The police looked toward me, waiting for me to jump in and defend myself, but I was as dumbfounded as they were.
"Mrs. Jones, do you feel you're in any danger?"
"No," she replied.
"Well I'm afraid there's nothing we can do here." As they were leaving, one officer turned toward me and said, "I suggest you two see a marriage counselor." I slept on my office sofa that night without uttering another word, but I was certain Ann's thought and logic would be impossible for me to live with.

This thing with Harry was beyond a domestic dispute. Juanita's lack of concern or judgement was a severe threat to me. When I got home with the new car, I offered to take my wife and daughter for a ride. As we cruised around the city and along the Pacific Ocean waterfront, I explained my dilemma to Ann. The only safe solution I told her would be for us to immediately pack up and move. I also decided not to conduct in any future criminal business with my 'half-stepping' ex-brother-in-law. By the end of that week, we had moved our family to another three bedroom apartment near Los Angeles International Airport.

After that little episode involving the false stolen car, I found it more pleasurable to stay away from home. Our marriage suffered from my lack of commitment for the next three years. I never forgave Ann for calling the police. I would often think about it, and even argue every few months, but I never let onto the true magnitude of my resentment.

Things changed in the spring of '75. Ann became pregnant again. By the end of that year, our second daughter, Rochelle, was born. It was my first experience in the delivery room during childbirth. The wonder of such an event restored my love for Ann.

The accident game soon became hotter than a two-dollar pistol. Cappers, lawyers, and doctors were going to jail by the truck load. The term 'Capper' is what the police used to identify a person who sold accident cases to attorneys. It's illegal! They were arresting too many people because of poor 'game' planning. Too many stupid guys were in the business. Drug users and habitual gamblers are the most unreliable hustlers. Drug users have brain damage and are untrustworthy. Gamblers are in constant need of money, and will sell you out. Not to mention the chiefs of stupidity, the violent, brain-dead, so-called 'gang members'. These were the guys who ruined the good name of 'hustling'.

Avaricious and ruthless lawyers and doctors were the reason for the downfall of the accident hustle. They would offer practically every person who entered their office money to refer accident cases. At up to $500 per head, idiots were out crashing their own cars into innocent motorists and buses. They were injuring innocent people. Although they arrested none of the people I worked with over the years, I decided to lay low. Since there was no way of determining who was under investigation, or who was an informant, I terminated my relationships with every accident hustler I knew. I moved my welfare fraud scheme from the back burner to the front, and recruited six more women besides the three already in motion.

To stabilize my financial position, I had Hamilton set me up with a credit rating strong enough to purchase an apartment building in Pomona, and a duplex in Pasadena, California. Between the two real estate investments, my bank account dribbled down considerably. No sooner than my blooming welfare scam was basking in the sun, a woman in Los Angeles got busted 'big time' for the same thing. Her name was Dorothy Woods but they labeled her, "The Welfare Queen." She collected public assistance in eight or nine fictitious names as a single mother, with more than 30 dependent children. From all I read about her in the newspapers, sister Dorothy was smooth. She earned my admiration. Just like so many wounded comrades before her, the betrayal of an untrustworthy friend brought her down. The shock waves of her exploits sent the county officials running around like chickens with their heads cut off in a mad rush to renovate the system. I alerted my crime partners of the imminent financial storm. As the week ticked by, I watched the progress of the Dorothy Woods investigation, seeking to capitalize on the county's mistakes and loopholes in the system.

Meanwhile, I decided to approach the insurance fraud business from a different avenue. An avenue not well traveled, not well known and, therefore, not well guarded. Instead of herding a bunch of potential informants off to make some easy money, I would become the only claimant. Rather than going to lawyers I knew, I would pick a fresh one from the telephone book for each case. Every name that I used would be a newly created name with several disability incomes, hospitalization, and medical insurance policies. The plan was to be hospitalized every time, by different doctors. The thought excited me. I would be away from home with no arguing and no fighting. I would just rest, read, eat, sleep, and be massaged daily while averaging $1,000 - $1,500 a day. My schedule stayed full between phony Worker's Compensation claims, auto accidents, and product liability cases. A patient with the proper insurance could stay in most hospitals following a minor accident from ten days to two weeks without a hassle from the insurance companies. My buddy, Gil was acquainted with dozens of insurance coverages through his position as an administrator of a busy medical center. I began setting up one-man accidents and allowing myself to be hospitalized in each case.

As a husband and father of two, it occurred to me that my family lacked financial security in case of my death. Most of the little money that came into my hands via crime went back into another crime. There was no bank account in my true name. Ann was limited how much she could put in the bank because of welfare restrictions. So, I invited a life insurance representative to our house to explain our options. After extensive discussion with the sales agent, the agent, Ann and me that I purchase life insurance for $15,000 for each child mutually agreed, $40,000 for Ann, and $75,000 for myself. There was also a double indemnity clause in case of accidental death.

Over the next several days following the signing of our insurance contract, I noticed Ann had become extremely paranoid. She wouldn't eat if I prepared dinner. Nor would she accept an offer of food from any of my relatives or friends when we were visiting them. She tensed up whenever I came near her. Finally, I sat her down and quizzed her. Soon she broke down crying, "I know you're trying to kill me."
"What makes you say something like that?" I asked astonished.
"Your mother is too," she wept.
"What's the matter with you?" I demanded.
"You can't fool me!" she affirmed. "That's why you bought all that insurance. You don't care nothing about us! You can't fool me!"
"I be doggone Ann!" I shouted, "Everybody should have life insurance, it's nothing *I* thought of."
"Well I don't want you having it on me and MY kids," she screamed. I started to reflect on other small weird things she had been doing.
"Is that why you've been sniffing on everything before you eat it?" I blasted. "Why you've been staying awake until all hours of the morning . . . getting up in the middle of the night and locking yourself in the bathroom for long periods. Is that where you've been sleeping?" I emphasized the word 'sleeping'. She didn't answer, just rushed from the room crying and locked herself in the bathroom.

I left the house disgusted. When I returned about two hours later, she was smiling and cheerful as if nothing had happened. A tasty dinner was cooking in the kitchen, but I was afraid to eat after all that. Instead, I had Ann dial our agent's number at Prudential Insurance Company. When she got him on the phone, I took the receiver and canceled our insurance. We ever mentioned nothing about life insurance within our household again.

Later that evening, Ann shared with me that she had been calling around town inquiring about a beautician job. I discouraged the idea of a job but encouraged her to rent a booth and become an independent operator. She was very reluctant because she didn't have personal clients.

"Look Ann," I interjected, "I'll help you. I'll tell every lady I know about you. I'll even put ads in the papers and pass out flyers." The subject went back and forth for a while but ultimately Ann got excited about the idea of her own booth and being her own boss.

"Okay Rick, I'll do it!" she exclaimed with exhilaration. "But what about the kids?" she asked. "Whom will we get to keep the kids?" "I know Rick!" she perked with pride, "You can keep them!"

"Now wait a minute Ann," I cut in, "I'm busy. Besides, I'm planning on going back in the hospital. Remember? Let me see," I continued and pondered as I spoke. "We could get a free full-time, seven-days-a-week babysitter." Ann leaned forward, giving me her undivided attention. "What we can do, Ann," I began, still measuring each word, "is use our mailing address as a residence for a live-in babysitter."

We maintained a small furnished one bedroom apartment about a mile away from our larger residence to receive mail, especially the welfare checks. Ann eventually rented a booth and became her own employer. We settled on one of six babysitters who applied for the job. Then suddenly, she made another major violation in the hustlers' wife codes of conduct. She left me in jail! Again!

One day I called home later than Ann expected. "Where are you, Rick?" she asked.
"I'm in jail. That's Where!" I replied. "Get me out. It'll cost $90."
"What are you in jail for?" asked Ann.
I told her the police stopped the car I was riding in because the driver made an illegal turn, when the police asked for my I.D. I accidently exposed a marijuana joint tucked away in my wallet. Ann left me in jail because she said, I should

not smoke dope in the first place. She hung the phone up on me. It was a very minor offense and later dismissed in court. Still, the idea of my wife not bailing me out of jail because she was against smoking weed. Oh I was furious! However, I didn't want to make the matter worse by fighting. However, my dislike for being home grew daily.

The viability of our marriage returned to infertile ground. My frequent visits to the hospital relieved the mounting mental anguish on both sides. Ann's major complaint was my drinking, smoking weed, and late hours. She never questioned me about the women I was seen riding around the city with, the few I brought home, or the private phone calls.

Although she felt that I was having sex with one or two of them, she was positive, and rightly so, I had no emotional attachment to any of them. Ann was aware of my well-established characteristic to have female friends without a sexual relationship, but none without having a business relationship. So she didn't worry herself about my fidelity. Ann once confided that her oldest sister, Hanna Mae, told her time-and-time again that all men were dogs and it's in their nature to sleep around. Since they returned home with the grocery and rent money, that's all that mattered.
"That's right!" I confirmed, "It's just nature."

We recruited our live-in babysitter through the local newspapers. Ann began renting a booth before the ad even hit the newsstand. "Booth for Rent" signs were common and easy to find. Her booth was in a busy shop. When the other beauticians realized how talented Ann was, they allowed her to do their overflow. From the very beginning, she was working until nine at night.

When our 'babysitter' ad caught the eyes of the readers, our phone began to ring madly. The ad was only placed in black community newspapers, and it read as follows: *"Couple with two small children have private living quarters to offer live-in babysitter in exchange for free rent. Must have drivers' license. Use of car for personal errands is available occasionally."*

Since Ann was working five days a week, I conducted all the interviews. At least six young women must have come by in two days. I selected a lady of about 25-years-old, with a four year old daughter. Her name was Harriet. Harriet was on the same level as Ann in attractiveness, but her daughter was the edge Harriet had over the other applicants. I figured since Yolanda was also four years old, the two could become playmates. Ann and Harriet got along so well that they visited each other frequently and took the children to the park, zoo, circus, or somewhere every Monday on Ann's off day.

Harriet loved the apartment we provided her, but she was extremely uncomfortable with me having a key. Sometimes I stopped by through the day to check on the mail. I knocked on the door occasionally to say hello or to make sure all was well. Once when she wasn't home, I entered the apartment and prowled through her belongings to learn her identity. Criminally minded people often become paranoid about their freedom. We suspect every stranger to be the police.

About a month later, I attempted to enter Harriet's quarters with my key, but it didn't fit. I immediately thought, "Harriet had changed the locks." I confronted Harriet about changing the locks without my permission and she blasted me.
"Your wife changed the locks!"
"What in the world do you mean," I demanded, "my wife changed the locks? I know *she* didn't change the locks!"
"Yes she did!" Harriet rebutted, "I told her that you're slipping in the apartment when I wasn't home and sniffing around in my underclothes."
"I wasn't sniff'n around in yo' underclothes." I did go through the drawer where her panties just happened to be. I went through all the drawers, closets, boxes and everything else, even dishes, but especially her papers.
"Yes you were," she said softer, "I wouldn't even mind if it were just you and I, but Ann is my friend." Then she added in a whining tone, "Mr. Jones, I'll have sex with you if you really want me to, but as soon as I find another place I'm moving out. I'll feel so guilty and dirty." I didn't know whether to accept her view of me as a pervert or admit that I was just *'plain, old'* paranoid. I elected the pervert.
"All right Harriet," I said, "You can stay and I won't sneak around in your

underclothes again. However, I do need a key in case of emergencies. Please accept my apology." Harriet gave me a duplicate key the next day, however, I never used it nor took her up on the 'watered down' sexual offer.

Spring of '76, a bank statement addressed to Ann caught my attention. I first thought it was a mistake. Ann never told me that she had an account at this bank. Usually I separated my mail and left hers on the bedroom dresser. Nevertheless, most of the time, her mail was magazines, sale papers, or letters from Mississippi, not bank statements. My curiosity prevailed and I opened the statement. Instantly I knew it was a mistake. According to the statement, Ann had $17,536 in the bank. I knew she had a separate Wells Fargo account and we shared a nominal Bank of America account. Her Wells Fargo account was in a fictitious name with only $8,000 as a balance. However, this was a Security Pacific National Bank account in her true name, and with more than twice the amount she had told me. To make matters worse, the account was more than four years old.

The truth was obvious. My wife had been secretly saving money since our marriage. This revelation dumbfounded me. Often I came home drunk and woke up with a $100 - $150 missing from my wallet or pocket. Whenever I complained to Ann, she would tell me that I was too drunk to remember accurately. She often said, I must've spent it by buying drinks for everybody, or my backstabbing friends ripped me off. Now the truth was out. Ann had been rolling me for four years. Rolling and clipping me, the way a robber does a common drunk. The truth brought tears to my eyes. I would rather have discovered motel keys in her purse than this. *That* I could rationalize. It's her body . . . I wouldn't like it one bit, but . . . it's her body. Women generally think just because they're not screwing anybody that it proves they're faithful. That's crazy! Trust means much more than not having sex with someone else. Trust means being up-front and trustworthy.

As hard as it was to do, I promised myself never to say anything to Ann about the bank statement. Gradually, the healing phase of our marriage declined from a guarded state to critical care. It was eventually placed on a life support machine with a weak battery. To achieve my own soul restoration, I mobilized more fake injuries and increased my time away from home through hospitalization. These medical excursions refreshed me physically and mentally. Not only could I relax and plan my next moves, but I enjoyed flirting with the nurses and physical therapy staff.

After a couple of months of being emotionally eaten alive by Ann's financial deception I didn't hold it back any longer. The kids were watching Sesame Street in the living room. Ann and I were in the kitchen, but emotionally miles apart.

I calmly said, "I know about your Wells Fargo Saving Account."

"What saving account?", she asked.

"Oh that's right," I corrected myself, "I don't meant Wells Fargo. I mean Security Pacific National Bank with more than $17,500 as a balance. You're too cold for The Kid."

"Rick, you must have gone crazy. I don't have money in Security Pacific Bank."

"Ann stop all the lying!" I snapped. "The game is over. I'm outta here!"

She stopped washing the pot and reached into a sink drawer and withdrew a butcher knife and just cradled it as if it were a baby.

"I'm not letting you hit on me." Then she turned and left the room to join the girls. I followed.

"Don't be walking 'round here with a knife, I'm not gonna bother you."

Ann swung swiftly around and backed into the living room. "I ain't lett'n you hit me," she threatened, "That's *my* money, not yours."

"Don't be going in there 'round the kids with that knife. Just put the knife down and I'll leave," I reasoned. My gestures were saying or sending Ann a threatening message. She raised the weapon up to shoulder height and screamed, "Leave me alone!"

"I'm not bothering you!" I yelled as I eased one hand in my pocket and clasped the canister of mace I often carried. Mace was something I carried and gave Ann, my mother, and sisters to carry for protection against attackers. Ann stood her ground and dared me to touch her. I wanted to calm her down, not fight. I felt guilty that she was behaving in such a violent manner. Yes, I had physically abused her in the past, but that had been more than two years ago.

I had long ago realized my violent behavior was a result of my childhood experiences. My mother often fought with her boyfriends. Those fights scared my sisters and me. As an adult I began to repeat the pattern. One day, after a fight, I sincerely apologized and promised never to defile our marriage in such a manner again. That was more than two years ago, and I had kept my promise.

However, today, Ann felt that I had a good reason to be angry and do her harm. She knew that I had her cornered in an ongoing fraud against me, and she felt any normal man would be raging mad. I wasn't, I truly wasn't. My frustration had been released long ago and I was just bringing this marital fiasco to a close. Still, I didn't like a knife being drawn on me, especially a 12-inch butcher knife, by a scared woman riddled with lies.

I withdrew the mace and sprayed Ann in the face. She doubled over as the knife fell to the floor. Ann coughed and gagged for air so badly that I helped her outside for fresh air. The kids and I were unaffected by the fumes but they hit Ann with direct contact. Once she got herself together, she snatched away from me and left the house coughing from the chemical assault.

By the time she returned an hour later, my car was packed with all my clothes and personal property. As much as I hated the idea of being a contributing factor to a broken home, I rationalized that the long term effect of our ugly relationship would be worse on the family if I stayed there. The separation was in the address only. I still came by at least three times a week to eat dinner or spend the night. Ann and I were closer during this period, but neither one of us was in a hurry to get back together.

About six months into our separation, Ann told me she was three months pregnant. She quit her job and got rid of Harriet. Ann said she wanted to be the only woman raising *her* children. Suddenly the thought of reuniting became important to my wife, but only until the baby was born, she reasoned. Since Harriet was no longer there, Ann felt she would have an easier pregnancy if I were by her side. Reluctantly, I agreed. However, I planned to move out again after the baby was six months old.

We didn't argue during the pregnancy. If we disagreed about anything, I left the house before we yelled at each other. Soon we felt this was true love. Though we behaved much better, I still resented her secrecy and untrustworthiness. Ann sensed that I never forgave her and would often apologize for her actions. She confessed that most of her decisions in our marriage came from her oldest sister Hanna who said, "A man ain't no good and will leave his family, in nothing flat." Ann later told me that nearly every time I made her angry or stayed out all night, she called her sister. Hanna told Ann to prepare for me to leave her and to hide away as much money as possible. Ann sometimes cried in bed and would explain her actions by saying she dreamed I left the family. Consequently, when my daughter Jennifer was six months old, the thought of moving out was no longer on my mind.

Two years later, Ann was pregnant for the fourth time. We purchased our first home (using phony credit, of course) in the Los Angeles suburb of Rowland Heights. Our oldest daughter, Yolanda, was now 7-years-old, Rochelle was four, and Jennifer was eighteen months. We were happy for the first time in years. Our home was in a quiet and beautiful community, about forty-five miles east of the city.

We moved there to spare our children the growing drug and gang culture. By this time, my welfare schemes were in full bloom. I organized a team of five welfare cheats, and we were bleeding the Public Assistance system as dry as we could. Ann had even gotten into the act and was receiving welfare checks in four different names for 12 children. However, I realized that the only reason Ann participated in my scams was to reestablish herself as trustworthy in my sight.

When Roxanne Catrice Jones (called Roxy) was born our family life was on an all time high. Ann and I expressed love for one another like in the days when we first began dating each other. The only problem was that I still drank heavily. A couple times during her last pregnancy, I was arrested for drunk driving. Both times, Ann rushed down to the jail and bailed me out. In my mind, this was the true test of love: A woman standing by your side when you're in jail or down in any way.

As far as I was concerned, there was hope for us yet. Ann's sister had not schooled her on how to treat a decent man, especially when you're married and have four children by him. We went on family picnics, drive-in movies, amusement parks, the zoo, and school plays featuring our oldest daughter. Ann joined a church. The family, minus me, went each Sunday. However, I showed up for special church programs when my children or wife was a part of them.

Occasionally, Ann and I would argue regarding my church membership. I replied by saying, "I am not a hypocrite, like you. Why should I sit up in church, singing church songs all day Sunday and rob from the automobile insurance companies, workers' compensation insurance, the welfare system, and rip-off furniture stores through phony credit schemes the rest of the time?" Ann would get so mad that she wouldn't bring the subject up for a month or two. Nevertheless, when she did, they would arm me with those cutting words: Hypocrite! Hypocrite! Hypocrite!

I often walked in on her crying for what seemed like no reason. When pressed to answer, she would state her dissatisfaction with receiving fraudulent welfare checks. "I love you, Rick. But I'm not going to let you send me to hell or jail." I would threaten her by saying, "You're in too deep to turn around. The law will lock you up and put the children in Foster Homes. I knew going to church would have a bad effect on you! That's why I don't go."

Gradually, God and church became our only division source. Though I was glad the girls were in Sunday school, I figured grown people were weak if they ran to church for guidance. Ann began putting her entire fraudulent welfare and accident income in church. I was furious! However, I didn't interfere since I told her, after she paid me 'my' 50 percent, I didn't care what her hypocritical, holy roly carcass did. The preacher and church members loved her and thought we were financially secure. They had the nerve to come by our house to convert me and increasing their church tithes, under the guise of 'saving my soul'.

One day Ann informed me that God told her to stop the cheating, and to leave me until I did the same. By this time, our youngest daughter, Roxy, was eighteen months old. I wasn't about to stop doing anything. This was my life. I didn't know anything else nor was I willing to learn anything new. Ann, on the other hand, was a beautician. She didn't need 'crooked' money to sustain herself. Additionally, she had a support group within her church. I strongly suspected that her little prayer groups and women's fellowship meetings were behind her decision. Her next step involved chasing evil spirits from the house with oil and burning candles. It seemed to me that the only evil spirit she was running away was me. Rather than leave my family, I allowed her to stop all her fraudulent activities and I pretended to pray about stopping too.

My wife came up with a new revelation three months later. Lead by the spirit, Ann confided in me that God wanted her to turn herself in for all her previous crimes and confess her sins. She would not be punished with eternal damnation, and the law would show leniency. I knew where she and God were going with this one. Both wanted me to do the same. We argued over this fine point night and day. I began to distrust her all over again. Eventually, for the sake of our children, I moved out. I told Ann since she allowed her church friends to break up our marriage, she had to pay the mortgage payment and all other house related expenses. She was very confident between her doing hair and God, she would not need anything or anybody. I secretly admired her strong faith, but there was no place in *my* life for such foolishness.

It did not surprise me that we got along better after the separation. Ann didn't bother me half as much about becoming an honest man and a Christian. However, she slipped back into her deceptive ways. Ann fell seriously behind in house payments. She kept me thinking that everything was fine and the bills were under control. I figured that since she was doing hair at home and some clerical work at her church, finances were in order. She didn't say anything for months. Finally, the court served eviction papers and we lost the house.

Deep down inside I was relieved, but pretended to be angry. I figured since Ann and, perhaps, her church members knew that the house was purchased with fraudulent credit I could never sleep in peace. That's why I totally disconnected myself from the house business. Ann preferred to stay in a motel until she found an apartment which accepted a single mother with four children. Meanwhile, the children moved into my two bedroom apartment. This arrangement was supposed to be for three days, however, two months later, the children were still living with me. Ann stopped going to church because she didn't want her church friends to know that she lost her home and I had the children. Finally, Ann found a small one bedroom apartment that would accept one small child. Ann got Roxy, and the other girls stayed with me. I strongly felt the older girls didn't like the idea of their baby sister living away from them, but they remained silent. In my heart, I felt that all the children would eventually return to living with their mother.

One rainy night, Ann was driving home from the grocery store with Roxy asleep on the front seat. According to the police report and witnesses, she made an illegal maneuver and caused a speeding eighteen wheeler trailer truck to crash into the rear of her automobile. Ann was killed instantly.

The county coroner's office called between two and three o'clock in the morning. Due to lateness of the hour, the call woke me from a deep sleep. I wasn't sure if I were dreaming or if this were a prank call or what. To the best of my recollection, the call went something like this:
"Hello, is this Mr. Jones?" asked the male voice on the other end of the phone.

"Yeah, it is. Who's calling?"
"This is Mr. Ashford of the Los Angeles Coroner's Office. Are you married to Annie Mae Jones?"

At this point I didn't know what to think or say. I knew the police played all types of games to trick you. That was my first reaction. I thought it was some kind of police trick. I decided to cautiously play along. Before I answered his question I asked, "How did you get my number?"
Mr. Ashford quickly replied, "The California Highway Patrol Officer discovered your name in Mrs. Jones address book as the person to call in case of emergency."
I questioned his answer, "Well how come the highway patrol didn't call me instead of you?"

"Mr. Jones," he replied, "there was a major accident on the freeway tonight and the highway patrol will have their hands full for hours." Then he asked again, "Are you married to a Mrs. Annie Mae Jones?"

I still didn't want to commit or incriminate myself in case this was a police trick. I mean, since Ann was always talking about turning herself in.

I replied, "Where's my daughter?"

"She's been checked out by the paramedics and seemed uninjured. Your daughter is now in the hands of the Los Angeles County Social Services. I have a number here for you to inquire of her exact whereabouts, but first I need you to identify the body of Annie Mae Jones. Is she your wife Mr. Jones?"

"I don't know," I slowly answered measuring each word. "My wife is not out this time of the night."

Mr. Ashford's impatience was beginning to show.

"The accident occurred several hours ago. They brought the corpse in only thirty minutes ago."

"Will you describe the woman in the morgue for me Mr. Ashford?" I asked, slowly beginning to grasp the importance of the call. He gave me a few general descriptions like height, weight, hair color, etc.

Finally, I interrupted him, "Mr. Ashford, did you examine the body, personally?"

"Yes, Mr. Jones."

"Well are there any birthmarks, scars or tattoos in common or unusual places on the body?"

He paused as if looking on a chart and replied, "There's a six-inch surgical scar on the abdomen and dark butterfly birthmark on the inner left thigh."

Suddenly, Mr. Ashford had me convinced. Ann was dead and Roxy was in the care of social services. Mr. Ashford gave me all the necessary information I needed to come in later that morning to identify the body and unite with Roxanne.

That morning after breakfast I gathered Yolanda, Rochelle, and Jennifer in the living room. When I broke the news to them, I did my best to emphasize the fact that their mother was in a better place. I highlighted the fact that their baby sister was fine and didn't receive a scratch. According to the mortician, I told them, their mother threw her body over Roxy's during the crash and that's why she survived. None of us really knew how we should have felt. The girls realized their mother was dead, but I didn't sense that they understood the true depth of what I told them. When you hear such news but don't see the body, the impact is different. None of us fell out crying but we all grieved and mourned her death. For me, I hadn't lost a wife or friend, only my kid's mother. My only thought was, how tragic to die so young. I figured God called her home early, since she loved Him so much.

My mother, her third husband, Nate, and Ann's brother, Wade, went with me to identify the body and reunite with Roxanne that morning. Nate drove while Wade and I sat in the rear. The reason I summoned traveling companions was twofold. First, I was very insecure about handling such a serious matter, and second, I needed moral support. I had never been asked to identify a dead body or salvage the property of a deceased person.

We first went to the Highway Patrol Station nearest the scene of the accident. According to the police reports, Ann was driving westward on the freeway when she pulled off the road to change Roxy's diaper. This was assumed because they discovered a soiled diaper balled-up and taped together on the front floor, and the baby was wearing a fresh one. The dome light inside her car was still on. The accident witnesses said the car reentered the flow of traffic at a slow speed without her headlights on. She drove into the path of a 18-wheeler diesel truck. There were skid marks from the truck 60 feet long. The truck crashed into the rear of her car and kept going over the trunk, roof, and hood with it's right nine tires. The truck flipped 75 feet onto its left side. There were tire tracks across our 1973 Buick Regal from bumper to bumper. Ann suffered a broken neck and died instantly. Roxanne was in the front seat next to her and was pulled from beneath her mother's body without injuries.

Attendants and police officers on the scene reported Roxanne didn't appear injured, nor did she cry as one would expect a two year old in a similar situation. Doctors later told me that being unaware of a tragedy was usual for a baby. Nevertheless, the lack of emotional expression from Roxanne worried me. The fact that she didn't cry during the entire accident or the aftermath wasn't something to be overlooked. There was no doubt that I would be seeking a child psychologist and retaining an attorney in the future.

The California Highway Patrol Officers released an envelope containing valuables found on Ann's body. They gave me an inventory list to check off the contents, which consisted of a watch, two rings, her purse, wallet, miscellaneous papers and $3,735.84 in cash. The money was used to defray incurred expenses, which included the mortuary, emergency medical services for Roxanne, and Ann's remains flown to Mississippi ten days after the accident.

I dreaded my duty to identify Ann's body at the mortuary. As she lay on an eight-foot slab and draped with a heavy dark sheet, I said my last farewell. There was a long gash across her forehead and her face had no blood stains. Movement in her throat seemed as if she were swallowing. I shouted to the mortician, "Hey look! She's not dead!" Mr. Ashford, the mortician, calmly explained what I saw was the movement of the fluids which they had injected to preserve the body.

As I stood there, I wanted to cry. It seemed like the right thing to do, but no tears fell. Memories of our good times didn't do the trick. All I could see was the woman who promised to expose all my criminal activities, in Jesus' name, to the police, was lying dead. In a way, I was relieved. Still, in the name of the love we once had, and in proxy for our children, I leaned forward, pressed my lips to hers and whispered, "Rest in peace." I could've sworn there was a single tear about to leave one of her shut eyes. I stared closely and silently, but no tear fell. After leaving the morgue, we picked up my baby daughter. Roxanne and I looked so much alike, the social worker in charge kidded me by saying, "No I.D. will be necessary, Mr. Jones. Seeing the two of you together is all the identification I need."

When Roxanne and I were finally home, it was daylight. I slept until 11:00 a.m. All my daughters were awake and watching television. I kept them out of school and preschool for another day. Yolanda fixed each of them a bowl of corn flakes. When she saw me, enter the kitchen, she managed a half smile and said, "Daddy, your cereal is in the refrigerator. Do you want some toast?" I returned the smile, walked around the table and gave each a kiss on the cheek. My head was clear of the side effects of drinking a half gallon of cheap wine the night before. The reality of single parenthood sank in. This reality seemed as cold as the lifeless lips I had kissed last night. I was a single parent. No more arguing over my decisions regarding the girls. No more worrying about Ann snatching them from school or my front yard without notice or permission. No more threats against my freedom. I felt I needed a permanent woman, one worthy of motherhood. But I didn't know a decent woman, nor an honest woman. It seemed like every woman I knew was either too wild, too square, or to churchy.

As I neared Hanna Mae's home, my visit into the past ten years, slowly ended. It seemed that I walked more than ten miles round trip. By the time I entered the 'after funeral gathering' of my departed wife, most of the guests had left and Yolanda was asleep. No one expressed concern about my extended absence. A card game was going on and they invited me to play. Though I declined, I did have a snack and engaged in light chitchat before retiring for the night. After a good night's sleep and early breakfast, one of Annie's uncles arrived to take Yolanda and me to the train depot. The funeral had been a tremendous emotional ordeal for my nine-year-old daughter. At last, we were returning to our home in Los Angeles. The train trip would offer us an opportunity to cover some serious and necessary issues.

The gravity of single parenthood grasped me with renewed perspective as the locomotive left the depot; the thought of it shook me up a bit. Most of the ladies in my family and female acquaintances were single parents. However, I never knew a male single parent. This was a bit scary. After all, this was 1981 and the image of Black fathers was constantly debased in the forum of public consensuses, which fueled my insecurity.

The fact that my own father took absolutely no part of my life detonated a charge in me to do better for my children. More than anything, the haunting memory of my childhood wishes affected me. Had I wished this horrible fate upon Annie? There were times in my youth that I despised the idea of being married, based on the poor examples from the adults in my life. Fatherhood, however, was a cherished dream. I recalled often wishing and perhaps sharing with childhood buddies, "If I get married, I hope my wife dies or runs off with another man. We wouldn't have to fight all the time and scare the children." This thought returned repeatedly. Was it my fault? Had a 11-year-old boy prophesied this ugly fate upon an innocent woman?

Thoughts of my death wish revisited me that night on the train while Yolanda and most of the other passengers were asleep. As I stared into the distant lights of the passing houses outside the window and wept in silence, my thoughts digressed into the years of my youth. This journey back in time was a quest for understanding, soul searching, and truth.

Chapter 3

*W*inter mornings in St. Louis, Missouri were typically at a freezing 5-20 degrees below zero. Snow, ice, and sleet was the greeting of the day. Mommy didn't have to worry about me eating breakfast before dragging off to school. I wanted as much hot oatmeal or grits in me as I could get to fortify me against that unmerciful chill that would waylay me. My gray tin lunch box usually contained two normal size sandwiches or one 'Dagwood Sandwich,' which is a triple decker, a piece of fruit and my good old thermos bottle which stored my traveling fuel, hot Ovaltine.

My standard traveling wear this time of year were two pairs of pants, three pairs of socks, a T-shirt, sweat shirt, and a top shirt, sweater and overcoat, heavy boots, gloves, wool cap and earmuffs. But if it was cold out, I mean really cold, then I would play hooky in the basement. More often then not, I would soon hear the signal knock of one or both of my sisters at the basement door. On rare occasions, they were accompanied by a girlfriend wishing to thaw out rather than go to school. They usually brought dance music, like Fats Domino singing, 'Blueberry Hill,' or The Five Satins, 'In the Still of the Night.' We would have a good time singing and dancing.

Being a single parent in the 1950's was a unique situation, which made my mother unique in more ways than one. Not only was she mother and father, but had two jobs. Convalescent homes, restaurants, and housekeeping were the mainstream occupational choices of the uneducated Negro woman of this era. Convalescent homes were the least favorite choice because of the brute manual labor involved with this job. They were called nurses' aides. Most of them were untrained. The supervising staffs were always white, and would routinely assign Negro nurses the heaviest and cantankerous patients,

45

according to my mother. The nurses' aides' duties consisted of feeding, bathing, making beds, dressing, changing soiled underclothing, walking, and appeasing overbearing relatives. The pay was a slave wage with no employee benefits.

Welfare was not a socially acceptable option, though a few scorned families received government surplus cheese, flour, butter, and dry milk each month. But for the most part, welfare recipients were 'in-the-closet.' My mother considered public aid disgraceful. "Every healthy person should work," she would say. This was not hypocritical lip service. Mommy worked two jobs for two neighboring convalescent homes and commuted by bus.

It was my proud pleasure to help mother anyway I could. She seemed to know how much I loved her, though as a child I vaguely remember saying it. At ten years old, I received a shoe shine kit from my maternal grandmother. My grandmother, whom we called "Mama," told me that I could earn money with it downtown. After that, I shined shoes on Saturdays. When I returned from work, I had a gift for my mother. Most of the time it was drinking glasses, dishes, or ash trays, although no one in our family smoked. Occasionally, I purchased white nurses' stockings or cosmetics.

One Saturday morning, my mother asked me if I wanted to go to work with her. She said that the gardener at the convalescent home quit and someone was needed to cut the grass and dig up the weeds. I knew she usually returned around 4:00 p.m. on Saturdays, which left enough time to still catch a few men at the train station downtown for a shoe shine. Mother didn't tell me how much money I would get. She said that was between me and the owner. We caught the bus. It was the longest bus ride I'd ever had. I'd never been so far away from home. No Negroes were walking the streets. The passengers on the bus, when we boarded in our neighborhood, were black like us. The farther west the bus went, the more Whites boarded. By the time we reached our stop in the city of Wellston, where my mother worked, I felt like we were space aliens. There were beautiful homes everywhere; trees without ceasing and new cars in every driveway. It blew my mind. I remember thinking to myself, "Holy Cow! This must be where, *'Leave It to Beaver'* lives." *'Leave*

It Beaver', was a popular TV show in the 50's about white kids in the suburbs.

When we arrived at the convalescent home, I was shocked that it strongly resembled the private homes on the street. The only noticeable difference was the sign in the front yard. No wonder, they called it a 'home.' After meeting the middle-aged white lady in charge, exchanging smiles and the usual chitchat, "Oh what a big strong *handsome* boy you are," she'd say.
"This sho' is a pretty house," I'd say . . . then it was time to get down to business.

"How much you gonna charge me to manage that yard today?" asked Miss Goldstein. Before I could answer, she snapped, "That's fine, it's all settled, I'll give you 75 cents per hour." What could I say? This was my mother's employer and I was afraid to embarrass my mother by rejecting the offer. To do so would be considered ungrateful. This was no more than a two-hour job. Big deal! My shoe shine prices were 15 cents per shine. Most customers gave me a dime tip. In two hours, I would have easily shined 10 pairs of shoes, and that would be more money than I would be paid here. Oh well, at least I got to see to Wellston. "That's fine, Miss Goldstein, I'll get started right away. Thank you, Miss Goldstein." That was the last time I went to Wellston.

Six months later, I noticed a 'Help Wanted' sign in the window of the local newspaper distribution center. I knew instantly they wanted a paperboy. They needed someone desperate enough to be out in the sub-zero weather before sunrise on Sunday mornings selling papers.

Anyone within two blocks of those early Sunday morning paperboys could hear their noisy newspaper wagons coming down the street, as they yelled any attention-getting bellow. Each paperboy had his own distinctive sound which their personal customers recognized. During the winter, the paper companies had a shortage of paperboys. Most of my contemporaries were opposed to this kind of work even in the best of weather because of rampant street robberies. Besides, a paperboy wasn't a hit with the girls, like a guy working in a record or candy store. I went into storefront office to become a paperboy. Oh I knew the job was mine. After all, there was ice on the ground everywhere.

When I told my mother about my new venture, she resisted the idea. Everyone was aware that paperboys were often robbed. I deceived her into believing my route was in a safe white neighborhood, and I would not be leaving home before 6:00 a.m. My persistency and pleads weakened her position. She conceded after thinking about it a long while.

On Saturday night, I usually stayed up late and watched good monster or cowboy movies on our 13" black & white television. This Saturday night would be the beginning of a lifelong change. For the first time, since I don't know when, I readily went to bed early on a Saturday night. The dispatcher told me to be there at 5:00 a.m. sharp. I went to bed with his words on my mind. My alarm clock went off at 4:00 a.m. I tipped out the house at 4:30. Excitement overwhelmed me to the point I didn't even care how cold it was.

I arrived at the distribution center, which was about eight blocks from our apartment, at 4:50 a.m. I'm sure of the time because there was a big clock in the window facing street traffic. From a block away, I detected several shadowy figures huddled around a blazing fire contained in a tin barrel. This was a common winter sight. I wondered why they didn't go inside to get warm. Just shooting the breeze, I figured. Without even trying the door, I headed straight for the barrel. After snuggling as close to the flames as I could without being cremated, I mumbled, "What's happening?" which everyone understood meant 'Good morning'. A couple guys returned the response. Half the guys around the barrel were close to my age. The other half were much older, maybe even 25-years-old. I knew one voice. As I looked up, I said, "What's happening, Boosty?"
"What's happening, Richard?," he replied.

Boosty was one of the baddest dressing dudes in school who was renowned and revered for his fine wardrobe. He wore snappy knit shirts, Stacy Adams shoes, Knox and Dobbs hats, leather coats of all colors, mohair and silk suits, trench coats, ties with fancy stick pins, and cuff links. Some of Boosty's jackets and sweaters even had his initials embroidered on them.

My main man Boosty, a stupid paperboy, I recall enjoying such a thought.

"You and me," Boosty said, in a *'I hope you can understand'* kind of voice. "You and me," I echoed, fully understanding. Boosty didn't want me to reveal his secret life. Everybody thought he was earning money as a 'booster,' which was our slang for 'rouge' or 'thief.' That's why we called him "Boosty," from the word 'booty,' meaning stolen goods. He wanted this to stay between him and me. What a strain we went through to impress others. In our confused circle, it was better to be thought of as a thief than a common laborer. But heck, I understood. I didn't want the girls to know I was a paperboy either. Boosty and me, I thought, stupid paperboys.

"What time do they open?" I asked. "We got ten mo' minutes," someone answered, "see the clock?" "Big Black never opens till five." a boy from the group added. "He's in there now, the lo' down nigga'."

Soon talk turned to football. Everybody had an opinion, but no one agreed. I never entered into conversations about sports unless it was boxing or wrestling. No team sport interested me. The way I figured it, the only way to know a man's true grit was to send him off alone. Without a team or a gang. Sports talk bored me and the next ten minutes seemed endless.

Finally, the door opened and we herded in like cattle. Big Black was not the dispatcher who hired me. Big Black, was the weekend manager and dispatcher. I found out later the white owner never worked on Sundays. Big Black was a tall burly man about 50-years-old. His complexion was dark as a berry.

Most of the boys and men were bigger than me. Even Boosty, at 13, was 6 feet tall and about 210 lbs. I was about 5'8", and weighted 125 lbs. at 12-years-old, but that was average. My mother and her friends were the only people in St. Louis who thought I was such a 'big' boy. As far as the newspaper business went, the bigger and tougher looking a guy was, the less likely he was to go home with empty pockets and a black eye.

However, the smallest guy was Tesler, a hard working short kid from my neighborhood. We were the same age, though I had him by 4 inches and twenty pounds. Everyone else was 200 lbs. and heavier. One boy, nicknamed Tank was 16-years-old, 6'3" and 240 lbs. Tank's real name was Tyrone. His brother, Alan, and I were friends. Tesler and Tank went to different schools than Boosty and me. The other guys were much older and probably not in school.

The dispatcher worked from a long wooden counter. Behind the counter where what appeared to be thousands of newspapers stacked in piles of about 500, and bundled together with string in packs of 50. The Sunday Post Dispatch was a thick paper. About 50 would take up half a wagon.

The wagons were made of wood with iron wheels, with no rubber on them so the sound of the wheels would be loud and disturbing to people. They were about 4 feet long, and deep enough to accommodate up to three packs of papers. A curved iron handle was on the front of it.

When Big Black called your name, you came up to the counter from the bench. He told you how many papers you sold last week, according to the chart in his hand, then you told him how many papers you wanted that day. If you asked for too many, based on your record, he refused and gave you what he thought best. You signed the book, got your favorite wagon, and left. The top sellers, like Tank and a few others, signed out two wagons full each week. Naturally, being new, I was the last name called.

"My rules are simple, Jones," the dispatcher growled as if he was annoyed. "You screw up and I put these size 13 boots in you junior-flip tail, any questions?"
"I didn't sayyyyay anyanyanything sssir," I stammered, as I usually did when nervous or lying.
"Big Black! Don't call me no cotton pick'n sir!" he roared. "You lil' skinny niggas' come in here begging Mista' Henry fer a cotton pickin' job, go out there . . . get your lil' butts kicked, money took, and it comes out my cotton pickin' pocket. Don't ya' come draggin' back in here with yer tail 'tween yer legs, cryin' 'bout being robbed, like that black dog Larry Turner. "You know Turner, boy?"

"Naaaaaanono, ssssirr, I meeeeean Bibibibig Bbbbblack," I managed. "I don't want no crap outta ya', ya understand," he yelled and slammed one of his big watermelon fists down on the counter so hard, I thought I felt the floor shake and myself pass gas at the same time. Then just as suddenly as he transformed into a monster, he transformed back into a human being. He calmly relit his two inch cigar and asked, "Wanna cup of hot chocolate fo' ya' get started?" "Nnnnnnnnnnnooono, I juuuuuuust wawawanna, getgetget started," I said.

He explained that the Sunday paper sold for 25 cents each, and I would receive 10 cents for each copy I sold. My starting amount would be 50 papers--I could ask for more if I sold out. My route was to start six blocks south and nine blocks west. When I got to Easton Avenue, I could start selling. Every street within a one mile square radius west of Easton was my route. He gave me a route sheet and warned me not to 'call-out' in areas assigned to others. Guys hated boys who crossed their boundaries. If a customer called me from a window and asked for a paper, tell them their paperboy would be along later. Those were my marching orders.

By the time I left the depot it was 6:30 a.m. The sky was just beginning to welcome the morning light, and the snow was coming down in gentle but steady drifts. Before I got to Easton at least three people called me from their doors or windows, "Oh paperboy!" I respected the route I was traveling through and yelled back to each person, that my papers were for prepaid customers and I had no extras. My route was in a neighborhood which was near a few friends' houses. I didn't mind my male friends seeing me sell papers, but not the girls. I was glad that I didn't know any girls around there. According to a clock on the 1st National Bank on Kings Highway Blvd., it was 7:05 a.m. when I sold my first newspaper to a man in a passing car. After that, sales went fast.

The 'yell' I decided to use went like this, "Yoooooour HEY Paaaaaapa!" Most of the responses were from sleepy female voices. I never knew so many half naked women existed. Most of them, however, had on thick robes, or handed me the money from behind the door. A few who were scantily clad, would unlock the door before I could reach it, and yell for me the enter while they were in another part of the house. As I stood waiting for them to come into the room with the money, I constantly peeped out the door to guard my papers, and life, according to Big Black. The women would return from the bedroom or den covering themselves with one hand while paying me with the other. They didn't seem to mind me having a clear view of their near nakedness. It was as if they were thinking, "He's only a stupid paperboy, why bother even covering up."

By 9:15 a.m., I sold my last paper and was headed back to the depot. I earned $5, and about $2 in tips. Big Black was still human and congratulated me. He even shook my hand. I didn't understand him a bit.

"Thaaathathank yayaya Bbbbbigg Blablablack," came stumbling pass my frostbitten lips, as I hurried out the door.
There were two more weekends before Christmas. Knowing that I could buy presents for my family pleased me more than almost anything. My greatest pleasure though, came from the anticipation of seeing those half naked ladies week after week.

The customers on my route began to know me and would buy their Sunday paper from no one else. My distinct 'call' became familiar to the entire route. By April '59, I was one of the top sellers, and I didn't stammer around Big Black anymore. Boosty shared with me that every time someone's tally came up short, Mr. Henry, the regional manger, took it out of Big Black's pay, for faked or real robberies. Larry Turner, whom I replaced, caused Big Black to lose a full two days pay ($20.00) by pretending some dudes stole 100 papers off his wagon. Also, Larry was a new paperboy, so Big Black took his rage out on me.

Boosty's secret life as a paperboy was safe with me. As a matter of fact, one afternoon Boosty and I passed each other in the hall at school, I was chatting with Irene Rogers, a 'stone fox', but she didn't date. Irene could pass for a 17-year-old but was 13. Boosty smiled at me and nodded. I responded with, "Me and You, Boosty." He said, "Me and You."

With all I had going, the new clothes, the regular gifts for my mother, the female attention as a result of the fine clothes, and more money than ever before, I was still missing something. What was it? When I figured it out, I was embarrassed to even think about it. However, I had to share my dark secret with someone. I chose Alan. He bursted out laughing when I told him I was beginning to dream about the 'practically' naked women I would see every Sunday. He thought I was lying when I described one of my customers with having one huge, and one tiny boob. He really laughed when I told him that she would cover the tiny boob while paying me, but freely expose the huge one. Then I told him about Connie, the sexy waitress who worked at the White Castle Hamburger Palace. She was also one of my customers. We knew Connie, but she didn't know us. Every time we ate there, we drooled just watching her.

"Alan, I ain't lying. She sleeps in a thin night gown without underpants," I whispered laughingly. "I even set her trash out, one Sunday morning." Alan was so convinced that I was lying he dared me to prove it. He even bet me a dollar. I told him, not only was I in no need of a dollar but I would get an eyeful next Sunday anyway. Alan's excitement grew daily.

Alan definitely loved seeing naked bodies. He even subscribed to a medical magazine called 'Causes and Cures' that showed pictures of healthy and diseased body parts. Though I didn't relish the idea of going on a peep show field trip with Alan or anybody else, I wanted to get an eyeful more often than on Sunday.

The most shocking experience I had, was the time I stopped for an old lady as I was in route to my own selling territory. The lady had called out to me on different mornings. Each time I yelled back to her, she wasn't on my route. However, this particular morning, I stopped to explain this to her. It was in the spring and still kind of dark outside. When I got to the front door, the skinny old lady was in a heavy terry cloth robe and head rag. The lights were off behind the lady as she stood in the gap of the half-open door. She immediately thanked me for stopping, and explained that they didn't get a paper until nearly noon.

Before I could say anything she asked, "Ya got change for a five?"
"No madam, I explained, "You're my first customer, and this isn't even my route."

"Well wait right here whiles' I find you a quarter," she said as she turned and disappeared through the doorway, leaving the door ajar. A hall light partially lit the living room. I saw the figure of a young woman on the sofa bed in the front room. Suddenly, a friendly male voice from the back room told me in step inside and shut the door to keep out the draft. When I was fully inside, I noticed three photographs on a mantel. One was the old lady, the other was an old man, and the third was Irene Rogers. She told me she lived with her grandparents. Irene said, they were old fashioned, and wouldn't allow her to date or have male company.

I watched her as she gently tossed to and fro in her bed. "Hurry up old woman," I thought to myself. I would have hated it if Irene woke up and saw me there. In that instant, her blanket dropped to the floor. She laid there on her stomach with her full length nightgown impersonating a short nightie. "Good Golly, Miss Molly!," I thought. "Her grandmother's gonna comes in and *think* I'm a young freak, and removed the blanket to bother Irene."
Then my thoughts flashed to, "Why don't you just stoop down and sneak over for a quick peek to see if she's wearing underpants." The next thought was to cover her. That's what I decided to do. As I eased toward her bed, the woman called to me, "Just a minute, honey." When I stooped to pick up the blanket I got a clear look. She *was* wearing underpants. I picked the covers up and was about to drape her. Suddenly she rolled over and exposed one of her bare breasts. One of her feet rested flat on the bed. Her thighs were slightly parted and her gown was draped loosely across her hips. Irene Rogers was a super duper foxy chick, *and* I saw her underpants. Good Golly, Miss Molly!

I quickly covered her with the blanket. Just as I returned to the doorway, the grandmother came into the room with a 50-cent piece, and told me to keep the change. With a final look at Irene, I thought, "What a fox!" I never told anyone, not even Alan, about seeing Irene Rogers, nor did I stop for the old lady again.

One day after school, Alan, two other buddies, Byron and Ned, and I were in our regular hamburger 'hangout.' Alan and I played the pinball machine, while the other guys were 'Bopping'. Though there were several girls available to dance with, Byron and Ned were fast dancing together. This was not, by any means, unusual in this era. The Marvalettes were on the jukebox, singing their current hit, 'Wait a Minute Mr. Postman.' (... de-liv-er the let-ter, the soo-ner the bet-ter, wait, wait..)

There were always dance contests around school, and it didn't matter who your partner was. Winning was the goal. Often boys and girls practiced with their gender. Regular partners knew each other's dance steps and together they could make up new ones. Byron and Ned were good. (...ya bet-ter wait, wait, wait a minute, Please Mister Po' ooooo-ooo-stman...) We came to 'The Doo Drop Inn' nearly every day after school. Every neighborhood had a 'The Doo Drop Inn', by another name, where teenagers hung out. The crowd here ranged from 13 thru 18-years-old. The pinball machine was a popular pastime at five cents per game. The juke box played records at five cents each, hamburgers were 20 - 30 cents, depending on your taste, french fries 10 cents and cokes 10 cents. They also sold candy bars. A Baby Ruth, my favorite, was also five cents. I often bought a snack for some of the other kids. After all, I earned about $7 every week. Money made me feel like a big man. I even gave my mother money sometimes, although she seldom asked for it.

"Why don't you get a job as a paperboy," I suggested to Alan. "If you want to see some naked bodies sooooo baddddd."
"You must be crazy! I hear about all those newspaper boy robberies from Tank," he reasoned.
"Alan just think a minute," I said, "I haven't been robbed in all the six months I've been working. Have I?"
"Well no," he said.
"And think about your brother, Tank. He hasn't been robbed and he's been working three years."
Alan laughed, "Ha ha so what, that's Tank, look how big he is."

"That's not why, I chuckled, look at Tesler, he's short *and* skinny, but never been robbed. And I'll tell you why."

"Why then?" asked Alan with a puzzled look forming on his face.

"I'll tell you why, since you wanna know so badly," I teased. "Because we get our work done and be back home before the robbers even get outta bed. We all start by 5:30 a.m. and be finished by 8:30 or nine. The guys that get jacked-up are the late ones. Not getting started until after 10 o'clock and still working their route at two and three in the afternoon. The robbers like to wait until late because they figure if a paperboy is out late, he has collected more money."

The pinball game was over and Alan had won another turn. "Okay, man," said Alan. "I'll make a deal with you. If you take me to see our sweetie pie at White Castle, I'll go talk to Big Black about getting a route this Sunday at five o'clock." Now, this was something worth thinking about. No one in Alan's family had been able to get him to earn his own money. Tank and I always told him about route openings to no avail. I guess we were also the main two responsible for his laziness because we gave him money or paid his way in the movies, to dances, and everything else. Alan was nice, and most guys helped him. Perhaps he was more slick than nice, but nonetheless, he was my best friend. Besides, we were friends because neither of us cared about sports. We enjoyed telling jokes and did lots of laughing. Alan didn't even like boxing. I owned a pair boxing gloves and wanted to box him for fun, but he always had an excuse. His arm was sore or he was too tired, etc. I often wondered if he could fight. I never saw him in an argument with anyone. Nobody picked on him, mostly because of Tank, although, he wasn't small. Alan and I were the same size. To hear Alan even hint of working was unreal. I knew he was serious because he adored Connie, the cute waitress at White Castle. The thought of seeing her nude was enough to drag him out of his tired, lazy ways. I was also excited because, he owed me nearly five dollars.

Dotty, a cute, short, and plump chick asked me to cha cha with her. She liked to start off the cha cha by standing close and embracing like a slow dance. That's how she got her steps going. Then she would dance 'in step' apart from you. I was once her boyfriend. We kissed all the time but that was her limit.

Therefore, I stopped visiting her. She didn't care. A lot of boys wanted her. The Duke of Earl by Gene Chandler played as we squeezed pass several other dancers to the center of the floor. (...nothing can stop me now, 'cause I am the Duke of Earrrrl, Duke Duke Duke of Earl Earl Earl Duke Duke Duke of Earl Duke of Earl Earl Earl...) I wondered if Dotty knew I was a virgin. I told her, if she wasn't going to do it with me, I would find someone else. I was still looking weeks later.

Alan and I agreed to meet back at 'The Doo Drop Inn' after the Friday night wrestling match went off television at 8:00 p.m. He admired 'Connie' for almost two years, since we stopped into that particular White Castle Restaurant and '*discovered*' her, as Alan considered it.
I, too, felt she was a very sexy chick, but Alan was more of a romantic. He would borrow a quarter from me or Tank and ride the bus across town for one bite size hamburger, if he knew Connie was on duty. Sometimes he would go by himself on the two-hour walk, with no money in his pockct, just to go in and ask Connie for a cup of water.

The first time Connie bought a newspaper from me was on a rainy morning. I was about an hour into my route. I had about 25 regular customers. On bad weather days I made more money because first time customers beckoned me. I usually bellowed with extra zeal on such days, "Yoooooour HEY Paaaaapaa! Yoooooour HEY Paaaaapaa!," I walked about ten steps and yell again, "Yooooour HEY Paaaaapaa!" Plus the wheels on the wagon also kept up enough noise to wake a jailhouse drunk.

Finally, I heard a male voice yelling from a second floor window in a nice brick apartment building, "Paperboy! Up here. Number 6." The front door to the building was unlocked and I carried one Sunday Post Dispatch Newspaper. It was about 7:00 a.m. Before I got to the last step on the second landing, the door with Number 6 opened, and a Negro man about 40-years-old, short and muscular appeared in a blue full length, loosely tied bath robe. He handed me a one dollar bill and I gave him the paper. I put the dollar in my right pocket and reached into my left for 75 cents change. He told me to just give him a quarter and keep 50 cents for myself. I thanked him and passed him the coin.

His robe fell open and he was nude underneath. I avoided making eye contact with him and quickly headed downstairs.

At the bottom of the steps, the door to apartment 2 was partially open with Connie standing behind it, with only her head and fingers in view. She asked, in a whisper, whether I had an extra paper. I knew her immediately, even with the rollers in her hair.

"Justjusjust aaaa mimiminute, let   Mmmmeeeme run out and check," I managed to get out. I smiled as I thought about Alan. The rain was barely a sprinkle now, and the papers were all still dry because of the plastic cover Big Black lent me. I was promptly back at her door. She was still in the same position. Connie stuck a five-dollar bill out to me and I handed the paper to her. I counted her change while she still had her hand extended. Connie then asked me to be her regular paperboy. I agreed and asked her name. Though I already knew her name, I'd seen her name tag at the White Castle at least 10 times. "Connie," she said, "what's yours?"
"Richard," I answered, I apparently was getting relaxed with her fast because my stammering was passing. At that moment, I spotted a small bag of trash in the kitchen and without thinking I blurted out, "Want me to take that trash out?" Oh my ! I thought, I 've gone crazy, why did I say that?
"How sweet! Are you sure you don't mind? I hate going out in this weather for anything," Connie said, as she opened the door a little wider. "Come on in."

I regretted making a fool of myself, but my true colors were exposed. She now knew I was not only a stupid paperboy, but one who's a sucker for a smile. Alan sure would laugh at this spectacle. No sooner than I was inside, she walked ahead of me toward the kitchen which was a straight shot in the small apartment. Connie had medium-brown smooth skin. Her face was oval and without a blemish. Her eyes were big, hazel and sexy. She was about 25-years-old, with reddish short hair. She stood about my mother's height but weighed a little more. Her breasts were big as Big Black's fists and her hips seemed to be wider than her shoulders. Connie walked just a couple steps ahead of me, wearing a long red night gown. I didn't think anything of it until she got to the kitchen door frame. The light in the kitchen made it possible for me to see right though her silk gown. She was exposed!

The two medium sized trash bags seemed to be three or four days full. Connie picked up one bag. As she bent over, the top of her gown revealed the entire top half of Connie's body. Her swaying breasts offered a peek-a-boo glimpse of her lower body. When she straightened-up, one of her shoulder straps fell and dangled on the side of her upper right arm. The front right side of the gown dropped a few inches lower. Connie nonchalantly readjusted the strap and extended the trash to me with both hands, teasingly saying, I was nice. I stood smiling but scared to speak because I felt a stammering attack coming on. I must've been in a momentary trance, because the next thing I knew, Connie was unlocking the back door about 8 feet away. "You can go through here," she said. "The trash cans are against that wall. Put it in the can marked Apartment 2. And thank you so much. You can get to the front through the driveway." She stood with the door wide open as I walked through, daring not to look into her face or engage in any talk. I just smiled. "See you next week Richard," I heard her say as the door eased shut behind me. I saw no other body that day that compared to Connie's.

On my weekly trips, I knocked at Connie's door, usually between 6:30 and 7:00 a.m. I could see from the door her trash area was always clear and didn't need emptying. Even if it did, I never offered, and she never asked. Most of the time she paid me while standing behind the door, with only her head and upper body sticking out. Occasionally, Connie would open the door before she had her money ready, in which case, I got an eyeful as she walked from one side of the room to the other looking for change.

Once, as Connie was getting ready to go to work, she hurriedly told me, she had been called unexpectedly to work. This particular time, Connie had apparently just stepped out of the shower when I rang her doorbell. She called out my name from the other side of the door before opening it. The door opened a couple inches. She began walking swiftly to a corner chair to get her purse. Then spoke without looking at me. All that time, she only had a blue towel wrapped around her wet body, and a white towel wrapped around her head. When Connie got to the chair, her back was to me. Connie bent over, opened her purse, and stayed in that position for at least a full minute while she continued talking and fumbling for 25 cents. The towel didn't cover her cheeks at all. It was as if her bare derriere was talking to me.

"That's her apartment over there, Alan," I said pointing a finger at the first floor window from across the street. The small four-unit building consisted of two upstairs and two downstairs apartments. Connie's one bedroom apartment was on the first floor.

Alan looked at his watch and said, "She should be home by now." Connie's long hours made me think about my mother's long work hours. I remembered thinking, maybe someday Connie would have a son to give her money. I never thought about her being married first.

It was a warm night, about 9:00 p.m. On such a night, you could very well expect most people to have their windows open. Connie was no exception. We could see the front windows opened from our position across the street. The shades on all three front windows were pulled all the way down. We began walking quietly toward the building, as if someone could hear us tip-toeing across the street. I lead the way. However, no sooner than we were in the driveway, Alan tiptoed pass me. He was moving too fast for me to catch up without making noise, so I followed behind him. He made a right turn at the end of the building. By the time I got there, I barely got a glimpse of him before he made a left, which took him to Connie's side of the building. I felt uneasy with Alan's behavior. He could trip over something as fast as he was moving, and we would get caught. At the same time, my heart was pumping with anticipation.

When I got to the other side of the building, Alan was already crouched beneath Connie's bedroom window, beckoning for me to hurry. I was there in five seconds. Before I could speak or catch my breath, Alan hushed me with one finger to his lips, "Shhh." Then he whispered, "I can't see anything." "No wonder," I shot back. "The shade is down." At that moment, a light in the next room came on. I knew it was the bathroom.

60

The bathroom window was a few feet farther down the building, and about four feet above our heads. We anxiously crept along and positioned ourselves beneath it. A sudden burst of running water could be heard. Then what was once a low musical melody in the far distant of her apartment was becoming louder and clearer from the bedroom window. "She's in the bedroom," we whispered in unison, and spontaneously assumed our crouched position and crept back as if we were Siamese twins, joined at the hip. The radio was playing Chuck Berry's Madeline (Oh Mae bel ine ...) We could hear Connie singing along with the songs. We could hear bath water running. We could hear crickets chirping, but we didn't come to eavesdrop. We came to peep. Another song played, then another. Suddenly the water stopped. We dashed, in upright positions, to the bathroom window.

Once there, we bickered, using silent lip movements and hand gestures, over who was going to stand on the other one's shoulders. I surmised since I'd seen Connie's private parts before, and Alan hadn't, I gave in and silently stooped. Alan, bubbling with excitement, climbed aboard. With both hands against the wall, I crawled to a full stand. The show was on! Connie was the only performer, and Alan was the only audience. There were no intermissions. No applause, and no encore. The bathroom light went out in about 15 minutes. Never before or since did I see Alan so happy.

Saturday mornings was always a treat in my household. That was the only day of the week my mother would surely be off work. Her other off day was what she called 'a floater'. Usually the days floated from Wednesday, Thursday or Friday. Saturday was special for each of us. We looked forward to our family breakfast together. All the rest of the days, we were off in different directions.

By nine o'clock, the entire apartment would smell of hot biscuits. My mother made a special kind of biscuit. Each one was thicker and wider than your hand, which dripped with butter. We also had crispy thick bacon, the kind with the rind. No matter how long you chewed it, the taste and favor were still there. There were home fries smothered in dark pepper spiced gravy with onions. I had flapjacks, my favorite kind of cooked egg. Rice, grits, orange juice, milk, or hot Ovaltine completed the feast. This day was set aside to discuss our problems, achievements, school, and future plans.

Our table came with five chairs for the price of four. The empty chair around the table was reserved for visitors, or one of mothers' occasional 'live-in' boyfriend. The empty chair had two long term occupants within the past three years. First there was Henry, a tall, slim, middle-aged man, about ten years my mother's senior.

Henry was ahead of his time. The women libbers of the 70's would've voted for him as their national poster boy. However, this was the 50's, when *real* men liked to watch wrestling or football, not soap operas. An era when *real* men went fishing, not water house plants. Henry shared in the housework, ironed his own clothes, and, from time to time, even cooked on Saturday morning. He really listened when I decided I wanted to talk to him, which wasn't too often. He even came back weeks later and asked how I resolved a particular problem. If he detected I changed a grade on my report card, he wouldn't tell my mother, but discussed it with me privately.

My mother would go out with her girlfriends without Henry once or twice a month. When she came home after partying, there would usually be some fussing coming from their bedroom. Henry could barely be heard, but mother could be heard loud and clear. My sisters and I stayed alert for a fight, so we could assist Mommy, as we were accustomed. However, Henry never gave us a good reason to turn on him. Poor Henry! His tenure expired after about eight months.

The second 'live- in' boyfriend was Clyde 'Evidently' Wabash. He filled the chair after a three-month vacancy. Held in there really good too. Close to an eighteen-month term. Elaine and I nicknamed him 'Evidently' because he overused the word, especially when he was scolding us. For example: "You 'evidently' thought no one would find out you played hooky," he would say. "What your mother tells you 'evidently' doesn't matter," he would say on another occasion. Ol' Evidently, was all right. He treated my mother well, that's the main thing I liked about him. If they argued, I never heard them. I think Mommy seemed to respect him more than his predecessor. Seldom did she go out with her girlfriends at night anymore. They went out and came in together. Evidently was approximately 15 years older than my mother.

Mr. Wabash had a grown daughter whom Tammie became good friends with. Tammie always chose older girls as her friends. Although our newly found stepsister, Nina, was nearly 20 years old, with her own apartment and a baby, Tammie and she spent a lot of time visiting each other. Their friendship lasted beyond that of the union between our mother and her father.

Elaine and I couldn't contain our laughter at the dining table during dinner whenever the word 'evidently' was used by 'Evidently.' He used it at least once during each meal. We would have to cover my mouth with both hands to keep from spitting food across the table. One time, I didn't make it. Maybe our behavior had something to do with him leaving us. When I got home from school one day, my mother very calmly said that Clyde left that day. I never knew, asked, or cared why. And Mommy went out with her girlfriends that night. Mommy was a fine dressing woman. Her shapely figure was the envy the neighborhood women and the weakness of the men. Her smooth dark chocolate skin, pretty face, and prefect white teeth, made her the world's most beautiful woman.

The table was set by Elaine, and the food placed on the table by Tammie on this fine Saturday morning. My only chore in the kitchen was to sweep and take out the trash. The girls took turns washing dishes. On Saturday, however, we helped each other. Mommy was always the first to say grace at the table, but today she asked me to say it. "Jesus Wept," I said with my eyes shut, head bowed, my hands clasped, and mind wondering, "Why the switch?" Tammie said, "God is love, and Elaine repeated me, as usual. Mother bowed her head and prayed. *"Dear Lord, thank you for this lovely day and the food you've put on our table. Thank you for the good blessings you've shown each of us. Please keep this family in your grace. Amen."* Saying grace before each meal was customary with my mother, although she very seldom went to church or encouraged any of us to go.

This was a rare move to ask me to lead in the blessing of the food. By family tradition, it's the head of the household who leads in grace. Usually that post was held by mother or the man campaigning for a permanent seat at the table. Was this her way of preparing me for manhood? I wasn't buying it. I'd been dethroned before. It really didn't matter to me anymore who wore the honorary title of ' Little King' for a season. They were still subject to 'The Queen,' who was the ruler of The Castle.

Tammie lifted the tray of home fried potatoes with both hands, "You're not gonna eat up all the home fries this time," she jokingly directed to me.
"You just shut-up!" I snapped back, "Don't nobody say nothing when you drink all the milk."
Mommy and Elaine laughed.
"Where's the butter, Miss know-it-all?," I giggled while looking at Tammie.

"You can't even put servings on the table right, and always worrying 'bout what I eat."
"Yall stop fuss'n," Mommy said. "Anybody would think you ain't use to nothing."
"All I want is some butter for my biscuits, I ain't fuss'n," I said, "Tammie might be fuss'n, not me." "There the butter is," Elaine jumped in pointing, "Right in front of you."
We all laughed.
After a few minutes of eating and talking about everything and nothing, Mommy said in a high-spirited voice, "Wanna hear some good news?"
We all eagerly said, "Yeah!"
"Well, the convalescent home has given me a raise and an extra day of work each week."
We all expressed joy, knowing the more Mommy worked the less likely a new boyfriend would move in. "Between both jobs," she excitedly continued, "I'll be bringing home $85 a week." "Mommy, that's almost one hundred dollars!" Elaine screamed out loud with one hand rushing to cover her mouth. "Here's the best part . . . " Mommy paused a moment and looked scornfully at me and my older sister, and then turned to Elaine and pleasantly continued. "We're moving, and it's on a nice part of town. . ." I disrespectfully interrupted and asked, "Do I have to change schools?" Tammie added, "I don't wanna move.

I can move in with Nina."

Mommy turned her scornful glare back to us, and spoke in a cold, controlled tone. "We're all going together."
"Where's it at Mommy?" Elaine anxiously wanted to know.
"It's on Goodfellow Avenue, near Soldan High School," she answered. "I don't know anybody over there," Tammie pouted.
"What about my paper route? I can't come that far every Sunday early in the morning," I said.
"Listen you two," Mommy snapped, in her you're getting on my nerves voice. "Say no more about it. The rent is already paid and we move in next Friday. That's it!"
Tammie jumped up from the table like a Jack-n-the Box, and pushed away her plate, "I'm not hungry anymore," she grunted.
"Me either, this ain't fair!" I shouted scooting my chair back. By this time Mommy's eyes were getting glassy. We knew this look well. This was a danger sign. We had gone too far.

My mind was racing to think of a trick to deflate the storm brewing. "De De De De flapjaaacks waaaaa-was de de delic licious, mmmmmMommy me me me," I mustered up.
But it was too late. Tammie was so disgusted that she didn't heed the building tension in the atmosphere, *or she just didn't care.*
"Why do we have to move so much!?" she demanded, as she snatched her body toward the kitchen sink to begin the dishes. "We never can keep any friends, always moving, every few months seem like."
Elaine's glass of milk was missing her mouth and flowing down the front of her dress, but she didn't notice, *or she just didn't care.*
The grip Mommy had on our long handle, iron, serving spoon was tightening as her first teardrop fell.
"I I I guess I I will ta take th th the tra trass tras . . . "
Before I could finish, I yelled, "Ahhhh!" and fell backward onto the floor. My mother barely missed my head as she swung the spoon, like a ping-pong paddle, across the table. I ducked in self-defense.

Instantaneously, the severity of the situation struck Tammie like lightning and she braced herself. Elaine and I would take our punishment, lick our wounds, and cry ourselves to sleep. But not Tammie! She was defiant! At fourteen years old, she was shorter than Mommy by four inches and lighter by 20 pounds. My mother stood about 5'6" and weighed about 120. They both were fierce and savage fighters. In the dozens of clashes this dueling duo had, Tammie never backed down, surrendered, nor won. Today would be no different.

"I do the best I can," screamed Mommy with tears now flowing she threw the spoon at Tammie. "You ungrateful puppies!"
The spoon made a swishing sound and collided with Tammie's' back at great velocity. The force of the impact caused my sister to groan with more bitterness than pain, though it caused me to quiver with chills and Elaine to drop her glass of milk.

Mommy's attention turned from Tammie to the broken glass on the floor. Elaine started to cry, "I'm sorry Mommy, I'll get it up, I'm sorry, I'm sorrrrry, I'm sorrrrry." "Shut up, you bubble eyed heifer," Mommy growled.
Elaine had big eyes, resembling her father. She was often put down by neighborhood kids, and also by me, but never by Mommy, unless she was uncontrollably mad. At such a time she would say anything.
We had different fathers and didn't look at all like siblings. Tammie was considered cute, but had short nappy hair. Her complexion was lighter than Elaine's and mine. Elaine was skinny with bumps on her face. Her complexion was toned between Tammie's and mine. And I had a big weird shaped head and my nose was compared to a pig's snout. Just as my mother had been among her siblings, I was the darkest child. However, my rich pigmentation was never a target of ridicule.

"I'll buy buy bi ya ya anoth another gla gla asss, Mommy," I said protectingly, but was ignored. Mommy's attention ricocheted back to Tammie, who stood well grounded at the sink with both hands grasped tight upon the edge of the counter.
"Don't! Roll! Your! Eyes! At! Me!," Mommy roared at Tammie.

Tammie snatched her head away, now looking straight out the kitchen window, still in her frozen position.

"Pick! That! Spoon! Up! And! Waaash! It! Off!," Mommy continued.

Tammie stood frozen.

Mommy walked toward Tammie, taking short deliberate steps. With each step, she spoke another daring word.

"Pick! That! Spoon! Up! And! Waaaash! It! Off!"

At the last word, Mommy was standing close enough to kiss Tammie, but that wasn't likely to happen, with her hands on her hips. Tammie didn't budge or blink. Her grip on the counter intensified.

"I brought you in this world," Mommy screamed, "and I'll take you Out!" With that she grabbed Tammie by the hair and yanked hard as she could, and shouted, "You nappy headed, heifer!"

Tammie cursed and screamed as they fell to the floor. They rolled from the counter to the table then back to the counter.

Elaine was in a frantic state. I stood by helplessly shouting, "Mommy stop! Stop! You're gonna hurt her! Mommy stop!" I was too afraid to separate them, too concerned to run, and too mad to stammer. Elaine fled, and promptly returned, yelling, "Mommy, Andy's on the phone!"

Mommy released Tammie, rose from the floor, and left the kitchen. As she calmly walked out, she called us awful names and ended with, "I wish you dirty imps were born dead. I oughta send you to live in a reform school for incorrigible kids." We'd heard it all before, but nevertheless, each time hurt more than the last. Tammie's nose was bleeding, and clothes were torn. We all pitched in cleaning the kitchen while whispering how much we hated our mother, and how much she hated us.

Mommy often told us, if it wasn't for us, she wouldn't have to work so hard or put up with different men. In anger, it wasn't unusual for her to curse the day we were born, or she might say, "I should've flushed you ungrateful imps down the toilet." I felt guilty every time she brought home a new boyfriend.

Mothers' love was ambiguous, at best. She always provided Christmas toys, gave us birthday parties, and ran to our rescue in time of need. Without the slightest hesitation I witnessed Mother jeopardize her life, health and freedom on our behalf.

Chapter 4

*T*hough the news of our future move wasn't well received on impact several hours earlier, the shock had finally worn off. For me, a long solitary walk usually helped me to sort things out. I left home at 2:00 p.m. A paperboy should like to walk and be alone with his thoughts. My conclusions on the matter at hand were swift. Besides, choices were none existent. We were moving next Friday. Case closed! Starting Monday, I would stop by the A&P Market and pick up empty boxes for packing. With Elaine and Tammie doing the same, we would have all we needed. Two years was long enough to live in one spot anyway. And as far as friends were concerned, heck, there's a potential new friend in every house, and a bunch in every school. It was 5:30 p.m. when I realized I had walked to Union Station, nearly 10 miles.

June is a fine month for walking around town. Girls wearing short-shorts were everywhere. Smiling and looking sexy, just hoping I spoke to them just so they could ignore me. I knew their tricks, but fell for them just the same. I took my memo pad from my pants pocket, flipped it open and turned the pages one at a time. Ummm, six. I've collected six new girls' phone numbers today. Not bad. Of course, the real test of success was in proving their accuracy. I was good at getting a girl to give me a number, not always her true number, but a number, nonetheness. Usually at least three out of five were right. But all I met were nice girls, like Dotty, the type that didn't go all the way. I wanted meet a *fast* girl. One who was dumb, hot, and had no big brothers.

When I got home Saturday night, it was only eight o'clock. I wanted to walk back, and collect more numbers, but the Cass Street Bus was irresistible. It was comfortably full. No one had to stand and I got a window seat. The route home, on the bus, was much different from my pedestrian route, so, a window seat offered me a fresh view. It was very relaxing to watch the people on the street, the cars and houses as the bus went by.

The seat next to me was empty, and, as always, I hoped a cute girl would board and sit next to me. Instead came a middle-aged lady with three small children. The entire family stuffed in next to me. One was crying, the other two fighting, and their mother seemed to be lost in space. I politely got up and changed seats. The window seat was taken, but the senior Negro gentlemen who occupied it had witnessed my dilemma and said compassionately, "I'll be getting off in a few more stops." "Thank you," I replied, appreciating the gesture. True to his word, he vanished within a five minute span.

The window seat was once again mine. I stared out the window, as I thought of saying goodbye to my schoolmates, my neighborhood friends and, above all, my newspaper route. I wondered if Alan would really show up tomorrow morning to ask Big Black for a job, as we had agreed. It was now the warm season, and routes were seldom available. Alan could have my route, if he only showed up. I'd kept my end of the bargain. He saw Connie in her birthday suit. Alan was so happy that he couldn't wipe the grin off his face for the first three blocks. He didn't even speak, just grinned. And every time I looked into his face, I laughed.

Finally, Alan opened up. "I saw her naked, Richard, she was actually naked. Right before my eyes, not a thread of clothing." From the serious expression on his face, I knew he was in his private heaven. After another three blocks of not talking, we came to our dividing point. We stopped and faced each other, each grinning for different reasons, then gave each other five, and Alan said, "See ya' tomorrow at the paper depot." "Be on time! No later than 5:00 *a.m.*, that's a.m. Alan," I said teasingly. As we parted company, he called back, "I'll leave with Tank."

A boy child of about 4-years-old said hello as he plopped down in the empty seat next to me. He was one of the three rascals who boarded with the middle-aged mother I was trying to escape. Now she and the younger two children shared a seat, while I shared a seat with her oldest child. I looked around the bus for an empty seat, but all the other seats were taken. At the next stop, a well-stacked girl of about 16-years-old boarded the bus. She wore a pair of cut off jeans, which were too short, a tight half blouse that fully revealed the size of her bosom, and heavy make up. She stole the attention of everyone on the bus. Slowly and unsteadily, she switched down the aisle toward me, searching for a vacant seat.

I nudged the kid next to me with my leg and leaned nearer him, then ordered him in a low, menacing tone, to go sit with his mother. She sat on the opposite side of the aisle several seats toward the front. This chick turned the head of every passenger she passed, including the kid's mother. The brat turned to me and stuck his tongue out as my chance switched by.

Three rows behind me were two teenage boys about my age. The one in the outside seat asked her, in a flirting manner, "Hey, good looking, wanna sit on my knee?" She giggled and said, "Ain't nowhere else to sit." As she lowered herself onto his knee with the whole bus gawking, she winked right at me. My watery eyes slowly turned toward the heartless kid next to me as I sincerely hoped he lived to be a ninety-year-old *virgin*. I was tormented by their laughter, three rows back, until my stop at Newstead Avenue.

Sunday morning I was up and out of the house by 4:30 as usual. My last Sunday rising this early. I would be able to sleep late like everybody else, I rationalized. But I also had to admit I would miss walking along a quiet avenue during the daybreak hours. There is no sight as beautiful as viewing the sunrise. As I walked along, I sometimes imagined that I was in heaven, on my way to talk with God about the troubles on earth.

Against the backdrop of the moonlit morning, I could see several shadowy figures in front of the newspaper depot. There were two small groups. Before I got within 50 feet of the depot, one of the shadowy figures left his pack and was walking toward me. After a couple moments, I realized it was Tank.

"Hey man! ," Tank called out and waved his arms. "You're a miracle worker. How in the world did you get Alan to get out of bed this time of the morning?"

"Magic words, Tank," I answered.
"I still can't believe it!," Tank said shaking his head.
"What did Alan tell you?" I asked.
"Nothing, except a promise is a promise," he said, still shaking his head.
"What's happening?"
"Nothing Tank, except a promise is a promise," I mocked, as I moved closer to the other guys. Tank followed.

Some of the bunch were arguing and bragging about great Negro baseball players like Leroy "Satchel" Paige, Jackie Robinson, Hank Aaron and Willie Mays. The others were gathered in a small circle crooning. Boosty sang lead with Tesler, Mudbone and Alan brought up the background sound with bass and doo-waaps. It was 4:50 a.m. Big Black was inside counting newspapers and tying them into bundles. Mudbone, as he was called because he was dark skinned and bony, only showed for work when the weather forecast called for a nice day. His customers were constantly complaining and asking for a more dependable paperboy. Big Black told me that Mudbone was his wife's nephew, and that was the only reason he wasn't fired. This was the first time I ever saw Mudbone before nine o'clock in the morning. He was usually just getting to his route around the time I was finished for the day. I was on Mudbone's route when I discovered where Irene Rogers lived. He'd been robbed twice in the last six months. I joined in the sing-a-long as they finished Yakety Yak by the Coasters.

"Hey, Boosty, you sure can croon," I said, raising a high flat palm.
"That ain't nutt'n new," Boosty joked in this deep bass voice as he rolled out a flat palm. "Gim'me five." Our palms met with a smack. The others gave one another five. "I KNOW I'm BAD!", Tesler snapped. "I don't care what nobody say." We laughed and joked for a couple minutes, and were in the middle of singing another tune when the door opened.

Everyone wandered in, signed the book, and wrote the number of papers they wanted to take out. Eight guys were there at five o'clock. There were about 25 paperboys who worked at our depot. Most showed up much later. The top seller on the list was Tank, beside his name he had written 300. The lowest seller was Mudbone. He asked for 50. I asked for 200, Tesler 200, and Boosty 250.

After I signed the list, I called out to Big Black who had his back turned to me. "Hey Big Black, this is Alan, Tank's brother. I'm giving him my route." Big Black stopped counting papers, looked over his shoulder and said, "What you say?" Everyone stopped moving and was completely quiet. "This is my last day. We're moving outta this neighborhood, and I want Alan to have my route," I called back.

All the guys started questioning me about when and where I was moving. Alan said repeatedly, "You didn't say you were moving, you didn't say you were moving." "I know I didn't Alan," I said "I just found out yesterday myself." I looked toward Big Black, who was still motionless, then repeated, "Today's my last day, we're moving this coming Friday."

"Alan can't just walk in here and take a good route from Me!," shouted Mudbone from across the room. "I want that route!" "You have a route," I yelled back, "and you don't even show up."

Mudbone was getting louder, "I've just been waiting for a DECENT route," he continued. "Alan has to build a route like everyone else." "Then build OURS!" Tank shouted. Big Black moved toward his messy desk, "Wait a cotton pickin' minute, all y'all, he growled, "I'm the BIG SHOT that decides who gets what." He ruffled through the drawer and withdrew a folder. "Let me see what we have here," he mumbled. "Ummm, three routes are open," said Mudbone's uncle-in-law, as Mudbone looked on half smiling. "Mudbone's right," Big Black said, while still looking at the folder. "The guys already working here get to choose opening routes before any new paperboy." Then he turned toward his nephew with a twisted grin and said, "Except for YOU! You lazy no-count leech. Who the tarnation do you think you are?" Big Black roared, "Late half the time, other half, don't show up at all! If you wasn't Lulu's nephew, you trifling sucker, I'd break your bony neck."

Big Black was apparently thinking about the money Mudbone had cost him. Suddenly, Big Black charged Mudbone and pinned him to the wall with one hand pressed against his chest, and his other fist drawn back. Tank and Boosty rushed and grabbed Big Black. "Pay me my cotton pickin' money," he roared at a trembling Mudbone." "I will, I will," Mudbone swore. "That's why I'm here, that's why I need the route. You charge me $5.00 per week, I can't pay that unless you give me a better route," pleaded Mudbone. I'll pay you back every penny of that $20.00, that's why I'm here so early!" Big Black returned to his work area. As he counted papers he glanced at Alan and said, "You're getting a good route son, don't screw it up. Walk with your partner this morning, learn the ropes." Big Black then turned his attention back to counting papers. "Forty-five, 46, 47, 48, 49, bundle."

At exactly 5:30 a.m., Alan and I left the depot with two wagons full of papers. Usually I hooked one wagon behind the other in train fashion and pulled them. That day, however, I had a helper and we each pushed a wagon. We agreed that Alan would handle all the new customers alone, but I would introduce him to my regulars. I warned him never to sell papers on another route unless the customer approached him in a car or on foot. Many paperboys were bitter enemies over that very issue. I told Alan not to go down Irene Roger's street because the low down people on that street complained to the police about the noise the wagons made so early in the morning. A peace disturbing fine would then be charged to Mr. Henry, the depot owner, who in turn would charge it to Big Black, who, in turn, would charge his fist in your mouth. I didn't tell Alan that Irene lived on that street and if he traveled it, her grandmother may call him, and then, he may get a weekly peek at Irene Rogers in her underpants. We both had a crush on Irene, but neither had the nerve to tell her.

We started on my route about six o'clock. After the first few window calls that Alan handled, he began to appreciate the early morning privileges of a paperboy. The first door we visited together was at the quaint home of the middle-aged, shapely single woman, who usually appeared naked from the waist-up, with one breast fully exposed and the other covered by her forearm. The doormat read: 'Love'. I often wondered if her name was 'Love' or if it a message. I never had a reason to call her by any name because she was the only person who answered the door. Since this was my last morning, I wanted to know her name. With her newspaper in one hand, I rang the bell. Within a few seconds the door opened.

"Good morning," she said and smiling as always. Today the woman wore a half-slip, pink slippers and a blue heavy cloth robe.
"Good morning," I said smiling. "This is Alan, my replacement."
As she spoke, she adjusted her robe even tighter around her waist. "Replacement? Why are you being replaced?"
"I'm moving out of this area," I replied. "It's too far to come."
"Alan," she asked, "will you be an early bird, like this young man? I prefer an early bird," blushing, she continued.
I had never noticed it before, but there was a fluffy cat walking around the front room. Alan saw it right away.
"What a beautiful cat," Alan said. "What's her name?"
"Casey," she said. "We have three more kittens, would you like one?"

Alan's cat Cisco, was killed by a hit and run driver last year. I knew he was going to say yes. Personally my entire household hated cats. "Yes madam," Alan gleefully said. "My name is Mrs. Love," she said, and took two steps back. "You boys come on in and take a peek at them." I declined, and told Alan to hurry. Someone had to stay with the wagons. When I returned to the curb, there was a man standing on his porch waving me to come over. I grabbed a paper and trotted over to him. As I left his porch, someone called from two houses down the street. I got two papers and delivered them.

By the time I returned to the front of Mrs. Love's home, Alan was leaving, carrying a spotted kitten. I looked at him and the kitten with a small degree of disgust. "Don't let that cat get near me," I blurted. "This is Poncho," he said with a grin. "Cisco told him not to go near mean ol' paperboys." One of Alan's favorite TV show was 'The Cisco Kidd,' which aired every Saturday morning. The Mexican star of the show, Cisco had a sidekick named, Poncho. Thus, came the names for Alan's cats, Cisco and Poncho.

As the morning sales picked-up, so did my confidence in my friend as a reliable paperboy. Alan practiced my unique and familiar call, "Yooooour HEY Paaaaaapaa!, Yooooour HEY Paaaaaapa!," and windows seemed to be opening everywhere with sleepy voices yelling out, "Oh Paperboy!, Oh paperboy!" After several blocks of hot sales and shooting the breeze about cute girls at school, Alan just blurted out, "Mrs. Love doesn't have one big boob and one lil' boob, ya' know."

"Yes she does!" I said with full assurance.
"No, she don't!" he countered. "No, she don't! She don't have but one boobie," he concluded with a puzzled expression.
"What ya' mean, one boobie?," I asked. "You must be blind!"

"You're the one blind, if you didn't see that flat scarred skin where a breast use to be," Alan said. We both stopped in our tracks. Alan went on to tell me how he came to discover Mrs. Love's secret. He said that when they reached her service porch area, where three kittens were kept in a huge box, Mrs. Love stooped down to pick up a kitten. The front of her robe offered a full view of the flat scarred skin where a right breast belonged.

I thought back to all the times Mrs. Love came to the door naked from the waist up, covering what I thought to be her right breast. What I never figured out, however, was her reason for so openly exposing the left breast. Alan even said that after she scooped up a couple of the kittens and had them cuddled against her flattened right bosom, Mrs. Love seemed to deliberately position herself to reveal her left breast. He suggested that showing her healthy breast, made Mrs. Love feel like a woman. Whether Mrs. Love was born that way, or whether this was the result of an operation, became the topic of conversation until we finally arrived at Connie's apartment building. Alan also read books on biology and dissecting insects. Therefore, I seldom argued with him on scientific subjects, illnesses or the anatomy.

Alan was anxious to be introduced to Connie. However, the note on the door explained, her absence:

Dear Paperboy,

Please do not leave a newspaper today. I had to go to work.
Signed,
Connie K.

Alan appeared relieved not to meet her with me present. I knew he would be nervous, and I would certainly tease him later. I wrote on the flip side of Connie's note:

Dear Connie,
I am moving from the area. Your new paperboy's name is Alan. He'll be here before 7:30 every Sunday morning.
From,
Richard

By 9:30 a.m., we were back at the depot turning in our wagons. Alan was very impressed with the fact I'd earned nearly $15 in just a few hours. We both silently felt there was a chance our friendship would eventually drift apart. I suspect that's why Alan talked about something I had never heard from him before. He shared his dream of someday becoming a career military man in the Navy. Ordinarily, I would have laughed at such a ridiculous notion coming from him, but today was one of our last. He talked about marrying Irene Rogers and living in the Far East. I wished him the best of luck.

I recall sharing the idea with Alan of having children and being a bachelor father after two popular television shows of that time. These shows were: 'Family Affair', starring the white actor Brian Keith. And 'Bachelor Father'. This show starred another white actor, John Forsythe. He too was the sole guardian of two children. And likewise their family had a male butler, an Oriental. However, Alan laughed at my vision.

"Why don't you want a wife?" he chuckled. "I want a six or seven children and Irene around forever. That's how I want to live, you know." Alan had angered me by laughing but I tried not to show it.
"Alan, you must be crazy!" I snapped. "A woman will cheat on you and have children by different men. Even your precious Irene?"

"You're the one crazy," he replied. "You want children, but no wife. Instead, you want a man serving you." He laughed a bit more.

"I did say anything 'bout having no man serve me," I rebutted. "I just want the children, not the wife. Nor a butler! She can die in a car accident, or run off with my best friend. I don't care! All women just cheat on you anyway. I know women! And when they're mad at the children, they strip them naked, tie them up with rope, gag their mouths and whip them with an extension cord. Women are sneaky, Alan. You just don't know nothing." We both laughed, but I was serious. Alan, his brother, Tank and their little sister, Brandi had the same father, who was still married to their mother, and lived at home. So what in tarnation did he know anyway! Next Sunday when Alan was on the route alone, I would be in our new apartment, in bed. I hoped he would do well.

When I got home from school on Friday afternoon, the truck was already loaded. My mother's boyfriend, Andy, and two of his buddies were tying down the load on the two-ton flatbed truck with rope. Andy drove the truck with my mother and sisters in the cab compartment, and me in the back with his pals. Goodfellow Avenue was a long ride from our previous place. This area still had plenty of white families, however, they were moving out daily in droves.

Andy was the biggest boyfriend my mother ever had. At 6'5" and nearly 300 pounds, I remember thinking how tragic it would be for us if we had to defend Mommy in a battle against Andy. He could murder all of us with one hand tied behind his back. After awhile I suspected Andy was married, because he never came over late at night or stayed long during the day. Occasionally, he would have dinner with us but never breakfast. Yeah, he's married, I was sure. Every time Andy showed up, he had a bag of groceries, a case of sodas, or something. He was a big country man. He talked and laughed loudly. Always wore blue jeans, cowboy boots, and plaid shirts. Andy loved wrestling matches. We watched them together on Friday nights when he was over. We both knew all the wrestlers by name, but Andy also knew their performance records and the name of each wrestling maneuver. Wrestling got Andy more excited than football or baseball. He would dive onto the floor in our living room, imitating the referee on television; pounding on the floor with one of his big palm leaf sized hands, causing the dishes in the kitchen cabinet to rattle in his attempt to count out a pinned wrestler out. Andy's two buddies were also giants.

The men unloaded the truck within an hour. Our new apartment was located on the third floor. The three men did not have use of a hand truck or elevator, yet they didn't break a sweat. After they connected the stove, Mommy fried enough chicken for everybody. The men ate and drank beer while they argued over the wrestling match on television. The men were acting wilder than football fans.

My mother, sisters, and I were the real movers. We had moved at least eight times. I had transferred to at least eight different schools since first grade. At this time I was in the eighth grade. While the men were watching television, we remained busy, unpacking boxes, setting up beds, arranging furniture, hanging curtains, and putting away clothes. By 11:00 that night, we were completely settled into our new place.

Being true to my usual form, I rose early and left the apartment to survey the neighborhood. Early in the morning was the time for this because it's quiet, and there were few distractions. It was a time to learn where the nearest mailbox was located, the stores, the parks, schools, shortcuts, and where the bus stops were without hassles from the neighborhood tough guys. I walked for about two hours and was back home by 9:30 a.m. My morning journey had taken me through a dozen alleys, four schools, two possible hangout cafes, two small parks, the police station, fire station, two hospitals, six stores, a Laundromat, one bowling alley, one roller skating rink, many trees, fences and garage doors with names and/or initials carved into them. The words 'Goodfellow Boys' was hand painted all over the area. The names' Red; Moose; Daddy; McGoo; Otis; and Rat appeared and reappeared everywhere. This told me who would be the guys to reckon with.

Mommy was in the kitchen preparing our Saturday morning breakfast as she sang the spiritual hymn 'Amazing Grace'. Elaine was setting the table, and

Tammie was mixing frozen orange juice. As I walked into the kitchen, Elaine looked at me and asked, "Did you see a library?"

"No library, except the one I already knew about way over near Forest Park," I told her.

"How far is the wash house?"Tammie wanted to know.

"About two blocks."

"How far do I have to walk to and from a bus stop?" Mommy asked.

"Just to the corner."

"How far is Soldan High School?," asked Tammie.

"It's a thirty minute walk, or you can catch the Holoman Streetcar and be there in five minutes," I informed her.

"How much does it cost to wash and dry a load?," Mommy asked.

"Fifteen cents to wash and FIVE CENTS to dry?"

"FIVE CENTS to dry!," they all shout together.

"Mommy!," snapped Tammie, "on Newstead it's free to dry."

"I know, I know," Mommy said followed by, "um um um, we'll just have to dry some things in the kitchen.

"Any cute boys,"Tammy interjected (one fourth joking, three-fourths serious). Mommy immediately warned, "I don't want any kids in here while I'm at work, yall hear me?!"

"Yes Mam," we answered in unison.

"Can I turn the radio on Mommy?," Tammie wanted to know. "Yeah, that is all right," she answered.

As I washed my hands in the bathroom, it occurred to me that no one ever asked about a church. Nor did I ever take the time to notice one.

The rock-n-roll hits from the 1950's filled our kitchen as we enjoyed breakfast together. The conversation flowed from household finance to the latest dances. We wondered if the Negro kids on this side of town danced like we did or if they dance like white kids. American Bandstand was the nation's top teenage show. We use to laugh at the way the white kids danced. Chubby Checker had them looking like fools trying to do the 'Twist'. The 'Jerk' was my personal favorite. It didn't take much of a dancer to master the 'Jerk'. You just stood flatfooted with your arms raised and jerked your upper body to and fro in time with the music. The 'Mash Potato' was the dance craze enjoyed by all races. The forbidden dance, one that never was on television but everyone knew about was 'The Dog'. "Do the Dog!" Rufus Thomas use to cry out on radio. Even a shy boy who couldn't dance, would stand and pump and wriggle behind a girl doing 'The Dog'.

Conversation went from doing 'The Dog' to Mommy's job. She was only a nurse's aide and limited in the amount of salary she could expect, even though she did the duties of a Licensed Vocational Nurse. Mommy considered going to night school to get her license, but there were not enough hours in the day. She already worked two shifts half of the time. Mommy mentioned that she had heard that opportunities were better for Negro nurses in California, but didn't know anyone out there but Bernie, her first cousin. My sisters and I had never met Bernie, but we often heard the family speak of how well he was doing out West. After breakfast, the girls cleaned the kitchen and I took out the trash. A frail, plain looking Negro girl with bumps on her face was staring and smiling at me from a first floor window.

About noon, I decided to call the six new telephone numbers I collected last week from the girls I met while walking around. The numbers were on a memo pad I kept tucked in my wallet. My usual procedure was to call the 'three star' girls first. Three stars stood for high probability. Second, I would call the 'two star' girls. Medium probability. And finally, I would call the 'one star' girls. The probability rating marked by stars, refreshed my memory as to what I guessed my chances were to receive a right number.

Many girls would say they didn't have a phone, but would take your number. I always believed that to be a lie. Even if I played along and gave them my phone number, they seldom called me. However, if they told me they didn't have a phone, but it would be okay to call them at another number, I would trust them. About 90% of the time, the number was good. Bad numbers usually came from girls that were much younger than they were trying to look. They were probably under strict orders not to give the number out, but rather than say that, they would give a wrong number. Most girls wouldn't dare ask for a boy's number. They appeared easy if they did. It was a disgrace to a girl's entire household for them to be known as "easy." If a girl seemed uninterested in me, but offered her number, she received one star. Unfriendly but approachable, one star. The three star girls had more potential, in general, for a worthwhile friendship.

Last Saturday's phone number collection consisted of two numbers with three stars, one number with 'two stars', and three numbers with one star. My first two calls turned out to be right numbers. I talked to each girl about ten to fifteen minutes, but tore their numbers up after the conversation because each one lived too far for me to see on a regular basis. Also, boys from other neighborhoods didn't take kindly of an outsider coming in courting their girls. My 'two star' girl was a wrong number, and so was two of my 'one star' girls.

Stella Barns was a 'one star' girl, though I didn't remember why. I did recall her being cute, a bit skinny, with light skin and reddish hair. Our telephone conversation went well. I usually gave dull minded girls a check mark on the other side of their names to indicate they appeared a tad slow. This meant the chances of getting in her pants were greater, because all the boys knew that getting into the pants of a dumb girl was easier than a smart girl.
Stella Barns had one star on the left side of her name and a check on the right side. But now, in our telephone chat, I didn't detect any dullness in her wit. She was delightful! As we continued our chitchat, I also learned she lived near Goodfellow Avenue. Stella and I met downtown as she shopped to buy her father a birthday present. We walked several blocks together before going our separate ways. I told Stella that I had just moved to Goodfellow Avenue. She then invited me to her house which was only ten to twelve blocks from mine. We agreed I should arrive at six o'clock. When I finally hung up the phone, I realized that Stella and I had been talking for 45 minutes. That was a good sign.

At two o'clock, I left my apartment headed in the direction I had figured the tough guys hung out. Over my right shoulder dangled two pairs of boxing gloves. There was a small community park a few blocks away.

My instinct told me this was the place I would find a few of The Goodfellow Boys. In less than fifteen minutes, I arrived at the entrance of the park. There was a tag team football game going on. No referee, no uniforms, no official rules. These boys were all Negroes between the ages of 14 - 17-years-old. A few older guys between 17 - 19 sat at a long picnic table playing dominos and cards. Lots of teenage girls were around, some watched the football game, some watched the games at the tables, and some were in small giggling groups.

There were no young kids in the park being pushed in swings by their mothers, running around playing tag, or hopscotch. I immediately noticed that there were no white kids in the park, though this was a 60 -70 percent white community. I also noticed a few boys were smoking and shooting dice; a couple teenagers were locked in an intimate embrace on blankets in remote areas; and one all-girl-trio was singing.

Upon entering the park, I was certain that this was the Goodfellow's Turf, and I, an uninvited stranger, was violating their unwritten trespassing law. I would be dealt with severely, unless I made the first move. I could feel the eyes watching me as I dared to invade 'private property'. The singing trio stopped singing as I walked toward the older guys playing parlor games. As I passed the girls, I was careful not to speak to them. Speaking to the wrong dude's girl would surely be a stupid, no-win situation.

As I continued down the curved pavement, I came upon two teenage boys squatted in my path, shooting dice. Without a word, I went six feet around them to prevent the tumbling dices from coming in contact with my feet which, I knew would be an excuse to start a fight with me, claiming my interference changed the flow of the game.

Suddenly, a wobbling football that had been kicked out-of-bounds came within a few feet of me. A voice from the football pack yelled, "Hey! Throw that ball!" I picked up the ball and braced myself to throw it when a different voice yelled, "Don't throw him that ball, throw it to me!" Then the first voice countered, "You betta' not throw him that ball, I told you to throw it to me!"

"Darn!," I thought, "a butt-kicking trap." No matter where I threw the ball, the other would take offense and would be forced to defend his honor. Each of the two callers stood about 15 to 20 feet apart, waiting for me to throw the deciding pass.

Everybody in the small park watched and waited for me to decide which boy I preferred to battle. The two were approximately 100 yards from me. Other players were scattered around the field. About 25 yards behind them was a lone big fellow in a blue T-shirt standing with his hands on his hips. I yelled out to him, "Hey, Blue!," and cast the ball high above their heads into the mitts of the distant player. No one said anything, the game resumed. I could sense a degree of respect being sent my way in the breeze from every angle of the park. It wasn't the fact that I had thrown the ball about 125 yards. Most any guy could've done that. But the fact that I saved my butt a few moments longer impressed them. My stroll continued toward the card players, with my boxing gloves still over my shoulder. When I got within ten feet of the pack of gang members, who were now pretending to ignore me, I spoke to the whole bunch, "What's happening?"

One of the card players lifted his eyes to me saying, "What do YOU want?" "Looking for a gym to get in some practice," I replied staring straight into his cold eyes. A short dude standing next to me, looked me up and down threateningly and said, "You can get all the practice you want right here, right now."
The usual hissing sounds and fight agitation had begun.
"This dude thinks he's baddd," came a background voice.
"Let me have him, Moose," came another.
"No, he's mine," said the first guy I spoke to, the one with the cold eyes. "I'm the one he called out!" The dude growled as he slapped his cards onto the table and rose up slowly, hoping to send me running with his body language. Oh, I knew all the signs. After all, I've been the new boy on the block too many times not to know the game.

Boxing was a status symbol for young Negro men in St. Louis, Missouri during my youth. A boy could catch more girls and get more respect by his boxing skills than any other talent or ability. When I was about nine years old, we moved into the toughest part of town, the Projects. There were about 20 clustered ten-story buildings, all on an area of land less than 20 acres. On this land included parking lots, recreational centers, a playground, and a baseball field. Every four or five buildings were identified by another name. The Igoo; The Pruitt; and two others, that slip my memory. Anyway, we lived in the Igoo, which was an enemy of The Pruitt. There was a constant violent feud between the two. The other two project buildings went by the same unwritten code of genocide. The Pruitt Boys were the best fighters because they controlled the recreational center. During my neighborhood survey on our first day in the Projects, I wandered into Pruitt territory. I was beaten by a boy that was a champion boxer. I didn't even come close to winning the fight, but won respect by not running. This guy's name was Waldo, and he passed the word that I had an unlimited pass to go to the recreation center.

Waldo was about 12-years-old and had fought in the Junior Golden Gloves and on television. I never joined the boxing team or took any training, but I was a sparring partner for Waldo every time he felt like socking around a guy. He would choose me most often for a couple reasons. First, I was one of the few young guys in the projects, outside the boxing ring, that didn't run from him. Second, I was the only fighter outside the boxing ring that could prepare him for left-handed fighters, since I fought left handed. I didn't realize it at the time, but I was learning a lot of moves and tricks from Waldo. He and I always fought in boxing gloves, never bare knuckles.

When this cold-eyed card player stood up, I realized he was bigger than I thought. I untied my gloves and tossed him a pair. The football game stopped, the singers hushed, the dice shooters were on their feet. Even the lovers on the blanket took a break. The entire park was walking, some trotting, toward the imminent action.

"Knock that sucka' out Moose," one of the singers called out.
"If you don't knock him out, I WILL!" shouted the much smaller dude they called Red. Moose was about 5'9" and 190 pounds, more flab than muscle. I knew from experience, Moose would charge me like the Moose for which he was named. You can always put money on the fact that a much bigger opponent will have a false sense of confidence which will cause him to do things and take risk he wouldn't take with someone his size or bigger. It took

85

me two times getting knocked out before I learned to use my opponents' large frames to their disadvantage.

In a match governed by rules, I clenched repeatedly until the other boxer was tired out from his own weight. But that was in the ring, not in Goodfellow Park where there were no rules except, to "knock that sucka' out."
By the time we were gloved, everybody in the park had encircled us. An older young man, about 20, in a sailor suit, who I later found out was home on furlough and an ex-Goodfellow Boy named Al said, "I'll keep the time. Fight three minutes, rest one minute, no hitting below the waist, no head butts, no hitting after I call time, on a knock down the standing man goes to his corner, two knock downs in any one round the fight is over. This will be a five round match."

"Otis," Al called out, "You be this dude's second."
"What's your name dude?," a short muscular dark skinned boy of about 15-years-old asked me.
"Richard Jones, "I replied.
"I'm Otis," he said with a stoic expression, "Stay away from Moose's left, circle to your right, breathe through your nose, not your mouth, no rabbit punches, and don't go to showboating or you'll get knocked cold. I think you should know, Moose was the Champ of Booneville for the last two years."

I was wrong about these guys. They knew boxing. And Moose a champ! I heard about Booneville which was a detention camp for juvenile delinquents. Moose went to Booneville, and was the champ. Umm! Five rounds can seem like five days. Moose was good. But I don't think he could've taken 'No Mercy Percy', a friend of mine who boxed at the YMCA. Nor could he have taken my first boxing coach, Waldo, who was now boxing in the Olympics. They were more his weight and height, but I was the one in the park. It's a good thing I knew how to roll with a punch and block well or Moose would've pulverized me. Though I was faster and more accurate, his power punches made me hear thunder. We weren't in a ring so he couldn't catch or corner me. Most of his blows would hit me as I moved away. For every punch he landed I landed three or four.

After the second round, I was viewing my relentless adversary through one eye. In the fourth round I was knocked down for the first time. Moose tried to finish me in that round, but I had more ring savvy than he did. He kept charging me, throwing all power blows and missing most of the time. Every time he missed, I rushed him and clenched him. This not only gave me free rest time, but also angered him which caused more mistakes.

At the end of the fourth round, my lip was bleeding. Moose won every round if inflicting punishment was the measurement of fine boxing, but it wasn't. I landed five good blows to every one he landed, but he had me by 70 pounds which would've never been allowed in a true match.

In the fifth and final round, Otis told me to just stay away from him for the first two minutes, then go out fighting like a maniac. Excitement was in the air. Bets were being made, not on who'll be the winner, but whether I could go the distance. I could hear half the crowd chanting, "Moose! Moose! Moose! Moose!" And the other half screaming frantically, "Run! Run!" (Run meant to be light on your feet and cause your opponent to miss, not run like a coward). It seemed as if I was knocked down again within the first five seconds. Otis later told me it was after the first thirty seconds of the fifth round. I remember getting up in the fifth round while all the girls and half the boys cheered me. Moose came at me like a steam engine, and I noticed a trickle of blood was coming from his nose. Otis suddenly called time out.
He retied my gloves, giving me time to rest. He whispered, "Hit and run, hit and run." Otis was a good second, and knew the game. Moose wanted to win by knockout or by the 'two-knock-down' in one round rule, not by a decision. His honor, he felt, was at stake. He charged me so hard that he fell when his powerful swing missed and I side stepped him. This wasn't counted as a knock down, but it helped me because it gave me more rest time, and the fight was into its' final minute. When he got up, I surprised everyone except Otis when I rushed Moose. He was much more exhausted than I was hurt. We went toe to toe for about thirty seconds, then I hit and ran for the remainder of the fight.

"Time!" called Al. Moose raised both hands high above his head, confident in

87

his easy victory. I looked and felt like I had fallen from a mountain top. But I was still standing. I accomplished my mission. In my heart, I felt I had won, though the game wasn't over yet. I went over and congratulated the contest winner and thanked Al and Otis for conducting a fair fight. For the next two hours, I sat in the park playing cards with the Goodfellow Boys. Before I left the park at 4:30 p.m., I'd been invited to a party. Moose told me to meet them at Moms' Cafe on Goodfellow Avenue near the Holoman Tracks. I knew the cafe. We planned to meet at eight o'clock. The party would be at the home of one of the girls in the park. But for the moment, my thoughts were fixed on my date with Stella Barrs.

On my return trip home, an adult couple asked me if I wanted them to call someone for me. I smiled and told them, "This is nothing new for a boxer." With my gloves flung across my shoulders I continued on with a dance in my walk. The young girl who watched me dump the trash earlier was in her front window as I passed to go up the stairs to the main door.

"What happened to you!?," she asked with sincere concern, "I bet it was those Goodfellow Boys." "Don't go down there anymore, please," she pleaded. "They'll hurt you some more."
"Is sit in the window all you do?" I asked sarcastically.
"Don't say I didn't warn you," she said bluntly. I resumed my pace up the stairs as she left the window.

When my mother saw my face, she merely said, "I see you've made some friends." We all laughed. Elaine later told me that the girl in the first apartment had been upstairs and introduced herself. The two of them were the same age and would be going to school together. Her name was Gloria and she liked "me." Elaine said that Gloria lived there with her mother and baby sister, and she was scared of this bad neighborhood because the Goodfellow Girls had beat her up. I told Elaine to tell Gloria that she wouldn't get beat up if she wasn't so nosy. Then I warned Elaine against befriending girls that are afraid to go outside. However, since Elaine was scary and avoided as many fights as she could, she and Gloria were compatible.

Gates Avenue was aligned with large two story homes. All the yards were well manicured. The trees towered over the expensive brick homes. There was no old beat up cars parked on the street; no broken windows or boarded up doors; and no scribbling on walls. Small children were running and playing carefree. Many of the verandas were adorned with lounge furniture. I was surprised to see so many Negro families on Gates Avenue. Stella Barrs must be rich was the only logical explanation my rationale could offer. When I got to her address, I paused in awe, as I absorbed the majesty. There were "two" shiny new cars in the curved driveway, a convertible, royal blue, 1959 Dynaflo Buick, and a 1958 coal black Cadillac 4 door sedan. "Um um um," was all I could say. When I rang the door bell, the chimes played a musical tune. The ambience of it all made Beaver Cleaver's neighborhood in Wellston look like The Igoo Projects. A female voice came through a small speaker box near the door, "Who is it?," she asked. "Richard Jones, I'm here to see Stella," I answered, speaking probably too close into the box.

A few moments later, the huge door opened and there stood a beautiful heavy set woman, elegantly dressed in a long black gown with glitter all over it. She wore long elbow length black gloves that made her high yellow skin stand-out even more. The jewelry on her neck, wrist and fingers was probably worth more than my mother earned in one or two years. I was astounded. Behind the woman, I beheld the luxuriance befitting royalty. There was plush red carpet throughout the hall and on the staircase with highly polished banisters, highlighted by a grand and sparkling chandelier. The formal dining room had a table big enough for twelve and it was at least that many beautifully carved mahogany chairs encircling it with a two foot long and two foot high candelabra at its center. "Lordy! Why are you wearing those demon dark glasses," she snarled glancing at her diamond watch, "at 6:15 in the evening?" Instantly I remembered why I put a check by Stella's name. She had mentioned her father was a preacher, and she wondered if she should buy him another Bible for his birthday. I didn't want to go through the third degree boys got from dating a preacher's daughter.
"Th th Goo- Goodfellow. Ba ba boys be beat mmm me up," I uttered, "thi this mo' morn'n."
"Lordy! Lordy! those lil' hoodlums," she declared, "Come on in child." "What

ya' doing 'round here," she asked in a softening tone, "this morning?"

"Mmmm my fam family jus just moved in in yes yes yester da day," I stammered, "An and thi this mo' morn'n I wen went fer a wa walk an and two boys jum jumped me in the the pa park."

"They're ruining this fine community," she said with disgust, "Negroes can't have nothing. Their families should've stayed in the projects where they belong."

As we stood in the hallway, Stella walked downstairs, "Hi Richard," she called, "I see you met my Mother." Then she noticed my swollen mouth, bruised right jaw, and puffiness protruding the left rim of my sunglasses.

"Apparently you're not a fast runner," she said jokingly.

"Shame on you!," Mrs. Barrs snapped at Stella.

"Oh Mother!, he can take a joke," she rebutted. Besides, God protected him from serious harm."

"Thank you Jesus," Mrs. Barrs called out loud with one hand and face raised toward her ceiling. "Thank you Jesus."

"Well, well, who do we have here?" asked a portly gentlemen dressed in a tuxedo as he entered the hall from the dining room area. Mrs. Barrs cleared her throat and eloquently announced, "Pastor Barrs, this young man is Richard Jones. He's a friend of Stella's." Then she turned to me and reversed her introduction, "Richard Jones, this is my husband and Stella's father, Pastor Howard M. Barrs." We shook hands. Oh, he's a squeezer, I thought as he nearly crushed my hand to splinters.

"Why are we standing in the vestibule?" Pastor Howard M. Barrs wanted to know. "Lets' go into the sitting room and get acquainted."

"Where's Milton, Peggy? Why isn't Milton down here? Stella go fetch your brother! Mr. Barrs, told his daughter. He needs to know your friends."

"Daddy, do I have to," Stella whined. "I don't meet all *his* friends."

"That's different, you're a young lady," he halfheartedly affirmed. "Now do as I tell ya'," he said looking at me.

Stella offered no more resistance but instead smiled at me, turned, and ran up stairs, two stairs at a time.

"Well this is it," I thought, the dreaded 'Third Degree'. The ideal of having to pass their family inspection angered and insulted me. My sisters never had a father to screen their boyfriends in the sitting room. My mother never called me in to join an interrogation squad. What's all the fuss about, I wondered? I hope they're not expecting me to produce an engagement ring. No way!"

"Are the lights too bright for ya?," Mr. Barrs metaphorically explored, referring to my sunglasses. "No sir!" I replied. "But I am embarrassed by my eye injury." I figured I would be direct, relaxed and full of it, since I didn't care how this meeting ended up. If I just stayed calm, I could control my stammering. The challenge was intriguing. I inwardly smiled. "Come on Pastor Howard M. Barrs, Mama Barrs and Baby Barrs," I thought, "let's play the game." "In this house," Mr. Barrs stated with indifference, "we don't wear sunglasses. Do you mind?" He made a hand gesture to remove them.

"What happened to you?," he questioned with a sneer.
"It was those . . . " Mrs. Barrs was beginning to say, when Mr. Barrs cut her off.
"Let him explain Peggy, I'm sure it's good," he said not even facing me.
"I was attacked by some boys from this community sir." I began, "as I went looking for a church for my family to visit." "What!" Mr. Barrs snapped. "Those dirty little sinners!" We continued into the sitting room and sat down. Mr. and Mrs. Barrs sat together on a sofa and I sat on a matching leather recliner. "My first impulse was to get a baseball bat," I lied, "And go head busting, but the words of my dear departed father came to me saying, "Vengeance is the Lord's." The little I heard about the Bible came from my grandmothers' sermons during our visits as small children. She would buy us new clothes just for a special church service. If my sisters and I fought each other, or did anything wrong, my grandmother would have the guilty one sing church hymns to the offended one or else you got a whipping with a thick leather barber strap she called Dr. Kellogg. I was surprised I even remembered any of that stuff.
"What you doing in this community," Mr. Barrs probed with growing interest. Look'n fer a church fer my family?" Before I proceeded with my concoction, Stella and her short fat brother came in. Milton seemed to be a couple years

younger than me, a couple inches shorter, but about fifty pounds heavier. He wore thick rim eyeglasses, and carried in his hand a Dick Tracy comic book. Milton took one look at my face and pointed a finger and chuckled saying, "Did The Goodfellow Boys do that?" Milton asked with a laugh. Actually he laughed so hard that he doubled over, holding his fat belly. "Don't mind him!," Mr. Barrs quipped, "He's just overjoyed it wasn't him, for a change. Go head continue, continue."

The baby Barrs sat together on a love seat. Milton stuck his face into the comic book as if not to be concerned with my mishaps. "We moved on Goodfellow Avenue yesterday from Newstead Avenue. Our home church is Prince of Peace Baptist Church, where the Reverence Philip Mac is Pastor. We use to catch the bus, but now we're too far away." I thought to myself, I better clean this up fast, before he invites us to join his church.

"My mother has to work every Sunday. She's a supervisor at Angels Convalescent Home in Wellston. And I sell The Post Dispatch Newspaper every Sunday on the east side to help support myself. My two sisters will be riding to Prince of Peace Baptist Church with my grandmother. The Lord has worked it all out." "Amen," Stella and her mother said in harmony. "What happened to your father, Richard?," Mrs. Barrs asked with compassion in her tone and eyes.
"Go get our guest a coke, Milt," Papa Barrs told his son hastily, "And hurry back." "Now what lie could I tell," I pondered. "It's difficult to share," I said with a sniffle and choking back tears, "with strangers." Papa Barrs sprung from his seat and rushed to comfort me. "We're not strangers," he said putting one hand on my shoulder, "But one family-in-Christ." The thought flashed through my mind, "Come on brain, don't leave me now!" I had it! A lie easy to swallow. No, chop it up some, nobody will swallow a lie that big. I took a long deep breath. All right, here goes . . . "But Mr. Barrs, it's all, my fault," I said in three puffs as I buried my face in my hands and snuggled closer to Papa Barrs. It should've been me . . . Not my my my fa father."

Milton was back with the soda. He had even poured it in a glass for me. Sympathy was written all over him.

"Here Richard," Milton said as he pushed the glass toward me. "Ha," I thought, "even Fatso is breaking down with emotion."

I refused the soda, not wanting to slow my flow.

"It was a fire," I managed to say. "I'm all right," I added for the drama, and sniffed a couple times, as if fighting back tears. "The fire . . . The fire, the lady, her baby, the baby . . . my father, daddy, daddy." I sat there and actually began to cry. My phony tears were doing their job.

Mama Barbs, and both baby Barbs were all standing. Stella spoke, rubbing my shoulder, "What happened next?"

I reached out and accepted the coke from Milton, whose arm was still extended. As I took a sip from the glass, I realized I was also sipping the tears that had fallen to my lips.

"That's Good! That's Good," I thought.

Mrs. Barrs handed me a silk handkerchief. I swabbed my eyes then continued, much more in control of my emotions.

"I'm sorry." I mumbled.

"Just let it out, son, "Mr. Barrs impulsively said.

"My father and I had been fishing," I recapped. "This was last year. We were about an hour drive from St. Louis. We saw this farmhouse on fire. Dad sped to the sight and we jumped out and ran toward the blaze. As we got close, a white woman ran out the house screaming, with a child about nine or ten years old in her arms. They collapsed at our feet. My dad noticed the child was not breathing and begun to pray. The mother was coughing and gasping for air." Suddenly she was on her feet running into the burning farmhouse, screaming, "My baby, my baby." Dad thought she was hysterical, and called to her, "you've gotten your baby out! Your baby is out!" But she disappeared in the house. My father ran in for her and dragged her out. He kept trying to assure her the baby was safe. I ran inside searching for another child. I found the baby in a crib in the rear of the house. With the baby in my arms, I fled through a back door. Once outside I laid helplessly on the ground, struggling to breathe. When it was all over I discovered my father had ran back into the fire for me and died there. There was a long silence in the sitting room. Then Mrs. Barrs spoke, "It wasn't your fault, Richard, it was his time." "God called him home," Milton added. Stella was sobbing. Pastor Barrs said, "Let us pray."

I began to fully appreciate the duties of fatherhood. It's amazing how a mere hour in the company of light will illuminate a world of darkness. Mr. and Mrs. Barrs loved their children and were frightened by what their sheltered world was becoming with fellows like me. I was used to foul language, lying, roguish adults, loud women, violence, drunkards, women cheating on their husbands, men cheating on their wives, pimps and jailbirds around the house. Good work Mr. Barrs, protect your daughter from the likes of me. I was proud of myself knowing I'd done well under such scrutiny.

The five of us sat in their parlor, played checkers and sang church songs as Stella played the piano. The Pastor and his wife went and changed clothes because they were all going bowling at 7:30 p.m. Earlier, that day they attended a formal N.A.A.C.P. Luncheon where Pastor Barrs received a Humanitarian Award. At 7:15 p.m., I said goodnight to everyone.

That was more than enough time to meet The Goodfellow Boys at one of their hangouts, a cafe called Moms. Stella walked me outside and we stood there a few minutes sharing some laughs. I left feeling good about my visit.

When I got to my apartment building, I halfheartedly expected to see Gloria in her front window. I wasn't disappointed. "Hi," she greeted me, "Elaine and I are friends, and I have something for you. Here, take this," said Gloria, and passed me a folded piece of paper through her open window. Then she closed her window and pulled down the shade. I heard her say, "*Bye my little Richie,*" from behind the curtains.

I tucked the paper into my pocket and rushed upstairs. Andy and my mother were watching television. Tammie was gone to our play sister Nina's house. Elaine was gathering herself to go downstairs and visit her new friend.
Andy jumped to his feet and yelled, "What happened ta yo' eye?"
"Don't it look bad?," I joked. But I didn't stop to explain, I went on to my room and closed the door. Mommy told him I was out boxing.
"One of these daze, I'm gone sho' him how ta sho' nuff fight," I heard him say.

I was so comfortable at Stella's house that I had completely forgotten that my

94

sunglasses were in my pocket. A quick change of clothes, a quick sandwich, and I was gone. By 8:05, I was walking into Mom's Cafe. The jukebox was playing something by The Miracles. There were about two dozen teenagers there. No one was dancing. Just a few small huddles talking, eating, and two dudes on the pinball machine. "I overheard a boy say to another, "That's the dude that went five rounds with Moose." I looked around and recognized several faces. Otis was there, so was Red. "Hey, Richard Jones!," Otis called, "Come here, man, I want ya' to meet some dudes." I met seven or eight guys; they called me Richard Jones, because there were two other Richards'. *Cool* Richard,and *Hot* Richard.

This was the most crowded party I had ever been to, especially in a basement. Wall-to-wall teenagers. Red lights throughout. No food. No drinks. Just back-to-back music and cheek-to-cheek dancing. One of the Goodfellow Girls, a 16-year-old high school cheerleader named Tanya, lived in an apartment on the second floor of this basement party. Her mother allowed her to have a party there every fourth Saturday night.

The parties were called, "Waistline Parties." The person at the door would measure the waistline of each person before they entered, and the party goers would be charged two cents per inch. My admission was a mere 50 cents. Moose paid 68 cents. The money was given to Tanya, to help her mother maintain the household. There must've been at least 100 party guests. I made a mental note to speak to my mother and our apartment manager about having monthly parties in our large basement. This party was cool. Naturally, all the cool kids were there. I was being introduced to guys with bad reputations; guys that I've heard about through the years like, 'Stickman', a dude that was known to 'stick' his enemies with a knife; 'Armstrong', a dude known to be a 'strong arm' robber. Members of well-known high school singing groups, even a few well-known teenage amateur boxers was there. I'd been to a lot of weekend basement parties, but nothing like a Goodfellows Party. There were more girls in that basement than all the telephone numbers I collected in my whole life, including the wrong numbers.

Many of these party girls were *'fast.'* I saw them slow dance with different boys who 'grinded' and gripped them by the rear end. These girls didn't resist. They grinded back! I rushed to dance with those girls on the next slow record. On fast records, I kept a lookout for the girls who did 'The DOG' in a nastier than usual way. These girls would be so hot with desire that the only real challenge was to slip them away from the rest of the guys. The more popular you were, the easier it was for you to choose the girl you wanted.

There was no dope or alcohol. However, anybody who was 'cool' smoked cigarettes. The basement was thick with smoke and perspiration. Music, laughter, and chatter. Kissing, fondling, and trains. (Trains were when two or more boys waited their turn to have sex with one girl).

There were three or four trains running. A guy considered himself lucky if he was one of the first three guys on a train ride. I'd heard of girls letting boys pull trains on them, but I never was in the midst of one. Although it wasn't blatant, I could tell what was going on because every five minutes or so, I would overhear one friend whisper to another, "Who's on you?" Meaning who is the guy on the train behind you. And if the friend say, "Joe's on me," then Joe would be sought and asked the same question, "Who's on you?" Eventually, the sex seeker would find a vacant spot on the train. The risk, of course, was the longer the train, the less likely it was the girl would still be available by the time the last few guys got a turn. Most girls would get mad if they were asked to have group sex, therefore, the guys would only ask the girls who didn't matter to them. Sometimes unpopular girls did it just to be allowed to hang around the others. It was obvious at my first party with the Goodfellow Boys that sex was no problem.

As I slow danced with one particular girl for the third time, within the last five slow songs, I thought I would get even bolder. On our first dance, I grinded on her, and she grinded back. On our second dance, I grinded on her plus gripped her butt with both hands. Other fellows beat me to the next couple slow dances, but finally I got her back. We danced by dim red lights in a far corner of the crowded smoky basement. The song was, "Tears on My Pillow," by Lil' Antony and The Imperials (you don't remember me, but I remember you, was not so long ago, you broke my heart into . . . Tears on My Pillow,

Pain in my heart . . .)

This time, as I grinded and gripped her bottom, I started nibbling on her ear, then her neck, then I pulled my lips away and turned to ask her name. We ended up in a long kiss. After the kiss, she told me her name was Laura. I whispered my desire for her phone number and she whispered it in my ear. I told Laura that I would remember the number always, and we would dance again later. We went our separate ways in thick smoke.

I resumed my vantage point on the wall and asked one of the fellows, a boy everyone called Daddy, did he know Laura. He asked me to point her out. I spotted her sitting alone and refusing dance offers. Laura was a shapely, ugly girl with bad skin and crooked teeth. He said he had seen her around, but didn't know her. Daddy was one of the most popular members of the group. His natural leadership ability and his dancing talent caused everyone to admire him. He was about sixteen years old, tall and skinny with big eyes, dark skin and wavy brownish hair.

"I think she likes me," I told Daddy.
"Why do you say that?," he chuckled.
"Well," I began, "I know girls and she has been letting boys grind on her all night, but I'm the only one she kissed," I concluded with a smirk.
"A KISS!," he snapped, "That don't mean nuttin'. If you want to see how much she likes you, the next time you dance with her, put your hand up her dress." "A KISS!," he said, "A ROTTEN KISS!"

I worked my way over to her. I didn't say anything, but took her hand and lead her away as the next slow record was beginning. We embraced in a secluded corner and kissed as we danced. I slowly inched my left hand from her backside around her hip and up the side to the front of her blouse and squeezed her gently. She didn't resist. So I inched my hand back down her side, pass her hip. My hand roamed to the front of her skirt. She had both arms gently over my shoulders and around my neck. I slid my hand all over her body. Finally I whispered, "Let's go get some fresh air," in a suggestive manner. Laura said, "Okay." I thought, "Now where can we go?"

The rear exit was within a dozen steps. We joined the many other couples in the parking lot of Tanya's apartment building. There were several boys crowded around an old '51 Ford. The car was parked in the farthest corner of the yard and sat on the ground without tires. As we walked around the side of the building, I heard boys straightening out a mix-up. "No no no, Ed," the mediator said, "Kenny is on me, you're on Kenny and Moony is on you." Another voice from the pack interjected, "All I know is I'm next. That's all I know, hurry up Moose!"

Even on the side of the building there were couples cuddled together. I led Laura to the front, as if I knew exactly where I was going. We walked with our arms around each other down the street. My hand found a receptive resting place tight around her waist as we turned the corner. My eyes searched for an opportunity. "Let's go this way," I told her as we entered the first alley I saw.

Deep into the alley we stopped and leaned against the side of an opened garage and started to kiss. After a few moments of necking, I led her into the garage. She came along willing. We climbed into the back seat of the unlocked car parked there. In the darkness, I fumbled with her clothing, and she fumbled with mine, until we were nearly naked. "Good Golly Miss Molly!," I thought, "I'm about to become a man."

Back at the party, I told Laura I would call her tomorrow as we went our separate directions in the smokey basement. There was Daddy dancing with a very pretty, and skinny girl. Half the party watched his fancy steps. He had all the crazy turns. And his timing was second only to Mr. Please, Please, Please, James Brown himself. The hit song 'I'm Look'n for a Love' was playing. (I'm looking For a Love, to call my own. . . someone to get up in the morn'n and rub my head...I'm Look'n fer a luv ta call my own . . . I'm look'n here and there, I'm search'n every - where. . .) When the song ended, a thunderous applause erupted, mostly for Daddy. He smiled as he scanned the spectators.

The next song started immediately and everybody grabbed a partner. Daddy still had the same girl by the hand, but instead of dancing he began to lead her through the crowd. As he approached me, I called his name. I wanted to share my experience, and tell him it all happened because I did as he told me. Daddy's eyes picked me up, and he displayed a devilish grin. He cut his eyes to the girl he was leading away, then back to me and tossed his head as if to say, follow me.

"Come on, Richard Jones," he said, "you're on me."

As we entered the front yard and headed for a secluded place, a voice called from behind. "Hey fellas, wait up!" It was *Cool* Richard. He joined us and announced, "I'm on you, Richard Jones."

Chapter 5

*B*y June '61, we had lived on Goodfellow longer than any other place in our lives. When Mommy announced during one of our Saturday morning breakfasts, we were moving to California. We were not surprised. We had lived there *three* years. Besides Mommy had written to convalescent homes in Los Angeles regarding employment opportunities. Most of her replies simply stated that they were more interested in hiring LVN's or RN's. Finally, after dozens of rejections, four convalescent homes, in the same month, guaranteed her a position.

Many of the gang had been to detention camps. Stella Barrs had gotten pregnant by one of the Goodfellow Boys. Pastor Barrs sent her to live in Texas with his sister. A month before we left the city, the police came to my school and arrested me for crimes I committed with the Goodfellow Boys. The police, later that day released me to the custody of my mother. The court date was two weeks later. I only got a stern warning from the judge, with a guarantee to be sent to Booneville Detention Camp for Boys if I were arrested on any charge in Missouri for the next three years.

Alan was still a newspaper boy. My sister's friend Gloria became a regular "train ride girl" at the Goodfellow Boys parties. I was ready for a change. The move to California was timely indeed.

Several months earlier, before mommy began writing to nursing homes in California, I was arrested for the third time since we moved on Goodfellow. Every time mommy and I went to court, the judge asked her if she could handle me. "If not," he would say, "I can send him to Booneville." The first two-times mommy swore to the court, she could handle me. "He's really not a bad boy," she said. "It's those Goodfellows Boys he runs around with." Each time the judge granted me probation. But the last time we went to court was different. The judge sentenced me to three years in Booneville for riding in a stolen car. Mommy begged and cried. The court bailiff took me to the holding cell. My mother was still in court with the judge for 30 minutes more. I never found out what kind of deal she made with him, but I was released on probation two hours later. Shortly after that, mommy began searching for work in California.

My mother moved to California two weeks ahead of the family. Mommy went ahead to secure an apartment and earn her first paycheck. She returned riding in a new Cadillac car, driven by her cousin Bernie. We called him Uncle Bernie. We rode to California in style. Uncle Bernie, as it turned out, was nothing more than a pimp. Once we got to California, my mother saw very little of him, except on family holidays.

Meantime, in her two-week absence, our "play" sister Nina moved into our apartment with her two baby daughters until our departure date. Nina and most of her girlfriends were in their early to mid-twenties. The ones who were married would meet other men at our apartment. There were several young married women using our place for their adulterous liaisons. My opinion of female fidelity was less than honorable. They would sit 'for hours and talk about how no-good men were, but when a man showed up, they ran and powdered their noses; put on the tightest blouse they could find; stuff their brassieres with paper or cotton; applied false eyelashes; and flirted without shame. Even 16-year-old Tammie, and her girlfriends were quick to two-time their boyfriends. Being present while women were plotting against men, harden and distorts a boy's heart. I decided if I ever had children, I would rather be a widower than put up with a cheating and fighting woman.

The years swiftly went by. By 1970, we had been in California eight years. My sister Tammie was married, the mother of a baby girl, and already separated from her drug dealing husband. Elaine became the unwed mother of two boys by different men. My mother was now married to a painting contractor named Frank. I had served time in the county jail on several occasions for petty crimes, including four or five drunk driving violations. My daily routine involved criminal activity.

In 1970, I was also on the rebound after separating from a live-in girlfriend. Her name was Norma. After a short courtship, I moved into her small apartment, and moved out six months later. She was a divorced mother with two young sons. At 22-years-old, I was still an immature adult, searching for his place in the world. All of my troubles were drowned in alcohol, and so were my victories.

Nevertheless, I did manage to land a job within Crocker Citizens National Bank Data Processing Center, even with my alcoholism. However, while working one evening, the supervisor came and beckoned for me to follow her. I thought that was strange, just to beckon and not say a word. She walked into her office as I followed her. She was a fat Oriental woman about forty years old with a strong accent. "I gotta let you go," she nonchalantly announced. "Orders from head office."
"Are you sure?," I questioned, as if I didn't know that my drinking was affecting my work.
"Order from head office," she repeated. "Gimme badge!"
She stuck one hand out for my bank employees' photo I.D. badge that was clipped to my shirt pocket. I unclipped the badge, "There must be some mistake," I objected ostentatiously.
"No mistake," she snapped, popping her fingers and repeated, "Badge!" She reached over and removed the badge from my opened palms. "If you want full explanation, call head office tomorrow, nine o'clock."
It was an extremely long walk from her cubicle to the elevator, it seemed the room had grown twenty times its normal size during our meeting. None of the employees seemed to notice my leaving. Everyone worked with their backs turned or heads down.

As I walked out, I laughed to myself, knowing I was well prepared for such an occasion. I had recorded enough information from checking accounts to make a good living ripping off the checking accounts of innocent customers. My only "minor" problem was that I needed to work with a hustler who had the necessary women to work the female accounts. All of the accounts were those of the white female customers. I didn't know a single "white" female forger. Therefore, I would have to contact a hustler called "Pretty Willie." This fellow worked exclusively with white girls. Pretty Willie and I began a profitable relationship. A few days later, I met Annie, my future wife, while out on an evening stroll. Now, 12 years later, she was dead as a result of a traffic accident. And I was a widower with children. Had I prophesied my destiny? Was Annie doomed from the moment she married me?

Suddenly, a realization came over me. A loud and clear spiritual message, that only I could hear, engulfed me. As I stared into the early morning beauty of the clouds, the horizon, and the distant mountains, I was comforted by an inner peace. My guilt began to vanish. God has ALL POWER. He is omnipotent. Ann's fate was not mine to call. My 25-year journey down memory lane came to a much welcomed end.

The train exited a long curved tunnel of darkness and the fresh light of a new day greeted me. I finally understood who I was, and how I got to be me. Yolanda was still asleep in the passenger seat next to me. She looked so serene, and innocent I couldn't resist the urge to bend over and kiss her on the cheek. I said a silent prayer of thanks, and asked for the strength to be the kind of father my children could love and respect. Being a parent is one of the most important and powerful positions in the world. The responsibly of molding the character of four human beings was not one to take lightly. A corrupt and dysfunctional childhood will greatly affect their adulthood, which may trickle negative traits down for generations. I asked myself, "What kind of example would I set?" I had spent my life blaming my single mother and absent father for my failures and short comings. For a short time, I even blamed the white man. Now, at 34-years-old, there was no more time or space for excuses. It was time to be a mature man. Changes had to be made. This was a new beginning.

Wade stayed behind in Natchez, then later returned by airplane. Although our purpose for being away from home wasn't a leisure trip, the two-day train ride gave Yolanda and me a measure of relaxation. Unlike the plane trip, we laughed, played cards, told jokes, sang familiar tunes, and made up new ones. We shared our feelings and hopes for the future. There were periods along the way that we set aside banter and engaged in serious conversation. I assured Yolanda that she was not expected to assume the role of mother. She was merely a few years older than the rest and that did not make her an automatic babysitter. She needed to hear that from me.

On more than one occasion while in Mississippi, I overheard Ann's relatives tell Yolanda she was now the lady of the house. I withheld my opinion on the subject to keep down confusion. Yolanda and I also talked about the multiple coincidences that Ann's family shared with her. First, Ann was buried next to her mother. Second, both of them died at age 30. Third, both deaths involved motor vehicles, and each suffered massive head injuries. Finally, Ann was two years old at the time of her mother's death, which was Roxanne's age.

The train conductor yelled, "We'll be pulling into Union Station Downtown Los Angeles in five minutes. Unboard in five minutes!"
Yolanda said, "Whew, it's about time!"
It was a rainy evening in the City of the Angeles as we took a Yellow Cab to my mother's house. I instructed the driver, for Yolanda's sake, which route to take so she would learn early not to be suckered by cab drivers. Mommy prepared a special dinner party for our return. About a dozen friends and family members were there and greeted us with hugs and kisses.

Over the next several days, Roxanne stayed with her grandmother. Roxy was not potty trained because Ann did not think it was necessary to rush her. However, under my mother's guidance, about a week later, Roxy was potty trained and eligible to attend the Crescent Heights Children Center and After School Care with her sisters. The Center moved Roxy's name from the bottom of the seven-month waiting list to the top. She started preschool immediately. The administration knew my situation, The staff awarded my family special privileges such as combing and styling my daughters hair occasionally, and talking to them on subjects that were uncomfortable for me in my new role as a single parent.

I retained an attorney regarding Ann's accident. My lawyer informed me that his investigator discovered Ann was under a criminal investigation at the time of death. Ann had sent a letter to the Los Angeles County Welfare Fraud Division submitting evidence of an ongoing welfare fraud scheme but failed to surrender herself for questioning as requested. An arrest warrant was then issued for her. Two days prior to her death, welfare fraud officers made an attempt to take her into custody but never found her home.

My lawyer's investigator also discovered that I was out of jail on bail, awaiting sentencing on a forgery charge. Although he wasn't a criminal attorney, he felt sure that with the proper attorney, I would receive probation. Of course, he just happened to be acquainted with such a majestic mouthpiece. He told me not to worry about how much the criminal attorney would charge because the fee could be withheld from the wrongful death settlement. I bitterly told him, no thanks, and to keep his mind on the business at hand.

I welcomed wise recommendation on child rearing, and domestic duties from caring females. However, I soon learned that just because advice is coming from a good woman, it doesn't mean it is good advice. For example, Sandra, an attractive redhead neighbor, offered her feminine wisdom to Yolanda. However, I wished she had just kept her mouth shut. When I found out she told Yolanda to fold sheets of newspaper into the size of a sanitary napkin when she began her menstrual cycle to save money, I revoked Sandra's counseling privileges. I wasn't comfortable with the idea of allowing anybody to teach my children how to be poor.

When Ann was alive, I didn't take single my parenting seriously, because I knew Ann would there to back me up in a tight situation. But now the game was real! No safety net! Nor did I have to bicker over every detail involving my children. I could control what they watched on television, the reading material in the house, their church habits, and their mental development. That was the bright side. On the downside, I knew my girls would lack the prim and proper home training girls are supposed to have. The etiquette of table setting, dinner parties, ladylike manners, etc.

Before Ann was killed, I had been arrested on a forgery charge and was out of jail on bail. Since I was now without Ann's back up, the thought of being sent to prison worried me. I regretted being in the criminal life. "What an awful break for my children," I thought. First they lose their mother to death and now, in a short time, they'll lose their father to prison. Ultimately, I pled guilty. However, I assured the court I was in school the better my life. The judge postponed my sentence date for nearly a year to allow me time to finish school. When the day came that I appeared before the judge for sentencing, I came well-prepared. While out on bail for over a year, I created a new public image. I appeared in court with a certificate of completion from Abram Freidman Occupational Center in the field of Major Appliance Repair. Hamilton, the phony credit man, furnished the court with a letter of employment. I provided the court with a copy of Ann's death certificate in hopes of compassion. The judge congratulated me on my newly learned trade and steady employment. He expressed his faith in my ability to be a good single parent. I received three years formal probation, with no jail time. As the judge looked over my long arrest record, mostly alcohol related, he shook his head from side to side and told me to do myself a favor and stop drinking.

Over a year went by without me setting-up any accidents or phony welfare cases. We were living fairly well from three sources of income: (1) the one welfare check; (2) our monthly social security survivor benefits check; and (3) a weekly salary earned as a truck driver at a major appliance store. I found this job with the sole intent of setting up an accident but kept putting it off week after week, until the next thing I knew I had been there for months.

Working a legitimate job renewed my longing for street life. Though I had only been employed for a few months, I was constantly thinking of ways to sue the company. An easy lawsuit would be to fake a back injury. All I had to do was take off work one day, call in with back pain, go to my doctor, and have him or her fill-out worker's compensation forms. The company employed four other delivery drivers and each one worked with a helper. Every couple days, the manager would switch drivers and helpers so we would all learn to work together. I liked each man but avoided becoming personally acquainted with any of them.

Meanwhile, I began looking for a larger apartment. Every day I would drive around seeking three bedroom units. When I eventually found a desirable place, we moved in within one week. Sandra, my previous neighbor, with whom I had developed a *casual lover* relationship, came over every Friday night with Rubin, age 10, and Belton, age 7, her two spoiled sons. They slept over so I would have a babysitter when I went to work on Saturday mornings. Sandra charged me the nominal fee of $10 each week.

Every week Sandra would get drunk on beer and we would spend half the night arguing, and the other half making up. As a result, most Saturday mornings I was either late, absent, or working with a hangover. Subsequently, I was fired. I had been there for several months and now I was fired. I realized at that point, job related accidents should occur as soon as possible.

Sandra and I became distant acquaintances after I no longer needed her weekend services as an overnight babysitter. The small flame we had for one another quickly flickered and died. Nonetheless, I needed female assistance. To address this need, I placed an ad in the classified section of two black newspapers which read:

> *Wanted:*   *Widower with four young children seek live-in babysitter and lite housekeeper in exchange for room and board. No salary.*

While waiting for the ad to appear, I applied for another delivery job. I was hired on the first interview. Before the calls from the ad started coming in, I had another full time driving job. My accident crime partners were put on call. I rear-ended my crime partners on my second day of work and placed myself under Worker's Compensation medical care. At the time, I possessed a dozen sets of driver licenses. I planned to procure a new job every week or two and stage accidents.

Several women applied for the live-in position. I realized my stupidity level was high, and my sexual discretion low while under the influence of alcohol, therefore, I wanted to hire the one who appealed to me--the least. Two of them were so repulsive that I had a hard time trying to figure out which one to hire. The woman I hired was bigger than our large double door refrigerator and uglier than the frozen catfish inside. She was 24-years-old and had custody of her six-year-old mulatto daughter. I don't remember their names, so I'll just call them Big Daisy, meaning mama, and Little Daisy, meaning the daughter. Big Daisy was as dark as burnt toast and Little Daisy was high yellow, with a long mane. Big Daisy treated Little Daisy like a fragile goddess. Little Daisy transferred to the elementary school where my daughters attended, and was scheduled to ride the school bus. Big Daisy claimed there were too many sick children on school buses. Some child in the past had coughed on her child and made her ill. Therefore, she took her daughter to school each morning on the public bus. Once she got her to school, Big Daisy would sit on the school yard bench and watches her until the students went to class. After noticing Big Daisy interfere with a dispute over a ball between her daughter and another child, the school officials banned her from waiting on school property. Defiantly, Big Daisy began standing outside the school yard coaching Little Daisy about everything.

At home, Big Daisy combed and brushed each girl's hair every night before bed. This ritual took two hours, about 20 minutes for my four girls, and one hour and forty minutes for her child. Little Daisy would play with my children's toys without permission, and if they asked her to put the toys away she would stand in the middle of the floor and scream at the top of her voice until Big Daisy came running to her. Her mother would always resolve the conflict in her child's favor.

Once I bet Big Daisy $5 that she couldn't sit calmly on the couch for five minutes while her daughter and I went into the next room. She insisted she could do it. So the challenge was on. I took Big Daisy's daughter by the hand, led her into my girl's bedroom and left the door wide open. When Little Daisy and I entered the bedroom, I told the child to be very quiet. We were not in the room alone. All four of my girls were in the same room watching television. I sat on one side of room and Little Daisy the other. Then I began watching the second hand of my watch. Within 45 seconds Big Daisy appeared in the doorway panting as if she had run up ten flights of steps. She verbally attacked me saying, "This is crazy!" Then she turned her attention to her child, "Are you all right baby?"

Big Daisy didn't last but one month, before I got rid of her.

The same ad was placed again in the newspapers. And I got the same response. This time the girls were present during all the job interviews. We wanted to be sure that the next live-in person didn't have children and was a good cook. Big Daisy was a sorry excuse for a cook, and we didn't want to suffer through that again. Several nice looking women came by that the girls liked, but I could imagine myself chasing them around the apartment throughout the day, therefore, I took their number but kept the applicants coming. The most uncomely woman who applied was Arlene, a 29-year-old, childless divorcee. When Arlene walked in, I hired her in my mind before she ever sat down.

One day while Arlene was away, I prowled around her bedroom and I found a dinner plate under her bed with a razor blade, burned matches, a white power substance, and glass pipe in it. I called Harry and described my findings. He informed me that Arlene was a 'freebaser', which meant she smoked cocaine. When Arlene returned and saw the plate on top of her bed, she knew her secret was out. I told her she had to move. Arlene insisted that I honor our 30-day termination agreement. I refused. "Look Arlene!" I snapped, "I'm on probation,and you're jeopardizing my freedom by asking me to allow a base-head to stay in my house." I threatened that unless she was gone in 10 days, I would call the police. She reluctantly agreed to move.

Unfortunately, I dropped my guard and started drinking the next night while Arlene was home. I was half drunk and in a partying mood. After a couple shots of rum and my fourth beer, Arlene began to look, a little, like an ordinary woman. I said to myself, "What the heck! She was gonna be outta here very soon anyway." Arlene had been with us for two months and we'd never partied together. I'd maintained a casual but professional relationship. Every morning, I left to wreck some employer's truck, and stayed home in the evening like an average guy. Arlene didn't even suspect that I drank. But on this night, I was sort of celebrating another wreck. The accident went well.

I had racked up about twelve accidents in the past few months and was celebrating the victory. I now was receiving seven or eight weekly Worker Compensation checks in different names and at different addresses.

I kept teasing and kidding with Arlene until she agreed to dance with me. As the night progressed, Arlene relaxed her guarded posture. We slow danced and kissed with heated intensity. At about 1:00 a.m., Arlene casually excused herself and went into her bedroom. She returned a short while later wearing a negligee. We danced once more. Then I suddenly realized that I was extremely low on rum, and the liquor stores would be closed at 2:00 a.m. I decided to rush to the store. Arlene requested some cigarettes. I didn't even know she smoked cigarettes. I made her promise not to go to bed until I returned and we danced at least twice more. However, neither of us knew that we'd danced our last dance.

On my way to get booze and cigarettes, I got something else instead, arrested for DUI (Driving Under the Influence). My car was impounded. This inconvenience cost me bail, and money to get my car, not to mention a night in jail and a future date with a judge. I seldom spoke to Arlene for the duration of her one week deadline. It's embarrassing, for me, to look someone in the face after you know, *that they know*, what a fool you truly are. In my denial, I blamed Arlene for my new legal problems, but intellectually I knew that my drinking and lack of discipline were the culprits.

After Arlene moved out, I decided to be a single parent in every sense of the word, without the benefit of a live-in babysitter. Besides, my experiences with such arrangements were negative. Big Daisy, I discovered while prowling through her private papers, was under psychiatric care. She was taking medication for a paranoid/schizophrenic condition and went to therapy twice weekly. Her child was fathered by a white man who played drums and traveled with his band. I also discovered, too late of course, that Big Daisy was a habitual liar. We had verbally agreed that she wouldn't make long distant calls on my phone, nor would she accept long distance calls. However, one month after her departure my phone bill arrived with more than $450 worth of long distant calls. Big Daisy had been accepting long distance phone calls from all over the United States.

Arlene, on the other hand, was a different kind of nut. She smoked crack and watched soap operas all day. I distinctly discussed with her, at length, that I didn't want my girls watching such 'brain dead' entertainment. They were too young, and such TV shows are not concerned about the mental welfare of children. I explained to her that our minds are in a common state of reception. It's always receiving and perceiving. And the information you nourish it with will ultimately decide your fate. Arlene would respond by saying, "Yes, Mr. Jones. I understand, Mr. Jones. I will not watch the soaps in the presence of your children, Mr. Jones." Yet! Time and time again, I came home unexpectingly, and walked in on the entire household watching; *Search for Tomorrow; All My Children; The Young and The Restless; etc.*

I would order my children out of the room and chew Arlene out for going against my rules. She would defend herself by saying something like, "I can't make your kids mind me. I told them you didn't want them watching soap operas, but they wouldn't listen." Arlene sometimes would take the position of defending the soaps. "It's only a movie. There's nothing wrong with 'my stories.' They're harmless. I have been watching them for years, and there's nothing wrong with me."
Besides that problem with Arlene, she had no interest in a wholesome diet. I tried to sway her junk food addiction into nutritious meals for the sake of my children. Arlene didn't understand the influence adult behavior had over formative youth. "You can't tell me what to eat!," the grossly out of shape and asthmatic babysitter would say in her defense.

At last, we were refreshingly alone again. The girls and I were not church members, but they visited a church every now and then. Usually, they would go with my sister, Elaine, who picked them up once or twice a month. Although I didn't know much about Elaine's religion, Jehovah Witnesses, I allowed my girls to accompany her until I learned the members were not permitted to receive Christmas toys, or have a Christmas tree. I felt every child was entitled to a Merry Christmas. Therefore, I stopped Elaine from taking her nieces to the Kingdom Hall.

Ann's brother, Wade, owned a beauty salon. He heard about the trouble I was having keeping his nieces' hair looking decent and volunteered his services. Wade was a man of his word. We never paid to get their hair done, as long as they went to Wade's Beauty Salon.

The responsibility of building my daughters good self-esteem was paramount. I pinned all the art work they brought home from school to the wall. It wasn't long before apartment walls were filled to capacity with the creativity of Roxy, Jennifer, Rochelle, and Yolanda. Some of my neighbors kidded me by saying, our apartment resembled a kindergarten class. When I heard those comments, I often responded by saying, "As a bachelor, I had a huge bar with eight bar stools, a full liquor shelf in the living room, posters of bikini clad women in the dining room, and several marijuana pipes fashionably strewn about in plain sight but nobody told me that my apartment resembled a bar."

I didn't have to be a family therapist to realize a lot of my parental critics behaved poorly in the presence of own their children. Behaviors such as cursing, drinking, smoking cigarettes, weed, and using drugs. I wasn't about to allow any of these parental misfits contaminate my honorable intentions. However, I've got to admit, I still had my criminal lifestyle and drinking problem, that no one except a criminal court judge tried to persuade me to correct.

One of my favorite television programs to watch with my daughters called, "The People's Court." It was a real life small claims courtroom drama. The participants were not actors, but real court litigants. My daughters and I would view the show, not as couch potato spectators, but as jurors under oath. We would closely observe the plaintiff, the defendant, the witnesses, the evidence, and the comments of the judge, who was indeed a real judge. During the commercial break, we deliberated the case and had our verdict by the time the commercial was over, or before the judge rendered his decision. It would be a proud moment for the ones who decided the case in agreement with the magistrate.

Eventually, the principals used in deciding those court cases were adopted by our household for resolving family disputes. They learned that the person crying the loudest or the first one to run and tell is not necessarily the innocent one. Emotionalism has no place in what's right or wrong. The truth is the truth, regardless of how much you favor one side. Whenever one of my daughters was found guilty of violating a household rule or the rights of her sibling through our mock court preceding, discipline would be swift and rehabilitating. Seldom would discipline be in the form of physical punishment. Usually chastisement came in the form of the guilty party becoming responsible for doing the innocent one's household chores for a given period of time. Sometimes it would come in the form of the guilty sister losing their weekly allowance to the innocent sister for a given period of time.

We truly enjoyed our peaceful family. The girls were always laughing and creating games and puzzles. They often made me the butt of their practical jokes. I remember an occasion when they wanted to watch an hour long television movie that came on at 10:00 p.m. Earlier in the week, they asked my permission to stay up until 11:00 p.m. I was firm. There was to be no television watching after 9:00 p.m. The girls knew that I would not budge.

However, on the night of the movie, the older girls put 3-year-old Roxanne up to coughing uncontrollably. I thought we had some cough medicine in the medicine cabinet, but the girls had hidden it. The coughing started about 9:50 p.m. By 10 o'clock, I was on my way to the drug store. Before I got to the bottom stairs, of our second floor apartment, Yolanda called to me from the front door saying, we needed some cereal for breakfast in the morning. I fell right into the trap by telling her I would stop at the grocery store on the way back home and pick up some. After I had driven about three blocks, I realized that I had forgotten my wallet, which contained my money and drivers' license. They didn't hear the front door open when I entered the apartment. From the living room I could hear their television. I could hear them talking and laughing, even Roxy. They were watching, 'Dallas.' This was a very popular TV show during the early 80's, and this was the long awaited episode where the star of the show, J.R., was to be shot. This was the last show of the season, and nearly everybody with a television set had been primed and buttered up to tune in. Including my daughters.

When I walked into their room, their faces froze. I angrily turned the television off and began taking off my belt. All four girls started crying and pleading that they wouldn't do it anymore. I grabbed Yolanda first, since she was the oldest. She continued screaming, "Daddy I won't do it no mo', I won't do it no mo'. Please daddy, please . . . " Before I landed the first lick of the belt, it occurred to me that the children were promising not to be creative 'no mo'. Promising not to figure out how to get what they want in a harmless and crafty way. I realized I wasn't mad about what they did. Surely in my youth I'd done worse. My anger stemmed from being out smarted by four little girls. I stopped the flight of the belt in mid air.

"Stop crying," I demanded. "Stop crying! I'm going to the kitchen to get some water and when I come back, the only person that's gonna to get a whipping is the one still crying."

When I returned a minute later, they all were silent with a puzzled look. I broke the silence with laughter. "That was a very good trick," I chuckled. "You girls are good thinkers, that's good. But don't start whining when you get caught. That's not only being a sneak, but a wimp to boot. I don't like wimps, but I do like good thinkers. Now listen girls, if you choose to do wrong, consider the consequences. If you can't handle the consequences, don't do wrong." I continued to laugh and they all joined in, each claiming the trick to be their idea. I turned the television back on and left the room.

Chapter 6

*W*ith three children in elementary school and one in preschool, my evenings were not my own. For no less than two hours each night, I assisted the girls with their studies. If I wasn't doing that, I would attend a PTA meeting or some school theatrical production. Looking back, I can attest with all certainty that those were the most serene years of my life.

Each time I attended a school affair, I made it my business to extend a warm greeting to a particular single female parent who was always present with her two daughters. As good fortune would have it, two of my girls, Yolanda 11, and Jennifer 6, were best friends with her two girls. Sadie was 11-years-old and Rita was six. The girls often visited each other regularly, and even had weekend slumber parties together.

Their mother's name was Evelyn Fargo, and she was a very involved parent, which was quality that I admired. Evelyn was a cute, light skinned, woman, approximately 5'6",135 pounds, 30-years-old, with coal black short cropped hair, worn in a style called Jeri Curl. We were casually acquainted and only saw one another in connection with our children's school or social events.

After a year of acquaintance with Evelyn, I became aware that there was a man in her life. Though he never attended any school functions, I occasionally saw him waiting in the driver's seat of a blue Mustang when she picked her girls up from the Crescent Heights Children Center. Sometime when I picked my girls up from her apartment, I noticed the same vehicle parked in Evelyn's parking stall. Yolanda mentioned, in idle conversation, that Sadie's father didn't live with them. Therefore, I assumed the Mustang's driver was a current boyfriend. On more than one occasion, I walked Evelyn and her daughters to the car as a matter of security when she picked her girls up from our apartment at night. Never on these occasions was Evelyn boyfriend waiting in the car, but she was driving the blue Mustang. I concluded they worked and lived together. I also thought he must be a very detached and selfish man.

One evening during an Easter program at the children's center, I noticed Evelyn arrived driving an older model Oldsmobile Cutlass. We sat together and enjoyed the show. When the play was in the intermission, we engaged in conversation over punch and cookies.
"Where's your chauffeur in the Mustang tonight?" I joked.
"Don't mention him," she frowned. "That was the worst mistake I ever made."

"How long was y'all together?" I asked. I spoke without thinking. Now Evelyn would figure that I was either nosy or interested and I didn't want her to think either. "Just since the kid's father and I broke up last year," she answered. "That's about the time my girl's mother died," I replied. "I know firsthand how a single parent feels the need for a supportive mate." We returned to our seats, laughed and applauded in support of the student cast for the remainder of the production. Before we parted company for the evening, I asked Evelyn would she mind if I called her sometime. Her response was a pleasant surprise. "No, I wouldn't mind at all!" she said fondly. "In fact, it would be a pleasure. But call after eight. That's when I'm finished with the dinner dishes and everything else."

My day consisted of physical therapy treatments from three doctors. I visited each office two or three times a week. Gradually, I would be released from each medical office, the oldest cases first. An average physical therapy treatment, for soft-tissue injuries, only required two or three months of hot pads and massages. When I no longer had daily treatments, I began seeking new delivery jobs in different names, and creating more phony claims against Workers' Compensation insurance. This was an innovative method of insurance fraud. The investigators weren't dedicating much time to this type of crime, neither were other accident hustlers.

An on-the-job injury claim is handled much differently from your ordinary car crash or personal injury claim. The worker involved is automatically entitled to two-thirds of his weekly salary, regardless of fault, and a lump sum settlement about a year later. It didn't matter if the individual was an employee of 20 years or 20 minutes; they were covered by workers' compensation. I only sought low-pay driving jobs. For two reasons: (1) low-paying jobs are quick and easy to get, and I could mentally justify wrecking their truck or van because low wage employers thought little of their employees anyway, and (2) by driving a company vehicle, I would be assured a better opportunity to fake an accident than working around an office or warehouse all day with a bunch of dead hard Uncle Tom employees. I had no regard for a person that boasted how long they'd been on a job. To me that was like bragging about how long you had been a house slave.

After my daughters were in school each morning, I left the house about ten o'clock to make my physical therapy rounds. By one o'clock, I was through for the day. And when a doctor released me to return to work, I never did. Monetary benefits were not predicated on whether you resumed your employee/employer relationship.

My afternoon activities ranged from swimming, playing tennis, jogging, patronizing an Oriental massage parlor, or nude dancing clubs. Speaking of Oriental massage parlors, I was a regular customer who received royal treatment. Consequently, the absence of a sleeping partner in my personal life was moot.

Every evening, over the next two weeks, I chatted with Evelyn by telephone. One night we conversed so long that Evelyn only got two hours of sleep before she had to get up and prepare for work. As for myself, I slept until noon. Evelyn called me during her lunch break and asked me in a half-serious manner, not to call her tonight because she was too sleepy to hold a coherent conversation. She said that her girlfriends at work were teasing her, claiming that they knew what she'd been doing all night. We both laughed devilishly, knowing what they were implying. But the fact was, Evelyn and I never even kissed or hugged one another. We just enjoyed talking to each other on the phone so much that it equaled a pleasurable date.

Evelyn was fascinated with my life. She only knew normal working men, and was dazzled by stories of the hustling lifestyle. Since I was so candid with her, it wasn't long before she opened up and confided in me. She told me of her extramarital affairs. We talked about her ambitions, fears, love for her children, parents, insecurities, *and* her church hypocrites. It was unusual to be so daring and candid in such a short while. But our unique rapport kept us talking and revealing more of our hidden selves. I found it puzzling that Evelyn was a Sunday school teacher, and could be attracted to me. Evelyn never tried to convert me to Christianity or any other religion. That's what I liked about her most. As a matter of fact, I suggested that she begin taking my girls to church along with her daughters each Sunday. She was delighted to do it.

Mother's Day was just one week away when I asked Evelyn to reserve that Sunday for dinner at my place. She accepted my invitation. I spent the entire week planning a special meal for Evelyn and our daughters. The dinner was a sincere tribute to Evelyn as a mother and a single parent. I chose to serve Cornish hens, wild rice, spinach, a fresh green vegetable salad, cornbread, cranberry sauce, dressing, ice tea, and apple pie. I hired a professional soul food catering service to prepare our dinner, but I led Evelyn and her daughters to believe I slaved in the kitchen all day. And although I had sworn my girls to secrecy, I figured they told the Fargo sisters. During dinner, Evelyn commented how delicious something tasted and I told her, "I learned to cook by working beside granny as she slaved in the kitchen of rich white folks." All the girls giggled. When Evelyn asked about the ingredients in this or that, I would respond, "Granny would haunt me from her grave if I ever betrayed the family secret." The girls were now laughing so hard that Evelyn figured the whole thing out.

After dinner, the girls watched television and played games in their bedroom. Evelyn and I played backgammon in the living room. I'm not sure how it started, but Evelyn and I began playing for mouth kisses versus nose rubbing. If I won, we kissed--if she won, we rubbed noses. It wasn't long before our daughters were peeking in the living room and running away snickering. Overall, we had a fabulous evening.

119

Evelyn, Sadie and Rita said goodnight then left for home about nine o'clock. I wanted them to stay longer, but the next day, Monday, was a work and school day. I hadn't planned to call Evelyn that night. She left enough excitement in me to last until we got together again. We agreed to attend a jazz concert on Friday night. However, as I was cleaning up the house, Evelyn stayed on my mind and I hoped I was on hers. I finished the kitchen and was straightening up the living room when I noticed she had left her cigarette lighter. Although I smoked, I hated the idea of a woman doing so. I figured Evelyn's smoking habit was one of the weaknesses she spoke of when she told me the Bible said, "No one is perfect. No not one."

I telephoned Evelyn. "Hi Evelyn, what are you doing?"
Hi Richard, I was just thinking 'bout calling you to tell you what a nice time I had," she said in a merry tone. Her enthusiasm excited me. There was a pounding coming from my chest that I hoped she didn't hear. "Thanks, I'm so glad that you made it. As a matter of fact," I said, "I don't want to wait until next Friday to see you again."
I was delighted when she said, "I don't wanna wait that long either."
"Well, can I come over tonight?" I said in a suggestive way. Evelyn laughed and replied, "No, not tonight. I'm getting ready for bed and the girls are already sleep. Maybe tomorrow night."
"Well," I began, "if I can give you a good reason, then could I come over tonight?"
"What's the good reason?" she fondly inquired.
"First say yes, if I have a good reason," I bargained.
"Okay, if you have a *gooood* reason."
"I do," I said. "You forgot your cigarette lighter."
She bursted out laughing. Then said, "All right just for a minute."

It was about 10: 30 p.m. I checked on my girls before I left and found all four fast asleep. We had a three-bedroom apartment. My bedroom, and the two oldest girls shared one, and the two youngest girls shared the other one. Each girl's bedroom had a set of twin beds. However, on this night, Yolanda and Rochelle were asleep together in the same bed and Jennifer and Roxanne was sleeping together in the other bed. They were all in the same room. I didn't disturb their slumber party. It had been a full day. Earlier in the day we spent the afternoon at my mother's house. The girls gave her the Mother Day Cards they in school. This was the second Mother's Day that they were without their mother. They seemed well -adjusted and happy.

Tammie and Elaine were at Mommy's also. Each of them brought our mother a gift. My niece, Karen and two nephews, were there with hugs and kisses for their grandmother as well. Elaine's sons' Oscar, about 17 and Omar, about 14, always visited but didn't stay long. Elaine was jealous of her sons affection for their grandmother. The boys shortened their visits to maintain peace. Karen, who was about 19, always stayed around to monitor her mother's behavior. Tammie had the reputation of getting drunk and insulting Mommy. Since Tammie was an adult, she would publicly display a strong resentment for Mommy. We all excused Tammie's antisocial actions as a direct result of her nearly fatal bout with meningitis a dozen years earlier. But the truth was, her resentment preceded the meningitis. The doctors cautioned that alcohol and her medication was a dangerous combination. Not only was it potentially deadly, it made her act disgracefully vulgar, except in the presence of her longtime white lover, a married man, who came around like family.
Elaine would almost certainly add to the turmoil by flexing her massive inferiority complex. She would get disgusted with Tammie for getting all the attention through her insane antics. Elaine would also get angry with her boys for buying their grandmother a sweeter smelling rose than hers, or angry with me for calling her ugly and mistreating her when she was 6-years-old. All-in-all, this Mother's Day had been a full one for my girls, and I was sure they would sleep through my quick run to Evelyn's house.

The distance between Evelyn's apartment and mine was only a three minute trip by car, if you didn't get caught by the stop light. However, I arrived in about ten minutes because I stopped at the 7-Eleven store for a couple of Hava-Tampa cigars. My tap on her door was loud enough to be heard in the front room only. There was no purpose to knock any harder, since Evelyn promised to be waiting up.

She whispered, "Who is it?" The tone of her voice indicated to me that she wanted to keep her girls asleep as much as I did. When the door opened, I wasn't surprised to find her smiling. Still peeking around the edge of the door, she whispered, "You can come in, just for a minute." The robe she wore was so heavy and long it was impossible to know what she was wearing underneath. We sat on the couch and held hands as we spoke. I returned her lighter, and she thanked me with a peck on the cheek. When she said, "You better go now, I *WILL* see you tomorrow." Before I let go her hand or rose from the couch, I nibbled on her ear, then her neck. When she faced me and formed her lips to say stop, I kissed her lightly in the mouth. She returned my passion with her own.

Forty-five minutes later, she was back at the door peeking around the edge whispering, "Goodnight." We had spent the last forty-minutes on her living room floor. Her couch cried out with squeaks and cracks so much that the floor was the nearest alternative. Evelyn's last words as she eased her door shut behind me was, "Thanks for a wonderful Mother's Day."

From that evening on, our families began spending much of our leisure time together. We piled into my station wagon and went everywhere, especially on weekends and holidays. A few weeks later, I purchased a new 12 passenger van to enhance our traveling comfort. Evelyn and I loved dining out and concerts. I treated her to a spectacular theatrical production or exotic cuisine restaurant at least once a week. And on Saturdays, if we didn't go out on a date, we had dinner at each other's house, or went to the Pizza Parlor as a family of eight.

As I reminisce about the events and times surrounding our affair, I find myself blushing at our amorous overtures. For months, I would write a love poem for Evelyn every day, and when I saw her that evening I recited it. And more often than not, Evelyn would present me with a love poem or letter she had composed for me, while sitting at her secretarial desk at the Bank of America in Culver City.

The last fellow that Evelyn dated, the guy with the blue Mustang, was a security guard at the bank where she was employed. His name was Lee Draft.

Their break up, according to Evelyn, was due to his heavy drug usage. Though they still worked at the same location, they seldom spoke to each other.

Evelyn and her children's father were high school sweethearts in Dayton, Ohio. His name was Carl Fargo. An all-round athlete and handsome guy, 6'4", 220 pounds, Carl was the prize catch of the school. Evelyn was behind him in age and grade level by a year. When Carl graduated high school, he enlisted in the military. They were married before he went away. Evelyn graduated high school then joined her husband in Germany.

When they returned to Dayton two years later, Evelyn and Carl were the proud parents their daughter, Sadie. Carl worked two jobs, which left him little quality time for his wife. Evelyn yielded to temptation and had an extramarital affair. Evelyn told me that she was regretful for ever cheating on her husband, and she only had two adulterous affairs. The first was years earlier in Ohio. Carl never found out about this sneaky undertaking. The second was with the bank guard on her job. The affairs with the guard ultimately lead to her husband leaving. She further declared and sometimes with teary eyes that she'd made many mistakes in her life, but she would never repeat them. Evelyn promised God that her adulterous days were behind her.

Evelyn now sought solace in the church, repented her sins and became a volunteer Sunday school teacher. Evelyn told me she felt the women in the church looked down on her because she was unmarried with children. She said that during her prayers, she asked God to soften their hearts. Evelyn also prayed that God forgives Carl for beating her when he found out about her affair with Lee. She told me that, she thought, I was the answer to her prayers for a good man.

In September '83, Evelyn and I began living together under some unusual circumstances. Evelyn called me after she got home from work one evening. "Richard!" she screamed into the phone. "This godforsaken apartment is full of fleas!" She sounded as if she was being attacked by monster fleas from outer space. "We haven't been home but fifteen minutes," she shouted, "and already each of us been bit a dozen times. Ahh! Oh Jesus! I just got bit again."

Without thinking I responded, "Y'all get outta there right now and come on over." Evelyn hung up the phone without another word and five minutes later I heard the ringing of my doorbell.

Evelyn rushed right in and didn't stop until she reached the bathroom. As she was moving through the house, she mumbled something like, "I gotta wash my legs." Rita and Sadie sat together on the couch vigorously rubbing and patting their legs below the knee. Rita was crying, and it was clear that her older sister had been too.

After things settled down a bit, I discovered that fleas somehow had infested Evelyn's carpeting throughout her apartment. There were always a couple stray cats around her building but certainly they never came inside. This was a mystery beyond our understanding. Evelyn called her apartment manager and bitterly complained. She complained so effectively that a pest control service company was called and scheduled to spray her apartment the very next morning. Evelyn was so upset over the incident that she wanted to know if she could sue the apartment owner. I told her since they were acting immediately, that was all she could expect. "I bet that dirty no good Lee did it," she told me later. "He had a key to my house and when I asked him for it back, he claimed he had lost it. I told you he was a cold blooded dog."

Evelyn planned to go to a motel with her daughters, but I convinced her that they should spend the night with us. "It's the only decent thing to do, under these dire circumstances," I told her. "Why should you waste money in a motel when you have friends?" Evelyn ultimately agreed. Then we returned to her apartment and brought back enough clothes for the next day. Before we left my place, three hours later, I gave Evelyn a pair of my pants and heavy socks to wear for protection. We rushed in and rushed out with the necessary apparel and items. However, we didn't escape without receiving a few bites on our bare hands and neck. I thought Evelyn was blowing the picture out of proportion but fleas were jumping around her apartment like a jar of them had been dumped in each room. Tears streamed down Evelyn's face as we left her flea infested apartment.

During the short drive back to my place, Evelyn abruptly grabbed my steering hand as I drove, which made the van swerve, and implored, with a desperate gaze in her eyes, "Please don't make me go back." She began weeping uncontrollably. I pulled to the side of the road to console her. "That cold blooded dog must want to see me dead to do something like this. Fleas and mosquitos carry deadly diseases. I don't wanna go back to that job either," she sobbed. "What should I do?"

Trouble seemed to be Evelyn's shadow. Apparently, she was never taught or acquired the knowledge to deal with conflict. Her only defense was to flee. As we sat there in the van talking, I was astonished. I was no longer listening to a mature 30-year-old woman, but, instead, the frightened little girl that lived inside her body. "When Carl and I first came to Los Angeles, " she blundered in a barely coherent utterance, and crying all the while, "we were getting away from a mess like this. Men were calling our house and hanging up the phone on Carl. His women were calling and hanging up the phone on me. I begged him to move to California, so we could start over. Rita was just two years old." Evelyn was rambling in areas that had nothing to do with the situation at hand, least as far as I could tell. "Carl told me that he was the only man," she whimpered, "that would ever really love me. I have run him back to Ohio. I'm out here all alone. And this dope addict is trying to kill me."

At this stage of our relationship, we had known each other more than two years and had been romantically linked for four months. However, in that relative short time I was in love with her. The fear that she was showing reminded me of Ann. Her naiveness reminded me of Ann. And the fact that she was asking for my help, also reminded me of my deceased wife, Ann.

"Evelyn, listen to me," I began. "I would love it if you and your daughters stayed with us. I have a three-bedroom apartment. There's room enough for us all." I was smiling to assure her that I sincerely wanted to be with her and it wasn't just a case of sympathy. "And about that job," I said sarcastically. "You don't ever have to go back there." Evelyn interrupted me and said, "But I don't want you taking care of us."
I quickly replied. "No no no! Let me finish." She sat silent. "Now about that

job of yours..."

Evelyn's introduction to the accident game was made right there on the spot. I explained to her that I would call my insurance company first thing in the morning and report that I had I accidently struck a pedestrian, in the cross walk, by the name of Evelyn Alice Fargo. "Your disability occurred right here, on this corner of LaCienega Boulevard and 18th street, at this time," I said, while looking at my watch, "9:40 p.m. All you have to do Evelyn," I explained, "is go to the doctor and lawyer I send you. You'll very soon get weekly cash from state disability. The doctor will arrange for your payments to last up to three months. And during that time you may treat yourself to a much needed rest. Then if you choose to return to work, you can. At any rate, within eight months from this night, you'll be the recipient of an accident settlement of, umm let me figure." I thought for a few seconds, then said, "Six or seven thousand dollars."

After Evelyn called her job the next morning and reported her accident to her bank manager, I made an official report to my insurance company. While the girls were at school, we spent the day moving her out of the condemned apartment unit. The exterminator didn't arrive until we were walking out the door with last the chair. We were geared up in heavy socks, long pants, long shirts, gloves, head scarfs, and eye goggles. We also sprayed the apartment with an insect killer before we began moving things.

Evelyn washed all their washable clothes and took all the dry cleaning to the cleaners. We didn't actually finish moving, washing, and unpacking until 2:00 a.m. We slept until 11:00 a.m. Evelyn enjoyed getting up so late on a weekday. We spent the afternoon getting her a private mailing address at one of the proliferating public mail drops, signing her up with an attorney, and getting her to a chiropractor. The doctor diagnosed her with a slipped disk, blurred vision, head trauma, and back injuries. He put her on disability for one month, and scheduled to reevaluate her as needed. Within two weeks of Evelyn's unfortunate accident, she and the girls stopped attending church. I acted as if I didn't notice. But I was relieved. I didn't need was another holy roller hanging around, feeling guilty, and telling God everything I do.

I didn't give a hoot about someone suing my insurance company. That's why I bought insurance--to sue those white-collar crooks. Anyway, my insurance company didn't think too highly of me prior to Evelyn's accident because they were *already* making my monthly auto payments due to a previous accident claim. I loved Evelyn and didn't mind spending the entire day with her. The pleasure and privilege of making love to her every afternoon were a more rewarding payoff than the anticipated insurance settlement. When we came home from our daily physical therapy treatments, we practically raced each other to the bedroom.

Within a month of shacking up, the realistic thought of being innocently, or justifiably, accused of child molesting disturbed me. Here I was an alcoholic living in the house with six young girls. It never occurred to me before Evelyn and her two daughters moved in. But the fact was, I often walked around the apartment in my underclothes, and so did my four daughters. However, nothing of a sexual nature crossed my mind. Yolanda was eleven years old and still had and the body of a little girl. But on the other hand, Evelyn's daughter Sadie's body was developing early and I was aware of her blooming womanly features. Taking this into consideration, I was especially cautious not to walk around the house in my undershorts when the children were home.

During one of my drinking and weed smoking bouts I stayed up late listening to my favorite jazz albums. Evelyn had prepared an elaborate tray of hors d'oeuvres that were only half eaten and the second bottle of wine was only half consumed. Oh, I was having myself a real party. Evelyn went to bed ahead of me, as she usually did when she felt intoxicated. There's no way a dedicated alcoholic like myself is going to disgrace the good name of alcoholism by going to bed with wine still in the bottle. My party of one was alive and well.

Suddenly there was an unexpected wild storm. I heard the sound of rain beating heavily against the windows. I immediately went to the balcony and closed the doors. I checked the windows in the three youngest girls room, and covered the uncovered ones. Then I peaked in on the older girls, Yolanda, Rochelle, and Sadie. Their window was closed, but the cover had fallen from Sadie's bed. The apartment was now cold, due to the storm, therefore, I decided to cover her.

As I approached Sadie's bed, the vivid thought and image of Irene Rogers entered my mind. I recalled the day on my newspaper routine when I stood in Irene's living room, waiting on her grandmother to get the money for a Sunday morning newspaper. Suddenly, I saw Irene on the bed, instead of Sadie. What was more scary, Sadie was lying in the same position I remembered Irene to be in. I froze in my steps, and shook my head from side to side to regain my composure. I found myself easing toward her bed. Sadie was wearing a full slip and panties but no bra underneath. One of her breasts was nearly exposed. I began to feel sexually aroused. I mumbled, "Irene Rogers, I love you." Abruptly, thunder roared, and lightning flashed, illuminating the bedroom. "Sadie," I thought. "Oh my God, it's Sadie!" I quickly covered her and backed slowly from the dimly lit room. When I returned to the living room, I was sweating and heavily panting. As I sat on the sofa and relived the last few moments, I recalled hearing the warning of a criminal court judge saying, "Mr. Jones, do yourself a favor, and quit drinking." Then I heard Ann's voice saying, "Rick, you need Jesus in your life."

In bed the next morning, as Evelyn cuddled in my arms, I broke our silence by saying, "I think I'll quit drinking." Evelyn's head rose lightly from my shoulder and she replied, "Do you think you can? Just like that!"
"I'm gonna have to. I don't have a choice."
"Why are you talking like this?" she asked in a puzzled tone. "Did a doctor caution you?" She laughed following that question and so did I.
"No Evelyn, I chuckled, "this has nothing to do with my liver or health. Since I'm now the immediate 'male' figure for our daughters, my behavior may be a factor in how they relate to men. I should carry myself more responsibly."
I was quiet for about thirty seconds, when out of the clear blue sky, I added, "I think I'll stop smoking too." Then decided to have a talk with the girls. The ordeal of last night was still on my mind.

After getting out of bed, I put on my pajamas' pants and robe. I exited our bedroom and when across the hall to the bedroom of the three oldest girls. However, they weren't there. All six girls were lounging in the living room this

Saturday morning, watching cartoons and eating cereal. Roxy and Jennifer were still in panties and T-shirts, while the other girls were in robes, long pajamas pants, or full slips. When I entered the room, I told them I wanted to turn the television off for about ten minutes to tell them something important. No one objected. I came right to the point.

"Do any of you girls know what child molesting is?" I asked. Yolanda's hand shot up just like in school. A second or two later, two more hands raced for the ceiling.
"I know! I know!, yelled Rita and Jennifer in unison.
"My hand was up before yours," one girl snapped at the other. "Richard!" Rita said loudly, "whose hand was up first?"
"Quiet down you two." I replied. "Yolanda's hand was up first." "Goody for you!" Jennifer snapped at Rita.

"Okay Yolanda," I said, "tell us what child molesting is."
She smiled and cleared her throat. "Child molesting is when a man touches you in the wrong place," she said with a little laughter. All the girls bursted out laughing.
"You're right Yolanda, but it's nothing funny," I said. "I want you girls to report anybody whoever touches you in the wrong way, no matter who is it. Do you understand?"
"What's is the wrong way?" Roxy asked. More laughter in the room.

By this time, Evelyn entered the room with her robe wrapped tightly around her. She stood in the doorway and interrupted. "Sadie you know what child molesting is. Why didn't you speak up?"
Sadie frowned and said, "I didn't want to talk about that."

"This is serious," I quickly said in a louder tone. "Everybody just listen! Child molesting is when someone touches you anywhere that is covered by your bikini, swimming suit, or under clothes."
Then I paused a moment to allow this to sink in.
"If anyone in this world ever touches you there before you're 18-years-old, don't be afraid to tell me, Evelyn, your teacher, your grandmother, your father,

or even the police. No matter who it is. No matter what they threaten you with. Does everybody understand?" Everyone quickly answered in the affirmative. I turned the cartoons back on and Evelyn and I went into the kitchen. As she prepared our breakfast, I told her of the horrible sexual abuse stories I heard from young girls, when I was a youth. Most of the girls were molested by their mother's live-in boyfriend, or a stepfather, a male relative, and in some cases, by their biological father. "I want our girls to be aware of the seriousness of this thing. Do you agree?" I asked.
"I sure do!" said Evelyn. "And thanks!"

We both took a sincere interest in our children's survival skills. After the girls got home from school, three days a week, they had swimming lessons. None of the six could swim, though my girls had previously trained at the YMCA. All six girls complained with a passion. They whined about their hair being messed up every day, and missing homework and study time. But the fact was, no one enjoyed struggling in the swimming pool. However, within four months they were swimming fairly well and diving into the deep end of the pool. After another two months, Yolanda and Sadie earned junior lifeguard certificates. The girls also had weekend drama classes, girl scout meetings, and dance classes. To give our girls an academic advantage, we enrolled them in a Saturday tutoring and special study class for youth, at Los Angeles City College.

Each child, on their birthday, was privileged to select a resort for us to spend their birthday weekend. Jennifer's birthday was in September. We stayed in a hotel across the street from Knot's Berry Farm, a well-known amusement park. That particular Saturday and Sunday was spent on wild rides, and enjoying entertainment from the old west. Rochelle's birthday was next on October 9th, then Roxanne's on the 23rd. Rochelle chose the San Diego Zoo, and Roxy chose the Los Angeles Zoo. Then came Rita in December. We visited Disneyland and stayed in the Disneyland Hotel for three days. Yolanda, in April, chose Las Vegas, where we all stayed at the Circus Circus Hotel. While in Nevada, I chartered a helicopter and the pilot gave us a sky view of Las Vegas. When Sadie's birthday came in July, we cruised by ferry to Catalina Island, where we stayed for a three-day weekend. By this time,

Evelyn was four months' pregnant.

As a family, we were happier than ever, but as a couple Evelyn and I had a steep hill to climb. About a month after Evelyn moved in, I had to appear in traffic court to be sentenced on the drunk driving charge that I incurred while Arlene was my babysitter. The judge gave me 30 days. Before I began serving my time, I arranged for a florist to deliver Evelyn a dozen roses every Tuesday and Friday, while I was incarcerated. I phoned her every night from the sheriff's detention camp called, Wayside Honor Rancho. We told the girls, I was driving a truck cross country which required many overnight stays. I often talked to them when I called home. Upon my jail release, Evelyn and I spent the next two days and nights at a nice hotel near the beach. My mother allowed the girls to stay with her, while Evelyn and I were becoming reacquainted. It was my version of a 'shacking' couple's second honeymoon. However, it later led Evelyn into a state of depression.

One afternoon, I walked into the bedroom and found Evelyn sitting on the edge of the bed crying. When I asked, "What's the matter Evelyn?" She then verbally launched at me in anger, "You know what's the matter! Just look at me!, she argued. You must see me as some kind of tramp. Here I am sitting in your apartment. I must've been a fool to move in here." Then she shocked me by alleging, "You don't plan to marry me!" She sobbed between words. "I know you don't! I'm tried of living in sin. I'm moving back to my own apartment. I passed by yesterday, and the 'for rent' sign was still out." I sat down and tried to comfort her. I even asked her to marry me. She cried even harder, but accepted my proposal.

However, that was only the beginning of our quarreling. Almost every other day, I found myself trying to console another emotional concern: "No, Evelyn, you're not too fat; "I'm sorry Evelyn, the reason I didn't eat much tonight wasn't because I don't like your cooking. I just ate a burger before coming home."

But the most thunderous sign of her unique brand of expression that I remember, was an exhausting exercise of perplexity. Our apartment manager sent us a five-day notice that he was having the building exterminated to get rid of the roaches. We were supposed to take all the dishes out of the cabinets and wrap all our clothes in covers. No one did the preparations because every time I told the girls to do it, Evelyn interrupted by saying, she would do it. On the eve of the extermination, Evelyn stayed up late doing all the work alone. I was too tired to help. I had been out all day, and had driven more than three hundred miles working a check cashing scam. Although, I kept asking her to quit the chores and wait until I slept and could help her in the morning, she declined my offer and told me to rest. I even went so far as to get out of bed and walk into the kitchen, took her by the hand and asked her, "Evelyn, will you please wait until tomorrow? I want to help you but I'm just too tired now." She insisted that I rest down, and she would do the work alone.

The next morning, after the girls were at school, we were leaving the house before 10 o'clock, as instructed by the landlord. Evelyn walked out ahead of me at a pace that put a lot of distance between us. When I got in the driver's seat of the van, before I even started the engine she said, "You think you're slick, don't you?" I hoped she was playing. The next thing I knew, she was calling me a user and abuser because I *tricked* her into doing all the work, while I slept. We argued all that morning. Fortunately, we only argued (in the beginning) when the children were at school.

Eventually, she was bitter over the fact that her kids were coming to me with their homework problems, instead of her. When Rita or Sadie went to their mother for help and she couldn't figure out the problem, it would insult her, if I solved it. Later that night, she would cry in bed and restrict me from touching her. Evelyn even accused me of trying to win her kid's respect, by making her look stupid. It got so bad that I would misspell words on purpose when one of the girls asked me how to spell something. I knew Evelyn would double check me with the dictionary. It gave her delight to announce that I was wrong, and to spell the word correctly.

I encouraged psychological help for us. Oh, it took some doing! But eventually, we went to a seminar conducted by a marriage counselor. There were several couples there. Evelyn and I were the only nonwhite couple, but everyone was friendly. At one point in the session, the counselor asked by a show of hands, who actually sought out the seminar. Out of all the couples, I was the only man who raised his hand. In all the other cases, the women suggested or persuaded the man to attend. One of the ladies asked the marriage counselor, "What's the meaning of this imbalance!" He answered, "It's usually the one in the most pain that takes the first step toward healing." At different times, each couple and individual had an opportunity to state their concern or problem, while the others were at liberty to comment.

At the end of the session, before going our separate ways, everyone bid goodby and farewell. Evelyn and I noticed, that all the couples gave me an extra word of inspiration, such as; "Hang in there!" "Don't give up on her!" "Be patient!" Their final words to Evelyn were; "I think you have such a pretty smile." You two look so nice together." "Where do you get your nails done?"

Evelyn would argue one day that I didn't want to marry her. After I convinced her that I did, she would call the wedding plans to a halt a few days later. This happened at least four times. Evelyn continued to compete with me. It got so bad that if I was walking to go and pick the girls up from the after school care, she would wait until I had a five minute head start, then she would drive past me, blow the horn and yell, "That's all right, I'll do it!"

In August of '84, Evelyn suffered a miscarriage. This was a loss that held little shock value. During her brief pregnancy she continued to smoke cigarettes, and worry over insignificant matters. As if spilled milk meant more than the health of the baby. She would argue and even be prepared to fist fight me, at the sound of a bell. Evelyn's accident settlement cheered her up a bit. It was for $6,000. To make her feel more like an independent woman, I offered to help her purchase her own house. Within a month, Hamilton set up all the necessary paperwork for us to start house shopping. Evelyn and I were buying our own separate homes. We began looking in areas outside Los Angeles. The Los Angeles Sunday Times newspapers lead us to drive 70 miles to Lancaster, California. There were hundreds of beautiful track homes under construction. We were fascinated by the models. But Evelyn, like Ann, was a very selective shopper. Evelyn had to stay at the $50,000 level in order to afford the 10% down payment required to purchase a home. There were numerous two bedroom homes in her price range, but she wanted a three-bedroom home. A few months later, Evelyn was pregnant again. This time she cut back on her smoking, ate better, got the recommended rest, worried less and didn't do unnecessary heavy lifting, accept to rearrange the furniture in the house.

By this time, I didn't care what she did. I was fed up from the on again-off again wedding plans, and her fickleness. I had selected my new home, and didn't want her there nagging me when I moved-in. It was a two-story four bedroom, two and a half bathroom, double garage home, on fourth acre lot, and construction was underway. All the homes in the area of Lancaster near my house were being built, or brand new, many were less than six months old. My move-in date was tentatively set at February '85. Meanwhile, we continued living in Los Angeles.

Evelyn talked of having our baby and leaving me. She planned on getting out of California. I hated the very thought of that. The idea of having kids spread out so far that months or perhaps years could go by before you see them, didn't appeal to me. I was willing to put up with a portion of her wishy-washy ways, if it meant she would stay in California, preferably in Lancaster. After much discussion, Evelyn agreed to stay in California, if I gave her enough money to make a down payment on a three-bedroom house. But she wanted her house to be located in Banning, California, which is a good two or three-hour drive from Lancaster. The only way she would buy a house in the same town as my house, according to her, would be if we shared my house and used hers as a child care home for working parents.

Ultimately, I provided Evelyn with an additional $10,000 to give her more leverage in finding a house in Lancaster. Two weeks later, she put in an application for a *four* bedroom, two and a half bathroom, one story ranch style home with a small back yard. When Evelyn's home loan was approved, we really celebrated. Not with champagne and dancing, but with punch, ice cream and cake, with the girls at our Los Angeles apartment, with girls. Though I agreed with Evelyn to live as husband and wife, the arrangement didn't set well with my better judgement. Evelyn's home was scheduled to be completed by June '85.

There was no doubt that professional mental health or relationship counseling would meet an unwelcome reception in our lives. However, there was one longshot possibility that we had not considered, conducting our own group therapy sessions at home. The girls ranged in age from five to twelve years old. They had good morals and practiced common sense in their daily activities. I went to Evelyn with the idea of having weekly family 'Table' meetings for one hour to vent our frustrations about one another, ourselves, the world, school, work, household concerns, etc., and to also unite in resolving the difficulties. I stressed that we, as parents, must be willing and open to accept criticism from our children, as well as each other, without retaliation.

In the presence of the girls, Evelyn and I laid down the ground rules. Each complaint brought to the attention of 'The Table' must be in the best interest of family harmony to enhance the maturity, fairness, or appreciation of the party be admonished. We would point out broken promises, lack of duty, the use of profanity by any household member, unfairness in any form, aggressive behavior, disrespectful behavior, abusive verbal conduct, instigation of argument or confusion, etc. Also when someone pointed something out to 'The Table' they were automatically obligated to provide weekly follow-up reports. We stressed the value of praise. If we observed acts of kindness or personal achievement from a household member, that person must be congratulated. It was all agreed, we would begin talking mental notes and be ready for our first meeting in seven days. The girls were excited and bubbling with anticipation.

The week passed swiftly. Since the sessions were my idea, I figured I would sacrifice my dignity by being the initial fall guy. As we sat giggling around 'The Table' anticipating the no reprisal character slaughter on one another, I said, "Okay everybody remember let's do this with love in our hearts and truth on our lips. And let us not point at a person's faults simply because they told us about ours. That's holding a grudge." We moved clockwise around the table, pointing out my faults. Some even offered suggestions. I was surprised to hear some of the complaints against me. Nevertheless, it was refreshing and cleansing to see everyone jest in this therapeutic manner.

"To begin with," Sadie said as she flipped the pages of a tablet, "here you are, Richard, right here." Before she went down her list, she wanted assurance of amnesty. "I'm not gonna get in trouble, right?"
"No trouble, no trouble, just remember to be honest, good-spirited, and only say things that would generally improve my disposition and character, should I accept your suggestions," I said with a serious face.
Evelyn encouraged Sadie by saying, "Go ahead Sadie, you aren't going to get in trouble." The table fell silent.

"Richard, you're supposed to sweep the front steps every day and wash them down on the weekend, but you don't." There was a roar of laughter and girls saying, "Yeah, that's right!" Sadie continued. "And you said, you were going to quit smoking, but you still smoke those lil' stinky cigars."
Another burst or laughter, especially from Evelyn, and comments from all around. "Yeah, that's right!"
I jumped to my defense. "Now wait a minute! Wait a minute! I admit you're right about the steps, and I'll start cleaning them like I'm supposed to. But my Hav-A-Tampa Cigars don't stink!"
The dining area erupted with jovial pandemonium. Roxanne, Jennifer and Rita fell to the floor laughing. Yolanda spit water from her mouth in a failed attempt to drown her snickers. Rochelle blurred out, "Yes they do!" And she began laughing until she cried.
"Wait a minute," I said, "wait a minute. Let's have some order." When things simmered, I continued. "How my cigars smell is a matter of opinion. To some they stink, and to some they don't. But I never said I was going to quit smoking cigars. I was talking about cigarettes."
Evelyn was silent on this, but all the girls yelled comments to the effect of, "Smoking is smoking, all of it kills you. You're just trying to get out of it."

At last, I saw myself as others do. A hypocrite! I made sure they did their chores, but didn't do my own. I encouraged the girls never to smoke, and tried to discourage Evelyn from smoking, but I smoked 'little cigars' myself. Sadie had to quit there because we were limited to two complains and two compliments per person. Her one compliment was that she thought I was nice. The party being accused didn't have to make any type of promise or apology when they heard the charges against them. They were only to listen without a show of bitterness and consider them in private. I chose to make a public announcement regarding my smoking. "If any of you see me smoking anything, cigarette, cigar, pipe or anything, I'll give you a quarter." They liked that and considered it a challenge. Over the next several weeks I paid out about $2 in quarters, as a penalty for being caught smoking. Afterwards, I quit smoking completely.

The next one to launch complaints against me was Yolanda. She didn't think it was fair that I gave them only 50 cents for each 'C' they got on their report card. In those days, I had a grade incentive program within the home. When the children brought home their report cards, which was four times per semester, I awarded them or charged them as follows:
For each 'A' or equivalent, they received $7. For each 'B' or equivalent, they received $5, and for each 'C' or equivalent, only 50 cents. For a 'D' or equivalent, they owed me $5, and for a 'F' or equivalent, they owed me $7. In the event they ended up owing money, they worked it off with extra household chores. After a bit of a discussion, I agreed to raise the 50 cents to$1.50. Yolanda had no other complaints, and no compliments.

As the family therapy session went on, much more was mentioned by way of a complaint. One of the girls accused Evelyn and me for arguing too much, too long and too loud. They all agreed that it kept them awake and interfered with their school performance. I apologized for the disturbance and promised to be more considerate of them 'when' we argued. I purposely said 'when' rather than 'if' because I recognized that irresponsible arguments. Evelyn made the mistake of pinning the girls down as to who was the primary source of the disruption coming from our bedroom. It was obvious that none of them wanted to reply. I intervened, "The complaint was given during MY time in The Hot Seat and I say it's not important 'who'--only that 'we' work toward bringing it to an end." Evelyn wouldn't accept that as an explanation. She insisted that the girls pointed the finger at the culprit. By a unanimous decision she was identified as the most culpable. BOOM! BAM! POW! She flat out exploded. She jerked away from the table with tears rolling down her beet red face, "I'm gonna remember this!" she threatened. "I tried to treat all y'all nicely. I'm the one who cooks and washes yo' clothes. I'm the one that keeps him from beating y'all to death Now y'all tryin' to make fun of me," she whined. Boy! Was she hot! "I'm gonna remember this!" She then stormed from the room and we all sat dumbfounded. We heard the bedroom door slam. BAM! That was the first and last day of our Family Therapy Sessions.

The elevation of Lancaster, California is much higher than Los Angeles. Therefore, the winters are colder, and the summers are hotter. My house was a couple weeks behind the expected completion date. We moved in during the cool and windy month of March 1985. There were only eight occupied homes in the immediate area, with another couple hundred under construction. We were so proud. The home was as huge as the mansions seen on television, to us anyway. It was more beautiful than any other home that I'd personally known anyone to own. This stately 'American Dream' was twenty-eight hundred square feet of interior, with an extra high ceiling. All four bedrooms were on the second floor, and along the corridor was a ten-foot cut-away opening in the wall making way for a decorative encased banister which overlooked the spacious living room and dining rooms twenty-five feet below. The outside view of the home resembled a well-kept miniature yellow and white castle. There were still sporadic patches of melting snow on the surrounding landscape. This was the first time my children played in snow.

Whenever Evelyn and I had three consecutive days without tearing at each other throats, I sensed there may be hope for us. If our spell of harmony stretched into a week, I would actually reopen a dialogue regarding a future together. I shared with Evelyn my plan to continue setting up Worker Compensation accidents, averaging one every two months. With the settlements, from $6,000.00 to $8,000.00 per case in the lump portion, we could use the money to set up credit in different names, and make down payments on approximately six new homes every year. I explained to Evelyn, how I could use different names with fresh credit through Hamilton. We could furnish each new home nicely, and lease them exclusively to business executives and their families visiting or vacationing in or near the Los Angeles area. We would also have a couple nice passenger vans and cars to chauffeur them. In about five years, we would have bought more than 30 homes with each netting a $30,000 annual profit. With those profits, buy into a major hotel franchise. I planned on Evelyn and me becoming multimillionaires within ten years, ultimately owning at least 60 homes, and a major hotel.

Evelyn had a creative business mind, and she suggested, we would contact all the major corporations that Bank of America did business with throughout the world and send them our brochure and introductory letter. Evelyn suggested, that we purchase modest style homes for year round leasing to permanent California residents with steady income or retired couples on solvent fixed income. We also planned purchase large luxurious homes for short term leasing. Evelyn convinced me that I needed to create back up sources of revenue for each house we bought to cover all probable expenses, in the rare instance, we were stuck with a few vacant homes throughout the year.

Legitimate business deals was not my forte, and I hadn't considered the possibility of dry spells. However, when Evelyn put that on my mind, the only thing that popped into my head was setting up a barrage of fraudulent welfare checks. When I related this to Evelyn, it spooked her. She recalled the nationally publicized case of The Welfare Queen. "No way I'm gonna mess with county checks," she swore. "I heard that The Welfare Queen was sentenced to fourteen years. And I don't wanna go to prison. I would rather just keep my one lil' house and open a child care home," she complained. "Evelyn, we can't let the fact that some woman got busted for cheating the system scare us out of making money. If you aren't afraid to stick those cigarettes in your mouth, after all that science has told us about that, you shouldn't be scared of anything," I argued. Again, Evelyn and I slipped into a tit for tats argument, which ended with a week of celibacy.

When I brought the topic of welfare fraud up again, I shared with Evelyn in detail how several women and I ripped the system off from 1973 through 1980. I told her I only quit because every scam needed a cooling off period. It had been four years since I procured any new cases, but no one who worked with me was ever arrested. I didn't tell her that Ann was under investigation at the time of her death, because it was Ann's own fault and attitude that lead to her problems.   After a few nights, of sweet talk and loving, Evelyn reconsidered and was receptive to the county check scam.

The first thing I had to do was figure out how to meet and convince dependable ladies to get with my fraudulent program. I explained to Evelyn, it was easy to start off with a chick, who only flaked out on you later because of her jealous man, or greed. The best way to go would be to import some lonely women through Afro American newspapers.
"What I will do Evelyn," I said, "is place some lonely hearts ad in ten newspapers. The ad will read something like this:

'Black man, widower 39-years-old financially secure, 5'11" 175 lbs. interested in corresponding with ambition a young woman that may consider relocating.   Write: Richard Brooks P.O. Box 99999, Lancaster, California. '"

This method of meeting women gave Evelyn great concern. As I told her, "Some women must be lead on in order to get any production out of them. And there are others that we could be truthful with. Some will return to their hometown, others will stay. "Of course, Evelyn you must understand, I occasionally will have physical intimacy with the women. However, my emotions will be detached. It's all in the course of our joint wealth, and not for lust or love," I assured her. Evelyn assured me she would not have a problem with me doing what I deemed necessary to obtain our goal of becoming multimillionaires. She began to visualize herself owning a popular hotel and a string of rental homes. She sense of greed began to manifest itself.

It wasn't long before my pen pal mail was pouring in like a flood. Evelyn was well into her pregnancy and driving me crazy. Her house was just a couple weeks from completion. I wanted her out of my house so bad, I would drive down to the track where her home was being built, park my car and just watch the men work. Evelyn started having nightmares. Not nightmares involving me, but unresolved issues from her past. In addition she was depressed because her children's father Carl filed for a divorce. She was doubly depressed because another man, named Campbell, she used to date on her job had also gotten married. I wasn't even aware that she had dated two men in the same office. This revelation confirmed her unstableness, as far as I was concerned. The closer it got to her house completion, the more she began crying and begging for forgiveness for her mean and hostile behavior. Once in a fit of rage, she threw a sharp pair of scissors at me, because I said I would be glad when her house was finished and she moved out.

My decision to insist that Evelyn move into her own home wasn't solely based on my displeasure with her actions. Quite frankly, I think we could've worked through that. But it was the illogical excuses she used for us to stay under the same roof that concerned me most. "I'll change!" she pleaded, "Don't leave me! I love you!" Evelyn hadn't realized it herself, but I did. She'd never been on her own and was afraid. I don't know how or when it happened, but she was very insecure. She didn't love me, Lee, Carl, or her second ex-lover from work named, Campbell, and probably not her adulterous lover of years past. She just needed a constant shoulder to lean on. That's how I summed her up. Evelyn needed to be validated by others to feel complete. She had a hard time telling people no, unless she was angry, then she could scream, Hell no! She reminded me of the girls the Goodfellow Boys pulled trains on in St. Louis more than twenty years ago.

However, through Evelyn I finally understood those girls in St. Louis were not 'fast', but frightened little girls selling their soul to be accepted. Evelyn wouldn't grow beyond this cocoon if I patronized her weakness. She would never know true freedom or how strong she really was unless she gave herself a chance. If only she wasn't afraid to make a mistake. If only Carl hadn't instilled in her head, she wouldn't survive on her own. I didn't know Evelyn very well. Nobody gets to know a turtle with its head in a shell, no matter how long the turtle is in their pocket.

It amazed me for a while, how a Sunday School teacher could be so weak on faith. Didn't they have a good relationship with God? Couldn't God snap her out of her 'Poor Me' disposition? Evelyn hated my correspondence with the dozen of women from around the country, but she said, "No Problem!" Yet when I sat up at night writing letters, scheming, bonding and building confidence with my pen pals, she would be in bed crying and wouldn't explain why. Sometime she would spend hours in the bathroom. I rigged up a long handled mirror one evening and slid it under the master bathroom door to see what she was doing. I wasn't surprised to see her sitting on the floor with her head down. Evelyn once confided in me, she would spend hours in the bathroom to avoid Carl, and later to avoid Lee. And now it was my turn. Nevertheless, she would beg me not to make her move into her own house.

At the height of my letter writing scam, I was writing forty different women during one particular month. I had a way of weeding out the wrong types. I was looking for women that (1) had small children, (2) divorced, separated, (3) poor, (4) black, (5) depressed, (6) had experience with street life, (7) would openly write about her sexual fantasies, (8) had experience with drugs, (9) adultery, (10) manifest larcenous tendencies, and, (11) ready to make a change.

The initial list of forty was narrowed to eight. Six of which planned to visit me - at my expense. However, only two actually flew out to meet me. Needless to say, most of these two women considered themselves in love with me before we ever met. Prior to the first woman's preliminary visit, we had written each other for ten months. Her name was Doris. Evelyn was now in her own home with our infant son, Darren.

The gap in our relationship widened with the arrival of Doris. She was a grand mistake in judgement on my part from the beginning. Doris and I felt like good friends before she actually visited Los Angeles. Though, I had grown to sincerely adore her from a distance of thousands of miles, it would've been wiser to leave her there. Doris attempted suicide twice during our correspondence and had been committed to a mental lock up ward each time. She admitted to me that she was a recovering alcoholic and often went into jealous rages. One of her jealous rages caused the murder of her brother, who rushed to her rescue. As he defended her in a fight with an ex-boyfriend, one of her son's fathers, the ex-boyfriend shot and killed her 6'5" overly protective brother. She was so distraught over this tragedy, Evelyn and I agreed that it would be a good thing if she relocated and started a new life. I used to share most of the letters with Evelyn, in the hope she would feel unless insecure.

Doris was to arrive with more than a thousand dollars, of her own money, in her pocket. In which case, she could have rented an apartment for two months. I planned to arrange $2,000 per month in multiple fraudulent welfare payments her rent expired. However, when Doris stepped off the plane, she informed me that she had only $5 in cash, because she paid her mother three months back rent. Therefore, I had no choice but to take Doris and her two boys to a motel. I paid $500 for one week, and I gave her $200 for food. She promised that her ex-employer was going to send her severance pay of $1,000 in one week. When the week passed, she was still without funds. Consequently, I sponsored her another week. I decided after three weeks of paying her way that she and her sons could temporarily stay with me, until one of us came up with enough money to get her an apartment.

As usual, Evelyn outwardly supported this decision. In fact, I introduced Evelyn and Doris, because Evelyn thought Doris was in need of a friend. The three of us discussed the living arrangements prior to Doris actual moving into my converted garage. Evelyn even lent Doris her car to transport her belongings to my house. Then later, hired her part-time at her home child care business. After Evelyn and Doris became friendly, Doris gave me an ultimatum. I was to choose between her and Evelyn. As Doris put it, "I'm not going to be anybody's other woman." When I told her that Evelyn and I had an understanding and she wasn't going to come between us, she became so bitter that she moved out of my den and back into the motel the next night. A week later her fraudulent welfare money started coming in but she decided that she didn't want anything more to do with me, and threatened not to pay me back any of the money I invested had in her. Finally, Doris agreed to just stick around long enough to reimburse me and then she was going back to Baltimore. Doris and Evelyn got so buddy-buddy that Evelyn decided to quit also and return to Ohio.

Four months later, Doris slipped away like a thief in the night. I didn't find out about it until I came over to pick up my money. Her apartment was vacant. Evelyn told me a week later that Doris had left for good. The next week I received a letter from Doris informing me how no good I had been and how double-crossing and two faced my dear Evelyn was. She told me that Evelyn was now receiving the county checks I thought were discontinued. She even told me the mailing addresses where Evelyn had the checks delivered. When I confronted Evelyn with this information, she denied everything. But Doris proved to be telling the truth. Doris also told me in the letter that Evelyn was still in love with her ex-husband, Carl, and was planning to break up his marriage and get him back. Evelyn denied this also.

The next woman to arrive from long distance to meet me was a 26-year-old mother of two from South Carolina, named Lillie. She stayed in California for five weeks. She was too much of a hardworking, one man woman. I didn't want to lure her into something that she would've regretted. Besides, Lillie was too much in love with me to function properly. However, she had enough money to stay in a first class hotel. I figured that unless I showered her with the attention of a romantic husband, she would feel jilted and perhaps 'blow the whistle'. I sent Lillie back home, and gradually stopped writing her.

In the summer of 1986, I began giving driving instructions to Yolanda and Sadie every Saturday morning. We used my '85 Buick Regal since my older model station wagon had been totaled in an accident of convenience. The girls preferred being taught by me rather than their high school instructor because he was too strict and didn't explain himself well, they thought.

On the outside of town you could drive for miles without encountering another car. Yet, we often chose to drive around the track homes that were under construction where there were paved streets with unoccupied homes. This prepared them for driving in occupied areas. Both of them were studious on our weekly outings. Yolanda was a heavy on the accelerator, and Sadie was heavy on the brakes. I fondly called them 'The Heavy Foot Sisters'. My house and Evelyn's were only one mile apart down the main road called Avenue K. Each track consisted of 50 to 150 occupied homes but there was a construction site of 100 to 150 unoccupied track homes between us. This is where went to practice most often.

One weekend, Evelyn was staying in Los Angeles with her ex-co-worker and friend, Sharon as she often did after we'd grown apart. The girls and I were responsible for Darren. Sadie, Rita, and Darren stayed at my house on such weekends. On this particular Saturday morning, the Heavy Foot Sisters informed me that they didn't want to drive that day. They said they would rather walk to Sadie's house to study their homework. For those two to suggest walking a mile when a ride was available sounded fishy. Earlier I observed them in Yolanda's room whispering on the phone. I didn't let on that they were under my suspicion. A short while later, they left walking in the direction of Sadie's house.

At the pace they walked I knew it would take them 30 minutes. So, after they had fifteen minutes head start, I drove in the opposite direction so I wouldn't pass them on Avenue K. The route I took was about a five-mile trip. I came into Evelyn's track from the other direction. I parked my car around a nearby corner and dashed to the house on foot. After entering with my key, I hid in Evelyn's bedroom closet, and waited for Sadie and Yolanda. They arrived five minutes later and began playing loud music. In fact, the music was so loud, I could not hear a word they were saying. But I knew they were not studying.

After being cooped up in the closet, like an out-of-style overcoat, for more than 30 minutes, I determined that I'd been wrong and the girls weren't up to anything sneaky. As I was about to exit the closet, and offer a humble apology, the doorbell rung. Suddenly, the music was turned a little higher and I heard laughter coming from several male voices. Through all the talking, music, and laughing, I clearly heard the teenage couple who entered Evelyn's bedroom and sat on the bed. They began discussing whether or not the boy had a condom. He did not, but he tried to convince the girl she wouldn't get pregnant. Through my crack in the door, I could see them both, but knew neither. They were on the bed for all of three minutes, when the girl said, "All right, but don't get me pregnant."

At that instant, I flung open the closet door and yelled, "GET OUT! Get out right now!" The house erupted with confusion. Teenagers were running out the front, back, and side doors. There must have been 10 to 12 kids throughout the house. The couple I interrupted in the bedroom fell off the bed. When the young man finally composed himself, he was silent, but defiant. He acted like he was prepared to fight. And I'm sure he was, under the circumstances. I knew how he felt. I would've been pissed off too. He stood in the center of the floor staring me down and refusing to rush out. He began to ease away when he realized his friends had abandoned him. Yolanda and Sadie were outdone, and tried to slip out in the stampede. I caught them. After scolding them firmly, I made them walk back to my house. I called Evelyn.

Maybe it was childish of me, but I relished the thought of ruining Evelyn's weekend. When I got her on the phone, it was obvious that a party was in full swing. There were music, and the sound of men talking. Before I finished with my news flash, she cupped the phone, giggled and said, "Don't be like that, Campbell. I'll be off in a minute." Then my anger showed. "Isn't Campbell one of your ex-boyfriends from the bank? Huh! What are you doing so important?" She yelled back, "You're there! What can I do about it? I'm 90 miles away remember?" Then she slammed down the phone. This was the same woman who worried and lost sleep over a broken straw in a broom stick. Suddenly, she didn't care if her daughter was having an orgy.

The next day, when she did show up, I argued over her lack of concern. The kids were still at my house and she and I were at her house. I was furious. Not so much about the incident regarding the girls sneaking and having a party that was nothing. I had bigger issues with Evelyn. I hated the idea of not following through with plans. I could sense that none of the plans Evelyn and I made were to be fulfilled. Great plans gone! Evelyn and I had a short future and I knew it. Why would a single woman bring another child into the world of split parenthood? What about our multimillion dollar plans? These were the thoughts that zoomed through my mind while Evelyn and I argued over the small matter of her hanging up the phone on me.

"Ain't this a crying shame," I thought. "How could Evelyn, a woman that claimed to love me allow a psycho like Doris to manipulate her.?" As we stood toe to toe shouting at each other, I wanted to do something that would be beyond an apology. Something that flowers and candy couldn't overcome. Something to show her just how little I regarded her. I abrupt grabbed her by the shoulders, and with brute force, pushed her against the wall and pinned her there. "Don't you ever slam a phone down on me again!" And with that I spit in her face. She gasped. Shocked beyond words. Beyond tears. Her eyes were bucked and frightened. Immediately, I feel ashamed. Though, I dared not apologize. When I calmed down, my mind wandered back to the incident in my life that caused me to do this terrible thing.

Evelyn didn't know much about my dysfunctional childhood. She didn't know when I was 17-years-old my mother had spat in my face. In one of her bitter rages, she attempted to strike me in the face with her fist. In self-defense, I caught her fist in mid flight. Mommy tried to break my grip but was helpless. She cursed and kicked at me. I was afraid to turn her loose. I feared she would inflict the deadly harm she was verbalizing. All I wanted to do was leave peacefully.

It all started because I stayed out all night. When I returned, she ordered me to move out. I really didn't care about leaving, since I felt it was more like a prison, than a loving home, anyway. Therefore, without much ado, I packed a few of my clothing and was looking forward to asking Tammie and Harry for refuge, which I knew they would provide. Tammie knew Mommy's venom better than anyone. As I was about to leave, my tearful younger sister Elaine offered me the sandwich she was eating when I got home. She did this in a sly way, hoping Mommy didn't see the exchange, however, this act of treason was observed. That's when I was physically attacked. "Don't you eat my food," she screamed. "You no good wandering dog! Get out of my house. I'll kill you before I let you use me."

I caught her wrist in self-defense. Finally, she spat in my face. I'm no longer clear on how I got out of the house alive. I remember feeling sorry for Elaine for being stuck there and constantly being threatened with being sent to a reform school for incorrigible kids. Though I survived the ordeal, I was emotionally wounded. So I knew how hurt Evelyn felt. I regretted stooping to such a pit, but the damage was done. The scar from such a crude act would last at least 22 years. As I stormed out of Evelyn's house, I heard the spiritual voice of Ann say, "You need Jesus in your life."

That night Ann visited me in a dream. She was wearing the same beautiful gown that she was buried in. I saw her descending on a cloud, although she had wings. Ann's face was a young and vibrant as the day we met, minus her childhood acne. As she spoke, her lips did not move. Her every word echoed. "I forgive you, Rick. God loves you. Teach our daughters to love the Lord, and they will live forever." Everything she said, echoed. "God loves you, Rick. Quit your life of crime, before it's too late. You need Jesus." I woke up that morning and asked God to show me another life away from crime. However, no answer came.

Over the Christmas and New Years holiday, Evelyn and I were civilized with a guarded amount of warmth, but never intimate. If it wasn't for Darren and the business connection Evelyn and I shared, we wouldn't have saw each other at all. Our communication was almost all business.

One afternoon, Evelyn called me on the telephone, she was very excited, and insisted I tune my TV set to channel nine. When I did, it was immediately clear why she was so concerned. It was a news special-the District Attorney's Office had two of their deputies discussing a major welfare ring that was under surveillance. "An arrest would be made soon," I heard a spokesperson say. He even said, the ring of crooks lived in new homes and drove new cars. When the newscaster asked, "What city are the new homes in?" The chief investigator said, "We don't want to say at this time. We could be tipping our hand, if we did."

After the newscast, I called Evelyn back and tried to calm her down. "They're not talking about us," I said. "We're not the typical scammers those fools are wise to. They're talking about people who are receiving welfare and working under the table." Though we never talked about it again, neither of us forgot it.

Meanwhile, to call my relationship with my oldest daughter estranged would be modestly stated. Every since I foiled the girls' attempt to have their secret party, Yolanda avoided my presence as much as possible. Our rapport began to suffer at the onset of puberty. Perhaps these were the years a daughter needed the guidance of a wise mother most. Young girls must go through an emotional change, as well as a physical one. Yolanda always felt I was too strict, though I disagreed. For instance, Yolanda didn't get to go out on dates very often. When we moved to Lancaster, she was only 12-years-old and in junior high school. Her popularity soared within a few weeks.

By the time she graduated, the senior class of Piru Junior High School voted her their class president. As president she was invited to nearly every party a senior student gave. However, I had a rule which stated, she could not go out but one night every other weekend. That meant only twice a month. I told her on the weekends, which she couldn't go out, her friends could come over, and even stay overnight once a month. Occasionally, she did invite kids over but when I interfered with the dimness of the lights or the loudness of the music, she got upset. Gradually, Yolanda, by her own choosing, decreased her visitors. I once asked her why her friends didn't come over anymore, and she growled, "Because none of them like you!"

When Yolanda got to high school, Evelyn suggested that I allow her more freedom. However, I didn't consider Evelyn a woman of sound judgement. She permitted Sadie's boyfriend to visit every night, and take her out twice a week, This guy was 19-years-old, five years older than Sadie. A man, for crying out loud! But for the sake of fairness, I compromised with Yolanda. I told her she could go out every weekend. Every Friday night and Saturday night, and stay out to midnight. She also could go out on Sunday night, but had to be home by nine at night because of school on Monday. She was all smiles when she heard that, but not when she heard the conditions.
They were as follows: *Yolanda had to bring a progress report card home from school every Friday. She had seven classes and each teacher gave for her a grade for her performance that week. If progress reports showed any D's or F's she wouldn't be allowed to go out, have company, nor receive phone during that particular weekend. For every C grade that was on the*

progress report, Yolanda would lose one evening of going out. One C meant one day loss - Two C's meant two days - Three C's meant her entire weekend would be indoors. However, company and phone calls would still be permitted as long as there was no D's or F's. Also, for each A she would have received a $4 bonus and for each B a $3 bonus. Nothing for C's.

Yolanda was never a girl who jumped to hasty decisions. She told me, she would think about it and let me know in the morning. I told her to consider every weekend that she earned the right to go out, she would leave with at least $15, and up to $28 in her hot little hands. "Of course," I challenged, "that would only occur on weeks of a near perfect progress report card."

Yolanda accepted my offer, and for the first few weeks, she managed to get out on the weekend with a few dollars. She thought it was a very fair deal. Through the week, I noticed she studied more. However, one of her weakest subjects had always been mathematics, and it was a constant struggle for her to maintain a C average. One week, she slipped to a D, and was hard pressed to recover. According to our arrangement, she wasn't permitted to go out on that particular weekend. And if she did leave the house, it was only allowed during the day until 6:00 p.m. It wasn't long before I plummeted back to the bottom of her popularity list. Yolanda had her high school counselor call me after had been restricted from going out on the weekend for six weeks straight.

"Good morning, Mr. Jones, this is Mrs. Grayson, of Lancaster High School Girls Counseling Office. May I speak to you about your daughter, Yolanda?" "Yes Mrs. Grayson," I said, "I'll be glad be talk to you." As we talked further, I learned Yolanda was there in tears because I didn't allow her freedom on the weekend. Mrs. Grayson expressed it was her feeling, a kid Yolanda's age shouldn't be totally isolated from other kids and their social activities. "I don't think you're being quite fair, Mr. Jones," Mrs. Grayson accused. "Be that as it may, Mrs. Grayson," I said. "Yolanda isn't as deprived as you're being led to believe." By the time, I finished telling the counselor the whole story, Mrs. Grayson changed her opinion of me. I heard her informing my daughter her fate had been put in her own hands. She couldn't blame her father for the outcome. Finally, Mrs. Grayson encouraged her to talk to me on the phone and try a renewed compromise.

"Hello Daddy," Yolanda sniffled, "I wanna work out a new arrangement." I eventually, at the counselor's suggestion, lowered Yolanda's Weekly Progress Report Card standard to nothing more than one 'D' would be acceptable. As long as Yolanda got a C or better in all her other grades, she would be allowed to go out on the weekend. This didn't sit well with me, but I conceded. All this parenting of a rebellious teenage daughter was new to me and I figured a school counselor should know best. But soon, that one 'D' was joined by another, and another. Therefore, she was back to being grounded. Finally, one Saturday afternoon, after a couple weeks of no company or weekend dates, Yolanda proudly came to me and made an announcement. "Daddy, I have decided to get a tutor to improve in mathematics." I told her I thought it was a fine idea. She said he would be over later that evening.

This tutor of hers was supposed to be one of the smartest students at Lancaster High School. A few hours later, a handsome young man arrived and introduced himself as Mac, Yolanda's tutor. I could tell by the sparkle in their eyes, as they shyly glanced at each other, something was up. When Yolanda went up to her room to retrieve her study materials, Mac and I began to chat. I asked him a simple question. "Mac, tell me, if you were riding a train that left Los Angeles at 5:15 a.m., traveling none stop at 70 miles an hour, to a destination in the east, where the time zone was three hours different, and 2370 miles away, what time would you arrive? I slid him the pad and pencil that were on the dining room table. He looked at me mystified. He sat there for five minutes staring at the paper. That's when I told him to come back after he slept on the problem. When Yolanda returned ten minutes later, with her hair in a different style, she was shocked to find no Mac. "Where's Mac?" she asked curiously. I calmly replied, "I sent his dumb butt home." As she ran up the stairs in anger, I shouted, "Good try, honey!"

Evelyn was a very sneaky person. She prowled around in Sadie's room, read her letters, and eavesdropped on her telephone conversations. I admired Evelyn's methods because it usually kept us a step ahead of their schemes. While the girls were at school one day, Evelyn called me at home and said she just got off the phone with the school attendance office clerk. To her amazement, she discovered Sadie had been absent 13 days this semester. Evelyn knew this number was excessive. She encouraged me to call and inquire about Yolanda's attendance.

It was of no surprise to Evelyn when I informed her, 20 minutes later, Yolanda had been absent more days than I had knowledge of, 16 days to be exact. Evelyn told me not to mention it to Yolanda, until she brought Sadie over and we would confront them together. That afternoon about five o'clock, Evelyn and Sadie arrived. I asked Yolanda and Sadie to join Evelyn and me in the den. Once we were there, Evelyn took the lead role in the interrogation. "How many days have you two ditched school this semester?" They both remained calm and denied ever ditching school. Then Evelyn hit them with our findings. Each of them tried to explain it away with illnesses, cramps, babysitting once or twice, and anything else they could muster. It was obvious that both girls were lying. Their composure was beginning to betray them. Evelyn was on their case like bitter on a lemon. Sadie was on the verge of tears, but Yolanda was defiant. It was their demeanor that convicted them.

Finally they crumbled to a confession. I felt anger and victory, in a weird way. Evelyn and I were united again, if only to attack our children. Every now and then, I threw in a threat, but it was Evelyn who solved the mystery. Once the truth was out, I figured the next order of business was to administer appropriate punishment. But Evelyn wasn't finished with them yet. She hit them and me with a bombshell question. "Is either one of you," then she raised her voice, "VIRGINS?" "Ain't no need in lying," I interjected, "we're gonna find out anyway." I don't know what I was thinking when I made that statement. Yolanda sort of rolled her eyes in disgust in my direction.
Evelyn repeated the question with a roar of anger. "Dammit! Answer me. Have you two been having sex?"
In unison both girls say, "NO, we ain't been doing nutt'n." "Well y'all better be tell'n the truth," Evelyn swore," 'cause tomorrow morning you are going to be medically examined and a doctor will know. So tell the truth right now. Have y'all been having sex?"
Sadie began to cry harder. Yolanda snapped, "I'm not going to get checked

like a dog."

I rebutted her harshly, "Oh yes you are!"

"Mama, I'm not a virgin." Sadie said sadly.

"I'm not either." My daughter added.

Evelyn pushed it farther. "How long have you been having sex?" "Four months." Sadie answered. "Well well well," I thought to myself. "I had warned Evelyn about letting that 19-year-old man hang around her daughter. But no, she wouldn't listen. That's what she gets."

Then Evelyn turned to Yolanda and asked, "How long have you been having sex?"

My daughter said almost proudly, "Two years!"

I flipped out. I slapped her, and was trying to slap her again when Evelyn grabbed my arm and came between us. The truth hurts. That evening I discovered that my daughter's sexual activity begun during my alcoholic excursions. Yolanda told us while I was out partying for long periods of time, she slipped in boys, and told the other kids not to tell. She screamed cold chilling words, "You left us hungry! If it wasn't for Grandmommy bringing us food we might have starved. I started to call the county on you!" I was dumbfounded. "Shut up you little liar!" I shouted. Evelyn and Sadie looked upon my shame in silence.

The next morning, as promised, Evelyn took the girls to the doctor and had them examined for diseases and pregnancy. They were negative on both counts. Although, they promised not to engage in sexual activity again until they finished high school, both were put on birth control pills. Yolanda refused to reveal the name of the boy or boys she had been with, and I didn't try to force her since she had not been raped. The way the law is written, some poor horny young guy would be thrown in jail on statutory rape charges, like I had been as a teenager. Though I asked her the names, as if it really mattered, I was more proud of her steadfastness than angered by her promiscuity.

There wasn't much doubt who Sadie's first lover had been. I told Evelyn not to allow that man to come around again, but she merely cut his daily visits down to weekends. I wondered what Sadie's father would have done.

Chapter 7

*T*he morning of February 6, 1987, started like any other school day. By 7:00 a.m., Yolanda had already left for school. She caught an early school bus at 7:15 a.m. Evelyn usually dropped Rita off at my house by 6:30 a.m. to wait until 7:20, at which time Rochelle, Jennifer, and Roxanne left with her for their bus stop. While Evelyn drove Rita to my house, Sadie stayed with Darren and received the children being dropped off by their parents en route to work. It only took about ten minutes for Evelyn to make the round trip. Since Rita had begun school from my address, almost two years ago, her mother never reported to the school their new address, because her Rita didn't want to change schools.

Snow from the raging winter was still on the ground. The blizzard closed schools several times during my last winter in Lancaster. The girls were sitting around watching early morning television, waiting until the last minute to rush out for their school bus. It wasn't unusual for me to be up and at my desk at this time of the morning, working on some scheme or another, and this morning was no exception. My office was set up in the corner of my large master bedroom.

From my second floor bedroom, I heard a loud banging on my front door. My first thought was that one of the girls mischievous friends were trying to startle them. I disgustedly rose from my seat and went to the upstairs railing. I looked down at the door, as the girls sat silently and shocked, I yelled, "Stop beating on that door like that!"

Another knock immediately followed. Blam! Blam! Blam! Then there was the loud shout of an adult male voice, "Sheriff Department, we have a search warrant." Balm! Balm! Balm! "Open this door!"

"Go ahead Rochelle," I called down to my frightened but calm 11-year-old daughter, "open the door. They must have the wrong house." Within five seconds my living room was flooded with Sheriff Deputies. I immediately recognized one of the barging officers as one of the Welfare Fraud Investigators I had seen on the news special two weeks earlier. I turned and dashed back into my bedroom, grabbed the phone from my desk and began punching out Evelyn's number. Before the phone even rung once two cops were running toward me with guns drawn demanding, "Hang up that phone NOW!"

Policemen could be overheard commenting how disgraceful it was for me to be living a luxurious lifestyle while eating on food stamps. I sensed a twang of envy in the voices of the men and women raiding my home. There were other mumbled comments-how clean and well-mannered my children were. None of girls, at least not in my presence, cried or even appeared upset. I realized they submerged their fear and confusion. Yet there was a measure solace in the fact the officers were not raging maniacs. That's one thing that was in my favor. The cops treated me with all the dignity afforded a prisoner that wasn't resisting them. They didn't even handcuff me until two hours after they arrived. When they did, the children had already been taken away by a social worker.

Before the Department of Children Services staffer took the children away, they asked me if I had a relative or friend I could call to come for the children. When I mentioned that I could call my son's mother Evelyn, the officer replied, "She's under arrest also. We have officers at her house right now." Rita overheard the last statement and went wild with emotion. She cried uncontrollably and screamed for her mother. My kids had witnessed me being arrested before when their mother was alive. As far as they knew, it was just a way of life. I felt sympathy for them for having me as their father. As they were being taken away, each one looked back and said, "Bye Daddy." The sound of their voices saying those endearing words, sent chills through me.

Soon, another officer in plain clothes, entered my house. He seemed to be the

H.N.I.C. (Head nigger in charge.) I immediately recognized him as another Welfare Fraud Investigators from television. He identified himself as Mel Wesson, the lead investigator. He told one of his men, the woman was being very cooperative and was willing to tell everything she knew. I wasn't surprised to hear that. Evelyn wasn't a hardcore criminal. She was just a mixed-up Sunday school teacher. Just as Ann wasn't a crook, until I entered her life. All while the cops searched my house for more welfare fraud evidence, I was mentally asking for God's forgiveness for ruining innocent lives. I knew I was going to prison before they even handcuffed me, so my mind was at peace about that. As for my children, I took it for granted my mother would take custody of them.

During the search of my home, the officers discovered that I also was involved in credit and insurance fraud. They found 13 driver licenses issued by The Department of Motor Vehicles with my picture and a different name on each one. In addition, a credit file with bank accounts for each fraudulent name was uncovered. In my accident files, 32 unsettled cases were exposed. Most of them were not in any of my names but in the names of other people I had put in cases. My children's bank books were also seized. Finally, when they escorted me from my house, nearly three hours later, with my hands shackled behind my back, there were dozens of my neighbors standing on their lawns or peeking behind curtains. I was sure they thought I was innocent of whatever I was being charged with. The public attention embarrassed me just the same.

When Evelyn arrived at the Sheriff Station and saw me, she seemed a little relieved. Not because I was a source of comfort to her, but to know that I too had been captured. We happened to be in the booking area and sitting only a few feet apart. Evelyn told me that she learned that Doris was also arrested that morning in Maryland.

The officers in the booking room didn't go out on the raid and didn't realize that Evelyn and I were crime partners. Therefore, they didn't interfere with our conversing quietly among ourselves. Evelyn told me of the embarrassment she suffered as the cops called each one of her child care parents. A set of 10 different parents was asked to leave work to come pick up their children. She said while the parents were en route, the children were all in the living room with her sitting in handcuffs. The children kept asking, "Why are you hurting Evelyn?" Evelyn and the children were crying. When the parents came each of them gave her dirty looks. I could sense her shame. Her experience had been far worse than mine. She also said that when the female social worker left my house, she drove down to her house to ask if she had someone to pick up Rita and Darren. Evelyn said, "Darren was already crying uncontrollably, but they wouldn't take the handcuffs off for me to hold him. Then Rita came in with the social worker and saw the scene and . . . Ahh, Richard, it was awful. If I could have, I would've grabbed one of their guns and killed myself." She began to cry all over again.

Shortly thereafter, we were booked and locked up. Though we couldn't see each other, we were still close enough communicate. Evelyn was calling to me to do something, think of something. "Please get me outta here." She pleaded. At the time, I figured she was talking to me, but now looking back, perhaps she was talking to God. "If you get me outta this, I promise I'll never forsake you. Please help me. I'll be true and faithful to you." She begged so much until I called back, "I'll do whatever I can." Evelyn didn't answer.

The deputy who worked the cellblock told Evelyn we would be transported to the main county jail later that night. She would be going to Sybil Brand Women's Jail, and I would be going to The Men's County Jail. A little later, I heard him tell her, "Yo' bail is $10,000 each. "No madam," the deputy said, "for the third time I don't know where yo' children are. At some Foster Home, I imagine." I stretched out on the iron slab in my cell and went to sleep. It seemed like I'd been asleep only a short while when the deputy rattled my cage door and called my name. I figured it was time to catch the chain downtown. But I was wrong. "Jones you've been bailed," the deputy said without care. Then he walked down toward Evelyn's cell and said, "Fargo you've been bailed." I heard Evelyn yell, "Thank you Jesus!" Immediately, I thought, "If it was Jesus that opened the cell doors, maybe I should say thanks too."

As always, my mother was right there whenever I needed her. When I stepped from behind the third locked door that lead to the lobby, there she was. Since

I had been a troubled child in school, my mother was there to bail me out. Now I was 41-years-old, and there she was again. I greeted her with a hearty hug. I didn't see Jesus waiting for me. I saw my mother. So that's where my thanks went. "Thank you Mommy. Thank you so much, I love you," I said. We both knew this case was the 'Big One' of my criminal career. "Mommy, I'm sorry for the inconvenience." My mother had been crying, I could see it in her eyes. As we embraced, she shocked me by saying, "Don't thank me, thank God. I started to leave you here, but I prayed about it. It was God that sent me this time. Thank God, not me." I mumbled for the first time in my adult life, "Thank you Jesus."

Then I went immediately to Nate, mommy's husband, who was forever at her side no matter what. I give him a hug as well. At this moment, the same door that released me opened for Evelyn. Nate and Evelyn embraced. Nate was a very emotional man and the tears on his face said it all. Then Evelyn and my mother sort of ran into each others arms. "Oh Thelma," Evelyn cried, "I thought I would die if I didn't get out of there. Thank you so much!"

We left the jail and headed for my house. My mother told us she learned our arrest on the evening news. Before we got to my house, Evelyn asked them to stop so she could get a drink. Neither one of us kept liquor at home. I hadn't drunk any alcohol for three years. Everyone in the car would've understood if I made an exception on this night. I shocked everyone, including myself, when I declined the suggestion of a drink. Nor did I crave a cigarette or cigar. I knew then, for sure, I had quit drinking and smoking forever.

Evelyn was so distraught about the whole thing that she refused to spend the night anywhere in the city of Lancaster. So we gathered about four days worth of clothing from each house and headed for Los Angeles in my car. We all sat around about 20 or 30 minutes discussing the matter before we left. We were all concerned about the children's whereabouts. My mother had been told, that all seven children were in Foster Homes and a judge would decide their fate within three days.

Before we got on the freeway heading south, Evelyn asked me to stop at the liquor store again for a small can of whiskey sour and a pack of cigarettes. While in the store, I noticed the headlines in the Antelope Valley Press Newspaper, which read:

TWO NABBED IN WELFARE FRAUD RAID

I purchased the evening paper. Evelyn read it aloud as I drove.
To paraphrase it:

'Two Lancaster residents were arrested this morning in a raid. Richard O. Jones, 41 and Evelyn A. Fargo, 34 were the masterminds in a scheme that biked Los Angeles County of more than $500,000 annually. The scheme is said to extend through several states including Texas, Kansas, Kentucky, Alabama, Maryland, and Florida. Jones was the author of a lonely hearts' club scheme and lured women to Los Angeles for the purpose of furthering his illegal activities . . . Fargo operated a child care service out of her home which were licensed for six children but at the time of the raid twelve children were found in her care.'

It is alleged by welfare fraud investigators that the children were used the obtain illegal funds.

When we checked into a motel in Culver City about 11:00 p.m. Instead of resting, we went for a long walk. I tried to assured Evelyn the whole investigation centered around me and the court would be lenient with Doris and her. We stayed together in the motel for three days. This was the first time months we slept together. We didn't make love as humans know it. Evelyn and I copulated as petrified robots, in search of a hiding place. The saddest part of it all was, we didn't even like each other.

Each day, Evelyn and I would take turns calling the D.A.'s office to speak with Mel Wesson. He promised to advise the judge we were fit to regain custody of our children, while awaiting trial. Their investigation showed each of us to be exemplary parents. Wesson was sure that we could pick up our children at the end of three days.

The subject of Doris and the things she exposed to me about Evelyn came up time and time again, until Evelyn finally confessed she had been plotting against me with Doris. She also admitted rekindling a romance with Carl, although he was remarried, with a newborn baby. I tried to reason with her. "Your reputation as a decent woman is to only thing you've got." I said. "If you get yourself involved in an adulterous scandal before you go to court, the judge may throw the book at you. In which case your tears won't help you."

My real reason for trying to discourage Evelyn's long distance romance was because, in a case as serious as ours, we needed each other's loyalty. Unfortunately, the only way Evelyn could show anyone 'loyalty', would be to point out the word in the dictionary.

Evelyn phoned Carl when she knew his wife wouldn't be home. If the current Mrs. Fargo answered the phone unexpectedly, Evelyn could hide behind concerns of their children. When Carl phoned the motel, he was under the impression Evelyn was there alone. Emotionally, I guess she was. Usually, I would just quietly leave the room. It was understandable that she was frightened and sought a familiar shoulder to cry on. Besides, I realized that the two of them had some serious child custody arrangements to work out. Carl and his wife agreed, Sadie and Rita would move back to Ohio while their mother stood trial.

The H.N.I.C. allowed Evelyn and me to meet him at his office, and he released one of our bank books so we would have funds to sustain ourselves. We withdrew the necessary cash from our accounts and reimbursed my Guardian Angel mother for putting up the bail. The following day, Wesson gave us the approval to meet with a social worker at the Lancaster Department of Social Services Offices to reunite with our children. All the staff there was expecting us at the welfare office. They probably viewed Evelyn and me as a couple of dirty rats who were stealing their precious funds. Nonetheless, each of them knew we were good parents. I encouraged Evelyn to walk in with her head up, look the social workers in their eyes while talking, and walk out with her head up. Our reunion was bittersweet. We all hugged and kissed each other as a handful of county workers looked on. This was the second time I reunited with Roxanne at a social service office. The first time had been five years earlier, following her mother's fatal accident.

We later learned that Darren, Jennifer and Rita had been placed together in a Foster Home with of an elderly couple. Rochelle and Roxanne were placed together with a family with three other foster children. Sadie and Yolanda were placed together where they were the only children.

Evelyn's child care business was ruined by the arrest and publicity. She saw no reason to return to her own home. Therefore, she moved in with me. Once again we were under the same roof. Just so Evelyn would be aware of all the perils involved, I warned we may be forced into foreclosure, since we no longer were solvent. Therefore, the wisest move for us would be to dump the homes and cut our losses. Evelyn had no problem accepting this fate.

Both homes had 'For Sale' signs in the yard within two weeks. Our children were very resilient. Although everyone in Lancaster knew about the big raid, none of their friends or school teachers treated them differently. One of the local newspapers printed our home addresses which prompted a motorcade of spectators. Each night cars drove slowly pass my house. I purposely sat on the front lawn and waved to them. Of course, most people pretended not to be interested when they were confronted in such a bold manner. After three or four weeks the traffic died.

Nearly every weekend, Evelyn escaped to Los Angeles. Of course, I was never invited. After the Jones and Fargo Families were living together a few weeks, Carl flew to Los Angeles on vacation from work. He and I met at my house and had a casual conversation about his flight and the weather in Ohio. Evelyn seemed pleased we got along. His girls were delighted to see him. Carl indeed loved his children. However, during his one week stay in Los Angeles, he never made it back to Lancaster to visit his family. Evelyn happened to spend that particular weekend in L.A. When she returned, I asked her if she slept with Carl. She assured me she didn't. She even offered proof by saying, "You know I was on my period when I left, and I'm still on my period." I replied by saying, "That proves it all right!"

Within a couple months our houses were sold and we moved in with my *Guardian Angel* mother in Los Angeles. My mother held the patent on 'The Ambiguous Welcome Mat'. She would rush to the rescue of her children, and offer her love, support, money, home, advice, or anything else within her power. But her smile would twist into a scowl in a metamorphic flash and the welcome mat transforms into a 'Do Not Disturb' sign. Suddenly, your every move would be out of order. You eat too much, talk too loud, sleep too long, get too many phone calls, have too much company, use too much water, snore too loud, your contribution to the house is too little, you iron your clothes too much, wash your clothes too much or not enough, your kids are too noisy or they sit around and whisper too much, bottom line, Get Out of MY House! If you happened to be the type of person who's easily embarrassed by knowing you've become the talk of the town, then you're in big trouble.

My mother and I constantly verbally sparred about the kids leaving lights on or not eating all their food, etc. They were bathing and using electricity to such an extreme, that her utility bill went from $50 a month to nearly $300 a month. Mommy would become tearfully upset if I asked to see the bills. This would be equal to calling her a lair and cheat. So the subject would magically jump from expenses to integrity, which, of course, is a touchy subject when you're staying in the accuser's house. Every few days my mother would discover another expense and increase the rent by $50 or $60 a month. Within a short span of time, the rent soared from $400 per month to $600 a month. Her house payment, at the time, was less than $500 a month.

The summer crept toward an end and the time had come for my children to relocate to Natchez, Mississippi and live split up among several of their mother's siblings. The original plan was for my mother to keep the children during my imminent imprisonment. Though she loved them dearly, I grew more and more concerned about child brutality under her care. Evelyn's daughters were sent to Ohio to live with their father. Our choice for Darren's shelter was between few and none. The only choice was my mother. I figured, at three years old, Darren was too young to get on his grandmother's last nerve.

As with Evelyn's daughters, we had a quaint farewell party for my girls. When the Greyhound Bus left the station, I felt a great sense of relief. Though I wasn't sure when I would see them again, I was glad they were gone because the stress of hearing new complaints about their slightest movements wore me down. Moreover, I constantly found myself in bitter confrontation with either my mother or Evelyn on a regular basis. I truly loved my daughters, but knew it was an unhealthy environment to daily witness the character assassination of their father by the two adult women in their lives. However, I realized that in Mississippi they would endure and overhear a few cruel remarks about me also. But the pain would be less if it wasn't coming from my own mother.

Doris was flown in from Maryland and testified against me with a vengeance. As the evidence unfolded, it was revealed that I became a suspect when I applied for the birth certificates of a deceased family in a small Texas town. Suspicion arose when I negligently applied to the same state for both death and birth certificates. I was aware that when a person died in the same state in which they were born there was a good chance that the birth certificate was pulled, and the word DECEASED would be stamped on the document in capital letters and red ink. In this case, when I sent for the birth certificate of a deceased woman and the birth certificates of her two deceased children in Texas, the officials there discovered the people were dead. Therefore, they notified the Los Angeles District Attorney. The authorities in Los Angeles were advised by the county department in Texas to forward the documents to me and they would keep track of them until they determined my scam. Eventually, the deceased Texas family appeared on The Los Angeles County Aid for Families with Dependant Children computer. At that time, I became the target of a major investigation.

Our court proceedings were well underway when my lawyer told me that the District Attorney's Office was willing to drop more than $400,000 worth of the fraud charges. Instead of the D.A. asking for the maximum sentence of 11 years in state prison, they would ask for four years if I pled guilty. A typical plea bargain. Evelyn would get no more than one year in the county jail, if she pled guilty rather than face a possible seven year prison sentence. So Evelyn and I pled guilty. Doris was promised straight probation, with no jail time for her full cooperation. She was sentenced to three years probation that same day and flew back to home. In fact, she was such a willing witness for the prosecution that she was released from jail without bail from the very start.

Evelyn and I were ordered to appear for sentencing in two months. As a court formality we reported to The County Probation Office for an evaluation. The probation officer reviews your case and background then makes recommendations to the judge. The judges usually took their recommendations because they were the (so-called) experts in determining your likelihood for future offenses.

The manager of the Bank of America Branch where Evelyn was employed, several personal friends, and her pastor wrote endearing character letters in her behalf to the judge and the probation department. I composed a two-page letter accepting all the blame and asking for leniency in Evelyn's behalf:

7/20/88

Dear Honorable Judge Candace Cooper:

Since my arrest, I've taken a long and deep look at myself and must admit the reflection was no prize, no prize indeed. You've seen my criminal record. I have been involved in illegal activity for more than 25 years. The time flew by so fast, as time does, I never realized just how callous my heart had become.

Not long ago while I was shopping in a grocery store, I came out only to discover that another vehicle had put a dent in my parked van. The driver took off, just like I would've done, without leaving a note. The average person would've been a bit annoyed to find a thousand dollars worth of damage on their vehicle. But my first instinct was to call my insurance company and make a false report. I was so overjoyed that I whistled and sang out loud as I drove home scheming on how I and all my daughters, including Evelyn's two girls were going to fake injuries, as if we were in the van when a hit & run driver stuck.

I planned to encourage the girls to play along by enticing them with the *vision of getting a check in their own name for $5,000 or $6,000 and I would've been proud of myself for providing them with such an opportunity. When I pulled into my driveway, it dawned on me just how corrupt I had become. I was only minutes from converting six innocent children into criminals.*

Judge, when I met Evelyn, and so many other women of my life, my first inclination was not to make them my lover, but to make them my crime partner. A poor woman is easy prey. Especially if she's a single mother. I love a poor, uneducated, struggling, and a lonely single mother, ha, most hustlers do. Evelyn was a piece of cake, and Doris was cake with ice cream on top. Any hustler could've gotten them. If I had been a pimp, they would've been standing in your court with a prostitution case. But I'm a petty con man. Therefore, they stand before you with petty fraud cases. I'm not proud of myself anymore.

For the last few years, I have been tormented by the fatal car accident of Annie Mae Jones, my ex-wife and children's mother. She was also an innocent young woman when we met. Through her relationship with me, she not only went to jail but was fleeing from arrest on welfare fraud charges at the time of her death.

Evelyn didn't have a chance. I slipped new furniture on her, easy accident settlements, credit cards, gave her children bank accounts, swimming lessons, love and friendship. Evelyn's got an opportunity to buy her very own home for the first time in her life. And also to started her own business. She's not your typical crook, but she is my typical victim. Evelyn has already been humiliated beyond anything you can do to her. To sentence her to jail for being a desperate frighten woman is like throwing water on a drowning man.

Dear Judge Cooper, I know Evelyn Fargo well enough to categorically state, she is truly remorseful and it is highly improbable that she'll ever be lured into such a trap again.

Contritely yours,

Richard O. Jones

166

Eighteen months had passed, since our arrest. It was nearly over, the majority of this time we stayed with my mother. Evelyn and I slept in the garage apartment. The seven children shared the front house with our hostess. Though we paid rent, it was never enough. The stress and anxiety levels were high. Evelyn and I argued and nearly came to blows so often that, eventually, Evelyn moved to the front house, and I was in the rear house alone. The children were extremely unhappy. My mother's house rules were stricter than any of them had ever encountered. As I awaited my final fate, I was at peace. My children were uniting with new relatives.

Two months zooms by when you're awaiting an imminent fate. One morning, I woke up to find, the day had come, September 9, 1988. After the one year sentence was handed down to Evelyn, the bailiff escorted her to the lockup area behind a heavy wooden door. I felt bad for my son's mother. All she ever wanted to do was be an independent woman. It had been so important to her to own a home and business. She achieved her dream, I hoped she realized that. A year wasn't too much. With time off for good behavior, she would be out in less than seven months. The fact was, I felt Evelyn could use the time away from all her other worries, and like the judge said, to construct her life.

As I stood before the judge, I purposely tuned her out. I was thinking, what an attractive and intelligent woman she was, an African Queen and a judge at that. I actually felt proud being sentenced by a black woman judge. I wished more black women were in the courtroom to witness what a woman could achieve when her head is right. Finally, when I did tune in the sound coming from Judge Cooper's red judicial lips, she was saying, " . . . according to your plea bargain agreement, you've committed yourself to four years in state prison. And should you return and truly get your life together, I'll help you any way I can."

A four-year prison sentence only meant two years to anybody with an ounce of a discipline. All you had to do is serve your time without acting a jailhouse fool and you would be out in no time. I really didn't care. Two years would be good for me. Being in jail can be stressful or peaceful, depending on your attitude. That first night was pretty relaxing. Three times more so than what I had become accustomed to at my mother's house In jail or prison you knew the rules, and the rules didn't change. You didn't have to smile or pretend to be happy. You didn't have to talk or argue or even try to get along. All you had to do was *'Yo' Own Time,'* and that was fine with me.

The Los Angeles County Jail is much more of a dungeon than prison. In fact, once a prisoner has been sentenced, he actually looks forward to being shipped out. Jail is just cell living, sprinkled with flashes of television liberty. The men in county jail act and treat each other like animals. They fight over the phone, candy, television channels, card games, to impress others and establish reputations. Sports, whether on the tube or in the recreation yard, is a spark of frustration. Everywhere you go, two or more grown men are trying to kill one another. Of course, there are the bullies that must prove they're real men by engaging each other into homosexuality. It's not that any one of them is so horny. Just so ignorant their mind can't think of anything else. This mindless attitude is also the catalyst for race riots and gang activity. Knowing how to cope in a menagerie was the biggest challenge of incarceration. My policy in jail was never to play games with fellow convicts. No basketball, or sports of any kind, no cards, no dominos and don't seek to write anybody's sister. Don't do anything which will cause a convict to think you owe him a favor. You can't repay a parasite.

My stay in the county jail was one week before I was off to Chino Institute for Men. Chino isn't considered by prison authorities a regular long term prison, but rather a reception center. At Chino prisoners are categorized by their crime, their past, their so-called I.Q. and education. After determining your level of security risk, you'll be transferred to the appropriate prison. The security levels range from level one thru level four. At level one inmates may be sent somewhere with minimum security, no gun towers, or high walls. Level four prisoners were subject to constant supervision under the barrel and scope of a high powered rifle. After being there for two weeks, and living in a dormitory, my group of entries was called in for tests and evaluation.

About 200 of us were herded into a huge gymnasium. The testing was mostly done from books. It was over in about two hours. One good thing about jail or prison for a poor person, were free medical services, including dental. Let's face it, nearly everyone unfortunate enough to be in prison is poor. Also many guys that otherwise would never see the inside of an exercise room spent much of their time working out with weights and dumb bells. When I got to prison it dawned, on me one morning while walking pass the weight pile, why stupid people -mostly men- are called 'Dumb Bell'. I immediately saw the connection between the weight and the man. Most likely, in the free world, where people join exercise clubs, the intelligence level runs high because it's an intelligent person who takes the time to care for their health. These Dumb Bells mostly lifted iron for appearance sake. Their personal habits and lifestyle away from the exercise area were an insult to good health. Nearly all of them smoked cigarettes, used drugs, bragged of multiple heterosexual sex partners, a few sought homosexual sex and risked their health and life on a regular basis by engaging in violent prone activity for a few dollars or gang status. No wonder the weights were called 'Dumb Bells.' Which also brought to my attention why narcotics were called 'Dope.'

After I had been at Chino for six weeks, I was called into the office for review and test results. The officer in charge of assignments saw me privately. This was unusual because most inmates just got a computer printout of their assignment and status. I walked into the small dull office with one desk and a chair on each side. The captain introduced himself and we shook hands.
"Inmate Jones, I'm Captain Gaynor," he said. "Have a seat."
As I sat there, Captain Gaynor, a well-built white man of 50 something, with grayish hair, flipped slowly through my file which was on top of his desk. Finally after three or four minutes, the silence was broken.
"It's our duty here on this yard to observe all the inmates closely," he said. "And it has come to my attention that your behavior is independent of most of the other inmates. No cards, no sports, no complaining, no arguments, no backtalk, some mingling, but no friendships, you made one phone call a week, and received and send much mail."
I thought before I spoke.
"Captain Gaynor," I began, "There are many men here and few officers. The

only way you would know my every move is if I had been singled out. Why?"

"To be quite frank Inmate Jones," he answered, "we've been watching you because I've long wanted to start an inmate on inmate counseling program. We received the report from the probation department. They don't seem to think you even belong in prison. You've already reformed, but let's look at it like this, you're 41-years-old, which is older than half the men here. Your aptitude far surpasses the average con on the yard. I would like to offer you the choice of staying here as a counselor, rather than being shipped off to a hardcore prison where there're daily fights and stabbing on the yard. You will be housed in a privileged unit with three other select inmates; a politician, a doctor, and an accountant, they're all part of a special inmate program."
The officer continued, as I sat silently. "Instead of sharing the shower, TV, and radio, with a whole dormitory, you'll have your own of each. Unlimited phone privileges, seven day library access, plus a good pay number."
"Will you give me a moment to consider this?" I asked with a sincere and deep expression.
"Sure take a couple of minutes," he answered, "but I have to know before you leave this room. We can't have a person that can't make up his mind until he talks it over with this one and that one."
As I was considering the attractive proposition, the Captain said, "Oh, by the way, you're a-level two inmate. The fact that you have two rape convictions as a teenager, puts you behind the walls in any other prison."
"Are you trying to use a 25-year-old charge against me now? Man, I was in high school then, I'm old enough to be a grandfather now. Besides, if you read the full report you'll see that it was not what a man with common sense calls rape, anyway. I had been with each of the girls sexually before and after these ridiculous charges. Both girls were afraid of the punishment they would have faced for being caught acting out their natural impulses. It didn't matter to me. So I admitted screwing them. But I didn't understand the magnitude of pleading guilty."
Captain Gaynor laughed and shook his head.
"It's a bureaucratic shame, but it's still on your record. The way the prison system is set up, no inmate with a rape, arson, or escape, on their record can be a level one."

"If that's the case," I asked, "then how can you offer me these special privileges, which would enable me freedom to roam on the compound, plus access to female staff."

"I don't feel that you're a threat to anyone, Jones," he said, "but at your new location you'll be treated like any other level two inmate."

As I walked back to my dormitory, I was glad of my decision not to allow myself to be manipulated into accepting a country club type of prison arrangement. Two days later, I received a notice along with three dozen other inmates that we were being sent to Mule Creek State Prison in Ione, California. Someone said that Mule Creek was a location about 40 miles from Sacramento, California. Chino was only a 90 minute drive from Los Angeles but this Ione was nearly an eight-hour drive.

I wrote a letter to Evelyn. My had mother sent me her mailing address and we became prison pen pals. Evelyn expressed a great relief to finally being somewhere she could rest. She said that her life was becoming more focused. I was surprised that she actually thanked me for the experience and gave me credit for enhancing her ability to face life without running away.

The good news was that she expected to be released in one fourth of her sentence, which meant she would only have to serve three months because of an early release program open to first time offenders. Evelyn said that the sentencing judge would have to approve her request, and she had already written Judge Candace Cooper. If all went well, she would be out before Christmas. Evelyn also said her best friend in prison turned out to be Dorothy Woods also known as The Welfare Queen. It seemed that Sister Woods had been released from prison on her original welfare fraud charges but while out on parole she committed new welfare fraud.

About three o'clock one morning, the dorm officer woke me saying it was time to be shipped out. We were told to be prepared the previous evening. On the prison chain there were very few older men, like me, who were being sent to prison for the first time. The stocky, gray headed, middle-aged man that I was shackled to, bragged about this being his fourth time. He was extremely proud of his 18-inch arms and 48-inch chest. Several other men were equally as buffed. They all were prison iron drivers. One of them, a white convict with a muscular physique threatened to molest a young white boy when we got to Mule Creek. The young convict became so nervous that he befriended a muscular black inmate for protection. Everyone knew the predictable ending to that story.

"The con shackled to me in the next seat said in a husky whisper, "Don't worry about nothing. I won't let anything happen to you." I sat silently for a moment to digest his words and meaning. "Don't flatter yourself 'Hero'," I said sarcastically.

"Yeah, right!," he grinned.

A little later, perhaps about ten minutes, he asked, "It this yo' first trip?"

"Yeah, I don't get caught every time I leave the house," I snapped. "Look nervous ta me!" he said.

"You're a very poor judge of character," I told him. "I'm more at ease now than I've been in the past 18 months."

The Los Angeles County Sheriff Bus, with bars on every window, was under the control - I should say the full control - of three commando type marshals. One drove the bus, and the other two were positioned in a locked cage. One officer was stationed in the rear of the bus, and the other in the front. Both were armed with a short barrel pump rifle and a handgun on their waist.

The front cage guard was a stocky, about 6'3" and 230 pounds, bald, white dude who talked loud and acted twice as mean. In the back was a cute blonde blue-eyed shapely young woman that left no one wondering whether she would blow them away.

It sort of tickled me to see these big, cruel, weight lifting, gang-banging, murdering, tough guys, inwardly tremble at the roar of the big guard's voice. There were some unnecessary loud talking and giggling on the bus by three or four gang members. The young black men were cracking jokes about the foxy blonde guard in the rear. The front guard warned them once to knock it off. Well, you know how brothers are, especially when they're in a pack. One of them cracked in a muffled voice, "Drop dead Honky!"

The driver immediately pulled the bus to the side on the road. It was about 5:00 a.m. and still dark out. The big guard bursted out of his cage by kicking the door open which actually broke the lock. As he did so, he pumped his rifle.

"SHOW TIME! You stupid animals!" he shouted as he stomped in the direction of the four. "I can't treat none of you dumb ghetto NIGGERS nice! Blam! He hit the first one across the face with the butt of his gun. Before the guy could even holler, he struck his 45 automatic pistol into to convict's mouth. In that instant, the loud pump and clicking noise of the rear guard's rifle paralyzed the bus.
The little cute blonde screamed, "Just give me an excuse!" The male guard put his face within one inch of the inmate with the gun in his mouth and promised "I'll kill you faggot!"

This occurred directly across the aisle from me, and I could see tears swelling up in the frightened convict's eyes. Suddenly, there was another rifle pump sound coming from the front of the bus. The driver beamed his deadly weapon into my side of the bus. I felt the 'Hero,' next to me, begin to shake. He shook so hard that our chain began to rattle. Then the big white bald headed guard turned slowly, very slowly to each of the men in the pack of the disruptive four, and backhanded them in the face. One suffered a nose bleed and another a busted lip. This incident was more horrifying because the barrel of the handgun was still launched in the tearful tough guy's mouth. None of the four tough guys said a mumbling word. The guard roughly jerked out his gun and told the whole bus, "The next time we have to stop this freaking bus, the coroner's office is gonna have ta be called." As the guard was turning to stomp off, he stopped abruptly and looked the 'Hero' next to me directly in the face. Without a word, he smacked the "Hero' in the mouth. When asked by the victimized convict in a whining tone, "Why you hit me?" The guard growled, "So you won't sit here whispering for the rest of the trip, 'I wouldn't let no white man hit me like that!' Now shut up, Faggot!"

We rode for the next three hours without a sound on the bus. If any man who was on that bus tells you they were not scared, he's a dirty liar. That was the kind of mess that worried me. One of these ignorant loud mouths, could get me shot on the prison yard behind their so-called tough guy behavior. I detested these sneaky drug dealing, drive-by shooting cowards. And now they were gonna be my family for the next two years. I wished that I been sent to a prison where there were some mature older men--just there to do their time and get out; not a bunch a drifters and thugs that viewed prison time as a holiday.

Imagine, grown convicted men walking around with their pants nine inches below their waist, fighting over a neighborhood where none of them own property, hundreds of miles away. This is what was on my mind as we pulled into the prison yard about 9:00 a.m.

Just like I always heard, prison was a hotel suite compared to the county jail. I was even fortunate enough to have my own cell for the first three months. The assignment officer gave me a choice of three jobs: (1) in the kitchen, (2) picking up paper on the yard, and (3) working in the visiting room. The most beloved job in prison is working the visiting room because an inmate stands a pretty fair chance of catching a girlfriend. In the kitchen the appeal was that an inmate could eat better than the other guys. Walking around picking up paper was the least desired job because none of the cons wanted the other cons seeing them doing such lowly labor.

I chose the yard work because I didn't want my job to be envied by anyone. That may sound petty to the average person but I wasn't dealing with average people. If you worked in the kitchen, guys would come to you to steal or sneak them out something extra to eat. In the visiting room, guys will be trying to get you to slip someone a note or slip something into the units. Picking up paper on the yard meant you were just a flunky, and no one bothers you for favors.

Evelyn and I were still in communication when she was released after serving only three months. She was now enthralled in a legal red tape with the probation department for permission to relocate to Ohio. They approved the move two months later.

As I walked around the yard picking up paper five days a week, I soon realized the job had its advantages. I was one of the few inmates that could walk up on a group of cons, no matter what their race or gang affiliation without their conversation stopping or being altered. With my broom and scooper, I could eavesdrop on every discussion on the yard. Most of what I heard was drag about sexual experiences or big money and high rolling lifestyles. However, every now and then, I walked up on a smooth scam story. In which case, I lingered around and joined in the audience of listeners.

Often to sustain my welcome, I shared a juicy scam or two. The fellows enjoyed and respected my tales of crime. After awhile, a few guys were coming to me for advice on pulling off a successful con or fraud. It wasn't long before I began to have one or two walkers traveling the yard with me and even picking up a few pieces of trash. We talked about God, life, women, crime, law, business, and our children.

My knowledge of God came from a free Salvation Army Bible Study mail order course. I also was involved in a psychology course that I studied through the mail. I began studying psychology by writing to National University in Sacramento, and addressing the letter to the administrator. I requested information about where and how I could begin a mail order course of psychology and Christianity. The administrator replied with a short letter suggesting I contact the local library.

Her assistant, however, happened to be a psychology student working on her master's degree and was also a Christian Sunday School teacher. She didn't like the cold response her boss sent me. When she got home, she wrote me a personal letter. Ultimately, she and I became pen pals and later friends. Her name was Cindy Lester and she was slowly turning into my most reliable correspondence. Cindy mailed me books, although I sent her the money for most of them. Sometimes they were gifts. When she finally sent me a photo, which was about three months later, I discovered that she was a cute, brunette white woman with a full figure and magical smile. The guys considered me a 'Player' because a psychologist had become my friend.

One day the Holy Bible scripture Ephesians 4:28 jumped out at me and clung to my mind. It reads:

Let him that stole steal no more; but rather let him labour, working with his hands the thing which is good, that he many have to give to him that needth.

That passage pointed me in the direction of crime prevention. I figured that God was telling me to use my negative past to be a good service to HIM and society. The only thing I knew better than most people, including many criminals, was crime. I had over 25 years experience as a criminal, and now it was time for me to retire. The revelation hit me that I was in the perfect place and doing the perfect job to write a book on crime prevention. With all the cons on the yard sharing rip-off tales and what it took to stop them, I had a boundless source of esoteric tips.

In November of '89, once again in the wee hours of the morning, I found myself shackled to a chain of transferring inmates on a Los Angeles County sheriff bus with bars on every window. The only difference was, this time our direction was south on the highway. There were 50 or 60 prisoners on the bus. Only a half dozen of them were from the 'B' yard as myself. The rest of the guys, I never saw before. There were four yards at Mule Creek and each yard had its own housing units. Very seldom did inmates from one yard come in contact with those from another yard, unless they were sick and in the prison infirmary. This bus ride was much more subdued than my first. Probably because this load wasn't fresh from the streets and we all knew, 'What Time It Was.'

Cindy and I became closer friends and she had visited me twice. However, this move would create a bit of a hardship on her because I was being transferred a couple hundred miles farther from her home in Sacramento. My new home was Soledad State Prison, in Soledad, California. Soledad was an older institution with three security levels. A-level three yard where inmates lived in a cell and were monitored by guards with high powered rifles in gun towers. My ex-cellie, whose street name was 'Dirty,' warned me not to take a job on the yard, but to work indoors, if possible. The shooting incidents at Soledad were fives times more frequent than on the level three yard than at Mule Creek.

"But Dirty," I said, "I'm going to the level one yard."

"You must be on dope!" he snickered. "You may eventually end up on the level one yard, but all new inmates spend the first month or so on the level three yard."

Dirty was right. I stayed on the level three yard for two months. I was never transferred to the level one yard. Soledad had A-level two yard called the East Dorm. It was an Army barracks style living, enclosed in a small barbed wire yard with two gun towers. However, the living would be than on the three yard. Since my ultimate destination was the one yard, also called The Ranch, where no fences were in sight, no gun towers, no cells, and little violence, homosexual rapes, or drug use, I was looking forward to Soledad.

I accumulated, during my stay at Mule Creek, over 60 books. Mostly correspondence courses material in psychology, biblical, an alcohol and drug counseling course, and books from the Federal Government on crime prevention. My major regret was that I could only transfer 13 books because of fire safety. I made a gift of my literature to several inmates who expressed an interest.

Back home, problems continued as usual, but severe when during the early part of the year 1990. Tammie moved into my mother's rear house, where I had been living before my imprisonment. After being there only a few days, Tammie attempted suicide by fire and drugs. She swallowed a couple dozen sleeping pills, barricaded the entrance with furniture, some boxes that contained my clothes, that were in storage at my mother's house, then set the place on fire, and laid down to sleep. The fire department saved Tammie, and the back house, but most of my personals were destroyed. My nephew, Oscar, happened to be present at the time and was the fundamental reason his grandmother survived the ordeal. She fought desperately to break down the door in and effort to rescue her elder daughter. My nephew, Oscar, held her back with one arm, and with the other fought the fire with a garden hose until the fire department arrived. Tammie was then taken to a hospital and put on suicide watch. Elaine later told me that our mother was not trying to save Tammie, but her house.

My mother was one of my main correspondents and constantly kept me apprised on family matters. She told me that Evelyn and Carl went back together, but broke up again after two months. Evelyn was now seeing an old boyfriend who was so ignorant that he argued in the background every time my mother called their apartment in Ohio. He didn't want Evelyn to have contact with anybody. I had suspected something strange was going on because Evelyn didn't allow me to write her at home. Instead she received my letters at her mother's address. She never spoke of any problems. I imagined her locking herself in the bathroom and sitting on the floor for hours, as she did when we were together. Good old -NO PROBLEM- Evelyn, I never really knew or understood Evelyn, and perhaps never would.

My first cellie at Soledad, on the level three yard, was a young man of about 28-years-old, with the mind of an irrational 15-year-old. Naturally, he was a drug dealer and gang member. If profanity was stricken from his vocabulary, he would become mute. The cruelest punishment I endured during my entire incarceration was being celled with that lunatic. This young brother was a fiery eyed, peanut head, fool who loved to flex his undeveloped muscles. He often asked me, like a kid rushing home with a good report card, "Do you think my biceps or triceps are proper?" I wouldn't even lift my eyes from my Bible or any other book and answer, "Yeah, they're proper."

I called him King Lunatic, Jr., but it was only a thought, nothing I dared to share outside the solitude of my mind, especially to King Lunatic, Jr. He was a guy about three inches shorter than I and had what's known as a short man's or 'Napoleon' complex. The tin mirror above the sink was level with his nose. Therefore, he had to jump up to view his full face and jump twice as high to view his 'proper' biceps or triceps. I guess he stood about 5'7" or 8" and weighted about 150 pounds. He believed he was the toughest man on two feet. According to what I heard on the yard, he had been in a brawl with every cell mate he had, which were many. King Lunatic, Jr. also had physical altercations with a couple of the deputies. After I was in the cell with this pitiful man for four days, he accused me of trying to put him down by using big words.

"If you don't cut that white boy mess out," he swore, "I'll make you eat my fist!"

I looked over the top of my Bible and say, "Pardon me. What are you talking about?"

He jumped up from his lower bunk and stood in the center of our cell and proclaimed, "This is *MY* house. I was here first and you gonna learn ta' respect *MY* RULES!"

I could see he was stir crazy. Poor fool, been in and out of prison so much it had become *'his hood'*.

"If I exhibited an iota of tranquility or was derelict in my expeditious expression of appreciation, please accept my humble apology. This is YOUR domicile and I will evacuate," I said.

He didn't respond and silently returned to his bunk. About 30 minutes later, he engaged me in an unwelcomed conversation about rap music. King Lunatic, Jr. would name some group and ask me how I liked them. No one he named had I heard of, which pissed him off. I told him that I was more into jazz and not rap. He also took this information as a put down and started another argument. This time he was so loud that some inmates from other cells yelled up, down, and over to him. And he would yell back, "This cellie of mine ain't never heard of LL Cool J or Ice Tea or N.W.A. Ain't 'that a dirty shame'!"

None of the other cons replied, just remained silent waiting on his next move. I would pacify him by saying something like, "I bet you were one of the best rappers on the street. It's a shame how so many talented brothers aren't given an opportunity." He would say something like, "No bull man, no bull." King Lunatic Jr.'s name was Maxwell Porter. "Come on Maxwell," I said, "share a few with me. It's about time I caught up on the real world." And right away he started playing table bongo and making popping noises with his mouth and rapping a bunch of degrading lyrics about females and Black men. The Skinheads themselves have never said worse.

"Go Maxwell Go!"

Finally, before Maxwell retired to bed, he yelled to one of his buddies in another cell, "Hey, Homie, my cellie's all right!"

The next week, my request for a cell move was granted.

The next cellie I had was an older and mild mannered man, who introduced himself to me as 'Oop'. His response to why people called him Oop, was because of the song *'Alley Oop'* a hit in the 60's. Alley Oop was something Oop had to remind him of his younger and better days. We got along fine. Oop had a television which he let me watch any time.

Life on the three yard wasn't bad at all. There was a library, chapel, canteen and four housing units. Each unit housed about 600 inmates. I enjoyed walking the yard, though I didn't really know anyone, I didn't fell like a stranger in a foreign land. My ex-cellie King Lunatic Jr. would break away from the crowd he hung with and walked with me on the yard. He often talked about his life as a playboy. But when the time was just right I would turn the topic to his attitude. "Brother, you gotta realize," I said, "the system rejoices when you come to the pen or even live a fugitive lifestyle. You gotta stop letting other people's image of you control your behavior. You're an intelligent man, but you elect to act 'bad' because you've always been called 'bad'. Well, I call you 'intelligent'. So now it's up to you to choose who you want to make a lair, me or them." "But Jones I don't even read good," Maxwell replied, "so maybe you're the liar and they're right, 'cause I've always been able ta knock a nigga out. I bet you can't even guess how many white boys I dun punked out, 'cause I'm so bad." "You must understand something Maxwell, if you're proud that a bunch of men has made bowel movements and passed gas on you, what does that make you? Tough or sick?" " Jones! You're cold!" "Look Maxwell, you're an intelligent black man, and don't ever say you're not. Just count the number of rap songs you know my heart. Think about all the dances you can do. Think about all the women's telephone numbers you know. Think about all the sport teams that you know and the records of the players. That requires intelligence. Some dogs and monkeys are very intelligent. Intelligence only means the ability to learn quickly. Do you learn quickly! Of course you do! Now all you have to is choose more selectively what you learn. Now you tell me, who's the liar me or them?" Maxwell shouted, "They're a bunch of dirty lying fart holes, Jones. I'm as intelligent as they *is*." We busted out laughing.

On the three yard, I was on lock down one month because of my new arrival status. During to second month, the whole institution was locked down several times because of stabbings and shootings on the yard. My first two months there, four inmates had been stabbed (two fatal) and one inmate had been fatally shot by a high tower guard. At Soledad the only pre-shooting warning you got was a loud siren that could be heard all over the yard. Once as I was leaving the library, no sooner than I had gotten a few feet away, the siren sounded. Out of ignorance, I ignored it, and kept walking with my eyes glued to the pages of the Department of Justice Annual Crime Report.

Suddenly, I heard Oop call, "Jones hit the dirt!" Without looking around I hit the ground, as the gun fire erupted, and came to a crash landing. There were no less than eight shots fired by two rifles. When the sirens stopped, a loud voice came over the public address system and ordered everyone back to their housing units. As I rushed, not running, to my quarters, I noticed several Mexican gang members lying on the ground, bleeding from gun shot wounds and three of them still held knifes. We were locked down for two weeks following that incident.

After that lock down, I was moved to the East Dorm to await an opening on the one yard. It was a pleasure to leave the three yard behind. At the East Dorm the guards and the inmates were much more relaxed. The only thing I missed about leaving the three yard was the drama and writing classes that I had enrolled in. Teachers from a local college came to the prison once a week to teach courses. However, I had only attended one class each before I left the yard.

The East Dorm had no creative programs. I later discovered, a work-for-cash program was the only program offered there. I was assigned to the wood shop. We made furniture for use in state office buildings. If I am not mistaking, my pay was something like 70 cents an hour for eight hours a day, five days a week. Each month your earnings were posted to your trust account, and we could buy merchandise from the monthly canteen. I mostly brought stamps, writing paper, and of course, a few candy bars.

After work each day, I would shower and wait for the dinner line an hour later.

Following dinner, I usually worked on my book in solitude at my bunk. The cons notice which ones are loners and which ones are groupies. The loners are usually left alone, if they're not troublemakers. No one bothered nor disturbed me while writing. A few inmates asked why I spent so much time writing. When they learned that I was writing a book on crime prevention, many of them joined me during my yard walks and offered their criminal secrets.

There were only four guys from the East Dorm I deemed credible enough to extract information. The best con man on at the East Dorm was a black man about my age named, Maurice Phillips. We called him Phil. Phil was a high-roller by every sense of the term. The con games he worked on the streets kept him in expensive cars and the high rent district. He dealt with Persian Rugs, antiques, and art fraud. However, his forte was wire transfer.

In June 1990, my mother and oldest daughter, Yolanda came to visit me. Yolanda had completed high school the year before and left Mississippi within a few days. She became a student at Howard University in Washington, D.C. and lived on campus for one year. However, through her own procrastination and incomplete applications for federal grants, she was ineligible to continue the next semester without a large cash payment. Therefore, Yolanda was back in Los Angeles to attend a junior college until she saved the necessary tuition. My daughter stayed awhile with her grandmother and the rest of the time with the family of a girlfriend from college.

Though I was anxious to see them, I didn't bother shining my shoes or ironing my shirt. It still baffled me why guys spent so much time on their appearance in prison. Anything other than a bath, shave, and simple haircut, had to wait until I was free. Our visit lasted two hours but it seemed like only 30 minutes. We caught up on everything. They were glad to see me in such good spirits.

There are so many horror stories about prison, that most family members of convicts are overly concerned about their safety. My daughter even asked in a very sincere tone, "Are any of these men trying to bother you, Daddy?" I knew that she was speaking sexually and understood her concern. "No, Yolanda," I assured her. "Most of the men that get turned-out put themselves in that position. And the men who rape other men usually are frightened little fellows and feel that they have to do something outrageous to keep other frighten little men off them. If you understand that, and they know you understand that, then your problems are greatly reduced. Know what I mean?" "Yeah Daddy, I know what you mean," Yolanda said with a sigh of relief.

My mother grieved over Tammie's mental condition and the fact that she apparently hated her so much that she wanted to burn her house down. Elaine verbally attacked Mommy for being angry about her house. It had long been my feeling that my sisters carried a deep hurt from their childhood and it didn't take much for the pain to surface. Now don't get me wrong, our visit wasn't a sad one. We laughed till we cried on a couple occasions over incidents exchanged with one another. Memories of my mother visiting me when I was 17 at Camp Karl Holton repeatedly flashed into my mind. I wondered if Mommy saw me as a loser.

On the outside I smiled, laughed, and ate popcorn, but on the inside I felt empty. My mother and daughter had driven hundreds of miles to visit the closest a man in their life. Here I sat, practically, powerless and helpless. I couldn't even go to the toilet without asking a deputy's permission. This wasn't the way I wanted my beloved family to see me.

My only defense was to talk about my regal plans for the future. My anti-crime book, my poetry book in progress, my 'born again' conversion to Christianity, and most of all, my commitment to a crime free lifestyle. Never again did I intend to resort to crime, a loser's attempt to live an unearned good life.

Before my visiting time ended, another inmate beckoned me to the candy machine area where he swept the floor. It was a young drug dealer who worked in the visiting room. "Hey Jones, is that beautiful young lady your daughter?" He asked with a whispering grin.
"Yeah, so what!" I snapped.
He caught my negative tone and said, "Ahh man, don't be like that. Just ask her if I can write her."
I was insulted the fool even had the gall to ask me some idiotic junk like that.

I looked at him as if to determine if I were hearing things.

"What makes you think I would arrange for a drug user to be the father of my future grandchildren?" I snarled. "And if she did write to a loser like you, I would end up doing federal time for burning down every post office in the country. Don't turn our big sorry lips in my direction anymore."
When I rejoined them we only had time to kiss and say goodbye.

With only three months left until my release, I began writing letters to drug and alcohol treatment centers, seeking a position as a trainee counselor with their clinic. A list of substance abuse clinics was posted in the East Dorm Recreation Room for convicts seeking help for their substance addictions. I wrote to the ten clinics in the Los Angeles area. My letter was more of a resume. It informed the directors of my incarceration, drug and alcohol course, I studied in prison, my years as an alcoholic and how I had quit drinking and smoking nearly five years prior to my imprisonment. Of the ten inquires only five replied and three of those wished me well, but stated I needed a psychology degree to work in their facility.

The two facilities which responded favorably were the Crenshaw-Baldwin Family Center in the Crenshaw District of Los Angeles, and The Marina Mental Health Services in Westchester. Each clinic was guarded in their letter. Neither promised a job, but each invited me to arrange an interview with their office following my release. It was obvious to me, through my knowledge of the city, that the Crenshaw District clinic would be a predominately Afro-American staff and the Westchester clinic would be predominately white. I wondered whether they thought I was black or white or would it actually matter. No doubt, my chances would be better with the black clinic. However, I responded to both with an equal amount of enthusiasm. In two more months, I would know for sure.

My prison routine didn't change very much, though I had completed the 658 page manuscript for my crime prevention book. Each day after work, and practically all day on the weekends, I read brief histories of black achievers and composed history poems. I figured since black kids could remember profane rap lyrics so well, perhaps poetry could be an avenue to teach them their history. The poetry book that I was pulling together was called, AFRO AMERICAN POETRY TO GROW BY. This particular project was personally gratifying to me. The way I figured it, I would start a new volume after every seventy-five poems and strive to have them placed in elementary and junior high schools throughout The United States. The book of poetry highlighted black achievers such as Martin Luther King, Jr., Mahalia Jackson, and others.

Chapter 8

Saturday and Sunday were the most relaxing days of the week at the East Dorm, for most of the inmates, because the wood shop was closed. These were the days we shot the breeze and hung out on the yard. Everybody indulged in their particular pastime without a care. Some groups played cards all day, some basketball, others read, watched TV, slept, wrote letters, lifted weights, etc. Several of the brothers were now calling me 'Shorty' meaning my time was short before my release. Anybody with under a year left to serve in prison is considered short.

My two road dogs, George and Phil, and I walked the yard a lot. George arrived at the East Dorm from the three yard with me. We hung out together mainly because we were around the same age. George got married in the visiting room, and I was his 'Best Man.' He married his common law wife of several years; they had two children together. Now they were legally married and eligible for conjugal visits. That's when your wife and family can spend a couple of days on the prison compound with you in a provided cottage. The inmates call them, "Bone Yard Visits."

George was awaiting his first visit to The Bone Yard which would take place in about six more weeks, and that, coincidently, was the day of my scheduled release. We were both looking forward to September 19, 1990. George was trying to convinced Phil and me to work out with him so he would be in shape for the honeymoon.

"Come on Shorty," George said, "you gotta' be in shape anyway for when you hit the street. Them young girls ain't gonna be interested in an old man with a spare tire around his waist."

Phil and George laughed and Phil added, "That's right, Shorty, they want those hard bodies, someone that can go all night in bed."

I was only 10 or 15 pounds overweight but they were ribbing me because I was short more than anything else.
"Well let me assure y'all of one thing" I cheerfully responded. "If I'm with a chick to the point that I break sweat and she still wants more, then the next time she sees me, I'll tell her I'm under doctor's orders to take it easy on the delicate female body--I'm an animal."They cracked up.
"I don't blame you, Shorty," George said while chuckling, "I knew a chick once who was so fine and oversexed, she collected insurance money off two dead husbands. One was old. The other had a bad heart. Both died in bed with a smile on their face."

The six weeks flew by. I worked out with George part of the time and actually lost two inches off my 36-inch waistline. Though I didn't reach my goal of 32 inches, I was satisfied. However, my road dogs still teased me about the two-inch overlap saying, "Women don't wink at men coming out of the portly clothing shops."
And I fondly responded, "That's all right, I'll just stand out front the portly shop until a fine sister comes along that's looking for a kind ol' gent with a gut and a social security check."

My daughter, Yolanda bought me new clothes and mailed them to the institute. I was allowed to try them on three days prior to my release date. Cindy and her Mommy planned to be there to pick me up and take me to dinner before I headed back to Los Angeles. The big day for George and me had finally arrived. We were called to leave the East Dorm simultaneously.

Cindy and her mother, a woman I never met but had spoken to a dozen times on the phone, were a few minutes too late to pick me up from prison. If someone was waiting for you, you could leave with them. But if no one is there, by the time the prison transport bus left, all ex-prisoners must board to be dropped off at the local Greyhound Bus Station. A prepaid ticket in your name was held at the desk to take you to the city you're paroled to. In my case it was Los Angeles.

As I was waiting at the bus station for the next departure, Cindy came rushing through the lobby with her mother, Joahn a few steps behind. We all embraced like family. It was an endearing reception. I knew the few ex-cons who witnessed this reunion assumed Cindy was my woman and I was just another black man nuts about white women. Well, they were half right. I was nuts about Cindy but white had nothing to do with it.

When we first began writing one another, our race wasn't mentioned until several letters later. She was the first woman I befriended that I didn't harbor some secret agenda to bed down with or use financially. My affection for Cindy was purely innocent. Never before had a stranger embraced me with platonic love and warmth.

While I was incarcerated, through introspection, the revelation hit me that I had never truly loved or even liked women as human beings. However, I did truly like men. Men were like me. My friends. We could camp together, fish together, joke, play cards, hike, even become roommates, and there was never a need or desire for them to prove their affection for me by some sexual act or financial charity. But I didn't know one woman that I would buy a hamburger unless I wanted something in return. If I didn't get it, I would internalize that she was trying to 'USE' me. Seldom would I even speak to a woman on the street without mentally undressing her and glancing back at her behind. I realized that if truly loved women as human beings and not merely as objects of my sexual fantasy, I would befriend them for pure reasons, not selfish ones. Their physical appearance wouldn't matter. Their sexual preference, age, or the fact they were promiscuous or celibate wouldn't matter, if I learned to love women as human beings.

I made a firm commitment and accepted a personal challenge not to lure women into lustful situations, unless I had serious intentions of making her my one and only woman. I planned to seek a platonic friendship with at least one female, hopefully several. If I happen to meet and befriend dozens of females, I vowed not to taint our relationship with illegal money schemes or casual sex.

I wanted to feel an affinity with women the way I could with the male friends in my life. Cindy was my first chance to practice this new found discipline. If I was to ever attract a good friend, I had to learn to be a good friend. My prison experience provided me with an opportunity to take a deep look at myself.

It was about 10 o'clock as we drove along the Sacramento countryside. Cindy's mom, Joahn, asked me what I planned to do. Cindy answered before I could speak, without taking her eyes off the road, "Oh Mom, don't you remember I told you, Richard is a writer and a poet. He's gonna be famous, and on Oprah, you watch."

"Ah Cindy, I know Richard is gonna make it," Joahn replied. "But what I'm asking is, what about until then?"
"Well, Joahn, I don't know how it's going ta' turnout, but I have two phone numbers of mental health clinics that invited me to call them upon my release, regarding the possibility of working with alcoholics."
"I'm sure you'll get a position with one of them," Cindy said.

After about 30 minutes of driving along a scenic route of the ocean on one side and forestry on the other, Cindy finally said, "This is Carmel and the restaurant buried deep into this wooded area belongs to the superstar actor Clint Eastwood."
It resembled more of a ranch than a superstar's restaurant. Cindy parked her car facing a beautiful landscape of farm animals. After we ordered our lunch, we walked around the ground for about ten minutes. Cindy had a camera and we snapped a lot of pictures.

"Isn't Clint Eastwood also the mayor of Carmel?" I asked.
Joahn said, "Not anymore. He lost the last election."
When we finished lunch, Cindy drove me on a tour of downtown Sacramento, including pass National University College where she worked as an assistant administrator when we first began corresponding. However, since that time Cindy received her master's degree and was working for the juvenile court system as a child psychologist. Cindy was about five or six years my junior

and had been married to a lawyer for 13 years. He divorced her and married his law partner, a woman Cindy said she had befriended."But I won't allow that to sour my view of all women," she once said. I thought to myself, "Adultery is as common as a walk in the park."

After a brief stop by her apartment that I asked to see, my friends drove me to the Greyhound Bus Station in Sacramento. They waited with me for the full 40 minutes until my bus boarded. Our final embrace was sincere and spiritual. The three of us held hands as Cindy said a goodby prayer and thanked God for bringing me out of prison safe and sound.

My bus departed at 4:30 p.m. It had certainly been an adventurous day. I was headed for Los Angeles, which was a six-hour trip. The plan was for me to call my Guardian Angel mother (as usual) when I arrived, and she would pick me up from the bus depot.

As I reclined on the bus, I reminisced over the past two years. After a few miles I thought it was be nostalgic to read over the many letters I had received from my daughters. They had all been unhappy for different reasons. I begin to read Roxanne's letters first. She was the most unhappy in Mississippi. Her cousins, whom she lived with, would try to hurt her feelings by calling me a jailbird. Roxanne had been caught wearing her cousin's earrings without permission, so, every time something was missing or misplaced within their household she was blamed for it. Roxanne lived with one of her mother's brothers.

Jennifer lived with the Hanna Mae. And Jennifer's discontentment was based on the fact they lived too far out in the country. However, she liked the family and her new school. Rochelle lived with another brother and his family. Rochelle and Roxy lived near one another. Rochelle was also anxious to leave Natchez, Mississippi. Yolanda was now living in Los Angeles, however, she hated her short time living in the South. In her letters, she often claimed it was like living in prison.

The bus arrived in Los Angeles on schedule. The night was warm and I felt like walking. I enjoyed walking when I wanted to think. However, I knew my mother was expecting me to call and I didn't want to start off being a disappointment to her. She arrived at the bus station 20 minutes later. Though it was nice to be free and welcomed into someone's home, I sure wished it was the home of someone else. After our brief hug, and exchanges of smiles, the complaining began. My niece, Karen and nephew, Omar was staying at her home and were getting, as she would say, on her 'last' nerve. This was a clear warning of what was to come, but, my only alternative was a slop house where the parole department referred homeless men. Anyone would figure that if a man can make it through prison without any confrontations or disciplinary action against him, he surely could reside quietly with his mother . . . Right? Wrong!

It wasn't long before my presence joined Karen and Omar on my mother's last nerve, three days to be exact. Which was two days longer than I would have bet. I was extremely uneasy there and tipped around like a thief in the night in a futile effort not to disturb. I could not even get up through the night to get a glass of water without waking her up; the next morning I would certainly hear about it.

"I'm so tired. I didn't get to sleep until three this morning because that noisy neighbor next door had his music blasting. And then finally when I did dose off, somebody stomped through the kitchen, sliding chairs and slammed the refrigerator door. Lord, I don't know."
"Mommy, that was me," I would say, "just getting a glass of water."
She would look pitiful and say something like, "Did they allow you to get up in the middle of the night and slam refrigerator doors in prison?"
It was so easy to get set up for an argument. Even when fairness was in my favor, I would still lose.
Mommy would cleverly ask, "Am I in *your* house, or are you in *mine*?"
"This is your house Mommy."
"Oh I thought so. I was just checking."

Most of the time I could sidestep those argument traps but sometimes I blindly walked right into one. From the time I turned the shower on until the time I turned it off, my mother knew exactly how long the water ran. If it was five minutes instead of the allowed three minutes, I would hear about it from relatives. Elaine warned me, before I went to prison, that Mommy said, I had such a wild look in my eyes whenever she talked to me that she had become concerned for her safety and was sleeping with a loaded gun. It was impossible to be comfortable talking to her, wondering what she saw in my eyes and how she was going to react. Even now, two years later, I was still walking on egg shells.

After being released a week, I called the Crenshaw-Baldwin Family Center and spoke with Dr. Loretta Dunlap regarding our correspondence and asked for an appointment at her earliest convenience. My interview was set for 9:00 a.m. the next morning. I felt lucky. I then called my other contact, the Marina Mental Health Services and spoke with my correspondent Diane Kaufman, Ph.D. She and I discussed prison reform, alcoholism, rehabilitation, and my views on self-help groups in general before she gave me an appointment. The appointment was for the following morning at 11:30. I knew that both appointments would be easy to make, even by bus.

I had been busy all week sending query letters, seeking a publisher for my manuscript, Tips Against Crime, Written From Prison. I send off approximately 20 letters. My mother became annoyed with my letter writing and not seeking work, as she knew it. There was no convincing her this was work. Everybody in the family, including family friends, heard I had come home from prison to freeload. Thank God Karen and Omar was very encouraging regarding my success. I seldom mentioned or shared my poetry with my mother because that only fueled her suspicion of my freeloading intent. The check that I brought home from prison was $485, so I didn't need to borrow money, right away.

The morning sun found me out at 8:00 a.m. standing on the corner of Crenshaw Blvd. and Pico waiting for the number 210 south bound bus. The trip was refreshing. I loved looking out the window and girl watching. However, there were more strawberries (a female strung out on crack) wandering the streets offering herself to anyone with the price of another hit on the pipe than I ever imagined. I hated the fact that so many sisters had gone to the dogs.

Sex was one of the last things on my agenda and I wasn't tempted by short skirts and see-thru blouses. My concentration was steadfast on issues of substance; reuniting with my children, getting published, and landing a drug counselor position.

When the bus stopped at Stocker Avenue, I exited and walked west until I reached International House of Pancakes about two blocks away. I stopped there for a quickie breakfast because I still had 25 minutes to kill and my destination was only a five minute stroll. After swallowing my last bite of pancakes, I left with exactly five minutes to be there. Punctuality is something we're all judged by, whether you care or not.

At nine o'clock, I was opening the door of the Crenshaw-Baldwin Family Center. There was a fair skinned, petite, middle-aged woman with long black hair, and wearing eyeglasses in the reception window.

"Good morning," I said. "My name is Richard Jones and I have a nine o'clock appointment with Dr. Dunlap."

The woman rose and extended her hand through the window while saying, "Good morning Mr. Jones, I'm Doctor Loretta Dunlap. I see you're punctual. That's an admirable quality."

"Thank you, Doctor Dunlap," I said as we gently shook hands. "Please Mr. Jones, come on around here where can chat." Her office was empty of patients and staff members. There were at least a half dozen therapy rooms plus a large office at the end of the corridor. The waiting room was nicely furnished and could accommodate about 20 people.

Our discussion went on for over an hour, with only a few phone interruptions. Dr. Dunlap was a shapely lady of about 5'2" or 3". She told me that her clinic had been in the community for more than 20 years and their specialty was family mental health. Many of their cases were referred by the courts, such as child abuse cases. However, my proposal of establishing an anti-drug self-help group truly appealed to her and she had discussed it with her Board of

Directors who endorsed the idea.

"The only problem that I see Richard, is that the clinic has no available funds to sponsor such a project. In other words you can only be paid if you can bring in the funds to support such a viable idea. You may seek volunteers and write a grant. We're a nonprofit organization and our charter will be your auspice."

She paused and sat calmly the way psychiatrists do, waiting and measuring my reaction. Her hands were clasped in her lap. Dr. Dunlap was one of the best listeners I had encountered. It was almost as if you were her patient and it was her job to extract information by encouraging you to kept talking. Our meeting was over at 10:15. We agreed I would come into her office and work on my plans twice a week for four hours a day.

When I arrived at the Marina Mental Health Clinic, it was 11:25 a.m. There were several patients sitting in the waiting room. All ages, all sizes, all white. The young fat blonde receptionist looked crazy enough to be sitting in the waiting room, listening for her name to be called, instead of calling names of visitors. She had on more makeup than Bozo the Clown, and her lipstick looked like it had been applied by an intoxicated blind man with the jitters. None of her colors matched and she was smacking gum while smoking a cigarette. She just stared at me. I made the first move.

"Good morning, I have an appointment to see Richard Jones. I mean Diane Kaufman." I shamefully corrected.
"Well who are you?" she slowly shook her head from side to side and uttered under her breath, "Mm, they're all crazy." Then I noticed she wasn't even a blonde. There was about a handful of reddish hair hanging free from underneath the wig which drooped over her right ear. You *are* crazy!" I grumbled. "And I'm crazy too for standing here." With that, I did an about face and exited without looking back. As I exited the door the receptionist said loudly, "Of course this means no parking validation."

Every morning about six o'clock, I went for an hour walk, except Sundays. On Sundays, I liked to walk in the afternoon no matter what the weather condition. On my second Sunday of walking I asked a middle-aged, redhead, black woman wearing a white uniform, where I might find jobs as a hospital orderly. I figured she was a nurse. When I noticed her, she was pumping gas into her car at a corner gas station.

"Excuse me madam," I said. "May I ask you a question?"
She turned toward me and I could see tension building in her. I proceeded with measured caution.
"I was just wondering if you were a nurse," I called from the sidewalk and dared not to invade her space. Our distance was about two car lengths. She called back, "Yes I'm a nurse, but this is my church uniform. I'm on the Nurses' Board. Why?"
"I was hoping you knew some hospital orderly jobs available," I answered. "But if you don't mind, I prefer you direct me to a good church."

Gradually, she began to relax and invited me closer with a smile. I slowly moved in her direction as I continued speaking.
"I have only been in town for two and a half weeks from the Sacramento area and I would like to attend church services." She was elated. Her eyes were dancing with excitement. I told her, "I'm live around the corner on Crescent Heights near Airdrome with my mother. She doesn't belong to a church, so she can't recommend one."

Now we were standing six feet apart. I didn't dare move any closer. During our conversation, I discovered that her name was Margaret Brown, she was married and a member of Cochran Avenue Baptist Church. We felt that it was a coincidence that she also lived on Crescent Heights and just a half block from my mother. Margaret offered me a ride to church with her next Sunday and I accepted. We exchanged telephone numbers and bid each other a nice day. That's what was missing in my life, a church home.

The next Sunday morning I rose with church and Margaret Brown on my mind. We hadn't spoken to one another since our meeting but I was sure she hadn't forgotten our date. About ten that morning, Karen called me to the phone, "Uncle Rick, telephone," she yelled. I was smiling because this would be my first call from a woman, and, I was about to be chauffeured to church by one. I gloated as I asked Karen, "Who is it?" She had a surprised look on her face as she replied, "Pastor Percy Hill."

The man identified himself as Pastor Percy Hill and told me that he was calling in behalf of Sister Brown. He said her husband suggested that a man should offer me a ride. And he was happy to do so, if I still wanted to attend church services. "Yes sir," I said, "I'm serious about going to church." He read the address Margaret had given him and asked me if that was correct. I confirmed it and he told me he would arrive in about 15 minutes. It impressed me to no end to be driven to church by the pastor. I felt quite special. Though, the next Sunday and every Sunday thereafter, I made it to church on my own. Two months passed, before I saw Margaret Brown in church.

In the meantime, I was working with Dr. Dunlap three or four days and often several nights per week. My duties were answering the phone, making appointments, escorting her to many business meetings that required setting up exhibits, tables and displays. Dr. Dunlap was the president of The Association of Black Professionals from 1985 to 1991. Her presence was required at numerous functions and social affairs. I drove her around in her older model Rolls Royce. I often helped her do personal things, like moving heavy objects, at her North Hollywood condo.

We'd applied for various grants and funding from numerous resources to expand the programs and services at the center. Meanwhile, I was basically hanging around waiting on the response in order to establish an anti-drug/anti-crime self-help group. I had the assurance of Dr. Dunlap that she was 100 per cent behind me and was positive my ideas would result in a national phenomenon.

When Dr. Dunlap spent Christmas and New Years with me, I was sure she didn't have a love interest in her personal life. On Christmas she ate dinner at my mother's house and on New Years we went to a movie. Though we spent much time together there were never any touching, no hugs, no pecks on the cheek--just business, and platonic friendship--until March '91, that is.

I remember the exact month so well because I still celebrated my freedom by counting the months until I reached one year parole. And in March, I was half way. I had since moved out of my mother's house and was renting a room from a preacher, named Reverend McDaniel, for $500 a month. Reverend McDaniel was on the pastoral staff of The St. Jude Baptist Church in Long Beach. At Cochran Avenue Baptist Church, I joined the choir, and maintained perfect church attendance for six months.

On this particular night, Dr. Dunlap and I were having dinner at her home when it started to rain. The downpour was completely unexpected. Usually, I stayed no later than 10:00 p.m. because the last bus to my place ran at 10:20, and the bus stop was a 10 minute walk. We began eating about 7:30. Even dining with Dr. Dunlap was a challenge because of her nit-picky personally.

She sought to use proper English with every utterance. When she detected an improper use of the English language by her faithful assistant, immediate correction was of necessity. If I used a double negative, or got my potatoes and 'tatoes, tomatoes and 'matoes, crossed, she was on me like an elementary school teacher. This happened a lot because we were together ofteOO When we ate together she, never failed to criticize my table etiquette. I chewed either too fast, or too slow, or used the wrong knife to spread my butter, etc. She would engage me in conversation during a meal, and as soon as I responded to a comment, she would say in a very proper and soft tone, "Don't speak with food in your mouth Richard."
I remained calm and polite and said, "My dear Loretta, you also have food in your mouth."
She seldom responded to any criticism. I loved the way she could remain stoic under fire. I desired to achieve that level of self-control. She would continue chewing silently and then ask, "Would you care for more tea Richard?" I also admired the way she could sidestep a confrontation.

The rain was still pouring at 9:30 and Dr. Dunlap wouldn't dare consider driving me home or even to the bus stop in such a storm. "Oh my Richard," she said, "you're gonna get drenched out there. Would you like to borrow my umbrella?"

"Do you have an *extra* umbubrella? 'Cause I might not see you tomorrow or not until late Monday and you may be needing it." She smiled and said, "That's very thoughtful of you, Richard. If only you were as thoughtful about your grammar. It's not um-bu-brella, it's an umbrella. And will you please reframe from using so many unnecessary *'be's*. And yes, I do have another."

I learned to ignore the impulse to respond to every flag of criticism and instead view it as a flag of improvement opportunity. "Thanks Loretta, I often make that mistake. I surely appreciate your corrections."

Most of the time, I was more comfortable addressing her as Dr. Dunlap rather than Loretta, even in private. I dared not call her Loretta at the office or in the company of other doctors. Not that she ever verbally insisted on formality, I just sensed her feelings on the subject and acted according.

"Richard, I have a better and more sane idea," she said rising from the sofa and going toward the closet in her den.

"What idea Loretta?"

She reached into the small closet and retrieved two neatly folded blankets and a pillow and said, "You can sleep right here on the floor."

"Yeah thanks. I was hoping you took pity on me."

We both laughed. We were always laughing about something. Dr. Dunlap considered me so funny and witty that she once told me, "Though you hold no degree Richard, you're one of the most interesting and delightful people I've worked with."

One of the reasons she was so taken by me was that I showed her how I could work at the Center and be paid by the government. During this time the government had a Job Placement Training Act (JPTA) Program in effect. The JPTA reimbursed an employer 50 per cent of the wages they paid an employee in training. Therefore, I applied for the program through the Crenshaw-Baldwin Family Center as my employer. My starting salary, while in training was alleged to be $12 per hour, 20 hours a week as a Community Liaison Officer Trainee. The clinic would write me a check each week for $240. I would cash the check and return $120 to Dr. Dunlap in cash. The JPTA Program reimbursed the clinic 50 per cent of my wages, therefore, the clinic would eventually receive all their money back. In essence, Dr. Dunlap had free labor. I didn't mind the low wages because I had bigger plans for our relationship when one of our grants came through. That's when all my time, effort, and sacrifice would pay off.

The blankets were spread on the floor near the sofa. I suspect she thought too much of her sofa for me to sleep on it. Certainly I wasn't going to make it an issue. Instead, I made a move in another direction.
"Would you like a massage Loretta," I asked in a nonchalant tone. Her face sparkled and her speech danced its way into my ears, "Oh that would be heavenly."

This would be the first massage I'd given in more than three years. She excused herself from the room and went upstairs saying she would be right back. Dr. Dunlap's home was a tri-level condo. Her living room was on the first floor, the dining room, den, and kitchen on the second, and her bedroom and office on the third.
Doctor Dunlap returned in about five minutes, wearing silk long pants pajamas. I last saw her in a business suit.

"Hey, Hey, Hey!" I teased imitating 'Fat Albert'.
"You sure know how to relax."
"I felt so confined in that stuffy outfit," she said. "If I was home alone, I would've tossed it at the door."
I though to myself, "So this is Loretta, pleased ta' meet ya".
"Now what about that massage you were talking about?" she said lowering herself to the pallet.

Dr. Loretta Francis Dunlap had a colorful past. Throughout her childhood she had very few friends because she was so studious and proper, according to her. She had a twin sister, Rosetta, who died while in their twenties. Her sister always had many more friends. The kids would only play with Loretta because of Rosetta, or, if Loretta helped them with their homework. All the adults loved Loretta, because of her precociousness, especially the school teachers. As expected by everyone, she received a full academic scholarship.

Dr. Dunlap had shared her past, with me, during our sequestered late night office hours. "When I arrived at The University of California Los Angeles (U.C.L.A.) in the early 50's," she said, "I was one of very few black students on a four-year scholarship. My scholarship was for Advanced Science, however, the school awarded me additional benefits for competing on the swim team. In those two areas, I was the only black student.

This is where the story gets colorful. During one of her swim meets, she was introduced by her coach to a middle-aged handsome black man. As it turned out, he was an influential and wealthy person. They went out to dinner that same day. Within a week, he persuaded her to move into her own apartment, off campus, at his full expense.

Throughout her college days and several years thereafter, he took royal care of all her needs. She said that they would spend little time together because he was out of town a lot. When he was in town, most of his time went to his wife and children. Which was perfect with her because she had more time to study and plan her career. When they went out, it was in a chauffeured limousine. She rubbed elbows with celebrities and high ranking city, state and government officials. Dr. Dunlap said she lived shrouded with guilt that her sister and parents had her on such a scholarly pedestal, all the while, she was nothing but a well-kept mistress.

"What really haunts me, Richard," she said, "is knowing I sold my virginity. I honored it, fought for it, cherished it, lost boyfriends over it. I was saving myself for my wedding night. I sold my innocence within two days of sampling the crumbs of wealth." What compounded Loretta's inner grief was the memory of her sister's death. Rosetta, the single mother of three children, by three different fathers, had been arrested for soliciting prostitution. Rosetta committed suicide rather than face in humiliation of disgracing her family. Her children were raised by their elderly and poor grandparents because Loretta refused to interrupt her career by returning to Arkansas in loving pursuit of her sister's children.

When her Sugar Daddy died in the late 1960's, he remembered her in his will.

With her inheritance, she established Crenshaw-Baldwin Family Center in 1971. She later married an Afro-American Navy Admiral in 1973. Who was from a wealthy family in South Carolina. However, he was a mama's boy and insisted they live with his widowed mother, who owned a huge estate. They had full time servants and dressed formally for dinner every evening. Her husband was killed in a naval accident. Admiral Dunlap's widow now received many governmental benefits. Dr. Dunlap always spoke of him very highly and said that her six-year marriage was the happiest time of her life.

"There were only three men of any significance in my life," claimed Dr. Dunlap. The third was a Black Muslim Minister. They met at a Sickle Cell Enemia Fund Raiser sponsored by the Crenshaw-Baldwin Family Center in 1983. They began to date and eventually he became the administrator of the clinic. Dr. Dunlap said that not only was he extremely handsome but was an eloquent powerful speaker and had superb letter writing skills. He absconded six years later after embezzling the clinic into insolvency. Minister Luther X's treachery explained Dr. Dunlap's paranoid suspicion of my every move around the office. Whenever she observed me glancing in her direction while she was reading something, she accused me of trying to read over her shoulder. She was careful not to let me know the security code, safe combination, or handle any medical payments. When I heard the story about Minister Luther X, I fully understood why and had compassion for Loretta's suspicious disposition.

I love giving an appreciative woman a massage. And under the best circumstances, a massage can be more erotic than other more common pleasures. However, when you're caressing a woman with tensed emotions and a half dozen 'Don't-touch-me-there' signs mentally tagged all over her body, this is tantamount to being allowed to sit down to a sumptuous meal with you hands tied behind your back and mouth gagged. Yet, your eyes and nostrils may feast lavishly. Thus was the case with massaging Dr. Dunlap.
As she laid prone on the blankets, with her pajama top and bottom on, I was only secure enough to allow my fingers to tip along her spine, shoulders, neck, and legs--nothing else. Every time I dared into private areas I could feel her body tighten. After 10 minutes of this child play I ventured into deeper waters. I kept the conversation flowing with office business.

Dr. Dunlap moaned with pleasure and purred, "How lovely." When I began to feel her hips rotate under the palm of my hands, my heart nearly stopped. Dr. Dunlap's hips moving could only mean one of two things. She was beginning to relax or we were having an earthquake. A quick glance around the room confirmed we were not experiencing the latter. Boldness entered my hands like an electric volt and I freely began to squeeze through her thin material. I continued my aggressiveness for a few minutes, then asked her to roll over. From the supine position, I began massaging her more sensually with no resistance. Loretta laid there humming lightly with her eyes closed. When Loretta felt my hands beginning to take liberties, she snapped back into Dr. Dunlap.

"Why thank you Richard," she said in her cultivated tone. "That is quite enough."

We resumed our conversation about office business and other manners from my place on the den floor on the second level, with her in the bedroom on the third. Finally, I yelled up, "May I come upstairs and make my pallet closer to you." "All right come on up!" she called back. My pallet was spread next to her bed like a throw rug. I was wearing only my undershorts and T-shirt. We talked about five more minutes, when she said, "You may get in the bed if you promise to restrain yourself and allow me to sleep." "Sure, no problem!" I said and quickly got into bed. I didn't make anybody contact or attempt anything. After about 15 minutes Loretta curled up under my arm and laid her head on my chest. As we talked, I unbuttoned her top and caressed her more. Loretta's body was very fragile, every few minutes she was complaining that I handled her too roughly. She stopped me several times and gave me detailed instruction. "Are you sure your hands and nails are clean? You're handling me too harshly, Richard. I better not get an infection. Slow down. Be careful there! Oh my! Oh my! Oh wait, I'm not ready! Mmmm, ahhh, that's heavenly."

As the weeks went by I came to know Loretta's body and could make love to her without complaints. Though I didn't consider myself in a fulfilling relationship, I had better sense than to grumble. It was a feather in my egotistical hat. In fact, I was so proud of my accomplishment, I invited

Yolanda to have dinner with us on one occasion, at the impressive home of Dr. Dunlap. My daughter was also overwhelmed that her uneducated father was romantically linked to a successful woman, a doctor at that.

During the seven months since my prison release, I worked diligently pulling my poems into book form. Finally, I self-published my first book of poetry called, Afro American Poetry to Grow By. The best thing I had going was my membership in a poetry group called, The Frontline Poets. It's president, a portly, short, brother about 50-years-old named Sunji Ali, taught me the performance side of poetry. It was during my first meeting with the Frontline Poets that I recited my work for an audience. Once a month, we performed at The Goodlife Health Food Store in the Crenshaw district. The Frontline Poets were also regularly invited to perform at schools, libraries, and museums.

My book, Tips Against Crime, Written From Prison, was accepted by Sandcastle Publishers of South Pasadena and was released by June '91. The sales from this book, my book of poetry and paid performances provided enough money to send for my children. Though we wanted to reunite immediately, I waited nearly a year, until school was out for the summer so their education would not suffer interruption. Also, I couldn't afford to reunite immediately. I had become a columnist and given a by-line in The San Diego Voice and Viewpoint Newspaper. My column was an anti-crime column called, 'Watchdog'.

My children were on an Amtrak train, on their way from Mississippi and were due to arrive in two days. I recently moved out of the Reverend McDaniel's rooming house and rented a two-bedroom apartment. My mother lent me $2000 and bought me some furniture. Mommy put no restrictions on my pay back date. She merely told to repay her when I was able.

Dr. Dunlap and I were drifting apart. She felt strongly that I should leave my children in Mississippi until my finances were stable. I knew her true reasoning was not in the best interest of my family. Dr. Dunlap rightfully assumed, I did not intend to maintain long hours away from home. Therefore, I wouldn't be available around the clock to her clinic or our quasi-affair.

On the eve of my daughters' arrival, The Frontline Poets performed their standing engagement at The Goodlife Health Food Store. The Rose Gale Trio backed us up with their jazz ensemble. The audience consisted of 35 to 40 people, which was a pretty good crowd considering the size of The Goodlife. One third to one half of the audience were Frontline Poets. And there were a few nonmembers waiting for the open mic session of the show, so they could recite their material. Most black poets wrote poems about the black experience. Some material was angry, while some was spiritual, and there were the Love poems, and poems of personal experiences. I appreciated them all except for those which were vulgar. If I had my way, a fourth of the Frontline Poets would have to polish up their act or sit on the sidelines. And some of those open mic readers wouldn't be allowed to open their mouth except to say, "I'm leaving."

However, Sunji Ali and his vice president, Dadesi X, though very spiritual brothers, tolerated an excessive amount of alley trash in the name of 'Free Expression'. On this day, I planned to introduce my new self-published book of spiritually inspired poetry entitled, Do You Really Know What Time It Is? This book had earned me a column in a Christian newspaper named, The A.C.C. Church & Community Newspaper. My column was also entitled, 'Do You Really Know What Time It Is?'

When Dadesi, the emcee, introduced me as the next performer, I was still undecided about which poem to perform. Then it came to me since there were many black women in the audience who wore long manicured fingernails that were most likely done at one of the many oriental nail shops. I had recently composed a poem that spoke to the issue of African American women respecting themselves, truly caring for their children, being conscientious about their health and paying less attention to the superficial. It would be the first time I recited this piece. I was a little concerned that sisters would become embittered. However, I decided to go with my feelings. I knew the poem had a message and someone needed to hear it.

I scanned the crowd and found five attractive women at the same table. Each appeared to have just left church, based on their dressy attire. The timing was perfect.

"I would like to recite a poem that was written for the love of my people," I told the audience. With that statement there were a few amens coming forward and scattered applause.

"This is a message that is desperate for an open mind and hungry ear." I paused in silence for about five seconds to build up a level of anticipation.

"The title of this poem is, *'That's Why You Ain't Got Nobody'.'*" There was a barrage of laughter, especially from the table of five. I quickly twisted my body toward to the jazz trio behind me and shook my head from side to side, meaning 'no accompaniment.' Another three seconds of silence. Then I got my flow on . . .

"There are markings and scribbling sketched on your skin
Oh tattooed woman, what has America done?
Your sensual mouth bears the bitter taste of the tobacco leaf
The delicate brain of your children is gasping on second hand smoke. Your
once ivory white teeth are stained. And the tenderness in your words have
vanished on a cloud of profanity. YOU HAVE come a long way baby!
The glitter that was once in your heart, is now upon your finger and toe
nails
Applied by dainty oriental hands-in your African community
Paid for with the tears of your welfare check, the sweat of your low wage
job, and the deferred college aspirations of your child
You must look gorgeous, you say! Therefore, heads may turn your way.
What have you done to embellish your mind? Your spirit? And your soul?
The man you sleep with, sent by your psychic friend, is not yours
He belongs to the World of Slave Mentality
On loan from the revolving doors of promiscuity, another woman's children
call him daddy. And the lies he whispers are drifting on the wind. Your
children once again are confused.
Someday a prince will take you away? You dream, you wish, you pray. But
of course, he must be the supreme gift to womankind
Tall, muscular, handsome, great job, and ah yes! Treat you ALMOST
special
Have you forgotten that it was YOU! The Mother of Humanity! Queen of
Civilization! The Goddess of Beauty! That danced along the riverbank in the

moonlight
The passionate imagination of every warrior, and the envy of every swan.
Now you dance bare and trade your god-given womanly jewels for drugs,
trinkets, and illusions.
YOUR Crown! What have you done to your crown?
Your proud, prominent native hair that spoke stately to our GOD,
announcing your presence
I AM HERE MY LORD!
Who is this press and curl colored girl?
Beautiful African woman, it's time to awake.
You're more than an image in the lake
And your children are watching!

Woman, woman, God's gift to the land.
The nectar of life is in your hand

God gave you breasts to nourish a nation,
But man says your breasts are his Erotic Shrine . . .
And you forbid your baby. It is all vanity under the sun.
And ah! Little woman of independent means, long days at the office. With
platinum credit cards. Your children call you 'Stranger'.

You stuff their dinner in a micro wave oven
You have no time for mother/child lovin'

Oh my wayward African Princess, what has America done?
You first must love your soul, not in words only
But with the boldness of thunder, and the shyness of a breeze
A living sacrifice unto God. For God ordains the steps of a virtuous woman
. . . That's Why You Ain't Got Nobody!

"Thank you," I told the shocked audience. The applause was mixed. Many
didn't know what to think. However, two of the women at the table of five,
wanted to buy it. I felt good about that piece.

The Union Station in Downtown Los Angeles is a very historical building. It's huge with long tunnel passage ways from the train to the station lobby. The walk can take up to ten minutes for a healthy person. The ticket counters put me in the mind of the check-in desk of a gigantic hotel. There are park benches every 50 feet or so along the walkway but closer together in the lobby. Many movie scenes have been shot from The Union Station and just being there reminded me of an Al Capone movie.

I wondered why no shoeshine boys were there as I had been at the Union Station in Downtown St. Louis 35-years-ago. Perhaps the boys these days thought the only way to hustle was to steal or sling dope . . . I wondered.

The time was 2:13 p.m., which meant the train was nine minutes late. Though I tried not to worry, worry I did. It had been three years since I had seen Roxy, Jennifer, and Rochelle and now the darn train was nine minutes late. How safe are trains anyway? Perhaps they got on the wrong train or maybe I miswrote the information their Aunt Hanna Mae me. I tried to relax by reading a newspaper, but every few minutes, I found myself looking at the big wall clock, and my watch . . . 2:28. Just as I was approaching the huge hotel counter there was a herd of people coming down one of the quarter mile tunnels. My feet automatically stepped in that direction. Some of the other waiting people joined my rush toward the crowd.

I spotted my darling trio and began to trot toward the pack of travelers. None of my girls broke into a trot, or even a fast step, but they couldn't hide their bulging smiles. Oh these girls are trying to keep their cool, I thought. How ladylike of them! Roxanne was now 11-years-old, Jennifer was 13, and Rochelle was 15. Three years had matured them a great deal. They all looked a great deal alike. A middled-aged blacked female passenger who walked in proximity of the girls smiled at me as I was rushing toward them. As I passed her, she joyfully said, "There's not doubt that you're their daddy. They're such lovely and well-behaved girls."

Each girl was carrying two suitcases. Hanna Mae was supposed to ship the rest of their belongings by United Parcel Service. After we hugged, kissed, and exchanged warm verbal greetings, we headed toward the main exit doors. Once outside, I hailed a taxi. I told the driver the exact route to take. Which was to continue east on the Santa Monica Freeway until we reached Arlington, make a right turn and continue to Country Club Drive, make a left and continue three blocks. It was my duty to teach my girls to be aware of price hiking cab drivers.

After we unpacked the suitcases, we were just about to walk to the pizza parlor two blocks away. When Jennifer opened the door for us to leave, there stood their grandmother, Nate, and Yolanda. By coincidence, Nate was holding two pepperoni pizzas.

Soon after their arrival, perhaps one week later, I applied for Social Security Survivor Benefits in behalf of my children. Within three weeks I was receiving $120 a month for each daughter in my custody. This totaled $360. I allowed the girls to manage their money. Roxy however, spent her money unwisely and was usually broke before the next pay period. Therefore, I sometimes would issue her a weekly allowance.

The girls were surprised to see me going to work every day. This was the first time in their lives that I held an honest job. The fact I was working in a doctor's office as an assistant struck them as funny. However, I could see they were proud of me, and that made the low wage position seen like ten times more than it was. The real shocker came on Sundays. None of my daughters had ever known me to attend church. Now I sang in the choir. As I lifted the name of Jesus in song, I could see my daughters, sitting in the congregation, snickering. They didn't know how to handle the shock, and I didn't sing well, my 'barking' messed up the flow of the songs. They told me they could hear me over the entire choir singing off key. I laughed and told them, "I won't go to hell for singing off key, and I won't get to heaven by singing on key."

Soon Yolanda and my niece, Karen, would show up on Sundays just to tease my singing. I didn't care. If my obnoxious crooning would bring more people to church, I would howl from the church steeple. A few weeks later, Roxanne and I got baptized on the same day. The entire church lifted our souls in prayer. I was sure God's hand was on my family. No longer was I concerned with seeking a female role model for my children. However, I didn't want my parental disciplines to be harsh or too masculine. During Sunday school, I discovered in The Holy Bible, King James version, Titus 2:3-5; instruction is given for female role models:

The aged women likewise, that they be in behavior as becometh holiness, not false accusers, not given to much wine, teachers of good things; That they may teach the young women to be sober, to love their husbands, to love their children. To be discreet, chaste, keepers at home, good, obedient to their own husbands, that the word of God be not blasphemed.

Whenever I was unsure of how the handle a family situation, I consulted with a spiritually mature mother at Cochran Avenue Church. Sister Patricia Hill, the pastor's wife, was one of several women who assured me that I could always come to her for advice. Often, I did just that.

Eventually, I dropped out of the choir because my work shift changed. Dr. Dunlap insisted working late Thursday evenings, which precluded choir practice. She was understanding about my not being all the time, but she fought hard to interfere with my church commitment. She offered me extra work hours on Sundays, which meant no church service for me. I declined the offer. The clinic's contract with JTPA had expired and Dr. Dunlap was now paying me from her payroll account. Dr. Dunlap was becoming more irritable and impatient. Our proposals and grants applications were rejected. The office needed a bonafide grant writer and I wasn't qualified. Ultimately, she asked me to aid her as a volunteer and seek other means of employment, until some benefactor approved one of our grant applications. Of course, this terminated our business relationship and severely hindered our personal one. Eventually, I placed an ad in the church bulletin as a handyman. Many members gave me work. Besides this, I survived on book sales and poetry performances.

In April 1992, all hell broke loose when an all white jury in Simi Valley, a suburb of Los Angeles, brought in a not guilty verdict for four white Los Angeles Police Officer charged with, attempted murder and excessive force. The alleged victim was a black man named Rodney King. The assault on

Rodney King was video tape recorded by a witness, and aired repeatedly on nationally television. The opinion of the public, black people in particular, was the cops were guilty. A major riot followed that took many innocent lives. Fires, looting, and total destruction in many communities throughout the nation lasted for weeks.

Finally, when the smoke cleared, things were back to business as usual. My answer to the problem of police brutality was to teach young black boys to reduce their likelihood of being the victim of this cycle of injustice. Education, clean living and a crime free lifestyle was the solution, as I saw it.

While listening to a Christian radio station, hosted by Dr. Roy Petitt, I heard about this Afro-American Big Brothers' organization called, The Rites of Passage. Dr. Petitt, who was the pastor of The Miracle Center Apostolic Church in Los Angeles, invited parents to register their boys and adult males to volunteer as mentors. I called the number within the next several days and spoke to Dr. Petitt. He welcomed me to come to their next meeting Tuesday night at seven o'clock. The Miracle Center was a huge beautiful church on Western Avenue near Adams. At my first meeting there was about 18 boys who ranged in ages from 7 to 16. There were two groups in progress, a classroom for boys and another for girls. Both were taking place on the second floor of the two story building. The Rites of Passage is an all male's program, but The Miracle Center took their church involvement to a co-ed level.

As a mentor, I sought to recruit boys and girls, including my three, into the program. My daughters complained that going to the group each week interfered with their homework. After a few weeks, I allowed them to stay home on the nights of the meetings.

For the next several months, all was well. The girls were doing terrificly in school and were involved in various church programs and clubs. My daughters and I went swimming, to church functions, and poetry readings together. In fact, more than once, each of them recited a poem during the open mic session. I would bribe them, of course. Jennifer even recited one of my poems before the whole church congregation. I was proud of them and I think, they were proud of me.

In January '93, I enrolled in a Public Access Cable Television Production course in the city of Eagle Rock. After completing the short course, I began to produce a Public Access Cable Television Show called, 'Tips Against Crime'.

Toward the end of February '93 The Frontline Poets were invited to perform at The Bilbrew Library for a Black History Program. This location is very historical. Many poet greats performed there including Maya Angelou. The Bilbrew Library has an extensive collection of Afro American Literature. Many of Los Angeles finest rising poets were on hand such as; Yvette LaVerne Sang'iewa who introduced her first book entitled, 'Soliloquy, Design of My Life'. Lady Zita also introduced her new book entitled, 'Message to My People.'

The Multi-Culture Room at Bilbrew was packed. Sunji Ali invited dozens of people, including the print media. All four of my daughters and two of my friends from church were there. They were Gaynelle Hughes, an aspiring writer and poet, and her twin sister Gaynetta Hughes, who was the co-producer of my cable television show. Gaynetta was also the single mother of two well-behaved girls, Tonetta, 13-years-old, and Helena, 5-years-old. I often sought parental advice from Gaynetta.

This was a perfect setting for me to give wings to a new poem. When my turn to perform came around, I opened by asking, "Has anyone noticed the change of Aunt Jemima's image on the pancake box?" The audience seemed amused. "Has anyone noticed that she has lost about 60 pounds and not wearing that disgusting red polka dot head rag any more?" This time there was laughter. "She's wearing jewelry, make up, and looking sweeter than a chocolate chip cookie." Someone yelled, "That's right brother!" "It reminds me," I continued, "how the black woman has gradually strengthened her position in this world. She is no longer limited to being a maid, cook, or a mammy." Laughter and affirmations filled the room. "She's now the Chairperson of

Board, in Congress, a Heart Surgeon, an astronaut, the mayor, president of her own company, and principal of schools. Just to name a few. I dedicate this poem to the black woman on the rise." There were continued affirmations and background chatter.

"Ladies and gentlemen," I said, "allow me to introduce to some and present to others, *The Liberation of Aunt Jemima.*" As I began, many guest and poets were laughing, but giving me their full attention.

Times certainly have brought about a change
And to a few, it might seem strange
Black women are soaring with ambition
No more, barefoot, pregnant and in kitchen

And she's not slaving like an ox
Have you seen her the image on the pancake box?
Purse full of credit cards, fancy car
And the girl ain't even a movie star
Not long ago I was on the bus
Eating fried chicken from the Colonel
Staring at a girlie magazine, and full of lust
Sitting next to a sista' reading a 'Wall street Journal'

I said, "Pardon me baby, where are you on your way?
I would like to know our name, if that's okay
Your perfume, I surely adore...
I believe we met somewhere before"
She says, "I'm on my way downtown to City Hall
I must chair a council meeting and that's not all
Then I'm flying to the United Nations
To advise on a classified situation

Sorry, but I fail to remember you
Were you ever in Zaire, Sudan, or Istanbul?
Or perhaps it was Rome, England, or by chance

It was Chad, Morocco, or Paris, France
You see, I'm multilingual and travel a lot
And the universe is 'My' melting pot
But once a month I take the bus
Just my way, of staying in touch

Nefertiti is my name,
And universal peace is my game
I attended Benedict College in South Carolina
and earned my Bachelor Degree
Then I went to Fisk and received my Masters,
in Nashville, Tennessee
At Howard University in Washington, D.C.
That's where I earned 'My' Ph.D.
I have offices in Dallas, Chicago, and Mexicana
A penthouse in New York, and a home in Atlanta
I play a harp, and pilot a jet . . .
Now tell me brother, where do you 'think' we met? ..."
I rung the bell, got up and left
Aunt Jemima done got besides herself!

The crowd laughed and applauded for two minutes. We had a fun packed afternoon. This was a buying audience. I sold 25 books of poetry. One customer bought six. We met a week earlier at the Good Life Health Food Store, when she purchased one book from me, following a poetry performance. She told me the new purchases were for six of her co-workers. "When I shared my copy of your book with the women at work," she said, "six of them gave me money to buy them one. I knew you would be here today. That's why I'm here, for my friends."

"That's delightful of you," I blushingly replied, "but how did you know I would be here?

"Are you kidding? The Frontline Poets 's name, and this event has been all around the radio."

She then handed me a six ten dollar bills, along with a list of six names. She

smiled and said, "Will you autograph them."
"Sure Shirley Williamson," I said with a smile.
"How do you know my name so well?"
"You wrote me a check last week, remember?"

Chapter 9

*C*hurch and poetry had become the most enjoyable and consuming part of my life. In my spare time, I wrote several newspaper poetry columns. One of my poems that appeared in the <u>A.C.C. Church and Community Newspapers</u> was so well received by the readers that several bookstores, cards and gift shops requested it in frames for their stores:

"IF I WERE. . ."

If I Were a cloud, I would cry for you
With crystal rain when you were blue
I would deflate the raging storm
Forecasted to bring you harm
Then send a rainbow, to ask for your smile
I would watch over you, If I Were . . . A Cloud

If I Were a mountain, you may climb
My highest peak, a view sublime
Skip along my rolling hills
Pick the lilies from my field
You may eat my berries, bathe in my fountain
I would be your rock, If I Were . . . A Mountain

If I Were the wind, I would send a breeze
To blow your hair, anytime you please
I'll place gold dust at your feet
To cool your heels from the summer heat

There's no beginning, there's no end
What my breath would bring, If I Were . . . The Wind

If I Were the moon, I would visit you each night
And in the midst of darkest, I would give you light
Through the window of your bedroom, I would beam you a kiss
It would so break my heart, should you turn to resist
I would write you name in stars, every night in June
To show you I care, If I Were . . . The Moon

If I Were an ocean, I would give you my beach
To walk in the sand, when you're searching for peace
You may play in my waters, all the day long
I would be soever gentle, though I am strong
I would sway your body, in a smooth lazy motion
And wave as you leave, If I Were . . . An Ocean

If I Were a poet, I would write a poem
That would cuddle you, and keep you warm
With all the comfort of a God-driven carriage
Headed for glory in an upward bound marriage
This gift of love, I would bestow it
To you with words, If I Were . . . A Poet."

I diligently sought publicity for my crime prevention book. I was interviewed by newspapers, magazines, and made guest appearances on cable TV shows. One of my biggest newspaper victories was when The Antelope Valley Press paid me to write anti-crime articles for their April '94 Annual Crime Prevention Tabloid. It was a thrill because this newspaper printed the most notorious and slanderous articles about me seven years earlier, regarding my arrest. Various crime prevention groups in the Lancaster area were now requesting Richard O. Jones to speak. My invitations to speak throughout Southern California were beginning to gain momentum because of an article in the July '94 issue of Turning Point Magazine.

<u>Turning Point</u> is an African-American quarterly magazine that highlights' people, places, and things of interest throughout Los Angeles and surrounding areas. The only problem with all the activity was that it is extremely time consuming, and my speaking engagements were free or nearly free. Other poets and speakers assured me that I was merely 'paying my dues.' I was expecting a breakthrough anytime. Nevertheless, it never came. What did come, however, was an ever increasing gap in my two younger daughters' respect for me. Since I was so busy reciting poetry, and *speaking free*, I couldn't dedicate much time to handyman work. I began using the monthly social security income to supplement my income. Yolanda, who had a job and her own apartment, understood my situation and had faith that I would make it someday. Rochelle was a senior in high with her own job and money, and didn't suffer from lack of clothes or other personal needs.

Roxanne and Jennifer grew furious at my inability to fulfill their wishes, namely a weekly allowance and extra money for their clothing. Both of them gradually stopped speaking to me anymore than necessary. The household became a source of bickering and confusion in three short years. They accused me of stealing their Social Security Checks to selfishly pursue my personal dreams, instead of getting a real job like a real father.

My situation didn't allow me to give them the monthly cash. Roxy and Jennifer began to wish they had stayed in Mississippi. I feared they might run away. Things got so bitter within the home that I again sought advice from various women at church. Sister Patricia Hill convinced me that I should treat the girls with more respect and allow them a say so in how the money is dispersed. She said, "Try sitting and calmly explain your situation, Brother Jones, and ask them for suggestions. Perhaps when they realize you care about their feelings, they will care about yours." I tried that. They wanted their money. Gaynetta Hughes told me, "If I were you, Richard, I wouldn't give them anything. You feed them, and pay the rent, which is enough."

The girls went to their grandmother for advice. She told them I should be ashamed of myself for taking their money. She also reminded them of the times she had to bring food to them because I was off somewhere drinking.

Their people in Mississippi told them by phone, I was misusing their funds and they were always welcome to return to Natchez.

Some church women put their heads and hearts together, and came up with a plan to help me. Three of them, who had the extra space, offered to give housing to one of my daughters until I established myself. I graciously accepted. I moved out of my apartment and returned to Reverend McDaniel's rooming house. While there, I worked on my plans to earn a decent living through my poetry, crime prevention books and engagements.

Sister Annie Jackson, and her daughter Melissa welcomed Jennifer in their home. Roxanne was good friends with Cynthia Allen's teenage daughter, Eboni, therefore, Roxy moved in with them. Both women were single mothers. Rochelle moved in with Gaynelle Hughes, a sister of Cynthia Allen and Gaynetta Hughes. Gaynelle had no children, but a big and loving heart. In Gaynelle's heart, there was room to house many. Rochelle had only a couple months before she would be finishing high school and turning eighteen. Her plans were to attend a local college and live on campus. Her short stay at Gaynelle's home was one of peace and comfort. Gaynelle and I were close platonic friends and recited poetry around town together. The loving attitudes of my spiritual sisters, made this crisis less distressing. None of these Christian women accepted rent money from me. However, I helped with their grocery bill and gave the girls weekly allowances.

Jennifer adjusted well to the new arrangements, however, her younger sister developed deeper issues. During the short time Roxy lived with Cynthia and her five children, Eboni, 13; Terrance, 10; Wilma, 7; Brian, 5; and Ernestine, 3; our relationship was in its worst state. I attributed Roxy's decline in parental respect to the way I mismanaged her childhood. We were separated again. This was the third time I had caused our family to scatter like a busted bag of marbles. When I got arrested, the girls went to different Foster Homes. When they went to Mississippi, each sister moved in with different relatives in separate houses. Now they were back in Los Angeles and in less than three years, they were separated again.

I could feel their growing contempt for me daily. It was in the little things that she did, and the little things she didn't do. For instance, there was a time when Roxy kissed me, not only goodnight, but also, goodbye when she or I left the house. Now she didn't even speak in a warm tone when I visited Cynthia's house. In fact, she would leave the room when I entered the house. There was a time that she would ask to attend my poetry readings or just walk with me to the store. I wanted to blame somebody. My mother would be an easy target, she did not welcome Roxy to her home. Perhaps I'll blame the publishing company. My crime prevention book was not doing well because the publisher wasn't promoting it properly. It's the fault of the Black Christians in Los Angeles. I've been writing spiritual poetry in The A.C.C. Church & Community Newspaper for more than one year and the churches are not responding fast enough. Black people don't support each other! Nevertheless, none of those excuses set well with my soul. Roxy knew the source of our problems and so did I.

As time went on, I found it difficult to look Roxy in the face. I would avoid eye contact when we talked, I and only spoke to her when it was necessary. Just five years earlier, I had houses, several healthy bank accounts, new cars, and didn't have to answer to anybody. Now in the blink of an eye, I was dependent on Social Security funds which was intended for the welfare of my daughters. It also took some swallowing of pride to visit Jennifer. Her demeanor was warmer than Roxy's. I knew she hated our situation, but she managed to hate it with a smile . . . and that helped.

Jennifer though, did not hold her tongue on the money issue. She fought her case like an attorney. I often teased her about being the lawyer of the family. This stems from a time soon after they returned from Mississippi. Jennifer purchased a mail order hair growth product that promised your satisfaction or double your money back. She had not informed me of the $13 purchase until she had some complaints. One morning, she came to me upset with a ball of hair, as large as an egg, in one hand. She carried a small jar of yellow wax in the other. "Daddy!" she said in a furious tone. "This stuff is making my hair fall out!" I took the jar from her hand and asked, "Where did you get this mess?" She stood there in silence and tears began to fall from her eyes. I asked it again, but firmer, "Where did you get this mess?"

Rochelle yelled the answer from the next room, with laughter in her voice. "She ordered it from a magazine. I told her not to do it." Roxy and Rochelle were now laughing aloud. I yelled at them for being so insensitive, and yelled at Jennifer for ordering anything by mail without my permission. The next day, I took her to Wade's Beauty Shop and he treated her for hair loss.

Two weeks later Jennifer's hair had started to grow back. A short time after she approached me and asked with a smirk on her face, "Daddy, where can I cash this check?"
"What check?" I asked.
"This check." Jennifer gave me a company check for $26, made out in her name.
"What is this check for Jennifer?"
"It's for lying and breaking off my hair," she said with a bit of an angry tone. "I wrote a letter to this company and told them my hair broke off. They wrote me back and asked me to send them the rest of the hair stuff. And yesterday this check came in the mail." I had her sign the check, and proudly gave her the money. As she did, I yelled out to Roxy and Rochelle who were watching television in the next room, "I don't hear yall laughing. What's the matter?" There was no answer.

One of my worst fears was realized the day I violently attacked Roxy. Though she definitely provoked it, I felt that I created the opportunity and fueled her frustration. It exploded the day I reported Eboni's disobedience to Cynthia. Eboni was on punishment for something, and as part of her punishment she was not to have company or leave the house for three weeks. However, during this period I had observed Eboni with company in the house and outside while her mother was away. Twice I warned her if she persisted to ignore her mother's orders, I would tell. The next time I caught her, I was making an unexpected visit and saw her outside talking with her friends. When she looked up the street and recognized me coming, she ran into the house. Again I gave her a firm reprimand and said, "I should tell her mother." This time she shocked me by arrogantly saying, "I don't care! Tell!"

When Cynthia came home and I told her, Eboni changed her tune. I guess she didn't expect the heat Cynthia was putting on her. Cynthia was on the verge of, not threatening her or adding to her punishment, but kicking her butt. Out of fear, Eboni denied she was outside. Well, to get to the bottom of it all, Cynthia called us face to face. I repeated my story and Eboni said I was mistaken. The girl I saw outside was not her. She flat out denied ever saying, she didn't care if I told. All the kids in the house, including Roxy, knew that Eboni was outside, but nobody spoke up. While Cynthia was still trying figure out who was lying, Roxy sprung from her seat and charged me like a bull. She stopped just two feet from my face, and screamed, "Don't you lie on MY FRIEND! She wasn't outside!"

For a moment, I was frozen . . . but when I thawed four or five seconds later, I slapped her across the top of her head twice with an open hand. She ducked, and I barely scraped her. Roxy fell backwards onto a chair, then I straddled her, and whacked her six or seven good ones. I ordered her to pack her things. Cynthia and her children look on in shock. To this day, I do not know if they were shocked at Roxy's behavior, or mine. All the way to my rented room, neither of us spoke to the other. The rooming house was an all male residential home, however, Reverend McDaniel allowed my daughter and me to occupy my room until I made other arrangements. The preacher said joking, "There are only two reasons I'm allowing her to stay. First, from what I know of you, Brother Jones, I know this is an emergency. Secondly, the two of you look so much alike, she's got to be your daughter."

He gave fair notice that these arrangements couldn't continue, because there were several single men in the boarding house and he didn't want anything to happen to her. I thanked him and promised to find an apartment soon. Roxanne slept in the bed, and I took the reclining chair. The next morning, Reverend McDaniel told me he also owned apartment building, and asked if I could afford $750 a month for a two bedroom, one bathroom unit.
"How much will it be to move-in?" I asked.
"Well, Brother Jones, I charge 3 x $750. That is first month's rent, last month's rent, and security deposit. The total is $2,250 in all."

Reverend McDaniel and I worked out an arrangement. I would manage the 24 unit apartment building and he would cut the rent by $400 a month. One week later, I had a two-bedroom apartment for only $350 a month, which was $150 a month less than the single room rent, and $350 a month less than our last apartment. The building was very well kept and only four blocks from Cochran Avenue Baptist Church.

Again, Jennifer, Roxanne, and I were together in our own apartment. This time we had a little extra money but not enough to give them the entire Social Security check. I put them on an allowance of $20 per week, but neither was satisfied. Rochelle graduated high school by this time and was a resident student at Cal State Northridge.

Jennifer found a part time job at a clothing store, therefore, her attitude toward me took on a softer disposition. She also was able to cope better because she knew her time in my custody would not be much longer. Every time we disagreed, she would throw it up in my face that she would be going away to college soon. In other words, she would finally be rid of me.

Because of Annie's fatal car accident, an out-of-court settlement was reached several years earlier. A trust fund was setup by the court and insurance company that awarded each daughter a lump sum of money on their 18th birthday. So far, Yolanda and Rochelle had received their money and gone to college. Jennifer was only a few months from her world debut.

In January '94, my business affairs began to show me a glimpse of promise. A community weekly newspaper by the name of The L.A. Watts Times accepted my proposal to write a 'Tips Against Crime' column. This newspaper reached 10,000 readers weekly including many local politicians and business leaders. I had been featured in several other newspapers, but those were articles written by staff writers. This was a column with my own by-line.

I knew the power of a good newspaper. In July '93 The Los Angeles Times 'City View' did a full page story on my anti-crime activities, including my book, cable TV show, and my infamous background. That article prompted calls from three national news programs; 48 Hours, A Current Affair, and CBS News. Two local news program producers invited me to lunch to hear my story and pick my brain.

However, my past crimes weren't bloody or hideous. No dead were bodies left behind. I wasn't an ex-robber, a drive-by shooter, gang member or drug dealer, therefore, they didn't feel the viewers would be interested in my rehabilitation.

After my third Watts Times column I received a call from Gil Confrancesco, field producer at CNBC. He selected stories for their national cable TV show called 'Money Tonight'. Gil ordered a copy of 'Tips Against Crime, Written From Prison ' before contacting me. He wanted to do an expose' on 'The Moving Van Scam'. This was a scam written in my book which told people how they could be ripped-off by fraudulent moving companies. My incarcerated buddy Maurice Phillips gave me this scam. Gil told me that he wanted to talk to the actual con men. He was prepared to interview them in prison. I knew several convicts who would be willing to be interviewed on TV, including Phil. At the direction of Gil Cofrancesco, I contacted Phil and he agreed to take part in the project. Gil got approval from the prison warden and the show was on.

The first half of the interview was with me in the sanctuary of Cochran Avenue Baptist Church. The second half was at Chino Institute For Men, where Phil was being held at the time. The show aired nationally and the response was promising. My publisher received a few requests for my book within three days after 'Money Tonight Show' aired. I thought it would be much more. Apparently Gil thought I had something valuable to offer his viewers because he contacted me within a month to reenact a scam from my past.

This particular scam was called, 'Dumpster Diving'. This is a deception preying on hard times. A person pushing a grocery cart through alleys and along the curbside with cans and bottles in the cart can rip you off through a phony credit scam. We've become so accustomed to seeing homeless people ruffling through trash that it seldom warrants a second look. However, there's a growing number of con artists who disguise themselves as homeless transients and go through your trash seeking discarded receipts containing your credit card numbers or bank statements. With your account numbers, a creative crook can rip you off - big time. To spotlight this crime, Gil had me to dress the part and play the role. Armed with a shopping cart, I was able to collect enough information, (in a woman's name) for one of CNBC female staff members, to go on a $4000 shopping spree. Before we left the area where the discarded information was collected, Gil, myself, and the camera man went to the woman's door, whose name, address, and credit accounts numbers appeared on the discarded property. With the cameras rolling, Gil explained to her he was the producer of 'Money Tonight' and we were doing a scam story on how people can be robbed through their trash can.

I then introduced myself as the producer and host of *Tips Against Crime* cable TV show. I explained that I was dressed down to appear homeless which enabled me to rummage through dumpsters without arousing suspicion.
"We would like your co-operation," Gil said, "to do exactly what we would do if we were actual criminals, as Richard directs us. All the merchandise, if we're successful, will be returned to the store and your account cleared. We just want you to be aware of it all and not call the credit card company. However, if the credit card company or any store calls you and ask if you've authorized use of your credit cards, tell them NO." I walked Gil's crew step by step through the scam from getting the phony I.D., to obtaining instant credit. Everything was done on camera. When the show aired, it was a success. And my crime prevention book sold another few copies within a week. But where was the stampede, I felt should have followed? Apparentl,y I was doing something wrong, but I didn't know what.

Jennifer and Roxanne became more arrogant than I ever known them to be. Our parent/child behavior and rapport could have easily earned us free round trip airline tickets to appear as guests on a 'no brainer' TV talk show. Both girls were extremely argumentive with me on every issue, especially money. If I told them I didn't have it, I could hear them mumbling, as they walked away, "You oughta stop writing poetry and get a real job."

On several instances I sat with them and explained my predicament, as Sis. Hill suggested. "Look girls, I know you wish I would go out and get a regular job. You've got to understand, I'm 47-years-old and never really had a regular job. I'm too old to be stacking boxes and sweeping floors all my life. That's why it's important to me to make a success of my writing.
Sure! I know how to rip people off, but I'm no longer in that lifestyle, and I struggle every day not to return to crime. Just look at me! I'm not spending money on new clothes, liquor, drugs, or having a good time. All the money I get my hands on goes to planting seeds for MY future, which will also benefit you two. We're all sacrificing together, which is what a good family does. Look at history! Families that struggle together, make it in the end." I stressed, "The long run."

Those two daughters of mine would not compromise. One day, I explained to Jennifer so long that we talked through a full length two hour TV movie. I had planned for three days to watch. Before I knew it, I missed the whole movie. Jennifer was still being stubborn and sassy. The problem was with me, I knew that. I raised them too loose. My mother often told me that over the years. It was important to me that children are given the opportunity to voice their true views without reprisal.

Finally, I yelled at Jennifer, "Look Stupid! Just SHUT UP!" She looked shocked but still wanted to be heard.
"Daddy you're being unfair," she complained. "You shouldn't be using our social security money to print your books."
"I told you to SHUT UP! This conversation is way overdue for a conclusion. We've been talking for over two hours. Now just shut up."
"You want everything your way," she snapped. "It's our money..."
Before I caught myself, I slapped her across the face.
"Now SHUT UP you ignorant puppy. I wished your mother had aborted you," I screamed. Jennifer stood in shock for a few seconds, then ran into her room in tears. Immediately, I ran behind her asking her forgiveness. She slammed the door to her room. I stood on the outside her room and asked for forgiveness. "I'm sorry Jennifer. Please believe me. I didn't mean that. I don't know what came over me. I'm sorry Jennifer." I turned the door knob

and discovered the door was locked. Roxanne yelled from inside the room. "What are you gonna do now? Break the door down?" I slowly lowered myself to my knees while tightly gripping the door knob, and pleaded.

"Jennifer, Roxy, please forgive me. I'm sorry! I know you have a reason to hate me. Don't ruin your young beautiful lives by hating. Hating destroys the heart of the hater, not the person who's hated. I'm sorry. I will never hit you girls again. Not even if you make me mad. God knows I'm sorry." "Jennifer angrily said, "Don't be sorry, just give us our money." "Yeah," Roxy said. I didn't reply. My eyes were watery and I began to tremble a little. It scared me. However, I didn't rise. I prayed aloud.

"Dear Gods, in the name of Jesus, please forgive me for my sins. I know my girls are good girls, Lord. Thank you for good girls Lord. They take after their mother Lord, thank you for that. I don't mean to be abusive and unreasonable. Please help me. Let Roxanne, Jennifer, Rochelle, and Yolanda know I love them. Please help me Lord. I want to be a blessing to my family. I tried to find work God. You know I have. I admit to selfishness. I admit I'm scared. I don't know what to do. I thought my poetry was from you God. I thought you wanted me to write. If that's not what you want Lord, I will sweep floors, clean toilets, and give up this writing idea. Tell me, show me, guide me, Jesus. Please give me back the love of my little girls..."

I prayed continuously for 15 or 20 minutes, when slowly rose and went to my room and laid down. Within a minute, I heard the girls bedroom door open. Moments later, I heard them both say in unison, "We're sorry, daddy." I didn't get up or look up. I was exhausted, yet relieved. A few seconds, later Jennifer entered my room. Her eyes were red from crying. Jennifer spoke in a soft tone. "I forgive you Daddy. I know you were just mad." I wanted to embrace her, but before I rose, she quickly and quietly left my room.

Each day I spent hours scheming and mapping plans that would bring me into the public spotlight in a positive way. A great portion of my meager income was cast upon infertile ground. There were small public relation firms that I had paid, but didn't have the means to have a kid scratch my name in dirt. After a taping of *'Tips Against Crime,'* with guests Officer Stephanye Payne, of the Los Angeles Police Department and Arthur J. Gray, of the Los Angeles County District Attorney Office, Mr. Gray asked me what I planned for future shows.

When I told him that I was thinking about looking up the district attorney investigator who arrested me, and the judge who sentenced me and inviting them to be guests on the show, he asked their names. "The Judge is Candace Cooper and the D.A. Investigator is Mel Wesson," I said. Officer Payne promptly interjected, "Oh I know Judge Cooper very well. She's working in the Santa Monica Municipal Court Building." Deputy D.A. Gray said energetically, "And I know Mel. He's now working the Hardcore Gang Unit in Compton." When I thought about it, I wasn't surprised they would all know each other.

Black people have a secret society of fellowship in every profession. These four were no different. Perhaps I was now one of them. The thought made me feel proud. Even more proud than I had ever been as a small time hustler. The two officers had given me enough information to go on with the ground work for the future show. At first, it was only a fantasy to host a TV show with the judge and the D.A. investigator responsible for my incarceration. I figured, such a show would be a first. But I'd procrastinated, hoping my show had become popular enough to warrant asking them to appear on it. However, Officer Payne and Deputy D.A. Gray encouraged me saying, they were sure Judge Cooper and Mel Wesson would do the show. They even supplied me with the telephone numbers. I felt God had a hand in it all and was telling me the time was right.

The next day, I called both numbers. I left a message with the clerk in Judge Cooper's Department. "My name is Richard O. Jones," I said to the clerk. "I'm the producer and host of the *Tips Against Crime* cable TV show at Continental Cablevision in Westchester. Judge Cooper sentenced me to prison in September '88 on major welfare fraud charges. I served two years. Now, I'm working in the field of crime prevention and I would like Judge Cooper to be a guest on my show."

"What is your telephone number please?," the clerk asked. "And when are you taping the show?" I gave her my telephone number and told her the date of our taping was in two weeks, March 15, 1994.

My next call was to the Compton District Attorney's Office Hard-Core Gang Unit. Mr. Wesson wasn't in, but a clerk took the message. I explained, Mel Wesson had been the chief investigator in my arrest and conviction for major welfare fraud. The invitation for Mr. Wesson to appear as a guest on my cable TV show was extended, and I left my telephone number.

Late that afternoon, I received my first response. It was Judge Candace Cooper herself. We spoke on the phone for about ten minutes before she very graciously accepted my invitation. Judge Cooper requested that I send her a letter regarding my show and other pertinent information. Thirty minutes later, Mr. Wesson called. Though I wasn't surprised they remembered me, it still flattered me to have left an impression on them which lasted over six years. Mel Wesson and I talked like old friends. After checking his calendar, he accepted my invitation. However, he also requested a letter for his reference. The following letter was composed and mailed to each of my future guests:

March 2, 1994

Dear Judge Cooper / Mr. Wesson,

Thank you for accepting my invitation to appear as a guest on Tips Against Crime TV Program. When you arrive, please enter through the studio entrance which is located on the parking lot. The show is scheduled to begin taping at 6:30 p.m. at the following place:

> *Continental Cablevision*
> *5314 Arizona Place*
> *Los Angeles, CA 90045*
> *Date: March 15, 1994*

Day: Tuesday
Time: 6:30 P.M. - 8:00 P.M.

Continental Cablevision is very near the intersection of Sepulveda and Continela, one block behind Dinah's Restaurant on Sepulveda.

The program will address concerns such as: (1.) Being a good witness; (2.) Proper conduct in court; (3.) Sentencing, probation and restitution (4.) In particular, why judges impose such astronomical fines and restitution, and are defendants exempt from such after probationary period? (5.) Parenting to avoid the lure of anti-social behavior in young children. Your co-guest is scheduled to be Mel Wesson, Chief Investigating Officer of my case in '88 / Judge Cooper the presiding judge in my case in '88. Again, thank you for your support and participation in this program. I feel the three of us may pave the path of a new wave in TV programing. Please feel free to call me anytime.

Sincerely Yours,
Richard O. Jones

This was the most exciting moment in the history of my year old program. Until this show, my guests had been authors on crime prevention, police personnel, attorneys, ex-criminals, psychologists, psychiatrists, (including Dr. Loretta Dunlap) and crime victims. This was different! Perhaps the first in the WORLD! An ex-convict, with an anti-crime TV show, and his guests are two intrinsic forces of his imprisonment.

I strategized my best approach to having major news networks' cover this story. It was decided, by the no-count public relations firm I wasted my money on, which we would fax all the local channels an invitation to this phenomenal event. About 12 were contacted, five accepted, and none showed up. However, Gil Cofranesco of CNBC came and recorded a fraction of the show. I found out later the other networks didn't attend my taping was because the Soul Train Annual Awards were taking place at the same hour. Just a case of poor planning. The public relations firm should have known this and advised me to tape on another date. If I had known the Soul Train Awards were taking place on that same evening, I would not scheduled a show. Everyone love the Soul Train Awards, even me.

As a photography backup, I invited my friend, Cynthia Allen, and my publisher, Rene Rolle-Whatley, and instructed both of them to bring their 35mm cameras. With two photographers, I figured, a few good shots were likely. When the judge and investigator showed up, the five of us sat around a table in The Green Room (the lounge area) chatting.

The conversation focused on me and my activities. I was so enchanted by just sitting there in a social setting with the judge and investigator who once held my future and freedom in their hands, I forgot to ask them any questions about themselves. Instead, I spent all the time listening to them tell Cynthia and Renee what a great guy both thought I was. Like a 175-pound sponge, I soaked it all in.

Mel Wesson told Renee and Cynthia how he investigated me to find out if my children were abused or neglected, but the more he looked, the better the picture of my parenting skills got. All my girls were doing excellently in school. Our home was clean, and there was plenty of healthy food in the house. All of their medical records were up to date, and their teeth in good condition. They were all polite, had bank accounts, and respected their father. I thought as I sat there listening, how much different I was as a sober parent than an alcoholic one. The one my mother always reminded me of.

Wesson bragged, in all his years of raiding houses this was the only time he remembered not finding any addictive substances like drugs, alcohol, or tobacco. He went on to say, "Plus there were no porno magazines or videos, nor did Richard subscribe to any adult channel cable TV. We checked it all out."

Cynthia asked him, "Why is all that checking necessary?" The judge took the question. "Before a judge returns children to the home of suspected criminals," she said, "the court wants to know as much as it can about their home environment. It was obvious, Richard was an exemplary single parent, male or female."

I excused myself to check on the set. After all, I was the H.N.I.C. The director informed me the set would be ready in five minutes. When I returned, the conversation had turned to everyone's personal lives. The judge was married with one child. The publisher was married with one child. The investigator was single with no children. Cynthia Allen, a real estate broker, was divorced with five children. I recall thinking as the ladies talked about their children, would they think I was such a good parent if they knew how much my 14-year-old daughter hated me. The distance between Roxanne and I were steadily increasing and it seemed as if there was nothing I could do to turn it around.

When the taping began, I realized, I had not prepared my questions. I even forgot the ones I put in my letter to them. We spent all the prep time gabbing about me, and now here I was with the cameras rolling and fumbling for solid ground. To be frank, I didn't realize just how far I had stuck my foot into my mouth, until I saw the tape.

Twenty minutes of the 28 minute tape was about me. When one of my guests asked me something about myself, I stole the time It was a miracle I didn't stand up and take a bow. Occasionally, I glanced toward the back of the studio and saw Cynthia and Renee giving me the 'cutthroat' sign, suggesting I was talking too much. However, I didn't catch on until too late . . . I had my flow on!

Though I am forever grateful for doing that particular show, it was no masterpiece. Nobody told me a T.V. host interviewing himself, was like the proverbial lawyer that defends himself, had a fool as a guest. I made a vow, following that program, to seek a host and stop producing and hosting myself. Perhaps at some time the future, the judge and investigator would grant me another opportunity.

With hindsight I realized that I was nervous and tense in the presence of Judge Cooper and Mel Wesson. Also, I was trying to impress them instead of sharing with the TV viewing audience. Two weeks later, I sent them a copy of the show on video tape and a copy of my book of poetry, <u>Do You Really Know What It Is?</u>

In June '94, when school was out for the summer, I sent for my son, Darren, now nine years old to visit us. Darren arrived on the day I was on a church program to recite a poem in honor of Pastor Hill's Ninth Anniversary. My son's flight was due in at five p.m. I was scheduled to recite at seven p.m. It had been two years since we were together. We had a grand reunion at the airport. Before we left the airport, we each ate three chilli dogs. Darren loved chilli dogs. The time got away from me and the next thing I knew it was 6:30 p.m..

Suddenly, I remembered my previous commitment. We went directly to the church. We got there at 7:10 p.m. Though, I offered to drop Darren off at the house, he opted to come along with me. It was about 8:30 before I addressed the congregation. After I gave thanks to The Lord for blessing me, I asked Darren to rise so I could introduce him.

He and I were not sitting together, because as a deacon. I sat on the front pew. Darren was seating several pews behind me, next to my friend Martha Acorn. Darren remembered fondly from his last visit two years earlier. However, when I looked in his direction, I noticed he had fallen asleep. Because of the time difference, it was after 11:30 p.m. in Ohio and way past his bedtime. Martha signaled me to let him sleep. Several church members knew Darren and he felt comfortable in their company. I paid proper tribute to my pastor and recited my piece, then gathered my son and we left the service.

During the entire two months Darren was in Los Angeles, he only saw Roxanne two or three times. She pleaded to be allowed to go to the city of Riverside to babysit for the summer for another one of Cynthia's sisters. Her name was Annette. Therefore, Roxy had left for the summer before Darren arrived. Annette was a Registered Nurse, unmarried and the mother of a 10-year-old child who was born with a crippling disease and was wheelchair bound. It was obvious to everyone Roxanne's motivation for wanting to babysit 70 miles away, was to get away from me. I felt helpless and ashamed, but I didn't know what to do. However, Jennifer, Rochelle, and Yolanda spent a loving amount of time with their brother. Except Roxanne, everybody in the family showed him a good time.

Cynthia and I had begun dating, so Darren and I were often at her home. My son and Cynthia's 11-year-old son Terrace became buddies. Terrace was two years older than Darren. I took both boys swimming five days a week. Darren and I also went to many poetry readings. Darren even recited a couple of my poems and one he composed about Dr. Martin Luther King, Jr.

Annette and her daughter often visited Cynthia on the weekends. This was when Darren chances were best to see Roxanne because she came to Los Angeles with Annette and her daughter.

Terrance was the only boy I brought Darren around on a regular basis. Though Cynthia's son was short on discipline, he was big on heart. Most of the time, they played well together, but were completely different in many way. My son enjoyed computer games and readings. Terrance enjoyed wrestling and climbing trees. However, Darren maintained his character and Terrance maintained his. When I realize this, I also realized that Eboni's misbehavior couldn't influence Roxanne to any great extent, if she was well-grounded the first place. In my search for explanations, I once considered Cynthia's daughter Eboni partially responsible for Roxanne disrespect toward me. Some children do, however, copy the negative character of their peer group or friends. This was not so. Somewhere down the line, I missed a turn on the road called, 'Parenting'.

Although, none of my other children had oblivious resentment for me, Roxanne and I were definitely in need of family counseling. Perhaps she was suffering from something connected with her mother's accident. After all, she was in the car with her.

In August, just two days before Darren was scheduled to return to Ohio, apparently Roxanne was suffering from emotional problems. My mother called me. By the trembling and anger in her voice I knew it was serious. "What is wrong with Roxy?," she demanded. "She just called here crying uncontrollably, saying she wants to spend the day with Darren before he leaves but she has to return to Riverside."

My mother wanted to know, why was I forcing her to spend the summer working. After a short conversation with my mother, I called Cynthia's house and asked to speak to Roxanne. She was still crying as I tried to talk to her.

Since I couldn't make any sense out of what Roxy was saying, I asked to speak to Cynthia. "Isn't anything wrong with Roxy," Cynthia snapped at me. "I told her if she don't wanna go with Annette she don't have to. Annette is on her way to pick them up. Now Roxy is sitting here crying, saying she needs the money because you won't buy her any school clothes."
"Okay Cynthia," I said, "when Annette comes, just tell her Roxy can't go." Cynthia screamed into the phone, "You tell her yourself! I'm not getting in this. Annette has to work tonight and she was depending on Roxy." She slammed the receiver down. Bam!

When Annette arrived, no one called me, and Roxy went back to Riverside. I waited until the next day and called Annette's house. She said perhaps Roxy underestimated the many duties involved in keeping a child in braces and a wheelchair. Since she's so unhappy, I'll bring her back home tomorrow."

The next day Annette brought Roxy back to Cynthia's. A good friend of Cynthia's named Vickie, with her daughter Roxy's age named Erica, brought Roxy home. Instead of Roxy spending Darren's last day in Los Angeles with him, she begged to return home with Vickie and Erica. Roxy claimed to need to rest because she had worked all summer. "Erica has a swimming pool where I could swim and relax," said Roxy. Vickie assured me that Roxy would be safe. Overall, Darren had a good visit and was unmoved by Roxanne's absence.

I arranged for family counseling at Southern California Counseling Center, which was not far from our apartment. This facility staffed student psychologist. The licensed doctors were only there for their select private patients and to monitor the soon-to-be psychologists. The fees for services were based on a sliding scale. The less you told them you earned, the less you paid. My fee was $6 per visit.

So there we were! Every Wednesday the three of us went to a counseling session. From 6 - 6:50 p.m. we sat in the psychologist's office and talked about our home problems. I did most of the talking. The girls didn't want to be there, and Morgana, the middle-aged, white female, soon-to-be, psychologist seldom contributed anything to discussion. I might as well have been sitting on a log chatting with three chipmunks. From time to time Roxanne and Jennifer would be urged to say something by our therapist. However, nothing they said helped their cases regarding my unfairness about their money.

Morgana discovered, I had corrected or was working toward correcting many of my faults. For example: I had long ago apologized for cursing Jennifer when I lost my temper. As far as striking them was concerned, I regretted it and sincerely, humbly apologized.

Regarding giving them money, I agreed to increase their allowances . . . which I had done before counseling. I gave them both $300 to buy a few school clothes. Also offered them $25 per week each if they helped me clean the church every Saturday morning, which had become my part-time job. Both girls declined that offer. I explained to all three chipmunks,"It's hard for me to just give a child money when they reject an opportunity to earn wages." However, this statement was mostly for Roxanne's ears because Jennifer still had a part-time job in a clothing store. I had even taken a turn at doing the dishes two days per week to share the housework.

After three weekly counseling sessions, I got a telephone call from a woman in Cleveland, Ohio. Her name was Joyce Bryant and she was the owner of Safety First Security Company. Ms. Bryant explained that she was the only black woman in the State of Ohio who owned her own security company. She wanted me to come to Cleveland to speak at a home safety seminar.

"I was at the library doing some research on crime prevention," she said, "and ran across your book; Tips Against Crime, Written From Prison. Mr. Jones, I'm so glad to be talking with you I don't know what to do! When I finished your book, I tell you, I couldn't put it down, and saw your picture in the back, Mr. Jones, I screamed." (There were laughter and excitement in her voice. Ms. Bryant was a fast talker.) " I said, Oh My God! He's black! Mr. Jones, I was so happy. To think that a black man would take his time to write a book like yours that'll help so many people..."

"Huh, excuse me Ms. Bryant." I abruptly interrupted. "How did you get my telephone number?" Of course, she had gotten it from Renee, I knew that. I just wanted to appear precautious.
"I called Sandcastle Publishing," Ms. Bryant explained, "and spoke with a Renee Rolle-Whatley, the publisher. The telephone number is right in the back. We discussed the likelihood of some readers wanting to converse with the author."

Our conversation ended in an agreement for me to come to Cleveland for two days and speak to three groups for a fee of $600 plus all expenses paid. Also, a $150 donation, from The Safety First Company, was payable to Cochran Avenue Baptist Church Mission Board. Mrs. Bryant had no way of knowing it, but she had just agreed to pay me more money than I ever received for a crime prevention lecture. Before this engagement my record high was $400, from a large Catholic church. My only regret about this trip to Ohio was, it wasn't in Evelyn's hometown of Dayton. My trip in Ohio was scheduled for October 19, 1994, which was two weeks away. Three days after our telephone conversation, I received a letter of confirmation from The Safety First Company, signed by the president, Joyce Bryant.

At our next counseling session, I told Morgan, I would not be attending the session on the 19th, because of business plans. Not only did I share the news with the therapist, but I told several church members, my mother, children, and friends. Everyone was excited for me, except Roxanne. She couldn't care less. However, something happened on October 12th, one week before I was scheduled to go to Cleveland, which got a raised eyebrow out of Roxanne.

It occurred one morning while I was at my desk composing a poem for The A.C.C. The telephone rang. I answered on the third ring. The very businesslike female voice on the other end said, "Hello, may I speak to Richard Jones?"

"Speaking, may I help you?" I replied.

"Hello Mr. Jones," she said. "My name is Judy Banks, I'm an associate producer of *The Oprah Winfrey Show.* Do you have a few minutes to discuss your activities?" Our conversation lasted for 40 minutes. Judy asked me about various scams I had perpetrated. Each one I shared with her was one she wasn't familiar with. I told them in a humorous way. She spent about as much time laughing, as I did talking. Finally, after about 30 minutes she asked, "Would you appear as a guest on *The Oprah Show?*"

I hoped our chat, would consummate with an invitation. However, I had been misled by other national shows before. When they discovered there was no 'gun play' or 'molested children' in my past, their interest fizzled. But this was OPRAH! Judy told me, while researching for their upcoming show on scams, she came across The Los Angeles Times July 25, 1993, article regarding my anti-crime activities. After reading the article, Judy knew I had a cable TV show in Los Angeles. She then called several cable stations, until she finally spoke with Steve Vargas, Public Access Coordinator at Continental Cablevision, in Westchester. Steve gave her my telephone number. Perhaps this would go all the way.

"Sure Judy!" I said, "It'll be my pleasure. When are you taping?"

"That's Grrr-eat!" she exclaimed. "We're taping next week on the 18th. We'll fly you to Chicago on the 17th, and you'll be in the studio the next day." Suddenly, I remembered my engagement in Cleveland. I would have to leave for Ohio immediately after the taping. The next day, Judy called back and said the executive producer wanted to see a copy of my book and a video tape of my cable show. A messenger was sent to my house a few hours later. Within 48 hours, I had airline reservations for Chicago.

During Sunday service, Pastor Hill made a public announcement. "Our own Deacon Jones, will be flying off tomorrow to be a guest on *The Oprah Winfrey Show*," he said. The whole congregation gasped. After church many people asked me to tell Oprah, how much they loved her or how good she looked, etc.

I allowed Roxy and Jennifer to stay home alone during my absence. They had earned the privilege. I didn't let their resentment toward me cloud my opinion of their character.

Everything was as Judy had prepared for me. A limousine was waiting. The hotel was spectacular. She also arranged for a driver to take me directly from the show to the airport for my flight to Cleveland.

Although the bed in my hotel suite was very comfortable, I couldn't sleep. The night passed slowly. At three a.m., I took a bath. At four a.m., I was up ironing my clothes for the second time. At five a.m., I was fully dressed and reading a magazine. Around six a.m., I got sleepy. Rather than lay down, I left my suite. The hotel restaurant, I discovered, did not open until 6:30 a.m. I took a walk to kill some time and calm my nerves. When I returned, the restaurant was opened. At 7:30, I was scheduled to meet a limousine driver in the hotel lobby.

As I waited in the lobby fantasizing vacationing in such an opulent hotel, four limousines drove into the circular driveway. Then, one of the desk clerks called out, "Guests of 'Oprah', your drivers have arrived." Nearly 20 people were waiting. We piled into the four cars. I rode with a white ex-convict, who was scheduled to speak on the show.

The ride from the hotel to Harpo Productions, which I discovered was 'Oprah' spelled backwards, was about 20 minutes. We passed a security check point upon entering the building. All the guests, at least those who arrived with me, had to walk through a metal detector.

In the Green Room, a staff member walked over to me and extended her hand and said, "Hi Richard, I'm Judy Banks." I was smitten at first sight. Judy was an attractive, robust, golden tone, sister who reminded me of Judge Cooper. Judy chatted with me briefly, "How was your flight? I hope you slept." Before I answered she politely excused herself, and scatted off to other duties.

As I sat in the Green Room, mingling with other guests, Ann's, my late wife, serene face formed in my mind. I could hear her saying, "God wants you to cleanse your soul. Going to church isn't enough. I forgive you Rick. Tell the others, you are sorry, before it's too late. God has something better for you. God wants you to cleanse your soul. Take care of God's business Rick, before it's too late. Tell the ones you abused, you are sorry, before it's too late." I rubbed my face with both hands and shook my head rapidly from side to side. The image and voice of Ann slowly faded.

The show was about 35 minutes in progress when the other ex-convict and I were invited to join the other guests on the 'Scam School' panel. Oprah stood among the audience. Most of the people who left the hotel with me, were victims of crime, or worked at some police agency. They were scattered throughout the audience to ask questions. Oprah, as I already knew, was an expert interviewer. There was no fumbling for questions for this cookie.

She had questions fed to her through the Teleprompter. Immediately after my introduction and displaying a copy of <u>Tips Against Crime, Written From Prison</u>, on the screen, she set pace by asking me specific questions. I knew I was trapped and wouldn't be able to get into any real scams, just the comical stuff I shared with Judy on the phone. So I relaxed and went with the flow. On stage were: an insurance fraud investigator, a Chicago police detective, the other ex-convict, a former crime victim, who had wrote a book on how to avoid getting ripped-off", and last, but not least, me.

The other author, stole the show. Oprah's film crew worked, with this windbag, for a few days, before the show. He pushed himself off as a scam expert. His expertise came from library research, not streetlife. This guy had the cooperation of banks, restaurants, and other establishments in using their property and uniforms to setup his cons...bless his heart. At various intervals during the show, film clips were shown of him conning unsuspecting people. A few of his quasi-victims were in the studio and were now laughing at themselves on camera.

The insurance fraud investigator, had surveillance tape of seemingly healthy people, engaged in heavy physical labor, while they claimed to be disabled, and were collecting workers' compensation from the insurance company. The audience was amused and impressed with all the hidden camera coverage. The other ex-convict's role on the show was not clear. He had very little to offer. The police detective was the real expert, and gave good advice to the public. During commercial breaks, and after the show, Oprah came over and chatted, off camera, with each of her panelist. Surprising, I enjoyed myself but it was not a serious crime prevention forum.

Upon leaving the studio, I saw Judy Banks for the second time. She was at curbside directing the group from the hotel into certain limos. She beckoned me to board the rear car along with three other people who were also heading straight to the airport. When I got closer to Judy, I extended my hand and thanked her for the opportunity. She told me I'd done well and she were glad that it was she who invited me. Out of the clear blue, I asked, "Do you like poetry?" Judy looked shocked and answered, "Oh yes! Do you write?" "Yes, and if you don't mind," I said, "I brought two copies of one of my books. Will you accept one as a gift and give the other to Oprah?" She smiled and said, "Sure, thank you." I gave her two copies of, <u>Do You Really Know What Time It is?</u>

On the flight from Chicago to Cleveland, I kept thinking about my vision of Ann at Harpo Production in the Green Room. What was the message? Who had I abused? Surely God must know I've repented my past ways. I was doing everything I could think of toward raising my children properly. Surely God knows that. I'd apologized to them. What was the vision telling me? Gradually, I dozed off.

When the plane landed, I went directly to the baggage claim area, where Joyce Bryant would be waiting. There was a nicely built, 30 something, brown complexion woman standing near the exit. "Youuu whooo, youuuu whooo, Mr. Jones," called and waved this attractive business dressed woman. I knew Joyce would recognize me because my picture was in the back of my book. We greeted each other warmly with a hug. We rode in her personal car. Joyce and I also ate dinner together. After dinner, Joyce took me back to my hotel accommodations in Shaker Heights. My stay in Ohio was an active one. Joyce had arranged two radio interviews, one TV interview, three speaking engagements, and one book signing. Between engagements, she took me around to meet her friends and family. Three days later, when I was leaving Ohio, Joyce's father drove me to the airport. It was definitely more personal than the quick brush I had received in Chicago.

Two college instructors, from Southwest Community College saw me on *The Oprah Winfrey Show,* while taking a break in the teacher's lounge, they ran and got the Assistant Dean. The teachers thought I would be ideal for the crime prevention workshop the school wanted on campus. I was contacted by the school administrators and offered the post. In July '95, I began instructing a six weeks, summer class at Southwest on Crime Prevention. My book, Tips Against Crime, Written From Prison, was approved my the dean as required reading for every student taking my course.

Meanwhile, my daughter, Roxanne moved out of the house for the time being. She had become a recluse by isolating herself in her room. I discussed this with the Morgan, who suggested I allow Roxanne to temporarily live with another relative. She eventually moved in with her oldest sister, Yolanda, who had a one bedroom apartment in Burbank, 35 minutes away.

Roxanne's new home was too inconvenient for us to continue weekly counseling sessions in Los Angeles near my apartment. Morgan suggested I get Roxy's name on the waiting list at Children's Hospital in Hollywood. There she would be seen by a licensed psychologist. When I registered my daughter for child counseling, I was warned that the listing list was extensive. The hospital clerk advised me to call back every week to see if there has been a cancellation.

Jennifer stayed home with me until she graduated high school in '96. Then she swiftly moved on campus at The University of California, Berkeley. She chose to major in Law. I was not surprised.

Rochelle transferred from Cal State Northridge to Bowie University in Maryland. She strongly considered becoming a medical doctor.

With the girls gone, I found myself eating more junk food. My weight sky rocketed from, my usual, 175 pounds to a portly 195. I joined the church walking club, spearheaded by Ruth Bailey, Cochran's secretary. During my five years at Cochran, I witnessed Ruth lose nearly 40 pounds. She was now the embodiment of motivation, personified.

A half dozen church members met each Saturday morning at Pan Pacific Park to walk. After being a member of the club for three weeks, I noticed a change in my weight. I had *gained* four pounds. My mind was constantly on Roxy, and to cope with the stress, I ate everything I could get my hands on. Every couple weeks, I called Children's Hospital to see where we were on the waiting list.

Meanwhile, I increased my walking to six days a week. One morning about seven o'clock, as I walked around the track of Southwest Community College, a woman called my name. When I turned in the direction of the voice, I saw Shirley Williamson waving at me. "Wait up!" she yelled. We both were dressed in red, white and blue sweat suits and wearing white tennis shoes. I stopped until she caught up to me. There were many other adults on the track, some walking, some jogging.

"Mind if I join you," she said.
"Please do! It's good to see you again."
"Good to see you again *too*," she said, with an emphasis on *too*. "How long have you been coming here?"
"This is my first," I said. " I usually walk in Pan Pacific Park near my church."

"This is my first time *too*," she said laughingly, with double stronger emphasis on *too*. "I usually walk around The Forum in Inglewood."

"Well, this only means one thing," I said.

"What's that?"

"Since we're wearing patriotic colors, at the same place, for the first time . . . it means, we need to be together, for the sake of America."

Shirley let out a laugh and said, "That's why we're here--too much apple pie." We laughed so loud the couple walking ahead of us began laughing. The man turned toward us and added, "We've all had too much American pie." I was drawn to Shirley's sense of humor.

As we walked, we got to known each other better. She began telling me how much she loved my book of poetry. I thanked her again for purchasing my books for her co-workers. I discovered Shirley was married, but separated for nearly a year. Her husband left while she was at work one day and never turned. "When Mr. Williamson abandoned me, " she said, "I almost lost my house." She consistently referred to her estranged husband as Mr. Williamson. Shirley was the second woman I had ever known to call her husband, 'Mister'. The first was Garrison's wife Liz . . . but she was Filipino. She even called me Mister Richard. After Shirley referred to her husband as Mr. Williamson for the sixth or seventh time, I asked her why didn't she call him by his first name.

"I only call him Mr. Williamson when I'm talking about him," she said, "but never to him."

"Why? He sounds like a dog to me."

"Everybody says that. But we all make mistakes. Mr. Williamson treated me fine for over 15 years. We have nice home, and he owned a small, successful plumbing business."

"So what! That was then. This is now," I reasoned.

"What you don't understand Richard is Mr. Williamson is not himself right now. He's on crack cocaine. He left me because he loved me. Rather than stay with me and keep fighting, which caused me *two* miscarriages, he had the decency to leave, before we killed each other. I won't desert him until he's dead, or I hear it from his own mouth he doesn't want me."

"How long was he on drugs before he sneaked out on you and the kids?"

"What kids? I didn't say we had kids. Anyway," she impatiently added, "Mr. Williamson was on drugs for eight years. Now tell me about you. What's driving you to be a glutton?"

After pausing a long time, I told her about Roxanne and me.

Shirley and I began meeting on the Southwest Community College track each morning for 45 minutes of walking. Then went our separate ways. Shirley was a good looking woman, about ten years younger than I. She was about 25 to 30 pounds overweight for her height, which was approximately 5'4". She worked at the telephone company as a supervisor on the swing shift. After walking with her about two weeks, we began talking on the phone, and later dating. Finally, I had regular female companionship.

Roxy had been gone approximately four months when Yolanda called and told me a serial rapist was loose in their community. She said a man raped two women living in their apartment building. Also, eight women throughout the neighborhood were sexually assaulted during the last couple of months. I heard about the rash of rape incidents in Burbank on the news. Most often, the rapist entered a home or apartment through an unlocked window. The police dubbed the guy as "The Mid-day Rapist" because he habitually assaulted women during the afternoon hours, when they were alone.

I tried not to become too concerned because both my daughters were usually away from home during the day, and they were together at night. Since schools would close soon for a two-week Christmas vacation, Yolanda felt Roxy would become vulnerable. We knew she liked to take a nap in the afternoon, while allowing a breeze to come through an open window.

Within a couple days, against Roxanne's tears, pleads, and strongest protest she was, to my relief, home again with me. During the first few days, we avoided each other as much as possible. This was merely our way of 'getting along. Roxanne stayed isolated behind her closed bedroom door as much as possible--even ate dinner in her bedroom, most of the time.

Though I was fully aware that my actions were as immature as my 16 year old daughter's, I allowed this estranged relationship to exist without confrontation. Not only did I feel helpless to amend the damage, but I was also preoccupied with writing newspaper columns, poems, and preparing anti-crime lectures. I didn't want to get sidetracked.

It was no secret that one of Roxanne's many resentments toward me was because our lifestyle was one of bare survival. After quitting my job with Dr. Dunlap, the money I earned working around the church, doing odd jobs for church members, lecturing, selling my books, and other speaking engagements, was just enough to take care of our rent and utilities. I seldom had enough money to provide my child with things important to a young girl--new clothes; money to get her hair done . . . The meager weekly allowance I gave her ($20) barely covered the expense for lunch and bus fare. As additional income, we received a monthly Social Security check for $190. Roxanne insisted, I give her the full Social Security check each month. Repeatedly, I explained to Roxanne the money I received, in her name, was to aid me in her care, not to be turned over to her like a paycheck. Of course, she was thoroughly disgusted with me. Now that Jennifer was away at college, Roxy carried the torch of hatred alone.

My daughters just did not seem to grasp the severity of my desperate situation. I didn't have a skill. Throughout my life, hustling and crime was all I knew. Now at the age of 49, I was trying to make it in a straight world. No hustle, no scam, just me and my writing. My poetry. My experiences. Somehow I had to make it work for me. They didn't understand that employers were not sounding their horns for older, unskilled ex-convicts. I dreaded the thought of being an old man working in a warehouse, sweeping floors, stacking boxes, or guarding a door.

Within a month of Roxanne's return home, I received a telephone call from Children's Hospital. There was an available time slot with a child psychologist, who could begin sessions with Roxanne as early as the next week. The sessions would be every Monday afternoon from 4 - 4:45 p.m. I knew Roxanne loathed the idea of therapy, but she had no choice in the matter. Our first meeting was to get acquainted more than anything else. The minisession took place on the 5th floor of Children's Hospital in Hollywood, with Doctor Howard Weinstein. Dr. Weinstein was a young Jewish man, about 20 years my junior. He dressed casually and spoke in a relaxed manner. Since all the paperwork had been done before this meeting, Dr. Weinstein had most of the background he needed to conduct this session.

We introduced ourselves and gently touched upon our concern and expectations. Roxanne did very little talking. Generally, only saying yes or no, with an intermediate grunt in the affirmative or negative. The allotted 45 minutes dragged by. Our introductory session was finished. Though Roxanne hadn't shared much, the little she did served as a starting point for her future sessions alone with Dr. Weinstein. The doctor made something clear to both of us--Roxanne's sessions were private! He did not expect me to question him regarding her every word. That was perfectly all right with me. I understood if she felt everything she said would only be repeated, she would never speak up or truly express herself in her one-on-one session. In addition, I had made my mind up not to drill her for information regarding her sessions. This only confirmed the doctor and I was in accord, at this point. However, during our introductory session a few new reasons (or excuses) for her resentment towards me were revealed. On the drive home I reflected on 'sound bites' of that session:

"So tell me how you feel about your father, Roxanne."
"I hate him!"
"Why is that so?"
"I don't know."
"Doctor Weinstein," I butted-in, "She usually claims it's because I won't give her more money and I rob her of HER social security check."
The child psychologist directs his response to Roxy.
"Is that true Roxanne?"
"That ain't the only reason," she snarled.
She cut her eyes at me and began to breathe deeply with her lips shut tight and puffed up. I looked at her with an expression that clearly asked the question, "Well, come on with it!"

She slowly turned her head in the direction of Dr. Weinstein, still looking like she was ready to fight and growled these words, "Every time I like somebody, HE (her voice raised on the word HE) runs them away." "What are you talking about, Roxanne?" I asked in an impatient tone.

"I'm not speaking to YOU!"

"Help me understand," the psychologist meekly interjected. "Who did your father cause to leave you Roxanne?"

She angrily answered the doctor, as she looked straight into my eyes, "First my mother! ...Then Evelyn! ...now Cynthia!"

"Wow," I thought, "this is heavy." The reference to her mother and Evelyn I understood. However, I didn't believe Roxy felt I had taken Cynthia out of her life. We belonged to the same church and saw one another regularly. Cynthia and I had mutually agreed, months earlier, our future as friends was much more viable than that of a romantic couple. As a result, we were in a stable and satisfactory platonic relationship. Perhaps Roxy harbored some idea of Cynthia becoming her new stepmother, and now I had sabotaged those secret wishes. I don't know! The doctor looked at his watch, and called an end to our introductory session.

Roxanne and I rode in the car together in complete silence, unless a question or statement of necessity was brought forward. On this trip home, I felt a little conversation was in order.

"Roxanne," I began, "since you think I'm so unfair, why don't we have our own therapy session at home with your sisters and anybody you chose to be there. This will give each of us a chance to be heard by other parties. Each person present may offer their opinion of what should be done to restore a sense of peace between us. What do you think?"

"I don't care what you do," was the cold reply.

"All right, it's all settled," I said. "When Jennifer and Rochelle come home from school, in a couple of weeks, for Christmas, we'll invite Yolanda, and your grandmother over for a family therapy session."

Roxy didn't speak, and silence resumed its usual seat in the car.

Shirley and I spent many evenings together at each other's apartment during

Roxy's stay in Burbank. Our love sessions were now restricted to her two bedroom house. Shirley didn't allow me to sleep there often, because she felt Mr. Williamson may pop up anytime. I once asked her, "Why don't you just get the locks changed?" She replied by asking me, "How would you like it if your wife got the locks changed on you, when you were sick?"

Roxy liked Shirley. They went to the movies with me. Shirley was trying to get Roxy to open her heart to me. I felt very good about Shirley's efforts, although nothing worked. Occasionally, when I caught Roxy in a semi-good mood, I would remind, her in a joking manner, "Shirley and I are dating but that doesn't mean we plan to share one another's Poligrip."

One afternoon, Shirley left a message on my answering machine inviting me over for dinner. She said, "I have something important to discuss with you." I figured that she was going to ask me to move in with her. I knew she was having it hard paying all the bills alone. As supervisor at the General Telephone Company, she made good money, but Mr. Williamson left her heavily in debt.

When I arrived, I was prepared to tell her I didn't want to live with her. I thought we had a good relationship, and we shouldn't rush things. Boy, was I in for a surprise! During dinner, Shirley brought up her husband. Immediately I sensed something different in her tone. Was she bringing our affair to an end?

"I hadn't told you before, but Mr. Williamson wants to talk to me."
"Has he contacted you?"
"Don't be mad. You're not going to get mad are you?"
"Why should I get mad," I said? "It's what you've being praying for, ain't it?"
"I haven't been praying for him to come home. I only prayed he would be all right. I would do that for anybody."
"Shirley, why don't you get to the point."
"You're getting mad. I can tell."
I didn't say anything. I knew I was on the verge of saying something ugly, therefore, I stuck a spoon of mashed potatoes in my mouth. As Shirley spoke,

I purposely kept my mouth full with food.

"Mr. Williamson sent me some flowers about two weeks ago. He sent them to my job. I left them at work and didn't say nothing to you because you would say that I was being stupid."

"Look! don't tell me what I was going to say. God don't even know what I'm going to say half the time. What makes you think you know?"

"I don't want to fight," she said. "I *AM* married to him. You knew that."

She then calmly reached beneath her plate and withdrew a small card. "This is the card that came with the flowers." She showed me the card which read: *I'm so sorry I hurt you. I hope it's not too late. (Signed) Al*

When I saw the card, my thoughts went back to the voice of my deceased wife, back stage at *The Oprah Winfrey Show*. I heard her voice again. "Going to church isn't enough. God wants you to cleanse your soul. Tell the ones you abused, you are sorry, before it's too late. I forgive you Rick. Tell the others, you are sorry, before it's too late."

Shirley went on to explain, Mr. Williamson began to call her at work about five weeks ago. He told her he spent the last six months in a drug recovery center. Before that he lived on the streets for nearly eight months, sleeping outside and eating wherever he could. He didn't want to return home the way he left. Therefore, he stayed away. About eight or nine months ago, he passed out from hunger, while bumming change at a gas station and was rushed to a nearby private hospital. When the hospital clerks discovered prepaid hospitalization and medical membership cards in his wallet, they proceeded to save his life. Without insurance, Mr. Williamson believed the hospital would have released him with a drug prescription and a recommendation to the L.A. County Hospital. He sincerely thanked her for keeping up his insurance. After 39 days of hospital care, Mr. Williamson was released. He then committed himself to their out patient rehab program. He was drug free for eight months, and had started another plumbing business which was five months old.

I listened closely without interrupting. Finally, I asked, "So what's the bottom line? Are the two of you getting back together or what? Shirley said, "I don't know what Mr. Williamson and I are going to do. That is up to God. But the question is, what are you and I going to do . . . I'm pregnant!'"

Months passed since Roxy had begun her mental therapy sessions. I considered it more of an exercise of futility than anything else. However, I was beginning to recognize a small positive change in her attitude. I attributed the change more to the active involvement of her sisters and her grandmother. Everyone spoke to Roxy about her disrespectful attitude toward me. It was gradually sinking in.

My daughters and I held two group family sessions before the change was apparent. Our sessions, though meant to be calm and productive, usually got loud and unruly. Yolanda had charge over the group meeting. This of course, was quite all right with me. It was the way I wanted it. Since I was the accused culprit, it was only reasonable for me to do more listening than talking. The rules were simple; anyone may say whatever is on their heart without fear or threat of reprisal. Only one person talks at a time. And we must stop and hug each other at the end of our 45 minutes session.

During the first session, Roxanne spoke and even cried while repeatedly claiming, she didn't know why she hated me. She admitted, under questioning by Yolanda, she couldn't recall anything I did to her to deserve her scorn. Jennifer suggested it was because I didn't give Roxanne enough money to buy herself clothes, get her hair done regularly, or purchase her personal female items, and such. She charged that I only gave Roxy enough money for bus fare and lunch during the school week. Roxy smilingly agreed. I began to call Jennifer, Roxy's attorney.

Rochelle mostly sat silently. When she did speak, her concern was that I should not expect her baby sister to do all the house work and all the cooking. Roxy again smilingly agreed. Yolanda came up with a couple of suggestions toward the closing of our 45 minutes. She said, I should give Roxy more money and share in the housework. I protested on the grounds I was too busy. As far as the money went, I just couldn't afford it. Well, they united in formidable rebuttal. At the conclusion, I conceded. We all have a good laugh

250

and hug afterwards, though, I really was not overjoyed.

Sacrifices had to be made. I lived up to everything promised. I asked Reverend McDaniel if he had work at his church. Within one week, I was working for St. Jude Baptist Church. I increased my daughter's allowance from $20 per week to $50 per week. However, she had to agree to do all the housework.

During our next session, a few months later, everything went a bit smoother, though we still had things to work out. Yolanda even brought up some unhealed wounds, she claimed I left on her. So did Jennifer. In addition, Jennifer felt I should send Evelyn money for Darren. Rochelle was quiet again, except to defend me by saying, I was doing the best I could and should not be criticized so harshly. I agreed. After our time was up, we all hugged and laughed. I offered to prepare dinner for everyone but no one accepted. So we went out to eat and chipped in on the check.

Shortly after that, I allowed Roxanne to stop going to the weekly sessions at Children's Hospital. Our relationship was good. She had accompanied me on poetry recitals and other speaking engagements. We went to plays and movies together. At home, we seldom sat in separate rooms to eat or watch TV. We didn't sit around talking and smiling at each other all the time, each had their personal projects and needed a degree of privacy. However, there was an obvious touch of God in the picture.

I saw very little of Shirley during her pregnancy. After I told her the prospects of becoming a father for the sixth time didn't appeal to me, she became angry. "If that's the way you feel about children you shouldn't have unprotected sex," she said bitterly. "Look Shirley," I replied, "you asked me, what I wanted to do about it. Right? I don't care what you do. It's up to you!" Shirley promptly rose from the table and said, "Don't you think you've said enough? I think you should leave. I'm expecting company."

After that evening, I didn't see her again for five months. However, I called her every few weeks, just to see how she was doing. She was angry with me for not being happy about her condition. I understood why she was elated. She had no children and her biological clock was running out of time. She had a good job, a home, medical insurance, good credit, retirement plan, and even a few stocks and bonds. I didn't have a darn thing in my favor. I barely got by. So bringing another child into the world, for me, was nothing to dance about.

When Shirley was approximately seven months pregnant, she invited me over to meet Mr. Williamson. They reunited three months earlier. Shirley told me her husband was working six and sometimes seven days a week rebuilding his plumbing business. He begged Shirley's forgiveness for his behavior and assured her that he no longer sought comfort in drugs. Shirley said, his brother and sister were murdered in separate incidents within a few weeks of each other about nine or ten years ago. Shortly afterwards, Mr. Williamson began to drink heavily. Gradually, he brought home marijuana and cocaine. His business and marriage started to suffer. It wasn't long before he was stealing money from his wife's purse. Shirley knew he was seriously addicted to when he violently attacked her over her pay check. She wanted to pay bills, and he wanted to buy drugs.

Mr. Williamson wanted to meet the man who had impregnated his wife, and discuss the future of the baby. Shirley and her husband sincerely loved one another. They wanted their marriage to last. They felt, since I was the father of her child, I should become cordially acquainted with the step father. I thought it was a very good idea. I wished more men were as responsible as Mr. Williamson. I finally understood why Shirley didn't allow anyone to disrespect him. She never told me his first name, and I never asked.

As I approached the front door, apprehension set in. However, I pushed myself forward. Shirley opened the door within ten seconds. I felt awkward. Was I expecting to greet her with a Christian hug, or a 'long time no-see' handshake? A warm friendly smile would have to suffice. "Welcome to the scene of the crime," Shirley joked. All of a sudden, her sense of humor didn't appeal to me. Shirley sensed my anxiety.
"Don't be uptight," she said.
"I didn't come here to be put in a trick," I replied.

She walked ahead to the dining room. I followed. Before I sat, a man about my complexion, height and built was coming through the kitchen door carrying a tray of snacks. I remained standing and waited to be introduced. When he put the tray down, Shirley said, "Gentlemen, through marriage or D.N.A. we're bonded forever. Let's make the most of it, for the sake of the baby." Then she introduced us. "Al meet Richard, the baby's father. Richard meet Al, my husband of 16 years." I extended my hand and said to Shirley, "I was expecting you to say meet Mr. Williamson." Al laughed and said, "I was expecting her to introduce you as Mr. Jones." We all laughed and sat around the dining room. Shirley immediately said, "You two have more than me in common." We waited for her to continue. After she sipped her soda, she said, "You're both from St. Louis."

Al screamed, "Richard Jones! I be a monkey's uncle! You're Richard Jones!" I yelled his name, "Alan! Alan Williamson! Man oh man! How in world have you been?" Then we shouted in unison, "I thought you were dead by now!" A hardy laughter followed.

Shirley sat dumbfounded for several seconds. Then she said sarcastically, "Are there any more men out here from St. Louis, I should be forewarned about?"

Alan and I tried to catch up on each other lives since our days in St. Louis. Too much time had passed. I was surprised to learn Alan had married *Irene Rogers*. The two of them began dating in high school, and married while they were in college. They had one child, who drowned in their backyard swimming pool at two years old. Each blamed the other for the child's death. Alan blamed Irene because she was home with the baby at the time of the accident. and such had been more responsible. But Irene had a drinking problem. Irene blamed Alan because she warned him about buying a home with a swimming pool. Alan and Irene divorced after four years of marriage. Alan moved to Los Angeles a year after his marriage ended. He met Shirley 20 years ago. Shirley had an apartment with a clogged kitchen sink. Her apartment manager sent her over a plumber, and future husband, to fix it.

Tank, Alan's brother was shot and killed, about 10 years earlier by a teenage street robber, in St. Louis. Their sister Brandi was so distraught over Tank's death, she began medicating herself to sleep each night. Three months later, she died of a drug overdose. The devastation of losing your only brother and only sister in such a short span of time, was too much for Alan to endure. He turned to drugs for comfort.

Alan asked me if I still remembered Connie and Mrs. Love, his first regular customers on the newspaper route. I laughed and assured him I did. He knew I was laughing about the time he saw Connie naked, but neither brought the incident up. He told me, Connie moved away within six month after I left. I asked him, "Whatever became of Mrs. Love?" Alan said, "Mrs. Love had her other breast removed, and died two years later." Alan kept the route for five years.

Regarding the child and business at hand, Shirley and Alan wanted me to give up my parental rights to the unborn child. Alan hoped to adopt the baby. Though it was a noble gesture on his part, I was not inclined to oblige. However, before the evening ended, I asked Shirley if she had any names picked for the baby. When she said no, I made a suggestion. "If it's a boy, name him Tyrone, after Alan's brother Tank. And if it's a girl, name her Brandi, after Alan's sister." We were in full agreement.

As the weeks passed, I received several invitations to recite poetry and lecture on crime prevention. The engagements were for pay, and a forum to sell books. I called a local television news program and left a message on their voice mail. This program was called *UPN News 13*. Each night this news program aired at 10 thru 11 p.m. The hour was broken down into several segments; Health Watch, Travel Watch; Crime Watch, Weather Watch, etc. During each segment an expert gave advice, information or tips.

My interest focused heavily on the Crime Watch Segment. Their tipster was a police officer. Naturally, I figured the public would be more informed if *UPN News 13*, occasionally allowed an ex-criminal to advise viewers, how to reduce the risk of being ripped-off. Therefore, I represented myself as author of <u>Tips Against Crime, Written From Prison</u>, a crime prevention columnist with The L.A. Watts Times Newspaper, and The California Crusader Newspaper. Finally, one of their reporters returned my call with an invitation to appear on their news program. This opportunity had great potential. I figured an enormous following of people watched their program. My mind raced with visions of book sales, and speaking engagements.

Over the next two months, I appeared on their program four times. My books sales didn't budge. Friends told me, I was only being used because the news program introduced me as an ex-convict and not as a 'safety consultant'. They did not show my book to the viewers, instead only made slight mention of it. Perhaps they're right, but I was elated. To me, it was just another stepping stone to a better place.

Everywhere I went for months, someone would say they saw me on TV and thanked me for the advice. Many people expressed interest in purchasing my book and wanted to know where to find it. I gave them the publisher's telephone number, but only a few calls.

During this time The A.C.C. Church and Community Newspaper office manager, Beverly Boxie asked me if I would recite a few poems for their Annual Pauline Awards. This event was known throughout the Los Angeles Baptist church community to be a gala affair. Usually, it was held in a top class hotel and the tickets sold for $60 to $70 each. The attire was always formal. The Pauline Award Banquet also featured great gospel entertainers and a fabulous dinner. The purpose of the Pauline Awards was to raise scholarship funds for high school seniors.

Beverly teased me saying, "Since you're getting to be a television celebrity, I figured we better snag you before you forget who we are." I was honored to accept her invitation. This would be an opportunity for me to perform for hundreds, perhaps nearly a thousand Christians at once. I thought about the many future invitations I would get from various churches, and the poetry book sales. My latest book, I'm in the Mood for God would make it's debut.

Beverly told me that The Pauline Awards Committee did not have the extra funds to pay me, but I could invite four guests. "No problem," I quickly replied, "I'll invite my four daughters." My private thoughts were, "Good this would be an opportunity to make them proud of me, if only for a night." Roxanne and I were still showing love and respect one another. Sometimes I would find myself wondering how God did it. I knew I was not the cause. Roxy was excited about my upcoming performance. Roxy phoned her sisters and invited them. They all shuffled their schedules to be there.

The Pauline Awards was over a month away, this gave me ample time to compose a special poem. For years, I wanted to do something to commemorate my daughter's mother. The title, **"When Mama's Gone,"** stayed with me, but the words were slow in forming.

While busy at the typewriter one morning, I got a call from Gil Cofrancesco. He informed the 'Dumpster Diving' piece, we shot for television a couple years earlier, had been requested by *The Today Show*. Also, *The Leeza Show* recently asked him if he knew an ex-con man type, who could give anti-crime tips on their national television show. "So what do ya think Richard? Would you like for me to give the producers of *The Leeza Show* your number?"

Though Gil had a good sense of humor, I knew he wasn't kidding about this. It seemed hard to believe. Two popular national TV programs in one phone call. "Sure Gil," I exclaimed, "Give it to them right away." We chatted on the phone a few more moments and then he said that he'd better hang up and pass along my phone number before they find someone else.

Within five minutes, my phone rang again. This it was one of the producers from *The Leeza Show*. After we talked for about 15 minutes regarding different cons and scams, the producer said their show was interested in re-enacting the 'Dumpster Diving' piece. I would be paid $200. By this time, in my Crime Fighting career, I learned to insist my book be not only mentioned on television, but also shown. I was assured this simple request would be honored. The producer laid out exactly what she had in mind for the show. Sunday morning, Reverend Mark Wrigley announced to the congregation that Brother Jones would be appearing on *The Today Show* and *The Leeza Show*.

The entire church reacted. Some applauded, some nodded approvingly and many congratulated me with hugs and handshakes after service. Cochran Avenue Baptist Church was always supportive.

The following Tuesday morning, at approximately eight o'clock, a black limousine arrived to transport me to Paramount Studios. Everything went as expected. Leeza Gibbons was a friendly and fun person to work with. She held my book in her hand on camera and advised her viewers that it was a very resourceful book that would benefit all readers. When the show aired millions of people around the United States saw my book, but unfortunately no one knew where to get it. Sandcastle Publisher did not market 'my book' aggressively, therefore, the big bookstores did not have it on their shelf. Only a select few stores, no more then 20 had my crime prevention book.

Alan was at peace with the fact his wife had become pregnant by another man. He told me, he knew in his heart, Shirley would have never sought the compassion of an extra marital affair, had he been there for her. I seriously agreed with him. Shirley was the type of woman I wished I had married while my children were young. She was the role model I wanted for them. But my attachment to her was a mere drop in the bucket compared to Alan's love.

Shirley was nearly 40-years-old and her doctors warned her this would be her last chance at motherhood, without high risk. After this she should have her tubes tied. She had lost two babies before. Shirley and Alan purposely avoided having children the first eight years of their marriage. Their plans were to wait until Alan established his business, for Shirley to graduate from college with a master's degree in business, and then buy a small house. Ironically, when these accomplishments were met, crack cocaine invaded their lives. One thing I had to admit, Alan planned for his family better than I had. All of my children were the result of unplanned pregnancies. When they were born, I didn't have a pot to piss in.

Shirley had been rushed to hospital the day before, but it turned out to be another false alarm. Alan called me from the hospital. He was more excited than anyone could image under the circumstances. He said, "Shirley was in with the doctors, but it didn't seem she was gonna be admitted. Richard, I ran two red lights getting her here on time, and now these dogs aren't going to keep her. She's in pain, and these dogs . . . I gotta go! They're wheeling her this way . . . "

"Through this godsend child, Richard," Alan told me as I was leaving his house on the first night of my visit, "I will see the love of my wife, hear the laughter of my brother and sister. Most of all, every time thoughts of drugs enter my head, this child will remind me to stay clean and sober forever."

My mother didn't know she was about to become a grandmother for the ninth time. She knew of Shirley through Roxanne, but I hadn't told anyone about her pregnancy.

When I visited my mother's house, we would usually sit in the living room and watch television as we talked. The news was on. It was the usual Los Angeles nightly reports of another baby shot by a gang member. That followed a report of a newborn baby found abandoned in a trash dumpster.

"Seems like a woman wouldn't go full term, only to abandon the baby," Mommy said in response to the latter report.
Suddenly, I asked without thinking. It just popped out.
"Why didn't you abandon us?"
Instantly, I saw the shock in my 68-year-old mother's face. Before she uttered a sound, I continued.
"You used to beat us near to death, and often wished we were dead. So why didn't you abandon us at birth?"
I watched her eyes as they frantically searched the room. My mother long ago taught us that when she starts to look around the room like that, she's looking for a weapon. Her eyes fixed on a heavy glass center piece on the coffee table a few feet beyond her reach. Then she spoke.
"If this is all you came by for, you can just get up and leave now."
"I didn't come by for this, nor was I born for what I got. Look Mommy, I'm confused, that is all."
"I'm confused too! Why come by here when you're confused? Go see a psychiatrist! Do you need therapy? I'm just sitting in 'MY' house, minding

my own business and you come by here . . . " Her next few words were so familiar, we spoke them in unison.

"...getting on my last nerve."

Big mistake on my part. She reached for the center piece, but I beat her to it and slid it out of her reach.

"Wait Mommy, please! I apologize! Let's talk! We must talk."

Now I could see tears forming in the corner of her eyes.

"Look Mommy, all I want is a few answers. We have never really talked. We laugh and sing. We kiss and fight. I know you've always tried to be there for us. And you were. I even think of you as my Guardian Angel. On the other hand, you've scarred each of us. Tammie, Elaine, and me! Why? We all turned out to be teenage alcoholics. Cruel to our children. Can't manage loving relationship. Each of us is a little bit crazy! Perhaps we can work it out. I don't visit as often as I would like. Elaine don't visit at all, unless she's borrowing or repaying something. All I want to know is why."

"Okay! You wanna talk! Let's talk! I beat yo' butts like mine got beat. I did it because I didn't know any other way. My mother use to drag me by my nappy head and beat me with anything she laid her hands on."

Mommy's tears their flowing freely, and her voice was getting louder. "As she was beating me for whatever reason, she often said, "When you have children, I hope they are ten times worst than you.""

She stood up from the sofa, but didn't reach for an object. Her tears worried me, they usually were followed by an attack. I knew she had weapons stashed all over her house. I just sat quietly.

"I was afraid you would turn out like Mama said I was, bad as they come," she screamed. "But Mama loved me. She would do anything to help me. Even from her grave she still helps me and talk to me. She talking to me right now, but I'm not listening. She says, I oughta bust you in your head with something. Oh, I want to mama, I know he needs it. But not this time. I ain't listening . . . You wanna talk! Let's talk!"

More than two hours passed before I told my mother about Shirley. Our discussion was so tensed and awakening, I nearly forgot my reason for being there. My mother had one sister and two brothers, which she fought with constantly as a youth. They were of a very light complexion, after their mother, and she took the dark hue of their father. Since her father didn't live with them, she was the darkest person in the house. Her siblings would call her ugly names in their childish anger and teasing. Though my mother was younger and smaller than her brothers, her pain and rage gave her the fury to conquer them in combat. Her anger overflowed into the streets and school. Soon she became known as the toughest girl in her class, school, and neighborhood. Fighting became her trademark. She protected her sister and fought with her brothers against their enemies. Although my mother's mother

was nurturing she was firm, and my mother was defiant. It was these attitudes that lead to her being send to a young woman's reform school for two years. By her release, she had taken on the form of a full-grown woman, though only 15-years-old. The men were mad about her. The females were jealous of her. Though she had dark skin, and most colored men of that era were crazy about high-yellow women, she proved to be the exception. Mommy could get nearly any man, and whip nearly any woman. Her good self-esteem was forever on high.

Mommy was impregnated by my older sister's father when she was 16-years-old. She disliked the rules of home and wanted out. She hoped this handsome 30-year-old night club entertainer would marry her, as he promised. The truth revealed him to be a married man, just out lying and having fun. He laughed in her face at the news of her pregnancy. Although, her mother welcomed her to stay home, she was too ashamed. While pregnant and living alone in a rooming house, my mother met and married, a watermelon man, my soon to be father. However, he turned out to be just another lying man. He flirted with every young woman that came to purchase from his produce truck. When I was less than a year old, my father left for a 14-year old-girl. After he was gone for two months, my mother realized she was pregnant again. She contacted him because she believed he still cared and would return as her husband. When she was four months pregnant, he did return. My mother confronted him with her findings that he had impregnated three other young women. She wanted to know why had he bothered marrying her. His response was to remove his belt and beat her. Though she was pregnant, they fought viciously. When he stomped out of the house, mother was left bruised, swollen, and bleeding. Later that night, she was rushed to the hospital and loss the baby.

Later Mommy met Elaine's father. "He was the nice until he got drunk," Mommy said. "He loved to fight and drink almost as much as he loved me." After a half dozen bloody battles, she ran away from him. At 19- years-old and the single mother of three children, my mother's heart formed a callousness for men that never died.

Sometimes she worked two full-time jobs. And when she thought we didn't appreciate her, after all she'd gone through, it was easy to scream I wish you were born dead or I ought send you to a reform school.
"I tried too! I tried to send y'all away, but the police station wouldn't take you," she cried. "Do you remember that?"
"Yeah Mommy, I remember that."

I found myself in tears before Mommy finished. She said again and again, "I beat y'all the way I did because I didn't know any better, and didn't want y'all to turn out the way my mother said you would." "I tried to make you a man," she moaned. "I allowed you to leave the house early at a young age, shining shoes, selling papers. I even took you to work with me and introduced you to Miss Goldstein. She hired you to work. Remember that?"

"Yeah Mommy, I remember."
"You were allowed to say grace at the table. Remember? I tried. I did the best I could."

Mommy said something I didn't recall hearing her say before. "Richard, I'm so sorry. Please tell Tammie, I'm sorry. Tell Elaine, I'm sorry. I just can't. I can't go through this again." We both cried. I sat beside her exhausted body and embraced her saying, "Mommy I love you, I love you. We all love you. But we never talked. We never knew! Now I understand. And I remember.

We moved so much because I was so bad. Disturbing the neighbors with loud parties while you were at work. I played hooky from school and even had girls in your bed, while you were working two jobs. I could have been a better son, but I just complained and never did anything to make your burden lighter. I took money from your purse and even stole items from the house to sell. Just so I could have extra money to jingle in my pocket. Remember the time you thought the house was broken into. I did that."

"I know," mother cried. "I know you did. But I didn't know what to do, so I did nothing."
"Mommy, please forgive me. I'm sorry for all the pain you've lived with."
Suddenly, I thought of Ann's words. "Tell the ones you abused you are sorry, before it's too late. God wants you to cleanse your soul. Going to church isn't enough. Tell the others you are sorry, before it's too late."

My mother and I sat together on her couch, holding hands and trying to smile. We cried together. I began to feel refreshed and free of the burden I carried for so long. That evening I discovered that it was fool hearted of me to blame my mother for the failures of my adulthood. In my youth, I was dependent and thought like a child. Now, 40 years later, it was insane of me to squander time looking for excuses. I had been wandering in the wilderness for 40 years. The biblical scripture came to mind. "And ye shall know the truth and the truth will make ye free."

"Mommy do you mind if I pray for us?" Mommy bowed her head and squeezed my hands but didn't say anything. I bowed my head and thought 'what a mighty God we serve'. *Oh Heavenly Father! Thank you for this day. I've been blind for so long, but now I see. Thank you Lord. Thank you for Jesus. Your son died on the cross that the world would love one another. We show our love for you Lord Jesus by loving one another. You said in Your Word that we cannot love you, which we never seen and not love the ones we see. There is no hatred or fear in my heart. There are no grudge or harsh feelings in my heart for anyone. In Your Word, you teach us that, we cannot expect you to forgive us, if we can't forgive others. Thank you Lord for my mother. Thank you for giving her the strength to endure my wayward soul. Thank you for giving her the love for her children that caused her to spare not the rod.*

Please bring us closer together as a family Lord. Touch the heart of my sister Elaine. Teach her to love and forgive. Teach Tammie to love and forgive. Teach my mother to love and forgive.

Forgive me God for walking in the steps of Satan for so many years. Spare me time to serve you. To do your will. Give my family the wisdom to serve you. I love you Lord . . . Thank you for the troubles I seen. Thank you for my mistakes. I know it was for a reason Lord. Thank you for putting Annie Mae in my life. She told me you loved me Lord. She did what you called her to do. She taught our daughters of your love Lord. Praise the name of Jesus.

Thank you for Evelyn. She told me of you Lord. She taught my daughters of your love. Forgive me for corrupting her. She loves you. Forgive me Lord. Bless our son Darren. Give him the wisdom to honor his mother and father.

Thank you for putting pastors in my life Lord. Thank you for Pastor Barrs, 35 years ago. Thank you for Pastor Hill. Through his preaching, many people are brought closer to you. Thank you for sending me to Cochran Avenue Baptist Church. It has been a haven in time of need.

My life would be nothing without you Lord. Thank you for everything. My children are healthy and smart. My mother is still with me. Forgive me for hating my earthy father Lord. Though he left us many years ago, you knew my mother would be better off without him. You proved to be all we needed Lord. Thank you Father. Thank you, Thank you. Thank you for putting a loving husband like Nate in my mother's life. Though he's dead now lord, let him know I loved him. Thank you for Shirley. Bless our child and make him or her a healthy, godly creature. Thank you for bringing Al back into her life. Bless their marriage. In the name of Jesus . . . Amen."

Mommy snatched her hand from mine immediately after I said, "Amen." "Thank you for Shirley! Bless our child! Bless their marriage! What are you talking about?" she asked with a puzzled look. I began laughing and could hardly stop. She sat silently and seriously waiting. Finally when I told Mommy about Shirley's condition, it cheered her up. The saga of Alan and me, struck her as amusing. Mommy said, "Nothing but divine destiny brought you into the life of Shirley and your friend. Now they will know the joy of parenthood. It can be beautiful, you know. But remember, your friendship with that boy was 35 years ago. Let that alone! Just go around, no more than once a month to see the baby. You'll stay friends longer that way." I promised Mommy, I would not rekindle a palsy walsy relationship with Alan or Shirley. I left my mother's home feeling better than I had felt in a long time.

On the evening of The Pauline Awards we all sat around my apartment making jokes about my verbal blunders on television. The ceremony was to begin in two hours. The drive to The Marina Marriott Hotel would only take about fifteen minutes. There was still plenty of time.

Jennifer's flew in from Northern California the day before the awards. She would stay a few days. Rochelle drove in from Northridge that was 35 minutes away. However, she would be staying over the weekend. Yolanda was in Burbank, but worked in the Wilshire district of Los Angeles, which was only 10 minutes from my apartment. She came over directly from work. All the young women brought their gowns and jewelry. Jennifer and Rochelle still fitted into their prom dresses. Yolanda, known to the family as the Mistress of Fashion, owned several formal dresses and brought at least three selections to pick from. Earlier in the week, Roxanne went shopping with her Aunt Elaine and purchased a very beautiful evening gown. I rented a tuxedo with all the trimming. We bumped into each other at the bathroom mirror while getting ready. At other moments, we found ourselves seated around the dinning table laughing and talking. I shared with them the events surrounding Shirley, Alan, me, and their unborn sibling.

In many ways, I didn't want this experience to end, not even for The Pauline Awards. It reminded me of happier times, when we sat around and played parlor games. The girls turned out to be intelligent, ambition young women. I was extremely proud of them. After much hustle and bustle, the time had come to leave the house.

The decision was easily made to take Yolanda's car since it was a brand new full size four door BMW. Yolanda drove, I sat in the front. My three younger daughters sat in the back. Yolanda, one of the original Heavy Foot Sisters, still had a heavy gas foot. We were there in ten minutes.

Once inside the spacious reception area, we mingled and conversed with other fabulously attired guests. There were more than 600 people present who represented approximately 100 churches. My daughters were impressed by the number of people who came over just to shake my hand and tell me how much they enjoy my column in *The A.C.C.* It was only three or four, but to them it seems like a lot.

Rochelle spotted members of Cochran Avenue Baptist Church. Gayetta, Gaynelle and Cynthia were there and several others. We all went over and joined them. I thought that nobody else from Cochran was there until we were joined by Martha Acorn. Jennifer and Martha had a special relationship because Jennifer use to baby sit Martha's grandson. The two of them lovingly embraced. The evening was getting off to a warm and spiritual start.

By 7:45 p.m., all the guests were seated at their assigned dining table in the Grand Ballroom. I arranged, through Beverly Boxie, to have Gaynelle, her boyfriend, Wally Church, Gaynetta, Cynthia and Martha seated at my table with my daughters, and me. There were television cameras and professional photographers snapping pictures and recording everything. The sumptuous dinner was served in a timely, ceremonious manner. There was much laughter and small talk through the ballroom. An array of Christian entertainment was on the program. Awards would be given to various individuals for exemplary Christian service, after our meal.

Finally, at approximately 10:50 p.m., after a brief introduction I was presented to the audience. As I stood at the podium I noticed for the first time at least five other people from Cochran throughout the Grand Ballroom. They smiled and nodded with approval. Gradually, I realized about 50 per cent of the room was applauding. A few rose to their feet, and I hadn't even opened my mouth. It finally dawned on me, I had fans!

The applause descended into a whispering hush after several seconds of my standing patiently and silent. "Thank you . . . Thank you very much," I said to them. "Can somebody say, Praise the Lord?" It seemed the whole room said, "Praise the Lord" in unison. And then I said, "He's worthy to be praised. Say praise the Lord Somebody." Again the glorious sound of, "Praise the Lord," came forward in harmony. The stage, upon which I stood, was quite huge. It was no effort for me to make eye contact with anyone in the room. I noticed a middle-aged gentleman and a young boy, both in white tuxedos, sitting at the same table. A father/son pair, I thought. After making an optical connection with the father and son couple, and got my flow on. "This poem is entitled:

Thou Art My Son

To every black father who loves his boy
You better talk to him and don't be coy
Tell him, Life is doing time without parole
So you better be mindful of how you stroll
I love you dearly, Thou Art My Son

And I won't see you ruined like the other ones
Don't drop out of school like a wimp that can't take
Study harder than before I KNOW you can make it

(At this point, I broke our eye contact and began panning my audience, using much body language, and playing to the tv cameras. I modulated for emphasis and maintained a caring but serious countenance.)

The eyes of the world are watching YOU!

(I point my finger directly in the direction of a teenage boy at the front of the room seated with what seemed to be a family group.)

And the odds are heavy you won't make it through

266

WHEN MAMA'S GONE

(I began to get my stroll on)

Infatuated girls will call you King of The pack
But take it lightly, or it WILL hold you back
Avoid the reputation of a promiscuous stud
It inflates an insecure ego, and turns a pure heart mud

(I had the audience full attention now. Many were encouraging me on with calls of 'Amen, Say it! Teach! That's Right! '.)

If you stumble into the cycle of crime
You might elude the law for a long-long time

But when -I SAID WHEN- you're caught, remember this
There ain't no future, in being a snitch . . .
Thou Art My Son

These words must come from a mellowed. BLACK MAN!

(I said the word BLACK MAN with an extra degree of force and authority.)

For a woman can't make a boy understand
What to do expect as a black male adult

And how to maneuver through this maze with the best results

Listen my son, I think you know
All that shines isn't gold and all that's white isn't snow

Be careful whom you consider a friend
The biggest smiles will do you in

Though you should always be forgiving, that's God's advice
But never let the same dog bite you twice

(That last line always gets a laugh, and this time was no exception. I elevated my voice for the next line to snap their attention back in place, as I panned the room and move freely about on stage.)

And when your heart is troubled and your mind seeks peace
And there will be times you're harassed by the local police
just reach with your soul and beseech The Lord
He'll see you through when times are hard . . .
Thou Art My Son

(The crowd continued sending nods and expressions of approval)

Avoid all substances that sedate your mind
Or your brain power will lag behind
Here's some useful information you should deem
And It will bring you racial pride and high self-esteem
To know your great ancestors were of royalty
And were embraced by honor and loyalty
In order to enjoy a life of dignity
You MUST study your BLACK HISTORY!

(My glance targeted the father and son in the white tux, again.)

Making babies don't prove that you're a man
Save your money son, invest in land

(My glance found several very attractive ladies at one table.)

Respect you mother and all womankind
But know a virtuous woman is hard to find
Don't be manipulated when females whine
That's a tactic some use from time to time

(I began winding down, relaxing my tone)

Remember these words even when you're old
Wisdom is more secure than gold
Now I can rest in peace because you've been told
Life is doing time without parole . . . Thou Art My Son

(With that I had finished and bowed my head saying . . .)

"Thank You!"

The crowd erupted with applause. Many were standing. The man and boy in the white tuxedos were both honoring me with a standing ovation. From my table, there were much excitement, waving and applauding. Only Yolanda was standing. I instantly realized this was her first time hearing or seeing me perform in public. I could tell she was very impressed. I waved toward my table saying. "Thank You!"

When the response to my performance simmered down, I introduced my next piece. I returned to the podium with microphone in hand. I reached inside my jacket and withdrew a white business size envelope and removed its contents. After placing the lone sheet of typing paper on the podium, I raised my eyes to the audience and spoke.

"This is a very special poem you are about to hear. It's in memory of my daughters' mother, my deceased wife, and the only woman I loved." The chatter lowered to a faint muffle. I lifted my head and focused on the magnificently grand silver and crystal candelabra hanging from the towering majestic ceiling. "Annie Mae" I said with my voice beginning to break, "When you went 'HOME' some 16-years-ago, our daughters were just baby girls. On this gala evening, in the presence of God and others, I present to you, four beautiful young ladies, whom you know well. If I must say so myself, they have done you PROUD." A burst of applause followed. My daughters were all smiling at me. The silence returned quickly. "The title of this poem is," I announced with stately decorum, "When Mama's Gone."

WHEN MAMA'S GONE

"A father's duty, if he's true

(my concentration and words were fixed upon The Jones Sisters)

Is to nurture love and take care of you
To never forsake or leave you alone

*(No sooner than I said that line I thought about how I didn't   leave
them alone, and the images of the past begin to visit me. I saw my kids
getting on the bus for MISSISSIPPI. I saw myself shackled and being
lead to the prison bus.)*

To be father and mother, WHEN MAMA'S GONE
While you were yet young, and still at play

(images of Yolanda and her mother playing Pattie cake)

God called your mother in His own way

*(My voice was beginning to crack again. I slowly turned my stare toward
the paper on the podium and soaked up a few more lines. I couldn't
understand this new emotion. One thing I did know, it was real. I
modulated.)*

Perhaps her destiny on GOD's earth
Was to give four beautiful babies birth

*(I noticed Rochelle was dabbing her eyes with a napkin.
She was crying. Not audibly. Just tears. Without
warning, I felt my nose begin to tingle. A
tear was imminent.)*

I've fallen short, I'm not the best

*(Oh how true I thought. Suddenly I became aware that
all eyes were locked on the poet on stage. And beyond
the stage nobody made sound.)*

But GOD's not finish with me yet

Being your father was MY destiny
                    (emphasis on MY)

He placed a mountain of faith in me

(I moved from the podium with mic in hand, toward their direction)

There were laughs, there was pain

*(images of us having a good time and image of us bitterly arguing came
simultaneously)*

There were times, I called your mother's name
The Lord gave me strength to carry on
To be mother and father, When Mama's Gone

(Roxanne was now dabbing her eyes)

Yolanda, Rochelle Jennifer and Roxanne

(My eyes were watery by now. I wondered if anyone knew.)

Some things we'll NEVER understand
And it is not our mission to second guess

GOD *(emphasis on GOD)* is the potter,
and He knows best

You girls have done your mother proud

271

(I saw them all in their Jr. high school or high school receiving a diploma in cap and gown)

She looks down from the clouds

She gave you your first ice cream cone
And you've done ME proud, WHEN MAMA'S GONE . . .

Thank You.".

Most everybody rose to their feet with applause. As for me, tears peered over my eyelids and threatened to fall. I swiftly returned the mic to the podium and embraced the male emcee, Joel Webster, Cochran Avenue Baptist Church choir director. Co-hosting with him was the very popular gospel and jazz singer Rose Mary Mallett, waiting to speak or present another artist. She also embraced me, and gave me a kiss on the cheek. I whispered to Rose Mary, "May I see you later." She whispered, "No way, I see all those lovely women at your table."

The remainder of the evening reached its mark within the next 30 minutes. My daughters and I had a great time. At least a half dozen guests that night commented on how similar each of us looked. Of course, we have heard that for many years. On the way back to my apartment I drove, while the girls talked and laughed so much until I no longer paid them any attention. The only thing on my mind was trying to figure a way to meet Rose Mary Mallett.

The telephone was still ringing as I fumbled with my keys at the door. Roxanne rushed in and grabbed the phone just in time. I heard her repeat herself twice.
"What? What? Okay, what floor? ...All right, I got it!"
"Who was that?" Yolanda asked.
Roxy directed her response to me.
"Daddy, it was your friend Alan. He said Shirley is on her way to
Kaiser Hospital, and for you to meet them there."

272

Someone yelled, "Shirley's having the baby!"

We went straight to the hospital. As I drove the girls discussed whether they wanted a sister or a brother. The choices were two to two. Rochelle asked, "Which do you prefer, Daddy, a boy or a girl."
"Twins!" I kidded. "One each!"
Jennifer added, "Why would you want two? You're not even doing anything for Darren and Evelyn. The baby, whatever it is, is lucky to have Alan."
"I can't argue that point. In fact, I agree, but you don't KNOW what I'm doing for Darren and Evelyn."
"Don't start anything Jennifer!" Rochelle demanded.

Jennifer put Evelyn on my mind. I wondered how she was truly doing. I use to love her so much that I wrote her a love poem every day. Now I go for weeks without even thinking of her. Evelyn is the mother of my only son. Jennifer was right. I should help her more often. The least I could do was call her and say I'm sorry. Sorry for the rage. Sorry for the dirty names. Above all sorry for spitting in her face, nearly 10 years ago. Now I understood what Ann meant by, "Tell the others, you are sorry, before it's too late."

When we arrived, Shirley was in the delivery room. I don't know how Alan did it. I lived 20 miles away from the hospital, while Alan and Shirley lived 25 to 30 miles away. Yet, he beat us there.
Alan brought a pack of cards. Jennifer, Rochelle, Alan and I played 'Pity Pat', while Yolanda talked to Roxy about college.

After we were there three hours, a nurse came in the waiting room and announced that the father could go in and see his wife and baby daughter. The room suddenly became eerie silent. The girls speculated who would go. Alan and I remained seated, each waiting on the other to make a move. Roxanne broke the silence. "How 's the mother?"
"Mrs. Williamson is well and fully alert," replied the young nurse.
Alan and I slowly rose simultaneously.

The nurse said, "Only the baby's father can visit now. For all others, there'll

273

be a short wait." The nurse turned and walked away. I extended a hand of triumph to Alan and said, "Congratulations, Mr. Williamson. You take good care of that baby." Alan shook my hand and pulled me close for a quick hug, just long enough to say, "You have another daughter, Mr. Jones, congratulations yourself." Alan then rushed proudly down the corridor behind the nurse. I was happy for Alan and Shirley. When the girls saw Brandi and Shirley later that evening, they all fell madly in love with their baby sister. I never saw Shirley smile so much.

The next morning, Sunday, I called Dayton, Ohio and spoke at length with Evelyn. I apologized for ever hurting her. I told her that I realized, that going to church was not enough. Evelyn told me that she had forgiven me years ago, but my apology was an affirmation, that I was the right man to father her son. We later went to church, Rochelle, Jennifer, Roxanne, Yolanda and me. As a deacon in the church, I sat separate from the girls. Deacon Bob Johnson led in song and I read a scripture:

Isaiah 40:28-31

Hast thou not known? Hast thou not heard, that the everlasting God, the Lord, the Creator of the ends of the earth, fainteth not, neither is weary? There is no searching of his understanding. He giveth power to the faint; and to them that have no might he increaseth strength. Even the youths shall faint and be weary, and the young men shall utterly fall: But they that wait upon the Lord shall renew their strength; they shall mount up with wings as eagles: they shall run, and not be weary; and they shall walk, and not faint. Amen.

Roxanne graduated from Hamilton High School in June '97, and became a college student with Business Administration as her major, at Xavier University in New Orleans, Louisiana. Roxy gives Shirley credit for her career choice. She lives on campus and we talk via telephone every couple weeks. At the end of every conversation just before she says goodbye, she says, "I love you, Daddy." I never thought I would hear those precious words from Roxanne again.

THE END

BOOKS AVAILABLE THROUGH

Milligan books
By Dr. Rosie Milligan

When Mama's Gone $12.00

Juror $10.95

Birth of A Christian $9.95

Rootin' For The Crusher, $12.99

Temptation - $12.95

Satisfying the Blackwoman sexually Made Simple - $14.95

Satisfying the Blackman Sexually Made simple - $14.95

Negroes-Colored People-Blacks-African-Americans in America- $13.95

Starting A Business Made Simple - $20.00

Getting Out of Debt Made Simple - $20.00

Nigger, Please -14.95

A Resourse Guide for African American Speakers & Writers - 49.95

..................................**Order Form**...................................

Mail Check or Money Order to: 1425 W. Manchester, suite B, Los Angeles, CA 90047

Name_____Date_____

Address_____

City_____State _____Zip Code_____

Day Telephone _____

Eve Telephone _____

Name of book(s) _____

Sub Total $ _____

Sales Tax (CA) Add 8.25% $ _____

Shipping & Handling $3.00 $ _____

Total Amount Due $ _____

❑ Check   ❑ Money Order

❑ Visa   ❑ Master Card   Ex. Date _____

Credit Card No. _____

Driver's License No. _____

_____   _____

Signature   Date